The Pawn

"There is nothing not to like."
— The Suspense Zone

"An exceptional psychological thriller."
— Bookshelf Review

"Riveting."
— *Publishers Weekly*

"An exhilarating thriller."
— Mysterious Reviews

"Brilliant."
— Ann Tatlock, Christy award–winning author

"Seriously intense."
— Pop Culture Tuesday

The Rook

"It's a wild ride with a shocking conclusion."
— *Publishers Weekly*, starred review

"Readers will be on the edge of their seats."
— Romantic Times, top pick

"Steven James has mastered the thriller . . . Best story of the year. Perfectly executed."
— The Suspense Zone

"Suspense thriller writing at its highest level."
— TitleTrakk.com

"Steven James hooked me with his debut, *The Pawn*. Now in his explosive sequel he has absolutely blown me away."
— The Christian Manifesto

THE KNIGHT

THE BOWERS FILES #3

STEVEN JAMES

Revell
Grand Rapids, Michigan

Published by Revell
a division of Baker Publishing Group
P.O. Box 6287, Grand Rapids, MI 49516-6287
www.revellbooks.com

Printed in the United States of America

Library of Congress Cataloging-in-Publication Data
James, Steven, 1969–
    The knight / Steven James.
        p.   cm. — (The Bowers files ; 3)
    ISBN 978-0-8007-3270-7 (pbk.)
    ISBN 978-0-8007-1898-5 (cloth)
    1. Criminologists—Fiction. I. Title.
PS3610.A4545K57 2009
813'.6—dc22   2009014944

For Jen and Kristin
Thanks for being patient

Don't you know how the tiger trainer goes about it? He doesn't dare give the tiger any living thing to eat for fear it will learn the taste of fury by killing it. He doesn't dare give it any whole thing to eat for fear it will learn the taste of fury by tearing it apart.

He gauges the state of the tiger's appetite and thoroughly understands its fierce disposition. Tigers are a different breed from men . . . the men who get killed are the ones who go against them.

—Chinese philosopher Chuang Tzu, 351 BC

1

Thursday, May 15
Bearcroft Mine
The Rocky Mountains, 40 miles west of Denver
5:19 p.m.

The sad, ripe odor of death seeped from the entrance to the abandoned mine.

Some FBI agents get used to this smell, to this moment, and after awhile it just becomes another part of the daily routine.

That's never happened with me.

My flashlight cut a narrow seam through the darkness but gave me enough light to see that the woman was still clothed, no sign of sexual assault. Ten sturdy candles surrounded her, their flames wisping and licking at the dusty air, giving the tunnel a ghostly, otherworldly feel.

She was about ten meters away and lay as if asleep, hands on her chest. And in her hands was the reason I'd been called in.

A slowly decomposing human heart.

No sign of the second victim.

And the candles flickered around her in the dark.

Part of my duties at the FBI's Denver field office include working with the Denver Police Department on a joint task force that investigates the most violent criminal offenders in the Denver metroplex, helping to evaluate evidence and suggest investigative strategies. Since this crime appeared to be linked to another double homicide the day before in Littleton, Lieutenant Kurt Mason had asked for my help.

But some local law enforcement officers tend to be territorial, and from the moment I'd stepped off the task force helicopter I'd seen how excited the four men from the crime scene unit were that I was here. It probably didn't help matters that Kurt wanted me to survey the scene with him before they processed the tunnel.

The mine was barely high enough for me to stand in, and narrow enough for me to touch both sides at once. Every five to ten meters, thick beams buttressed the walls and ceiling, supporting against cave-ins.

A rusted track that had been used by miners to roll ore carts through the mine ran along the ground and disappeared into the darkness somewhere beyond the woman's body.

As I took a few steps into the tunnel, I checked to see if my Nikes left an imprint but saw that the ground was too hard. So, it was unlikely we would have shoe impressions from the killer either.

With each step, the temperature dropped, dipping into the low forties. The time of death was still unknown, but the cool air would have slowed decomposition and helped preserve the body. The woman might have been dead for two or three days already.

One of the candles winked out.

Why did you bring her here? Why today? Why this mine?
Whose heart is that in her hands?

The voice of one of the crime scene unit members cut through the dim silence. "Yeah, Special Agent Bowers is inside. He's taking his time."

"I should hope so." It was Lieutenant Mason, and I was glad he was here. He'd been on the phone since I arrived, and now I paused and waited for him to join me.

A beam of light swept past me as he turned on his flashlight, and a moment later he was standing by my side.

"Thanks for coming in on this, Pat." He spoke in a hushed voice, a small way to honor the dead. "I know you're leaving to teach at the Academy next week. I'm hoping—"

"I'll consult from Quantico if I need to."

He gave me a small nod.

Forty-one, with stylish, wire-rimmed glasses and swift intelligent eyes, Kurt looked more like an investment banker than a seasoned detective, but he was one of the best homicide investigators I'd ever met.

It'd been a hard year for him, though, and it showed on his face. Five months ago while he and his wife Cheryl were on a date, their fifteen-month-old daughter Hannah drowned in the bathtub while the babysitter was in the living room texting one of her friends. Kurt and I had only known each other for a few months when his daughter died, but I'd recently lost my wife, and in a way the sense of shared tragedy had deepened our friendship.

Silently, we donned latex gloves. Began to walk toward the woman's body.

"Her name is Heather Fain." His voice sounded lonely and hollow in the tunnel. "I just got the word. Disappeared from her apartment in Aurora on Monday. No one's seen her boyfriend since then either—a guy named Chris Arlington. He was a person of interest in the case . . . until . . ." He let his voice trail off. He was staring at the heart.

I looked at Heather's body, still five meters away, and let her name roll through my mind.

Heather.

Heather Fain.

This wasn't just a corpse, these were tragic remains of a young woman who'd had a boyfriend and dreams and a life in Aurora, Colorado. A young woman with passions and hopes and heartaches.

Until this week.

Grief stabbed at me.

Kurt's comment led me to think he might have reason to believe this was Chris Arlington's heart. "Do we know the identity of the second victim?" I asked. "Whether or not it's Chris?"

"Not yet." An edginess took over his voice. "And I know

what you're thinking, Pat: don't assume, examine. Don't worry. I will."

"I know."

"We have to start somewhere."

I focused the beam of light on the heart. "Yes, we do."

Together, we approached the body.

2

The candles gave off a scent of vanilla that intermingled with the smell of moldering flesh and the sharp sulfurous odor coming from deeper in the mine. I wondered if the candles were the killer's way of trying to mask the smell of the body as it began to decay, wondered where he might have purchased them, how long they'd been burning.

Details.

Timing.

"I should tell you," Kurt said, "Captain Terrell's not thrilled this is going through the task force. He wants it local law enforcement all the way."

"Thanks for the heads-up." Even from three meters away I could see the heart's intricate, fleshy veins. "We'll deal with that later."

We arrived at Heather's body.

Caucasian. Mid-twenties, medium build, dusty brown hair. Fresh lipstick. I pictured her alive, moving, breathing, laughing. Based on the bone structure of her face, she would have had a lovely, shy smile.

Her skin was mottled and blotchy and there'd been minor insect activity, but the cool temperature had kept it to a minimum.

I studied the heart for a moment—reddish black and clutched in her hands. It looked so dark and terrible lying on her chest.

Then I let my gaze shift to the candles. Over the years I've found that having a clear understanding of a crime's timing and location is the most important place to start an investigation. I looked at my watch and then blew out the five candles encircling her legs. "Jot down 5:28 p.m."

Kurt wrote the numbers on his notepad. "Wax flow?"

"Yes." Later, we would have Forensics burn this brand of candle at this altitude and this temperature and compare the melting rate and amount of wax flow to determine how long these candles had been burning. It would tell us when the killer was last here. I didn't need to tell Kurt any of this; we were on the same wavelength.

I studied the position of the body in relationship to the way the tunnel curved to the left as it followed the vein of minerals winding through the mountain. It appeared that Heather's body hadn't been placed haphazardly in the mine. The killer had centered her between two support beams.

He wanted us to see her as soon as we stepped into the mine. He's framing her. Like a picture.

"Just a few more minutes," Kurt said, jarring me out of my thoughts. "Then I need to let the CSU guys in."

I leaned over her body.

Her eyes were closed.

No visible body art.

No ripped clothing, no sign of a struggle. Black slacks, brown leather boots, a yellow and orange flower-patterned blouse stained dark with the blood that had seeped from the heart.

I brushed away a strand of hair covering her left ear and saw that it was pierced in three places, but she wore no earrings. I checked the other ear. No jewelry. "Let's find out if she was wearing earrings the day she was abducted. If she was, check ViCAP for other cases of killers who take earrings as trophies of their murders."

He wrote in his notepad.

"Kurt, besides you, how many officers have been in here?"

"Just two." He pointed his light toward an intersecting tunnel leading to the east. "I checked the tunnels before they got here. It's clear. No more bodies."

Water dripped out of sight somewhere deep in the mine. Wet echoes crawling toward me.

"Do we know who owns this mine?"

He shook his head. "Up here, mineral rights change hands a lot. Get inherited, resold. It's hard to track down. Jameson's working on it."

I gave Heather my full attention again.

No contusions on her face, no blood in her hair, no ligature marks on her neck. *How did he kill you, Heather? Press a pillow against your face? Drown you? Poison you?*

"Let's get a tox screening."

"ME's on his way up to get things rolling."

The candle beside her right shoulder blinked out.

I moved my beam of light past the heart and directed it onto the slight folds and wrinkles in her clothing.

Kurt bent beside me, pointing first at her shoulders, then at her ankles. "No clumping or bunching of her clothes," he said. "He didn't drag her in here; he carried her."

"Looks like it. Either way, he took time to smooth out her clothes, to brush her hair. He spent time with her. Posing her. Making sure everything was just right."

I felt a renewed sense of sadness at her death and the death of the person whose heart now lay on her chest. Moving the beam of light across her body, I thought of how many killers return to the dump sites of their victims to violate their remains, to relive the thrill of the murder, but there was no sign he'd defiled her remains. And I was thankful, if for nothing more than that.

Why here? Why did you bring her here? When I'm in the middle of an investigation I have a tendency to talk to myself, and I didn't realize I'd done more than just think my two questions until I heard a woman's voice behind me: "He's sending us a message."

Then footsteps, quick, firm, purposeful. Careful to avoid shining the beam in her eyes, I tilted my flashlight toward the woman approaching us. In the corner of the light, I could see her naturally beautiful, cowgirl face and strawberry blonde hair.

"Detective Warren," I said.

"Agent Bowers."

At twenty-nine, Cheyenne was the youngest woman ever to be promoted to homicide detective for the Denver Police Department. She was smart, down-to-earth, dedicated, and I liked her. I'd worked six task force cases with her over the last year, and each time I'd become more impressed.

Even though I was seven years older, there was definitely chemistry between us, and she'd taken the lead and asked me out twice, but the timing hadn't been right. However, in light of the problems I was having in my current relationship, those two instances came to mind.

Her eyes whisked past me and found the body illuminated by Kurt's flashlight. "Ritualistic posing," she said. "He took his time to get it just right."

"Yes." I focused my light on Heather again.

One of the CSU members called loudly for Kurt. I saw his jaw tense; he spent a moment in quiet deliberation, then handed Cheyenne his light, excused himself, and stepped away.

I returned my attention to Heather, and as I leaned close to her face, I noticed something in her mouth. Gently, I pressed against her lower lip to peer inside.

A black device the size of a folded-up strip of gum lay on her tongue.

Cheyenne saw it too. Knelt closely beside me. Most of my attention remained on the crime scene, but some of it shifted to her, to the soft brush of her arm against mine.

We both scrutinized the object. "What is that?" she asked.

"I don't know."

"I'll be right back." She exited the mine while I used my cell phone to take pictures of Heather's face and the placement of the object in her mouth.

Cheyenne returned with plastic tweezers and an evidence bag. "CSU was thrilled to pass these along."

"I'm sure they were."

She handed me the tweezers, and I slid them carefully into Heather's mouth. Squeezed the object to remove it.

And heard a voice.

"*I'll see you . . .*"

I toppled backward.

"*. . . in Chicago . . .*"

A recording.

"*. . . Agent Bowers.*"

I caught my breath.

Felt my heart race.

I stared at the tweezers, at the small recordable device. It looked like the kind you find in some types of greeting cards. Depressing the sides had activated it.

"OK." Cheyenne let out a long narrow breath. "I didn't see that one coming."

My heart was still hammering. "Me either."

The message repeated. "*I'll see you in Chicago, Agent Bowers.*"

I waited to see if there was more to it, but those seven words just repeated every six seconds. Carefully, I placed the recording device into the evidence bag.

"He knows about Chicago," Cheyenne said, taking the bag from me. "About Basque's trial."

Tomorrow morning I was flying to Chicago to testify at the retrial of a serial killer named Richard Devin Basque, a man whom I'd caught thirteen years ago in my early days as an investigator. He'd been found guilty and had been imprisoned since then, but recently new evidence had emerged and now it was possible he might be set free.

I didn't want to think about that now.

The recording continued playing: "*I'll see you in Chicago, Agent Bowers.*"

The faint sound of dripping water.

For a moment I listened to the tunnel. To my thoughts.

Whoever left the recording not only knew I'd be in Chicago tomorrow, he knew I'd be here, at this crime scene today.

But how?

And how is this murder connected to Basque's trial?

Another candle blew out. Stale darkness crept toward us from deeper in the mine, and the heart Heather was clutching no longer looked red at all, but completely black.

Voices behind me. Kurt and the CSU.

"All right," Cheyenne said. "Here they come."

The recording continued repeating the message. I wished I knew how to shut it off.

As the team approached, I let my light drift from Heather's body and wander along the wall of the tunnel, where I studied the glimmer of light glancing off the minerals embedded in the mountain. Occasional fissures and clefts only a few centimeters wide ran through the rock.

An ancient, rough-hewn ladder disappeared down a shaft four meters past the body. I walked to it and aimed my light down. The shaft was barely wide enough to allow a person to descend. About ten meters further down, it terminated at another tunnel.

"Any idea how big this mine is?" I asked Cheyenne.

"Not yet, but some of these old gold mines run for miles."

Then the crime scene unit arrived, we left the recording device with them, and Cheyenne and I headed for the mine's entrance.

As I passed the men on my way out, I greeted them softly, but Kurt was the only one to reply.

3

Cheyenne walked beside me. "You think it's Taylor who left the message?" she asked.

Sebastian Taylor was an ex-assassin on the FBI's Most Wanted List who'd taken a special interest in me a few months ago and had started sending me taunting letters and cameo photographs of people in my family. He signed all the notes "Shade," the code name a pair of killers had used in San Diego on a case I'd worked in February. Trace DNA left on one of the envelopes told us Taylor was the one sending the messages and that he was actually the father of one of those killers.

Two weeks ago an officer had found tire impressions in the mud next to a rural mailbox that Taylor had used to mail an envelope. We didn't know yet if the tire prints were from his vehicle, but it looked like a good lead. Kurt's team was looking into it.

"This doesn't seem like Taylor's type of crime," I told Cheyenne. "And all of his previous messages to me have been handwritten, not recorded."

"Any other killers in the habit of sending you personal messages?"

"Not at the moment."

If Taylor was the killer and really was planning to see me in Chicago, I wanted to be ready for him. So, when Cheyenne and I reached the entrance, I pulled out my cell. "I'll call a buddy of mine at the Bureau. Put some things into play."

"Be careful, Pat." Her voice held deep concern. Deeper than

that of just a co-worker. "This one's different. I don't like this. Any of this."

"I hear you." A slightly awkward moment passed between us, then she returned to the mine and I speed-dialed Ralph's number.

◼

Special Agent Ralph Hawkins wasn't just the acting director for the FBI's National Center for the Analysis of Violent Crime, or NCAVC, but was also one of my closest friends. Even though he was based in DC at FBI headquarters, I knew that if anyone could get a team in place at the Chicago courthouse by tomorrow, he could.

As I waited for him to answer, I noticed that the sun had dipped almost to the mountains, and the day was beginning to fade. Just past the flat strip of land where the helicopter sat, untamed spruce forests bristled down the slopes. Beyond them, ragged snow-covered peaks jutted to the sky.

My cell reception died, and I headed toward the chopper. Tried again.

Nearby, a car rolled to a stop on the potholed road leading to the mine, and Dr. Eric Bender, Denver's chief medical examiner, stepped out. Thick glasses. Serene face. Eric was nearly six foot five and slim and had a sloping, sauntering walk that made him look like he was always slightly off balance. He must have noticed that I was on the phone, because instead of calling out a greeting, he just nodded to me.

I nodded back. I'd first met Eric last year, a month after I moved to Denver with my stepdaughter. Tessa didn't make friends easily, so I was thankful when I found out that his daughter Dora was also a junior in high school, and I was even more thankful when the two girls hit it off.

Eric disappeared into the mine just as Ralph picked up. I brought him up to speed on the recorded message and the possibility that it might be Taylor. "All right," he said. "I'll make some calls. Fly to Chicago myself. When do you testify?"

"One o'clock. Calvin's picking me up at the airport."

"Werjonic?"

"Yes."

"I'll meet you in the courthouse." Ralph rarely spoke more words than he needed to. "If it's Taylor, we'll get him." And he ended the call.

We could have extra screeners at the airports in the region, but I had a feeling that if Taylor wanted to get to Chicago he'd find a way. Still, I phoned my supervisor at the FBI field office in Denver and asked him to send out an FAA alert to all airports in the West and Midwest.

The task force helicopter pilot who'd flown me here from police headquarters stood leaning against the cockpit. He looked up from a copy of the *Wall Street Journal*. "Ready?"

"A few more minutes."

Lieutenant Colonel Cliff Freeman had retired from the air force last year at forty-four and now flew choppers part-time for the federal government. A family man with twin eleven-year-old boys, he had short-cropped hair, was still in good shape, and had a knack for choosing up-and-coming high tech stocks.

I returned to the tunnel to take one last look at Heather's body, and finally, when I was satisfied, I joined Cliff in the cockpit.

As we lifted off, I took note of the scarce trails and dirt roads that switchbacked down the mountains and through the nearby Arapaho National Forest. The exit route the killer had taken shouldn't be too tough to narrow down. I studied the topography of the area. Memorized it.

Then the sun slid behind the mountains and night began to crawl across the Rockies.

The recorded message echoed in my head: *"I'll see you in Chicago, Agent Bowers."*

"I'll see you too," I said to myself.

And we skimmed over the foothills toward Denver so I could pack for my flight.

4

17 miles southeast of Bearcroft Mine
8:12 p.m.

Over the years Sebastian Taylor had learned to be careful.

Careful while he'd worked for the CIA finding permanent ways to deal with problematic people; then careful for the next decade to keep his previous line of work a secret as he launched his political career; then even more careful during his four years as the governor of North Carolina, laying the groundwork for a future run at the presidency. Careful, careful. Always careful.

He stepped from the shower and toweled off, then picked up his Glock from the countertop beside the sink and eased open the door to his bedroom.

Always careful.

But most of all he'd been careful during the last seven months after his fall from grace, after murdering an ex-associate and landing on the FBI's Most Wanted List.

For decades Sebastian had done only what was best for America. But since his country had turned on him last October and started hunting him as a wanted man, he'd found room in his conscience for a different kind of loyalty and had discovered that money could be at least as satisfying a motive as patriotism.

Sebastian thought of these things as he finished dressing, armed himself, and then slipped on his handmade Taryn Rose Chester oxfords. Italian shoes were the best-made dress shoes in the world, and even though he was aware that he needed to keep a low profile with his purchases, he'd still allowed himself a few luxuries. A touch of the finer things in life.

Over the last few months he'd constructed a new identity, chosen a secluded home in the mountains thirty miles west of Denver, and then carefully covered his tracks as he planned his next move against a certain troublesome FBI agent who seemed to keep popping up in the wrong place at the wrong time.

Special Agent Patrick Bowers.

Sebastian finished tying his shoes, stood, and straightened his hand-sewn Anderson & Sheppard suit coat to cover his shoulder holster. Yes. The finer things.

Which was why he was going to see Brigitte Marcello again tonight.

Even though he was just over fifty, Sebastian kept himself in impeccable shape, which was helpful for someone who preferred his women younger. And at twenty-seven, Brigitte hadn't begun to sag and wrinkle and weather. She was still supple. Still beautiful. Still worth his attention.

After making love one night last month, she'd said to him softly, lovingly, "I can't believe I'm doing this. You're old enough to be my dad."

"And you're old enough," he'd said as he drew her close, "to be my true love," and then she'd melted into his arms and they'd had sex again. Yes, to get what you want from people, you simply have to tell them what they want to hear.

He picked up the manila envelope containing the photos of Bowers's stepdaughter Tessa. Slipped it into his briefcase.

A quick glance at his watch: 8:22 p.m.

Just enough time to mail the pictures before picking up Brigitte at 9:00. After eight envelopes, the FBI had almost certainly installed face recognition video surveillance at the post offices in the Denver area. Much better to let the feds track his letters to random homes around the city—just find a mailbox flag flipped up from someone foolish enough to put his mail in the box at night rather than in the morning, and then slide the envelope inside.

Careful.

Alert.

Sebastian Taylor was not a man to be trifled with.

He entered the garage, flicked on the lights, and walked to his Lexus RX, rightly called a luxury utility vehicle rather than a sport utility vehicle. Opened the driver's door.

And felt the blade, cool and quick, bite into his right Achilles tendon—

Felt the strength in his leg give way as the intruder slit the tendon in his left leg as well, cutting even deeper than before.

And even though Sebastian had been trained to deal with pain, he involuntarily gasped as he crumpled to the ground.

But by the time he landed, he'd already drawn his Glock.

He rolled to his stomach and aimed but realized too late that the man had rounded the back of the Lexus, and before he could turn and fire, the intruder was on him, slamming a knee against his back, pinning his chest to the concrete and grabbing his right wrist and forearm.

No.

Sebastian recognized the position of the man's hands and knew what was about to happen.

No.

But because of the awkward angle, he was helpless to stop it.

No!

With swift, precise force, the man bent forward while simultaneously twisting both hands.

There was a moist, thick snap as the bones in Sebastian's right wrist shattered.

The man removed the Glock from his limp hand and tossed it out of reach, toward the door to the kitchen.

And for a moment, Sebastian was aware only of the pain arcing through his arm, shooting up his legs. He lay still, trying to control it.

Failed.

Standing then, the man retrieved the straight razor that he must have dropped after slitting both of Sebastian's Achilles tendons. "I'm sorry about that wrist, Governor. You pulled your gun faster than I thought you would. You really are good at what you do."

Sebastian rolled to his back to see his attacker.

Black ski mask. Black sweatshirt. Jeans. Brown leather gloves. The blade that he held dripped bright, fresh blood onto the concrete. But who? Who was he?

Someone from his past?

A mark he hadn't hit?

Control the pain. Control the pain.

No, he'd always carried out his assignments to the letter. Never left any loose ends. "Who are you?" Sebastian asked, keeping all hint of his suffering from his voice.

For a moment, the man watched him as if he were a specimen in a jar and not a human being. "You can call me Giovanni. We'll go with that for tonight, how does that sound, Shade?"

How does he know who you are?

Sebastian narrowed his eyes. "Why the ski mask? Only cowards hide behind masks."

"You're a smart man. I located and disabled three of your video surveillance cameras, but it's possible you have more. I couldn't take any chances that the police would be able to identify me after you're dead."

Sebastian let the death threat slide off him. He wasn't going to die tonight.

The man who preferred to be called Giovanni studied the growing pool of blood at Sebastian's feet, then pulled a white handkerchief from his pocket and began to wipe the straight razor clean. "That wrist must really hurt. Those Achilles tendons too. I've heard only childbirth and broken femurs are more painful than having those tendons cut."

Sebastian knew that cursing, begging, crying, would not help in a situation like this. So, despite the dizzying pain, he kept quiet. Only listened, planned. Prepared to respond.

The man finished cleaning the blade, folded up the razor. Slid it into his jeans pocket.

Sebastian could feel his legs twitching. He tried to control them, to stop their involuntary shivers, but couldn't, and Giovanni must have noticed. "Nothing to be ashamed of." Sebastian heard a touch of admiration in the man's voice. "Really. You're handling the pain remarkably well."

Slowly, Sebastian pressed his left hand against the cool concrete floor. He needed only a moment to slide his hand down to get to his backup gun.

Careful. Yes, now was a time he was thankful he'd been careful.

The Smith and Wesson M&P 340 scandium framed .357 snub in his ankle holster was one of the most powerful snubs S &W made.

The finer things.

Not a man to be trifled with.

Giovanni picked up the briefcase that Sebastian had dropped when he collapsed, and set it on the workbench running along the side of the garage. "Governor, haven't you heard the stories? About the psycho who waits beneath people's cars in their garages and at mall parking lots, and then as they're about to step inside, slices those tendons to disable them? You should have checked beneath your car."

Sebastian saw him open the briefcase and remove the envelope containing the pictures of Tessa Bernice Ellis. He pulled a black magic marker out of his pocket and wrote something that Sebastian couldn't read on the envelope.

Get to the gun. Just get to your gun.

Giovanni retrieved a black duffel bag from beneath the Lexus where he'd apparently hidden it earlier. "You know the story of how the Achilles tendon got its name, don't you?" He set the duffel on the floor just out of Sebastian's reach. "Achilles. The greatest warrior in Greece, but he had one weakness."

Patience. Patience.

"There was only one place he was vulnerable—that tendon in the back of the leg, just above the heel. His one small weakness. And do you know what yours was? Pride. Hubris. You covered your tracks, but you never really thought you could be found."

With his broken wrist, Sebastian could only use his left hand. But he knew he could still fire a gun.

Slowly, he began to drag his leg across the concrete toward his hand.

"You were wary, but not attentive. Don't feel bad about it, though. Everyone has it. That one place the arrow will pierce."

Giovanni unzipped the duffel bag, then looked at his watch. "I wish I could say our time together is going to be pleasant, but unfortunately, things are going to get a bit messy."

Sebastian pulled his leg a few more inches toward his hand.

Just a little farther and you got it.

A little farther.

Giovanni took out a carpet cutter. Flicked out the blade. Set it on the workbench.

As Sebastian moved his leg, his heel scraped on the ground, prying open the gash in his Achilles tendon. He took a gulp of air to quiet the pain. Rested his leg. Steadied himself. Somehow managed not to cry out.

Giovanni pulled two lengths of rope out of the duffel and laid them neatly in front of him on the workbench.

Then a pliers.

Then a hunting knife.

Sebastian knew he didn't have much time.

He grabbed his leg, yanked it up, and the wound widened. His leg spasmed, and a dark, sweeping dizziness rolled through him, but he didn't scream. Just went for the gun.

All in an instant, Sebastian instinctively unsnapped the holster, retrieved the snub, and swung it toward Giovanni.

"I have a .357 aimed at your back." He was surprised how calm he sounded considering the amount of pain he was in.

Giovanni froze.

The tables had turned.

"Try anything and I will shoot." But before Sebastian killed him, he wanted to know who this man was. "Now, hands to your side, or I'll make sure you die very, very slowly. After all, like you said earlier, I'm good at what I do."

The man who preferred to be called Giovanni did not move.

Sebastian didn't want to kill him until he had some answers, but if the man didn't obey, he would squeeze the trigger and not let it trouble him for a moment. "I'm telling you, you don't want to press your luck. Hands to your side and face me."

Giovanni slowly lifted his hands and began to turn.

"Who sent you?"

No reply.

"I said who sent you? How did you find me?"

As Giovanni finally faced him, Sebastian could see a tight, barely visible tremble work its way down the man's throat. Still no reply.

"This stalling is going to cost you," Sebastian said. "Now, take off the mask."

Giovanni let his eyes flick toward Sebastian's Glock lying on the floor near the kitchen door. But that one look telegraphed everything.

As he lunged for the gun, Sebastian squeezed the trigger of his .357.

Click.

Nothing more.

Giovanni scrambled across the garage. Sebastian fired again.

Click.

Nothing. Again.

How could the snub be empty? You always keep it loaded. Always!

Giovanni rose, holding the Glock. Faced Sebastian. "How did I do there, a moment ago?" he asked. "Did I seem scared? I practiced, you know, in front of a mirror. I'm not that great of an actor, and I didn't think it'd be as believable if I improvised. But I had you going, didn't I? It looked like I did."

He aimed the Glock at Sebastian's face.

No!

Sebastian took a sharp breath.

Giovanni fired.

Nothing.

The man stared coolly at Sebastian and shook his head, disappointed. "Governor, please. Do you really think I would have let you enter the garage with either of your guns loaded? You're a very dangerous man. That wouldn't have been too bright of me. You shouldn't leave your snub on your bed. Or for that matter, set your Glock on your bathroom countertop. Someone might sneak into your home and empty them while you're taking a shower."

"Who are you?" Sebastian heard his voice slipping from confidence to fear.

Giovanni's only reply was to snatch up one of the ropes from the workbench and, with cat-like quickness, rush toward Sebastian. Before he could roll out of the way, Giovanni looped the rope around his uninjured wrist and yanked Sebastian's arm toward the workbench. A moment later, he'd secured the wrist to one of the bench's legs.

Now he was standing, retrieving the other rope.

Sebastian knew he couldn't let Giovanni tie his other hand. If he did, he'd be completely helpless. It'd all be over. He rolled toward his bound wrist and tried to grip the rope, tried to untie it, but because his wrist was broken, he had no strength to do it.

Then Giovanni came toward him again. Sebastian tried to fight him off, but his attacker gave his arm a fierce twist, and one of the bones in his forearm shattered. This time Sebastian couldn't help but let out a sharp, strangled cry of pain. The awkward bend in his suit coat sleeve showed where the bone of his arm was protruding through the skin.

"It's OK." Giovanni was pulling his arm toward the car. "Most men would have been weeping by now. I have great respect for you." He sounded genuinely impressed. "You're doing an admirable job."

Sebastian yanked at his bound wrist, but the knot Giovanni had used just grew tighter. With one last surge of strength, he tried to throw Giovanni off, but failed.

Within seconds, Giovanni had tied Sebastian's broken wrist to the seven-spoke, eighteen-inch aluminum alloy wheels of his hundred thousand dollar Lexus RX luxury utility vehicle, and Sebastian Taylor lay helpless, his arms stretched to each side, each wrist bound.

Giovanni examined the bindings to make sure they were secure. "There." Then he stood, stepped toward the duffel bag, and pulled out a crosscut saw.

"It's OK if you scream, just so you know, I won't think any less of you." He reached into his duffel again and brought out a thick strip of cloth. "Now, I can gag you until we're finished if you want. It might make things easier. Based on what I've seen, biting against a gag seems to help people deal with the pain. Either way is fine with me, though. I'll leave the choice up to you."

Sebastian was done playing it cool. He let out a string of curses and finished by saying, "You're a dead man. You have no idea who you're dealing with."

Giovanni put the gag back in the duffel bag. "All right, then. Let's get started."

Carrying the saw, he knelt and positioned its blade against Sebastian's left knee, just below the kneecap. Then he held the leg firmly against the concrete with his other hand.

"We have a long night ahead of us. I don't want to go too deep on this first cut, so I suggest not wiggling too much. It'll only make things messier and force me to take my time. I'm not sure you'd want that. But once again, the choice is yours."

Sebastian felt fear, deep and raw, shoot through him. He clenched his teeth, tried to brace himself for what was about to happen, felt a scream coming on, but then, before the man could draw back the blade, he heard the crunch of gravel outside the garage.

A car.

And a slight glimmer of hope. Maybe, just maybe, he could still get out of this alive.

Giovanni hurried to the light switch and flicked it off. Only the faint glow of the headlights and moonlight outside the window remained.

He grabbed the gag. "It looks like this is no longer optional, I'm afraid."

Sebastian started to call for help, but his cry was quickly cut off as Giovanni worked the thick cloth into his mouth and secured it behind his head.

Outside the window, the headlights blinked off and a car door squeaked open, then slammed shut.

Giovanni rose to his feet. "That would be Brigitte. Good timing. Very prompt. After receiving that text message I sent her earlier on your behalf, she must have decided to hurry over." Giovanni retrieved another length of rope from his duffel bag. "I believe you told her that there was a change of plans. That you had an unforgettable evening planned and could she please bring some Chinese takeout. I thought it'd be easier this way, having both of you at the same location, and besides, I like Chinese and I'm sure that by the end of the night I'll be famished. So this way it's convenient for everyone."

Sebastian tried to yell, tried to force the gag out of his mouth, but it wasn't possible.

In the dim light of the garage he saw Giovanni flick out his straight razor.

"You know, according to the story, I need to kill her first, let you watch, so we'll stick with that." He paused and looked down at Sebastian sympathetically. "Well, OK, then. I'll be right back." And then he disappeared through the door leading to the house.

Sebastian Taylor, the ex-assassin who called himself Shade, did not believe in the Almighty. If he had, he would have prayed, would have begged for divine mercy for all that he'd done in his secret past, but instead, he was left to only curse his captor and the world and his own carelessness. And he thrashed hopelessly against his bonds while his slashed tendons seeped blood onto the floor of the garage, permanently staining the heels of his $495 Italian leather shoes.

He heard the front door click open.

Brigitte had arrived.

The long and final night had begun.

5

I woke.

Showered.

Dressed.

Found my cell and saw that Cheyenne had left a voicemail: Forensics had matched Chris Arlington's DNA to that of the heart. "So, to put it bluntly"—she didn't sound insensitive, just forthright—"he's no longer a suspect." Yesterday it had seemed like a good possibility that Chris was the second victim, so her message didn't surprise me.

So now, the challenge: find a way to focus my thoughts on the upcoming trial rather than let my attention get diverted by the deaths here in Colorado. I often work multiple cases simultaneously, but putting one out of my mind while I work another is a constant struggle.

I took a moment to review my notes on Basque's case, then finished packing and brewed some coffee so I could survive the morning. I was halfway through a cup of Sana'ani—a robust, full-bodied Yemeni bean—when my stepdaughter Tessa appeared in the kitchen doorway, putting in her eyebrow ring for school.

"Hey," she said. She wore washed-out jeans, canvas sneakers, and a T-shirt that read "Live Green or Die." The row of short, narrow scars she'd given herself in the months after her mother's death was visible on her right arm, and the edge of her raven tattoo peeked out from beneath her left sleeve. Her eye shadow, lipstick, and fingernail polish all matched her jet-black hair, and gave an edge to her gentle features, making her look cute but also slightly threatening. The way she liked it.

"Morning," I said.

"I know you're not going to tell me where this trial is, but I'm gonna ask anyway." She grabbed a sweatshirt from the wall hook and flipped the silk scarf I'd bought her on my last trip to India around her neck. "Where's the trial, Patrick?"

Because of her sable hair and free spirit, I'd taken to calling her Raven at times—part of the reason she'd chosen that image for her tattoo—and now I said, "I can't tell you about the trial, Raven. You know that my work life and my family life have to stay—"

"Separate. I know. Just thought I'd ask."

She stepped around some of the moving boxes and poured herself a cup of coffee.

Neither of us knew who her biological father was and she didn't have any close relatives, so after her mother died, the two of us had grieved together, struggled together, and finally grown to love each other in a way that made me feel like her real dad.

I looked at my watch. With my FBI clearance I could go directly to the gate at the airport, so security wouldn't be a problem, but traffic might be. "Listen, I need to—"

"This one's different, though, isn't it?" She was staring at her coffee and twirling a spoon through it, though I didn't recall her adding anything to the mug.

I thought I might know where she was going with her question but hoped I was wrong. "What do you mean?"

"Like when you were preparing for it and stuff." She didn't look up from the coffee cup. "I watched you. I could tell. It's . . ."

She might have paused to search for the right word, but as brilliant as she was, I doubted it. I suspected she was waiting to let me fill in the blank—probably with the word *personal*—but instead I simply said, "Yes. This one is different."

A slight pause. She picked up the cup and walked past me toward her room. "C'mon. Help me with my necklace. I can never get that stupid clasp to work."

Getting to the airport would be tight, but I could tell that something more important than just the necklace was on her mind. I decided to give myself a couple more minutes.

By the time I'd reached her room she'd already set her coffee on the dresser and was digging through her jewelry box. "Who is it? This guy, this trial? At least tell me his name."

"Tessa, you know I can't talk about my—"

"Just his name."

"He's a killer, Tessa, that's all you need to know. I was the one who caught him, a long time ago. Before I ever met your mother."

"So what did he do to his victims?"

"He killed them."

"He did more than that or it wouldn't bother you this much."

"Tessa—"

"C'mon. You're always doing this, you bring something up and then you won't finish talking about it."

I blinked. "I didn't bring it up, you did."

She pulled out the black tourmaline necklace I'd given to her last October for her birthday. "Stop being argumentative." She handed me the necklace, took a seat on the bed, and watched me in the bedroom mirror.

"I'm not being argumentative." I draped the necklace around her neck. Tried to snap the clasp shut.

"Yes, you are."

"No, I'm not."

"I say you are being argumentative."

"Well, I say I'm—"

She smiled and gave me a slight eyebrow raise.

"Look." Teenagers shouldn't be allowed to do that. There should be a rule. "We'll talk about this later."

"Now you're avoiding my question."

I was still working on the clasp. She was right, it was tricky.

"Tessa, you hate hearing about dead bodies. Blood, any of that stuff. Which, by the way"—I pointed to the posters of her favorite band, Death Nail 13, and the framed picture of Edgar Allan Poe, his dark, troubled eyes staring at me from across the room—"what's the deal with these bands and Poe, anyhow? I mean, all he writes about is death and the macabre."

"Just one of my winsome incongruities, part of what makes me so adorable."

Winsome incongruities.

Great.

"You listen to death metal and sleep with a teddy bear."

"You're trying to change the subject, and it won't work. Just summarize for me. Broad strokes."

I finished with the necklace. Tried to think of an appropriate way to describe to a seventeen-year-old girl what Basque had done, and finally just ended up saying, "This man, he did a lot of bad things."

"Oh, really? A killer who did bad things? What an anomaly." She was still watching me in her mirror. "I never would have guessed that." Then after a moment, when I didn't respond, her voice became thinner, more serious. An edge of apprehension. "How bad?"

A pause.

"*Silence of the Lambs* bad," I said at last.

She looked at me through her mirror. "Are you scared of him?"

"Look, could we just drop it? I need to get to the airport—"

"Well, are you?" She turned from the mirror and looked me directly in the eye.

Admitting that I was scared of anyone didn't seem like the valiant-FBI-agent-thing to do, but I figured she'd be able to tell if I wasn't being straight with her. I took a small breath. "What he did to those women . . . He made me question things—about how much evil we're capable of, what each of us is . . ."

She gazed at me steadily for a moment, and I could see her insatiable curiosity wrestling with her squeamishness about death. "So," she said at last. "You are scared of him."

I gave her the truth. "Yes."

She was quiet for a long time. "Good," she said finally. "I'm glad."

I wasn't sure what to say.

A shadowy moment settled around us, and even though I really needed to get going, I didn't want to leave her alone with thoughts of murderers and death.

"Good luck on your exams."

"They don't start till Monday."

"Gotcha. And you're sleeping over at Dora's tonight, right?" When she nodded, I added, "Don't keep Dr. Bender up all night."

"Right."

When I travel, Tessa often stays with my parents, who live about fifteen minutes away on the outskirts of Denver. This week my father was on a fishing trip in Wisconsin with my brother Sean, but my mother was still here. "Call Martha if there are any problems."

"I will." She grabbed a gray canvas floppy hat from her bedpost and slapped it on her head. The hat looked like it'd been run over half a dozen times by a pickup.

"When you get back home in the morning, do a little packing, OK?"

She groaned with her eyeballs. "I don't get why we have to take so much stuff. We're only leaving for the summer, it's not like—"

"Just do some packing, OK?"

"Whatever."

"Which is really your way of saying, 'I love you and I'd be glad to do that for you, Patrick.' Right?"

A tiny smile. "Possibly."

We left her bedroom and on my way through the house, I grabbed my suitcase and computer bag from my room and then met her by the front door. "All right. I should be back by noon tomorrow.

We can grab lunch together." I set down my bags, gave her a small hug. "I have to go."

"Wait." She held me at arm's length. "Is there a chance he'll be released?"

"There's always a chance."

She gave me a solemn, unsettling look. "If he scares you . . . I mean . . . there's . . . Just do a good job, OK?"

All I can do is tell the truth.

"OK," I said.

Then I kissed her on the forehead, picked up my bags, and left for Chicago.

6

The Cook County Criminal Courthouse
The corner of West 26th and South California
  Avenue
Chicago, Illinois
11:52 a.m. Central Time

With the number of death penalty protestors and counter-protestors surrounding the courthouse, South California Avenue had been closed off, so Dr. Calvin Werjonic and I parked a block away. We stepped out of his car, and I shielded my eyes from the pelting rain.

Despite the storm, snipers were in place all around the courthouse.

Because of the possibility that Sebastian Taylor might show up, Ralph had coordinated efforts with the Chicago Police Department and the U.S. Marshals Service to provide coverage. But even with their help, I wasn't sure we'd be able to locate Taylor. He was one of the most elusive and dangerous men I'd ever met, and I didn't know too many people who were good enough to stop him.

The recorded message in the mine hadn't contained any specific threats against me, but if Taylor were here, I wanted to flush him out, so, even though there was a secure parking garage underneath the courthouse, I'd insisted that we not use it.

I wanted to be in the open, where he could find me.

Now, while I shuffled through my pockets for some change, Calvin, who was in his mid-seventies and looked like he was about to get blown away by the wind, tugged his London Fog trench coat

37

tighter around himself. "I'll meet you inside, my boy." His light English accent flavored every word.

"All right."

As he disappeared into the dark rain, lightning slithered across the sky, leaving a drumbeat of thunder in its wake. I slipped quarters into the parking meter.

Calvin Werjonic, PhD, JD, had been my advisor nine years ago when I started my doctoral program in environmental criminology. That was also the year I made the transition from being a detective with the Milwaukee Police Department to becoming an FBI agent.

For the next four years I'd buried myself in my postgraduate studies, while still working full-time for the FBI's National Center for the Analysis of Violent Crime. Tough years. Very little personal life. Only a few friends, but when I finally finished my degree, Calvin shifted from being my professor to becoming one of them.

Parking meter fed, I splashed across the street toward the courthouse, my eyes on the protestors. I'd thought the thunderstorm would have kept them away, but despite the weather it looked like three or four hundred people had shown up.

I wondered which of them might be FBI agents or undercover officers.

As I made my way to the building, I entertained the possibility that Taylor wasn't the one who'd left the recording device in Heather's mouth. In truth, it might have been almost anyone in the crowd.

I looked for any familiar faces, for anyone who was making unnecessary eye contact with me, or purposely avoiding it, but I saw nothing unusual.

There were at least 150 death-penalty supporters, some carrying signs with enlarged photos of the victims, others holding signs that read "An eye for an eye. A life for a life."

The people gathered on the other side of the street waved "Death Does Not Equal Justice" and "Rehabilitate, Don't Slaughter" signs. The two groups were trying to outshout each other.

Two visions of justice.

Two sides of the equation.

Thankfully, the police had cleared a path and blockaded it with wooden sawhorses, so I was able to make it to the courthouse steps. I jogged up them as the wind whipped through the channel between the neighboring administration building and the courthouse, sending rain pelting into my face.

7

Calvin was shaking the rain off his trench coat when I found him in the entryway. "Quite a scene out there," he said.

"No surprise." I brushed the water out of my hair. "Considering who's on trial." Even though we were inside, the temperature hadn't changed. The central air must not have been working properly. I guessed it was somewhere around sixty-two degrees. Maybe cooler.

Calvin was silent for a moment, then said, "I am a bit surprised they didn't recognize you, my boy."

"It's been thirteen years."

"Yes," he said thoughtfully. "I suppose it has."

I was scrutinizing the faces of the news reporters and bystanders in the lobby, trying not to look like I was staring. Some of the victims' family members wore black armbands. "Besides, killers are a lot more memorable than the guys who catch them. Nobody makes FBI agent or police officer trading cards, but three different companies make them for serial killers."

"That is a little troubling."

"More than a little."

A pack of reporters glanced in our direction and apparently recognized Calvin, because they began to flock toward us, eyes locked on him. He was used to media attention, being one of CNN's most frequently called upon criminology experts, so it didn't surprise me, but I like media interviews about as much as I like truck-stop coffee, and I think Calvin knew that because he walked past me to intercept them. "I'll see you in the courtroom," he said.

I thanked him and headed for the security checkpoint where six officers stood sentry beside the three metal detectors. One of the officers, a squat man with an uneven dome of sheared-off hair, motioned for me to step forward. It took me a moment to empty my pockets and send my keys with my lock pick blades, along with my Mini Maglite flashlight and some change, through the X-ray machine.

Before the officer could even ask for it, I handed him my ID and said, "FBI."

Then I removed my .357 SIG P229 and the knife Ralph had given to me—a Randall King black automatic TSAVO-Wraith—and handed them over as well.

The Wraith wasn't the kind of knife I would've chosen on my own, but Ralph had told me I needed a good one and had given it to me last month. Tessa called the Wraith "wicked."

Which was actually a pretty good description.

The officer, whose badge read Jamel Fohay, set my gun and knife on a table beside him, then stared at my ID while I laid my computer bag on the conveyor belt. "Fed, huh?" he said. "Big guy came through here a few minutes ago."

That would be Ralph.

"Agent Hawkins."

"You two here to testify?"

"He did last month. I'm about to."

He didn't seem to be in any hurry to return my ID, and the line of reporters waiting to get into the courtroom was quickly growing behind me, so I plucked the ID from his hand and he backed up as I stepped through.

He gestured toward my Wraith. "Two and five-eighths ounces. ATS-34 stainless steel blade. Made in the U.S. of A. Good choice."

"You know your knives."

"I work the evidence room," he explained, "whenever I'm not stuck babysitting this X-ray machine. See a lot of knives come through. Always glad to see a Randall King. Gotta leave it here, though. The SIG too. You know the drill." He placed them into a small metal locker attached to the wall. Turned the key. Handed it to me.

After all the times I'd been called in as an expert witness, I was all too familiar with courtroom proceedings and protocol. While it varies between jurisdictions, I knew that here in Illinois no one was allowed to have weapons in the courtroom except for the two officers who stand guard by the main door. Some states allow judges to have guns hidden beneath the bench.

But not Illinois.

As I gathered my personal items, I saw Officer Fohay's attention rove to the line of reporters forming at the checkpoint. "When you testify," he said, "remember those women."

I remember them every day, I thought.

But instead of replying, I picked up my things and headed toward the elevators.

Yes, I remembered them; and now more than ever, because a mistake I'd made when I arrested their killer might be enough to set him free.

8

Basque used an abandoned slaughterhouse.

That's where he brought the women. That's where he tortured them, always making sure he kept them alive long enough for them to see him surgically remove and then eat portions of their lungs.

Based on the medical examiner's reports, sometimes he'd been able to keep his victims alive for over twelve hours—a fact that still sent shivers down my spine.

When I found him in the slaughterhouse, he was standing over Sylvia Padilla, holding a scalpel.

I shouted for him to drop the knife, and he attempted to flee, firing a Smith & Wesson Sigma at me, nailing my left shoulder. When my gun misfired, I rushed him and swung a meat hook at his face. He ducked, and I was able to take him down and cuff him. Then I hurried to try and save Sylvia.

And when I did, he mocked her as she suffered.

And when her suffering was over, he mocked her as she died.

So then, my mistake.

I hit him. Hard. Twice. Even though he was handcuffed and wasn't fleeing or resisting arrest. And in a dark moment of rage at what he'd done, I reached for the scalpel to go to work on him, but thankfully, I was able to hold myself back. As it was, I only broke his jaw.

Later, for a reason I've never been able to guess, he told the interrogating officers he'd broken his jaw when the meat hook hit him, even though it never touched him.

At the time, I didn't want anything to jeopardize the state's case, so in my official report I didn't clarify things as carefully as I should have. "There was an altercation," I wrote. "Later it was discovered that the suspect's jaw was broken sometime during his apprehension." It was the truth, it just wasn't the whole truth. The physical evidence was enough to convict him, and the defense didn't make a big deal out of the broken jaw, especially since Basque himself claimed it was accidental. The specific circumstances surrounding the fight never came up during the trial. He was convicted, sentenced, and that was the end of it.

But that wasn't the end of it.

I still carried the memory with me. I'd physically assaulted a suspect and then omitted pertinent information in my report. It was a secret I wasn't proud of. And Basque knew about it. And when someone knows your secrets, he has power over you.

More than anything else, psychopaths crave feelings of power and control. So maybe that was it. Maybe that's why he'd kept quiet all these years. There was no way to know.

But one thing I did know: I didn't like Basque having power over anyone. Especially not over me.

I found Ralph waiting for me beside the elevator bank.

Even though he's not quite as tall as me, he's still over six foot, and with his broad shoulders he seemed to fill the entire hallway. Lately, he'd been trying to bench as much as he did when he was an Army Ranger, before he joined the FBI. Maybe it was a midlife thing, I wasn't sure. Last I heard, he was repping at 225—which meant he could probably max out at 405. Not bad for a guy who was pushing forty.

"Let's go up the back way," he said. He was popping some kind of small white snacks about the size of M&M's into his mouth. He pushed open a nearby door, and I followed him through a narrow hallway toward the back stairs.

"Anything on Taylor?" I asked.

"Nothing yet. If he's here, he's a ghost."

We passed a window and I saw the Cook County Jail encircled with razor wire fences lying just across an alley. That's where they were keeping Basque.

When I was still a detective with the MPD working the Basque case, Ralph was the FBI agent who'd been assigned to help us find him. After Basque's apprehension, Ralph had encouraged me to apply at the FBI academy. It was a few years before I took him up on his invitation, but eventually I did, and we'd been close friends ever since.

Ralph had shaved his head since the last time I'd seen him, and I decided it was worth a comment.

"Nice haircut," I said.

"Brineesha's idea," he grumbled, rubbing a huge paw across his head. "Said it makes me sexy. I feel like a cue ball."

"I agree with your wife. You're looking good, my friend."

Even though a few people crossed the far end of the corridor, we'd ended up in a relatively deserted part of the building. Maybe Ralph had chosen this route on purpose so we could talk without anyone eavesdropping on our conversation.

He popped some more of his snack into his mouth. "Lien-hua's gonna be jealous when I tell her you said that."

I felt a sting of regret as he mentioned her name. Lien-hua was the woman I'd been seeing for the last four months, a fellow FBI agent, a profiler. Ralph didn't know our relationship was in its dying throes, and it didn't seem like the best time to tell him, so I decided to change the subject. "What are you eating?"

The stairs they used to transfer prisoners from the jail to the courtrooms lay just ahead.

"Yogurt-covered raisins." He slid his hand into his pocket and drew out another handful. Tossed them in his mouth.

"You're kidding me."

"Brineesha got me hooked on 'em last week." He was talking with his mouth full. "Have you tried 'em? These things are amazing."

He offered me a handful from his pocket. A clump of lint joined them in his hand.

"No thanks," I said. "I'm not really a big fan of yogurt."

"Suit yourself." He tossed the entire handful into his mouth, lint and all. "You're the one missing out."

"I'll try to make do."

We passed a drinking fountain, and he nodded toward a restroom near the stairwell. "Hey, I gotta take a leak."

I thought of how I'd be stuck in the courtroom for the next few hours and decided I should probably make a pit stop too.

Ralph paused at the water fountain for a drink so I stepped past him and pushed the men's room door open and then stopped midstride.

Facing me, one meter away and flanked by a pair of mammoth Cook County Sheriff's Department officers, stood Richard Devin Basque.

9

As soon as I saw Basque I felt a tightening in my chest, a sharp flare of anger and regret, the past clamping down on me. *If only you'd kept your cool after Sylvia died . . . If only you'd gotten to the slaughterhouse sooner she might still be alive . . . If only you'd pieced the case together one day earlier . . .*

He smiled at me. "Detective Bowers." For some reason, I noticed that his teeth were all still in place, still flawless. His jaw looked perfect too; the surgeons had done a good job. "No, wait . . . it's Dr. Bowers now, isn't it? And an FBI agent? How time flies. So good to see you again."

I didn't reply.

Ralph wedged himself next to me in the doorway, blocking the path.

"C'mon," barked one of the officers, manhandling Basque toward the door. "Let's go." But Ralph put his hand on the man's shoulder. At first the guy looked like he was going to swat it away, but then he noticed the cords of muscle in Ralph's forearm and paused.

"It's OK, buddy. Let him be." Ralph removed his hand when he was ready. "We can talk for a sec. We're just here to use the john." But Ralph didn't enter the bathroom, just stood barring the doorway.

I began to wonder what he had in mind; I had a feeling he was hoping Basque would try something so he could take him down. Hard. I hoped that wasn't where things were heading.

"For the record, then," Basque said, "I waive all my rights to have my lawyer present. A chat might be nice."

"See?" Ralph said to the officers. "There you go."

Both of them sized up Ralph, and nobody made a move. They eased back, and we all stood facing each other.

To be safe, I decided I wouldn't speak to Basque before testifying and chance a mistrial.

He eyed me. Thirteen years in prison had hardly changed him. He still had the handsome, confident good looks of a big-screen leading man and the incisive eyes and disarming smile that had served him so well in luring his victims into his car. Just like Ted Bundy and so many other killers, Basque had used his charm and charisma as his most effective weapon.

Looks intact, his time in prison had only served to harden his features, lend a few creases to the edges of his eyes, and wrap him in a thick layer of chiseled muscles that flexed against the designer suit that his lawyers had undoubtedly purchased just for the trial. Overall, he looked as dashing and trustworthy and GQ as ever. Maybe more so.

A handsome, respectable-looking cannibalistic killer.

I used to get shocked when I met people who commit the most appalling crimes — torturing and eviscerating their victims, eating or raping decaying corpses — because the offenders almost never look like you'd expect. Instead of looking like monsters, they look like Little League coaches and college professors and church elders and the guy who lives next door — because all too often that's exactly who they are.

Basque shifted his attention to Ralph. Offered him a wide grin. "Special Agent Hawkins. I enjoyed your testimony last month. Very persuasive, I thought. And how is Brineesha? That's her name, isn't it? Pretty little thing. Taking good care of her, I hope?"

Ralph's face darkened. He stepped forward.

"Not like this," I urged him quietly, but I'm sure Basque and the officers heard me. "Not here." I motioned to the two men escorting Basque. "Take him away."

One of them tugged at Basque's arm, but he stood firm. After thirteen years of pumping iron all day, it was going to take both of them to move him. To make things worse, Ralph still blocked the doorway.

I could feel the air tightening around us.

"C'mon," I said to Ralph, but he didn't move. Neither did Basque or the officers.

Basque eyed me again. A smooth, charming smile. "All these years I was so hoping you'd visit me in prison, Patrick. But there are so many cases to solve, I suppose? I read about a number of them in the journals. You've been a busy man." He wet his lips. "Missed seeing you, though."

Ralph cracked his neck and said, "Yeah, it can get pretty lonely in there. I'm sure you found plenty of—"

"Sometimes lonely, my burly friend, but never alone." He met Ralph's gaze. "Not with the good Lord by my side."

Oh, I'd almost forgotten. Seven months ago in prison, Richard Basque had found Jesus, just like so many convicts facing a parole hearing or a retrial seem to do. The prospect of freedom must be a rather strong incentive for getting right with God.

Ralph's eyes became iron. I put my hand on his shoulder to pull him back, but if Ralph wanted to do something to Basque I couldn't imagine how I'd be able to stop him. The officers escorting Basque tensed as well. Everything was moving in the wrong direction. Basque let his dark liquid eyes drink in Ralph's growing rage.

"Last I heard," Ralph said. He had squeezed his hands into fists. "The Lord's by the side of the sheep, not the wolves. Someone like you is gonna burn in—"

"No one is beyond redemption, Agent Hawkins."

I grabbed Ralph's arm. "Come on. I need to get to the courtroom."

Finally, Ralph stepped aside, and the officers quickly directed Basque past us to the hallway. As they did, he called over his shoulder to me, "Patrick, when this is over I hope we can meet again under less awkward circumstances, perhaps break bread together. Partake of the body and the blood."

His words *the body and the blood* echoed down the hall as the door swung shut and Ralph filled the room with words I doubted Basque would find in his recently dusted-off Bible.

I glanced at my watch. Time had been evaporating. I needed to hurry.

We finished our business in the restroom, jogged up the stairs, and arrived at the courtroom just as a granite-faced female officer was getting ready to close the doors.

10

Everyone in the room was settling into their seats.

I'd never been in this courtroom before and couldn't help but think that, with its paneled walls, faux marble columns, and straight wooden chairs, it was reminiscent of the days when the building had been erected nearly a hundred years earlier.

In the subdued light everything looked imposing—the judge's expansive bench, the witness stand raised nearly two meters above the courtroom floor, seating for over two hundred people in the gallery. The scent of dust and old books filled the air.

At the defense's table on the other side of the room, a slim, intense woman in her early forties sat conferring with Basque. She had tight lips and stick-like fingers and was wearing the same charcoal gray pantsuit she'd chosen for an interview on Fox News last week. I recognized her right away: Ms. Priscilla Eldridge-Gorman, Richard Basque's lead lawyer. Her legal team sat beside her.

Thirteen years ago Basque had been tried and convicted in Delafield County, Wisconsin. Since then, he'd always maintained his innocence and eventually convinced a law professor at Michigan State University to look into his case. For three years Professor Renée Lebreau had her grad students review the trial proceedings and transcripts, and eventually they uncovered discrepancies in the DNA evidence and in the testimony of one of the eyewitnesses who claimed to have seen Basque leaving the scene of one of the murders. Ms. Priscilla Eldridge-Gorman demanded Basque's sentence be commuted, but after a careful judicial review, the Seventh District Court ruled in favor of a retrial instead.

And so, here we were.

A sharply dressed Hispanic man in his late thirties hastened across the room and slid into the chair beside me, interrupting my thoughts. "Good to see you, Pat."

"Emilio." I knew Assistant State's Attorney Emilio Vandez from a brief meeting we'd had last month in preparation for the trial.

He pulled a stack of file folders from his briefcase and set them in front of us. He took a long time straightening them. "It looks like we're in good shape for today."

"I'm glad to hear that."

Emilio set two pencils beside the stack and then carefully positioned them parallel to each other. He took a deep breath. "I don't know what's wrong with this AC though. I should have brought a sweater." Then he looked around the room as if he were searching for a clue as to why it was so cold.

I'd heard Priscilla Eldridge-Gorman was good, really good, and I began to wonder if Emilio Vandez was a match for her.

Then the bailiff called for all to rise, the judge entered from his chambers, and the trial of Richard Devin Basque resumed.

Twenty minutes ago, standing hidden and invisible in the crowd of protestors, Giovanni had watched Patrick Bowers enter the courthouse. Now, he returned to his rental car parked a block away from the police barricade.

He'd flown in and rented the car under a false name and worn a disguise while waving his "Death Does Not Equal Justice" sign.

No one knew he was here.

He drove to a nearby alley, called Denver's dispatch department, and left an anonymous tip reporting the location of Sebastian Taylor and Brigitte Marcello's bodies. Then he tossed the prepaid cell phone into a dumpster.

And so.

Everything was in place.

Through his contacts, he knew that Sebastian Taylor had tried to bribe members of the jury in order to get Basque set free. He still didn't know why Taylor had wanted Basque acquitted, and the governor had stayed remarkably tight-lipped throughout the night about his motives, even as things progressed toward more and more discomfort. But that didn't matter. None of it did. The jury wouldn't even be giving a verdict.

No, Giovanni had taken steps of his own.

He turned on the police scanner he'd brought with him to monitor the afternoon's events.

And waited for the story to unfold.

11

The trial, which had been scheduled to start late last fall, had been bogged down in a legal quagmire for months—postponed five times by judicial reviews and a slew of recesses and interruptions.

However, that was good news for me because it meant I wouldn't have to sit through an endless round of opening statements, arguments, and counterarguments. We could cut right to the chase. And after the preliminary trial rituals and an hour of questioning from Emilio, Ms. Eldridge-Gorman strode to the middle of the courtroom and paused for a moment beside the table containing the bags, photos, sketches, and other physical evidence to begin her cross-examination.

She slowly turned to face the jury. "Before we begin, I would like to remind the jury that we've heard from three of the country's leading DNA analysts, and each of them has corroborated my client's innocence. Mr. Basque is a victim of the system who has spent the last thirteen years in—"

"Objection, Your Honor!" Emilio Vandez was on his feet before Priscilla could finish her sentence. "Here we go again. Is she going to question the witness or just restate her case?"

The judge, a white-haired hawk of a man named Lawrence Craddock, glared first at Vandez, then at Priscilla Eldridge-Gorman. "Get on with your questions. We already know how you feel about the defendant. You've made it abundantly clear over the last four months." He took a long narrow breath that seemed to suck half the air out of the courtroom. I had the sense that he was going to say more, but he held back.

She nodded. She'd probably expected the objection and had simply taken advantage of the opportunity to reiterate her claims of Basque's innocence. Just another gimmick to manipulate the system to her client's advantage. I hated these games of posturing and showmanship. All too often they overshadow facts and evidence and end up undermining justice.

"Dr. Bowers," Ms. Eldridge-Gorman went on, "please state your name and position for the court."

"Special Agent Patrick Bowers. I'm an environmental criminologist for the FBI's National Center for the Analysis of Violent Crime. Currently, I'm based at the field office in Denver and when needed, I serve on a violent crimes task force working in conjunction with the Denver Police Department."

"But you used to be a detective."

"Yes. With the Milwaukee Police Department—for six years. I was the one who apprehended the defendant."

"Yes," she said stiffly. "You were. But we'll get to that in a moment. Can you kindly state your qualifications?"

I'd already gone through all this with Emilio, but it's typical for the defense to ask you to repeat your qualifications so they can try to poke holes in your testimony by diminishing or discrediting them in the eyes of the jurors.

Repeating my resume was the last thing I wanted to do, but I didn't want anything to interfere with the prosecution's case, so I decided to just get it over with. "I've been with the FBI's violent crime division for nine years and, as I mentioned, served as a homicide detective for six. During the last fifteen years I've assisted with or been the lead investigator in 618 cases in seven countries and served as an expert witness in 91 criminal and civil trials. I have a bachelor's degree in criminal justice from the University of Wisconsin–River Falls, a master's in criminology and law studies from Marquette University, and a PhD in environmental criminology from Simon Fraser University. I've also worked as a consultant for the National Law Enforcement and Corrections Technology

Center in Denver, Colorado, been on the board for the American Academy of Forensic Sciences, and served as a liaison between the National Geospatial-Intelligence Agency and the FBI to help integrate the military's geospatial research with that of the law enforcement community."

There. Done. Enough of that.

Ms. Eldridge-Gorman paced briskly toward me. The stark clacking of her confident heels ricocheted like gunshots around the room. "And isn't it true, Dr. Bowers, that five years ago you won the President's Exemplary Service Award for Law Enforcement Innovation and you've written two books on geospatial investigation, one of which won the Silver Badge Award for Excellence in True Crime?"

"Yes, that's correct."

"And, don't be modest now, you're one of the world's leading experts in environmental criminology and geospatial investigation."

I didn't like where this was going.

"Those are my areas of expertise."

"Your vita is quite impressive, Doctor." I assumed she was calling me doctor every chance she got to try to make me sound like an egghead. Another tactic. More games. She savored a moment of stillness and then added, "Congratulations."

"Thank you." It's never a good sign when the defense attorney starts congratulating you for your accomplishments. She flashed me a fabricated smile, and I knew she hadn't just been fishing for information but had already moved me closer to some sort of verbal trap.

"As a geospatial investigator you study the timing, location, and progression of crimes, correct?"

"Yes."

"And using computer models and geospatial analysis, you develop what is known as a 'geographic profile' to help narrow down the number of suspects or focus the investigation on one specific locality?"

"If the case warrants a geoprofile, yes. That's correct."

Looking past her, I saw Calvin in the back of the room. He wasn't here to testify, only to observe, and he must have noticed something because he was scratching busily at a pad of paper.

"And you use defense satellite information to study these locations." She consulted her notes. "A system called FALCON."

"Yes: the Federal Aerospace Locator and Covert Operation Network. It's the world's most advanced geospatial digital mapping program."

Her tone shifted from complimentary to condescending. "It's only fair to mention, however, that your approach is somewhat controversial, isn't it, Dr. Bowers?"

"Objection!" Vandez shouted. "Dr. Bowers's investigation techniques are not on trial here, Mr. Basque is."

"Her question is relevant," Judge Craddock responded harshly. "A technique can be controversial but still effective and well-established." He eyed her. "But Ms. Eldridge-Gorman will make certain that she doesn't insult or badger the witness."

"Of course, Your Honor." She thought for a moment. "Let me rephrase the question. Your investigative strategies are considered by some to be unconventional . . . ?"

"Investigations should be more concerned with discovering the truth," I said, "than with following convention."

"And you don't look for motive?"

"No."

"Or use behavioral or psychological profiling?"

"No."

"In fact"—she glanced at her notes—"you've even written, and I quote, 'I don't care why someone commits a crime. I would rather catch him than try to psychoanalyze him.'"

Actually, I was kind of proud of that one. "Yes. I did write that, and the rest of the paragraph as well: 'Investigators need to stop asking "why?" and start asking "where?" It doesn't matter why the offender committed the crime, our goal is to find out where he is.'"

"And you've even derided the use of DNA analysis. Isn't that correct?"

"I've never derided it, I just don't depend on it. Criminals watch CSI too. It's not uncommon for them to leave other people's blood, hair, saliva, even semen, at crime scenes to misdirect investigations. They're using the system against us. And they're good at it."

"So you prefer geographic profiling." She didn't offer it as a question.

"It's one of the most effective tools I know of for narrowing the suspect pool in cases involving serial offenders."

"But Dr. Bowers"—she flavored her words with slowly escalating sarcasm—"isn't geoprofiling only useful if there are five or more crime locations? Isn't that the minimum number needed for an accurate geoprofile?"

"The more linked cases, the more accurate we can be, yes. Given twelve or more locations we can be up to 97 percent accurate in narrowing down the most likely location of the offender's home base."

Now, she feigned ignorance. "But how do you know that a series of crimes are linked? If you have, let's say, sixteen murders in two states over two years, how can you tell that they're all committed by the same perpetrator?"

"Linkage analysis," I said, "otherwise known as Comparative Case Analysis, is typically the responsibility of local law enforcement. CCA is done through a careful review of offender initiated linkage, eyewitness descriptions, crime scene locations, victimology—that is, characteristics or relationships of the victims that point to a connection between the crimes—and physical evidence found at the crime scenes. With regard to the sixteen murders Mr. Basque is accused of, I analyzed the data myself and felt confident that the homicides were committed by the same person."

"But you might have been wrong?"

I peered past her to the morbid photographs spread across the evidence table. "It's possible. All investigations deal in terms of probabilities, not certainties."

I thought she might jump on that, but instead said, "And for your investigative approach to work, isn't it true that the offender must have a stable anchor point? Not just be passing through the area?"

She'd done her research, I had to give her that much. She was quoting almost directly from the fifteenth chapter of my book *Understanding Crime and Space.*

"That's right," I said. "Peripatetic, that is, transitory offenders, skew the results. Imagine a person standing in a closet, spray painting the walls while turning in a circle. If he left in the middle of the job, it might be possible to locate the precise location where he'd been standing by analyzing the patterns and density of the droplets of paint on the walls. But it would obviously be impossible if he walked around the closet while painting."

"Yes, but what if he *is* moving, Dr. Bowers? What if the offender is a commuter, so to speak? He drives to the city, commits his crime, and then returns to his home in the suburbs afterward. That's possible, isn't it? And that would make the geoprofile completely useless—or at best, inaccurate—correct?"

I'd heard all of these objections before, dealt with them in depth in my book, addressed some of them earlier in the proceedings during Emilio's examination. "Just like any investigative technique, geographic profiling has its limitations."

Ms. Eldridge-Gorman opened her mouth, but before she could respond I added, "But so does every method. Before you can match DNA you need to find some DNA. It's the same for fingerprints or hair or bite mark analysis."

After a quick breath I went on, "In the latest geoprofiling software, we've been eliminating some of the issues you just mentioned. We've included spatial temporal movement analysis that calculates the mean center of the crimes based on crime sequence and not just location. This helps us see if the anchor point of the crimes is shifting. Enhanced virtual temporal topographies reveal the synchronic and diachronic changes of crime patterns within specific locations. Also, we've added a Bayesian journey-to-crime model that incorporates current research about—"

I noticed the glazed eyes of the jury members.

Oh. That was brilliant, Dr. Egghead. Just brilliant.

Maybe I should have gone into my use of multivariate statistics too. That would have been good. Or spatial density analysis and the use of kernel smoothing routines to reduce the effects of the psychological barriers associated with mental maps. I'm sure that would have really impressed them.

Priscilla looked pleased that she'd lured me into using techno jargon. "So, in layman's terms," she said, "you've been improving the technology and refining your approach since my client's arrest thirteen years ago."

"That's correct."

"So you admit, then, that when my client was arrested, your investigative strategy needed improvement."

"That's not exactly—"

A slight grin. "Back to my question. If this technique only works with an offender who has a stable anchor point or home base"—she raised her hands in a dramatic display of bewilderment—"how do you know he's not mobile before you catch him?" Then she gave me a pretend smile. "The answer is you don't, do you, Dr. Bowers?"

"No—"

"So, your conclusions could be completely—"

I'd had enough of this. "Every investigation is a holistic process. You continually evaluate the evidence and revise your investigative strategy as needed." My voice had turned harsh, argumentative, and that was probably what she'd been shooting for. I tried to tone it down. "Geographic profiling is just one facet of a well-rounded investigation."

As I said the words "well-rounded investigation," I glanced again at the pieces of evidence lying on the table. Juanita Worthy's faded pink blouse, splattered with dark stains . . . the scalpel Richard Devin Basque had been holding when I arrested him . . . the enlarged Associated Press photos of the sixteen known victims . . . a map of the Midwest with the locations of each crime marked with red thumbtacks . . . a hatchet, still stained with blood . . .

Ms. Eldridge-Gorman went on, but the evidence had caught my attention and I was only half-listening to her. "Isn't it true"—she was pacing theatrically in front of the jury—"that when you were investigating the crimes for which my client was . . ." She hesitated, searching for the right phrase. "A person of interest . . . that you compared the timing of the crimes to the work schedules of the suspects to try and narrow down the suspect pool?"

I shifted my focus back to her. "Yes. The nature of these crimes would have required the offender to be present while they occurred."

But in my mind I was clicking through the items on the table, now removed from the plastic evidence bags: the Smith & Wesson Sigma that Basque had fired at me . . . the key to the slaughterhouse freezer where he'd kept four of the women's lungs . . .

Something about the positioning of the evidence on the table didn't seem right.

"Dr. Bowers." Priscilla Eldridge-Gorman stalked across the courtroom toward me. "Do you think justice is served when a man is convicted of first-degree murder based on his days off from work?"

She was twisting my research around, trying to make it sound ludicrous. And even though I couldn't believe any jury would give credence to her line of questioning, by the way the jurors were staring at me, it looked like at least some of them did.

The room still hadn't warmed up.

Still chilly.

The evidence.

Something about the evidence.

"Given the timing and location of the crimes," I said, "Mr. Basque's schedule would have allowed him to be present at the site of each of the murders."

Ms. Eldridge-Gorman held up a file folder. "And so could at least six other employees of the acquisitions firm he worked for." She slapped it down, loudly, onto the table. "I checked. And that's just one company. Thousands of people could have committed those crimes."

The recorded message in Colorado said, "I'll see you in Chicago."

Is Heather Fain's and Chris Arlington's killer in the courtroom?

I let my eyes drift from the evidence table to the faces of the people in the room, but Priscilla Eldridge-Gorman paced in front of me, blocking my view. "Did you actually witness my client attack Sylvia Padilla?"

One of the men in the gallery made eye contact with me and then quickly looked away.

"No. Mr. Basque was leaning over her body when I arrived."

The man was wearing a black armband, which meant he was a family member of a victim. *But which one? Which victim?*

"So you admit," Ms. Eldridge-Gorman said, "that it's possible my client heard Sylvia Padilla's screams, went to offer his assistance—like any conscientious citizen would do—and was reaching down to help the poor woman when you ran toward him." She looked at me sympathetically. "No doubt with the simple intention of fulfilling your duty as an officer of the law, and then when you aimed your gun at him, he understandably feared for his life and was forced to defend himself by firing his legally registered firearm. That's possible, isn't it?"

"He was holding the scalpel."

The man with the armband was still avoiding eye contact.

"My client found it lying on the woman's chest and was moving it so he could help stop her bleeding."

I felt my patience slipping again. "He mocked her as she died."

She held up a file folder. "According to the police report you filed, my client said, 'Looks like we'll be needing an ambulance, detective.' And then, 'Looks like we won't be needing that ambulance after all.' He was simply showing concern for her."

This was ridiculous.

I mentally flipped through the faces of the family members of the victims. It'd been thirteen years, and the man I was watching was shielding his face, glancing at his watch.

If I could just get a clear look at his face . . .

"Dr. Bowers," Priscilla said, once again interrupting my train of thought. "Is it possible you arrested the wrong man?"

"I'm confident we made the right—"

"But is it possible?"

"It's possible," I said impatiently. "Yes."

The man with the armband finally looked my way.

Yes. I recognized him. He was the father of Celeste Sikora, the second-to-last known victim, one of the women I could have saved if only I'd pieced things together a little faster.

"But," I said, elaborating on my answer, trying to quiet the growing frustration in my voice, "as I mentioned a few moments ago, all investigations deal in terms of probability rather than certainty. We don't live in a perfect world. The jury isn't asked to determine a person's guilt with absolute certainty but rather beyond reasonable doubt—"

"I am well aware of the legal requirements of American jurisprudence, Dr. Bowers."

Yes, Celeste's father, Grant.

Ex-military. I remember because he'd reacted so violently when I notified him that his daughter's wounds had been fatal that he'd needed to be sedated.

The trial, Pat. Focus on the trial.

"But as I was saying . . ." I continued speaking, but my attention was split. "The evidence strongly supports the conclusion that Richard Basque was—"

"Dr. Bowers." Her voice had turned to ice. "Did you physically assault my client?"

The room spun around me. Dizzy. A swirl of colors. Then everything dialed into focus.

She closed the space between us. "Back in the slaughterhouse? After you handcuffed him?"

So, Basque told her. She knows.

Grant Sikora looked at the clock on the wall. A bead of sweat glistened on his forehead.

You swore to tell the truth, the whole truth, and nothing but the truth.

"Did you break Richard Basque's jaw with your fist?" she asked. "Did you attack him after he was handcuffed?"

You can't let Basque walk. You know that, Pat. You can't admit that you hit him.

Time slowed.

Sweat? Why is Sikora sweating?

I looked from Grant Sikora to Priscilla. Beyond her I saw Basque smiling, as if the moment he'd been waiting for all these years had finally arrived. If I told the truth, he might walk, but if I lied I'd be committing perjury and going against everything I'd worked toward all these years.

Another bead of sweat formed on Sikora's forehead.

It's too cold in the courtroom to be sweating. Too cold. Unless.

"Dr. Bowers!" Ms. Eldridge-Gorman had stepped in front of me and now planted her hands on her hips, her two elbows jutting out like bony wings. "Are you having trouble remembering that night at the slaughterhouse?"

Grant Sikora began to discreetly make his way toward the side aisle. It's not unheard of for people to slip out of a courtroom while a trial is in session, so no one else seemed to take notice. Their eyes were riveted on me.

The evidence table.

The hatchet . . . the knife . . . the gun . . . a weapon . . . is he going for a weapon?

"I'll ask you one last time." Her words were cold stones dropping one by one into the still courtroom. "Did you or did you not physically assault Richard Devin Basque after he was in your custody in the slaughterhouse?"

Nothing but the truth.

Answer her, Pat. You have to answer the question.

My eyes flashed across the evidence table, scrutinizing, examining the positioning of the items. I noticed the Sigma's witness hole, the small groove that allows the operator to observe the brass case of the bullets if there are any chambered rounds.

Ms. Eldridge-Gorman's voice rang out, "Judge Craddock, please direct the witness to answer the question!"

Inside the witness hole I saw a brassy glint . . .

"Dr. Bowers, I advise you to answer the counselor's question."

That glint could only mean one thing.

Ms. Eldridge-Gorman threw her hands up.

That gun was loaded.

"Will you answer the counselor's question?" the judge said.

Sikora's going for the gun!

"No," I whispered.

"No?" the judge shouted.

Grant Sikora reached the aisle and ran toward the evidence table.

You can't let him get the gun.

Stop him, Pat. You have to stop him!

I grabbed the railing of the witness stand and launched myself over the edge.

12

My shoes slipped as I landed. I smacked onto the floor, and by the time I'd made it to my feet, Grant Sikora's hand had found the gun.

The next three seconds seemed to take forever and happen all at once.

I sprinted toward him. Time collapsed, then expanded. A series of terrible thoughts raced through my mind. *The gun's loaded. He's Celeste's father. He's going after Basque.*

Sikora raised the gun, and the two officers stationed at the courtroom's main doors drew their weapons.

I instinctively reached for my SIG. Found only an empty holster.

All around me, blurred sounds, elastic words that somehow slowed as they moved through the air, in between the creases of time. Screams . . . shouts . . . the frantic scuffling movement of people diving for cover . . . I felt like I was in a scene from a movie where the bullet slides in slow motion through the air, only this time the bullet hadn't been fired yet. And I had the chance to stop it.

The judge had disappeared behind the bench, and Richard Basque had risen from his seat and turned toward Sikora. Standing as still as death, he watched Grant sweep the gun in an arc toward the officers who were shouting at him to drop his weapon.

Out of the corner of my eye I saw Ralph on his way toward the gunman, plowing through the crowd of people seated in the gallery. But I was closer. A lot closer.

Priscilla Eldridge-Gorman's shrill voice cut through the room calling for Basque to get down! Get down! She threw herself beneath the table, but he didn't move. Just remained stoic and still.

I was almost to Sikora.

The two officers leveled their weapons. One of them fired and the bullet whirred past my face and shattered the wooden railing of the witness stand behind me.

I reached Sikora, but before I could grab him, he squeezed off a shot, and one of the officers wrenched backward with a sharp cry and crashed to the floor. The female officer who'd closed the courtroom doors earlier hesitated, glancing momentarily down at her partner.

Grant Sikora stared down the barrel, looking stunned that he'd actually pulled the trigger.

And then I was on him.

I snagged his arm and went for the gun, but he slithered free, whipped around, and leveled it at my face. "Out of the way."

Time caught up with reality and froze. I'd had guns aimed at my face before, but it doesn't matter how many times it happens, you never get used to it. I felt my heart slamming against my chest. *Easy, Pat. Easy.* I raised my hands to show I meant no harm.

"Put down your gun!" the uninjured officer yelled. Only then did I realize I was in her line of fire. She didn't have a clear shot at Sikora, only at me.

Out of my peripheral vision I could see the other officer laying sprawled on the floor, blood from the gunshot wound soaking through his shirtsleeve, but it was only his arm. It didn't look life-threatening. *Good. That buys us some time.*

"Drop your weapon!"

"Shut up," Grant shrieked. "Everyone, shut up!" He took one step closer to me. The officer on the floor was slowly drawing his weapon. "Drop your guns," Sikora yelled to the officers. "Or the FBI agent dies."

Three meters to my left, Ralph silently slid into position beside the prosecution's table. Everyone else except Basque either lay on the floor or knelt low to the ground. A few people peered over the edges of chairs and benches to watch things unfold. Neither officer dropped their guns. Basque still stood calmly watching everything unfold.

"Put them down!" Grant hollered. "Slide 'em here!"

I saw his finger on the trigger and felt my heart twitch. There was no way he would miss me from there. No way.

"Drop 'em!" Ralph bellowed. "Do it!"

Sikora didn't seem to care that someone else had yelled the words, he just kept his eyes glued on me. Kept his gun steady.

The two officers gauged the situation for a moment, and finally both of them shoved their guns toward us.

"Nobody else move!" Sikora yelled, then glanced toward Ralph. "And you. Back off. Now!"

"Easy." Ralph raised his hands and shuffled one step away from us toward the wall. "I'm backing up. OK?"

"Farther!"

"I am." One more step.

"Go on."

Two steps.

Sikora glanced at the officer standing beside her partner. "Get outside the door! No one comes in here. If anyone tries to, I mean anyone, if that door opens, Bowers is dead." He tipped his head to the left. "The bailiff and the judge, you go with her. Go!"

After a moment, the judge appeared from behind his bench where he'd been hiding. His face was etched with anger, but he said nothing. He and the bailiff followed the officer out the door, and then she swung it shut behind them.

Ralph and I still had a chance at diffusing things if only we could get close enough to take Sikora down, but to do that I needed to focus the man's attention on me. "It's Grant, right?" I said. "Your name is Grant Sikora? I met with you after your daughter's death?"

He eyed me, didn't answer. Took in two choppy breaths.

I pointed. "The officer you shot, he's going to be OK." I spoke slowly, trying to calm him down. "End this now. I understand you're angry—"

"No."

"You have a right to be angry—"

"No!"

"But shooting people won't help to—"

"Quiet!" Rage in his voice, but his jaw was quivering. A tear escaped the corner of his left eye.

He's sorry, so sorry.

"No one else needs to get hurt." I edged toward him. "You're not a killer."

He shook his head violently. "He killed her. He killed my Celeste."

Are there other agents in here? Where are they?

Sikora shouted past me, into Richard Basque's general direction, "You killed my daughter, you son of a—"

"Did she believe?" asked Basque, cutting Grant off.

"What?"

"The Lord said that those who live and believe in him shall never die. Did your daughter believe?"

"Shut up." Grant was shaking, possessed by grief and rage. "Shut up, shut up, shut up!"

His eyes locked on Basque again. He'd made his decision.

He swung the gun away from me toward the man who'd tortured, killed, and eaten his daughter.

My chance. My only chance.

Now or never.

Now.

13

I lunged toward Sikora and grabbed for the gun, locking my fingers around his wrist and pivoting at the same time. I pulled the barrel away from the crowded courtroom and toward the empty northern wall. And this time I made sure Grant Sikora couldn't jerk away.

He must have slipped his finger off the trigger because the Sigma didn't discharge. With strength fueled by adrenaline, he tried to pull free again. I twisted his arm around his back, trying to control him, to disarm him, but with his other hand he snagged something from the evidence table and slammed it against my side; a crushing heat, a burst of pain cruised through me and I wondered if he'd broken my rib.

Whatever he'd grabbed, Grant pounded my side again, but I wouldn't let go.

A flash of movement—Ralph on his way toward us, but it would be a couple seconds before he could help me.

Then I realized Grant was holding the hatchet Basque had used on three of his victims. Thankfully, he'd only been able to swing the handle at me and not the blade, but still, it hurt enough to make me gasp for breath.

As he swung the hatchet handle at me again, I sucked in a breath and chopped at his forearm, sending the hatchet clattering to the floor.

Now, for the gun.

We were facing each other with the Sigma between us. As we wrestled for it, Grant pivoted and we smashed into the witness stand.

"Drop the gun!" Ralph flipped the evidence table aside, scattering its contents. Rushed toward us.

Grant Sikora's face was set with determination, and I realized that if Basque had slaughtered someone I loved, I would have been just as determined, just as enraged as he was. "He . . ." His teeth were clenched with the effort of fighting me off, but he managed to speak through them. "He . . . killed . . . her."

"Please," I said. My side was throbbing so much it was hard to breathe. "Don't—"

"He ate her," Grant said. "Ate my Celeste—"

I felt the barrel pressing into my bruised ribs. I tried to pull it away, but Sikora pitched to the side. The soles of his shoes slipped, and together we crashed into the wall.

And that's when the gun went off.

14

Everything can change in an instant.

I felt the gun's jarring repercussion ride up my arm and jolt into my shoulder.

So this is it.

Time clicked forward.

After all these years, it ends like this.

I waited for the ache of the bullet's impact to sweep over me.

Felt nothing.

And then I saw Mr. Sikora's face.

No.

His eyes losing focus, his grip on my arm loosening.

No, please, no!

Liquid warmth spread across my abdomen, but the wound wasn't mine.

Ralph was beside me.

"Get an ambulance," I said. He rummaged through his pockets for his phone as I eased Mr. Sikora to the floor and onto his back.

After pulling the gun from his hand and sliding it away from us, I cradled his head as gently as I could while applying pressure on the gunshot wound with my other hand.

But I couldn't stop the bleeding.

"Don't let him . . ." Grant coughed, struggled for breath.

I wanted to tell him that everything was going to be OK, that he didn't need to worry, that the shot wasn't serious, but I'm not a very good liar. "Relax," I said softly. *Nothing but the truth.* "Help is coming."

He drew in a gasping, strangled breath but said nothing.

The blood on Grant's chest was frothy and bright, which meant the bullet had hit his lung, possibly nicked his heart. Even if the paramedics arrived within the next couple minutes, I didn't think he'd make it.

"The paramedics are coming," I said. Considering the recorded message in Colorado and the tight security here, I doubted that he'd loaded the gun himself. "Who loaded the gun for you, Grant?"

He struggled for a breath. "Hurry."

"They're on their way. Tell me a name. Who was it?"

He swallowed, took a coarse breath. "You have to get . . . hurry . . ."

Four officers came bursting through the door and swarmed around us. One of them retrieved the S & W from the floor, the other three aimed their weapons at Mr. Sikora's face.

"Back off," I said. "Give him some space."

They hesitated.

"Back off!"

As they retreated, Grant Sikora pulled me close. "Please." He coughed a fine spray of blood onto my cheek. I was sure I was the only one who could hear him.

"Promise me you won't let him do it again."

"Grant, you need to—"

"Promise me." Urgency. Desperation. "For her. For Celeste."

I had to say something. "I promise," I said softly. "I promise I won't let him do it again. Now, please. Tell me who loaded the gun. A name."

But he never heard me finish my request. As I was speaking, he closed his eyes, his hand fell away from my arm, and Grant Sikora died.

No!

If we were ever going to bring him back I needed to keep his blood flowing. I started chest compressions, but after a few minutes when the paramedics still hadn't arrived I felt Ralph's presence beside me, his hand on my shoulder.

"He's gone." Ralph's voice was as gentle as he could make it. "Pat." He knelt beside me, put a hand on my shoulder. "He's gone."

I kept going. Maybe he was wrong.

Two more compressions, three more, four more, but it wasn't enough, would never be enough. A crew of paramedics streamed into the courtroom, and as they took over trying to revive Grant, I leaned back, out of breath. My heart pounding.

I tried to relax, to calm my breathing, but couldn't seem to do it.

Throughout the courtroom the spectators and jury members were emerging from their hiding places. Richard Basque stood nearby, watching me. His deep, thoughtful eyes touched me, swept over me, a psychopathic mixture of coolness and warmth. "Thank you, Dr. Bowers." He spoke just loud enough for me to hear, then let a smile play across his lips. "I owe you my life."

That's it.

I rose and started for him.

This time it was Ralph's turn to hold me back.

"Let it be, Pat." I strained to get free, but he didn't let go. "Like you said before, not like this."

"I'm OK."

I tried to shake his hands off. Finally, he let go on his own and studied my face.

"I am. I'm all right."

"That's good," he said softly. "Because right now you need to be." He stayed within reach.

The body and the blood.

Still tense. Still angry.

The EMTs were using a defibrillator on Grant, but by the look on the face of the lead paramedic, I could tell that this was one patient he didn't expect to bring back.

74

A grieving father was dead, a remorseless killer was alive, and I'd made a promise I wasn't sure I could keep.

Everything can change in an instant.

———————————■———————————

6 minutes later

Giovanni watched the ambulance roll away from the court-house.

From listening to the police scanner he knew that it carried the body of Grant Sikora rather than that of Richard Basque. And he'd used his credentials to find out from one of the marshals outside the building that Special Agent Patrick Bowers had been the one to stop him.

Well.

Giovanni had expected, of course, that Sikora would be wheeled out of the building with a sheet over his head, but he'd thought that with his background as a gunnery sergeant in the Marines, he would have been able to accomplish his mission first. Of all the family members of the victims, he'd been the best choice.

But he hadn't been good enough to get past Bowers, which at least confirmed what Giovanni had already suspected—that Special Agent Bowers was the perfect choice for story number ten.

It looked like a slight change of plans was in order.

Time to get back to Denver.

To tell tale number five.

15

My side ached.

My heart ached.

And Grant Sikora didn't make it.

He'd been pronounced dead upon arrival at St. Francis Medical Center thirty minutes ago. The officer he'd shot would need a little time and physical therapy to heal but would eventually regain full use of his arm, so it looked like even though there'd been one tragedy, one had been averted.

Two, if you counted Basque escaping with his life.

The courtroom we'd been in had become a crime scene, so the bailiff had taken the jurors to the jury room, and all the members of the media and relatives of the victims had been ushered downstairs to the lobby. The medical and law enforcement personnel and a few people such as myself who were involved in the trial had moved to a smaller courtroom across the hall.

I located one of the Chicago police detectives and gave him my statement, although, with more than a hundred witnesses in the courtroom, there wasn't a whole lot of ambiguity about what had just happened.

Even though this wasn't the time or the place to sort through all the issues we needed to discuss, after coming so close to being shot, I felt the need to talk to Lien-hua, to hear her voice. I punched in her number, but she didn't pick up.

I decided not to leave a message.

I left my shirt, still soaked with Grant Sikora's blood, with one of the crime scene investigators, and while Ralph went to find Calvin to get a change of clothes from my suitcase in his trunk, I asked one of the paramedics to take a look at the bruises on my side.

A quick examination was all it took.

"You'll need X-rays to see if the ribs are broken," he said.

I'd been in my share of scuffles, so I already knew that the treatment for a bruised rib and a broken rib is pretty much the same—keep it wrapped, avoid straining yourself, and take lots of Advil. I figured I'd wait and see how much it bothered me before going in for X-rays.

"Thanks," I said.

He wrapped a snug dressing around my chest and gave me a cold pack to help reduce the swelling. "Take care of that, OK?"

"I will." As he was stepping away, I saw Ralph approaching, bringing me a fresh shirt and jeans. I accepted the clothes, thanked him, and went to find a restroom to clean up and change.

A few minutes later as I was buckling my belt, my phone came to life and I figured Lien-hua must have seen that she'd missed my call. I answered, "Hey, you."

"Hello, Pat." It was Detective Cheyenne Warren. "I heard what happened up there. I'm glad you're all right."

"That makes two of us." I realized that I wasn't disappointed it was Cheyenne rather than Lien-hua.

She got right to business. "It doesn't look like Taylor left the recorded message in the mine."

"What? How do you know?"

"We found him this morning, dead, along with a woman. I should say we think it's only one woman. It's hard to tell."

Her words could mean only one thing. "Dismembered?"

"Yeah. The killer dumped her in the water at the northern swimming beach at Cherry Creek State Park. Killed her at Taylor's house, though; we matched the blood at the two sites."

I let her words sink in as I returned to the courtoom. "Taylor had a house in the Denver area?"

"Up in the mountains. Near Evergreen. That's where he was be-headed—tortured first, though. We're still looking for his head."

Unbelievable.

The envelopes had all been mailed within the Denver metroplex, so I'd suspected that Taylor might be living in the region, but still, it was disconcerting to hear that he'd been that close to us and we hadn't found him.

"Suspects?" I asked.

"Not yet."

I was considering everything she'd just told me when the bailiff led the jurors into the room. I only had time for a few quick questions. "Besides the dismemberments," I asked, "are there any evidentiary links to Heather Fain's death?"

"No physical evidence yet, but there was an anonymous 911 tip, just like with Heather's body."

Judge Craddock and the two lead lawyers emerged from the judge's entrance.

I tried to think of any criminals I'd run into who could have found, overpowered, and killed Taylor, but came up short. "Anything else?"

"We're going to Taylor's house in the morning to finish processing the scene. Early: 7:00 a.m. It's about half an hour from downtown; maybe you can ride with me, reduce our carbon footprint."

Normally, it annoys me when people try to sound so progressively green by using the "carbon footprint" cliché, but from Cheyenne it just sounded natural.

"I'd come," I said, "but I'm not scheduled to arrive in Denver until almost noon tomorrow."

"So change your flight. Come back tonight."

It was a possibility.

I suspected the judge would call for a mistrial, but I wouldn't know for a few more minutes. "I will if I can. I'll call you back when I know more." Judge Craddock situated himself behind the bench and called for order. I needed to get off the phone. "Do me a favor. Text Agent Ralph Hawkins for me. Fill him in."

"All right."

I gave her Ralph's number, ended the call, and turned off the phone. After everyone had taken their seats, Judge Craddock faced the jurors and cleared his throat. "This incident involving Mr. Sikora bears no relevance to the trial at hand. We are conducting a trial concerning the defendant, Richard Devin Basque, not this man who just tried to shoot him. If this event is allowed to disrupt the judicial process, our justice system would be too fragile, too easily manipulated to be efficacious."

He took a deep breath. "And so, considering all of these factors, I am not calling for a mistrial. You will be sequestered until Monday. No news media. No outside contact. During the weekend we will provide independent, court-appointed psychologists to conduct, at no charge, confidential counseling sessions with any jury members who wish to discuss their feelings regarding the shooting. We will resume proceedings Monday at nine o'clock sharp when Dr. Bowers returns to the stand."

I could hardly believe his words, and by the looks of the jury members' faces, neither could they. I wasn't sure what would be normal in a situation like this, but resuming the trial on Monday—

"I will not let this grievous event train-wreck the judicial process. Not in my courtroom." He let his eyes click from one jury member to the next. "This trial will move forward. We will proceed and we will reach a verdict, and justice will be served."

Even though I was surprised by his decision, the more I thought about it, the more I found myself understanding the logic of it. The actions of Grant Sikora weren't at issue here, and shouldn't be allowed to affect the trial's outcome. And the longer we waited, the more likely the jurors would be to remember the shooting and forget details from the trial.

I expected Ms. Eldridge-Gorman to object to the judge's decision, which she did, quite vociferously. She would certainly appeal if Basque were convicted, and the state would do the same if he were acquitted. What a mess.

"Objection denied," Judge Craddock squawked. "Dismissed!" He slammed his gavel down, rose, and had his robe half off by the time he entered his chambers.

Just like me, the jury must have thought he was going to call a mistrial, because they sat in shocked silence, most of them staring blankly at the door to the judge's chambers, which was now slowly swinging shut.

I took a moment to think.

I really wanted to take a look at the crime scene where Taylor had been killed. It wasn't even five o'clock yet, so I could probably catch an earlier flight and still make it home tonight, then return to Chicago Sunday evening.

A quick call to the airline told me there was a flight that would arrive in Denver just after ten tonight, and I still had ninety minutes before the departure time, so, even with Friday rush hour, I figured I could make it.

I confirmed a seat assignment and was ending my call when Ms. Eldridge-Gorman crossed the room toward me. She came close and spoke quietly, only for me to hear. "I know what you did in that slaughterhouse, Dr. Bowers. On Monday morning I will move that you be held in contempt of court for refusing to answer the question today."

She might have been baiting me to see if I'd say something she could use against me when I returned to the stand next week. I didn't respond.

"If you tell the truth, the jury will discount your testimony and empathize with my client." A sense of dark satisfaction threaded through every one of her words. "And if you lie you'll perjure yourself. Either way, Richard will be set free, Dr. Bowers, and you'll be the one to thank."

Everything had suddenly become even more complicated. "Have a good weekend, Ms. Eldridge-Gorman," I told her.

"I will." She snatched up her briefcase and gave me a half smile. "And I will look forward to seeing you on Monday."

She strode away, and I noticed that Ralph had been watching us. He walked to me, and after she was out of earshot he asked, "What was all that about?"

"A misunderstanding." I'd never told him what had happened in the slaughterhouse, and now was not the time to get into all that.

His gravelly voice became even lower than usual. "Something you need to tell me, buddy?"

I considered my options, his friendship, the case, my future . . . and decided to let things stand for now. "No. It's nothing." I gestured toward the door. "You heading out?"

"I gotta give a statement to the press. Being the senior agent on site . . . You know."

"Gotcha."

He mumbled a few choice words concerning how excited he was about talking to the reporters. When he paused for a breath, I said, "I booked an earlier flight. I need to get to the airport."

"I'll give you a shout tomorrow."

I nodded, he lumbered away, and after I'd picked up my knife and SIG, I headed toward the back door so I could avoid the media drones swarming around the courthouse entrance. On the way, I called Cheyenne and told her I could make the 7:00 a.m. meeting tomorrow morning. "I'll swing by your place at about 6:30," I said.

"How about I drive? That is, unless you have power issues with a woman being in the driver's seat?"

I had the sense that she wasn't just talking about carpooling but decided not to go there. "All right. You can pick me up." Only after I'd said the words did I realize that they contained at least as many meanings as hers had.

"Sounds good to me," she said, a smile in her voice. "I'll see you at 6:30."

She'd never been to my house before, so I told her my address before we ended the call. Then I speed-dialed Calvin to let him know I was taking a cab to the airport and that he could just hang on to my suitcase until Monday. While I waited for him to answer, I exited the courthouse's back door.

And found him standing on the steps, sheltered from the drizzle by a broad gutter high above him, scouring his pockets, looking for his ringing phone. "Oh, there you are, my boy, I've been waiting for you." He found the phone, looked at the screen, then at me. "Shall we speak in person or on our mobiles?"

I stared at him. "How did you know I was coming this way?"

"I know how much you like to appear on the news. Come along. I'll give you a ride to the airport." He repositioned his coat and stepped into the rain.

But I hesitated. "I just changed my flight less than five minutes ago. How did you . . . ?"

"My dear boy, I can't give away all my secrets." He pulled out his car keys. "Come along, there's something I would like to ask you on the way."

16

For nearly twenty minutes Calvin wove through traffic without speaking. Maybe he was trying to give me an opportunity to deal with Sikora's death. Hard to know.

The rain was easing up, but the clouds hung heavy and gray above us. I knew the sun wouldn't be setting for a few hours, but already the day seemed to be withering into night.

We hopped onto the Kennedy.

More time passed.

A car swerved in front of us, and the driver flashed Calvin a rather elaborate finger gesture I'd only seen a few times before, on the streets of New York City. For a moment it reminded me of my years in the City, and of Christie, the woman I'd met there, fallen in love with there, married and then buried there.

Death.

Surrounding me.

Touching my life no matter where I turned.

And now this week, more of it: the two victims on Wednesday, the day before I joined the case . . . Heather Fain and Chris Arlington yesterday . . . Sebastian Taylor and the unidentified woman, and now Grant Sikora . . .

So much death in my past, in my present. I'd chosen this career, this life for myself, but sometimes —

"I heard some of the reporters chatting," Calvin said softly, interrupting my thoughts, "while you were giving your statement to the police. The media is already calling you a hero, my boy. They want to pin a medal on you."

"I'm no hero, Calvin."

"You saved a man's life."

"Who?" This was the last thing I wanted to talk about. "Basque? He deserved to die. Sikora deserved to live. How does that make me a hero?"

Calvin thought for a moment. He chose not to reply, and I felt his silence to be some sort of refutation.

"I was proud of you today," he said at last. "Proud to have been your teacher."

His words sounded conclusive, as if he were wrapping up one of his lectures rather than simply commenting about the day. It made me uneasy. "What's wrong? What's going on?"

Once again he chose not to reply, which was uncharacteristic of him. Now, he definitely had my attention.

A dump truck in front of us spit up a plume of sour exhaust.

Calvin pulled into the left lane to pass.

Silence stretched between us, and finally, when I realized he wasn't going to answer my question, I tried to guess what he'd been hoping to talk to me about. "Was there something I said on the stand that . . ." I searched for the right word. "That you felt was inaccurate or unrepresentative of—"

He swept his hand through the air dismissively. "Don't be ridiculous, my boy. Of course not. Nothing like that." I waited for him to continue, but once again I received only silence.

I'd never met anyone who chose his words more carefully or more precisely than Dr. Calvin Werjonic, but now he was being evasive. I didn't want to pressure him, but I did want to find out what was going on.

"Patrick, governments daily break international laws and treaties to look after their nation's best interests. And this is necessary because laws are established to serve something greater than themselves."

"Justice," I said.

"Yes."

I considered his words in light of the day's events. "But Calvin. Justice is a matter for the courts to decide."

"Yes, yes, of course. The right answer. The textbook answer."

I hadn't noticed earlier, but now in the cloud-darkened day, I saw that he looked frail and tired, like a mighty cliff finally eroding with time. "But not your answer?"

"The quest for justice leads not to an answer but to a dilemma: how far is one willing to go to see it carried out?" Calvin merged back into the right lane.

I was beginning to see how his words might be related to the trial. I hoped I was wrong. "Don't we vow to tell 'the truth, the whole truth, and nothing but the truth'? Justice isn't served when truth is censored."

"Yes, precisely."

Another surprising answer. "But?"

"But have you noticed that the attorneys for both the prosecution and the defense are not required to take the same oath? Rather than being bound to tell the whole truth, they are, I dare say, expected not to. Their legal obligation is to tell only the version of truth that supports their case. Only the witnesses, not the lawyers, have to vow to tell the whole truth. And yet, as you just noted a moment ago, justice is not served when truth is censored."

I wasn't sure what to say. Thick traffic closed in on us. Rush hour.

"We've lost sight of the goal, Patrick. Our justice system is concerned more with prosecutions and acquittals than it is with either truth or justice. You know it's true. It's just that we're reticent to admit it."

He was right on both counts: it was true, and I didn't like admitting it. Both the prosecution and the defense stick to the evidence and witnesses that support their case. If they discover evidence that would help the other side, they don't submit it to the trial—even if it might mean keeping an innocent man from going to prison or making sure a brutal killer gets locked away. That's what happens when a legal system values individual rights above the search for truth or the administration of justice.

Calvin went on, "But seeing justice done, isn't that why we entered this field in the first place? Isn't that more important than winning a case?"

"You're not justifying—"

A tired sigh. "I'm seventy-six years old, my boy. I don't have time left to either justify or condemn, only to reason and, while I'm able, to act."

It felt strange hearing Calvin say these things. Over the years, I'd questioned aspects of the judicial system myself but had never articulated my misgivings to anyone.

"Yes," I said, returning to his question. "That's why I entered this field."

We were nearing the exit for O'Hare airport, and I sensed that we hadn't yet made it to the crux of our conversation. "Calvin, at the courthouse you said you wanted to ask me a question."

"Yes, of course," he said. "Now, please understand that I mean no disrespect whatsoever when I make reference to your stepdaughter in my hypothetical example."

"Go ahead."

"Imagine that a man is on trial for first degree sexual assault. You are called in as a witness and you know that he is guilty and that your testimony will make the difference in the verdict."

I began to feel a little uneasy. "All right."

"However, the evidence is not sufficient for a conviction and you know that if you relate only the facts of the case, he will be acquitted and will sexually assault Tessa, or perhaps another girl her age. However, if you shade the truth in your testimony toward his guilt, he will be convicted. What would you do?"

His hypothetical situation left me very little wiggle room.

"Assuming my testimony was the only deciding factor." I felt my throat tighten. "I would lie to protect her." Finally, like a lens slowly coming into focus, I realized what Calvin was saying and how it related to the events earlier in the day.

"Yes." He nodded gently. "Because protecting the innocent matters more than anything else."

He turned his head and gazed at me. Despite his age, his eyes were as piercingly observant and incisive as ever, and this time he cut straight to the point. "Do you believe Richard Basque is guilty of those murders?"

There was no question in my mind. "Yes, he is. And probably more that we don't know about."

"I've reviewed the case, as you know. And I am convinced of it as well."

We came to the airport exit. Calvin took it.

A thought.

No, it couldn't be.

But maybe it was.

"Calvin, you loaded the gun, didn't you?"

He shook his head. "Sorry to disappoint you. There must be someone else out there thinking the same things as I am."

Maybe I shouldn't have believed him, but I did. After all, someone else had killed Heather and Chris and had left the taunting message in the mine. So then, Calvin's comments could mean only one thing: "You don't think I should have stopped Sikora."

He was quick with a reply. "No, no. I'm not questioning anything you did. I think you did the noble thing, the heroic thing."

"But not the right thing?"

"If you hadn't reacted as swiftly as you did, two people would be dead instead of one. They would not have taken Mr. Sikora alive, you know that."

I noticed he hadn't answered my question. "But if you're not questioning what I did, what are you doing?"

"Explaining myself."

He stopped the car in front of Terminal 1.

"What are you talking about?"

Calvin let the car idle. "For more than five decades I have told the truth and then watched as people whom I knew to be killers and rapists and pedophiles were set free." His fingers shook slightly. He laid them on the steering wheel, probably so that I wouldn't notice. But I did.

"And they molested again," he said. "They raped again, they murdered again. So many lives have been destroyed because I trusted that if I related the facts, justice would be carried out. But it wasn't. And now, the suffering of the innocent weighs heavily upon my conscience."

He looked at me, a gray fire burning in his eyes, a single terrible teardrop trailing down his cheek. "Perhaps I could have done more to help them."

"But perhaps not."

"True," he acknowledged. "But either way, it is too late to change what has been done. We can only change what is and what will be."

A police officer approached the car. We either had to move or I needed to grab my suitcase and head to the ticket counter. I could have identified myself as a federal agent, but my wallet was in my computer bag in the trunk and I didn't want to mess with all that. I just wanted to finish this conversation. "You're no longer sure you did the right thing by telling the truth all these years."

Calvin stared out the window at the rain. His silence was all the answer I needed.

I remembered his hypothetical question regarding the rapist: "If you shade the truth in your testimony toward his guilt, he will be convicted. What would you do?"

Truth and justice always wrestle against each other in our courts. For all these years I'd chosen the side of truth. So had Calvin. Maybe we'd chosen the wrong side.

"Promise me," Mr. Sikora had said.

"I promise," I'd told him.

I could feel something shifting inside of me. The confidence

I'd always had in the justice system suddenly seemed overly naive and optimistic.

"Do you believe Basque will kill again if he is set free?" Calvin asked.

"Yes."

"As do I."

The officer rapped a knuckle against the glass. I held up a finger to tell him to give me a moment, then I asked Calvin, "You're going to do something, aren't you?"

Silence.

"What is it? What are you going to do?"

He folded his hands on the top of the steering wheel. "I'm going to watch carefully." His words were decisive. Firm. "And see what happens next."

I searched for what to say. The officer pounded on the door and began to demand I step outside, which I finally did. He pointed to Calvin. "He needs to move along."

I exited the car, and Calvin rolled down his window. "I'll call you," I said.

"Yes, do. Ring me."

Then I retrieved my bags and watched as Calvin drove away, the taillights of his car glimmering off the wet pavement. A blurry, distorted reflection.

The officer was still standing beside me, and when I didn't move he said, "Is everything all right?"

No. It's not. It might never be.

"Yes," I said. "Everything's fine."

Then I entered the terminal, wondering if I should have just let Sikora kill Richard Basque, or if maybe I should have helped him aim the gun. Calvin's words stalked me as I made my way through the concourse: "I'm going to watch carefully and see what happens next."

Well, so would I.

17

Baptist Memorial Hospital
Denver, Colorado
7:51 p.m. Mountain Time

Disguised and dressed as a custodian, Giovanni passed through the lower level of Baptist Memorial Hospital toward the morgue. He carried a black waterproof duffel bag and was careful to avoid the hallways that had security cameras.

His flight had arrived nearly an hour ago, which had given him plenty of time to get ready.

Now, he picked the lock to the morgue, entered the room, and shut the door behind him. Set down his duffel bag. Unzipped it.

Then, he headed to the cold storage area where the recent arrivals were kept.

Giovanni had never served time for murder, which was a bit surprising, considering how many of them he'd committed.

And considering he'd even confessed to one.

But no crimes, not even that first one, appeared on his record because he was only eleven when he confessed to it and the court system decided that he was too young to understand his actions, that he was just a boy and so.

And so.

And so.

Instead of serving time in jail, he'd spent six months at a special hospital and then attended a boarding school and met with a counselor three times a week to talk about his feelings.

But neither his counselor nor any of his lawyers or the judges or court-appointed advocates had ever understood that he really *had* known what he was doing when he killed his grandmother two days before his twelfth birthday. He'd known very well. And even now, all these years later, everything was still fresh in his mind.

He unlatched the metal door that led to the cadavers and felt the sweep of cool air brush across his face, his arms, as he stepped inside. Just a few degrees colder than the mine—cool enough to store the bodies for a few days, not cold enough to freeze them solid.

He was responsible for eight deaths during the last week, or possibly seven, if the priest was still alive, so he recognized several of the bodies in the cold storage area, but he noted their presence without any emotion or even satisfaction. They'd only been characters in the epic story he was telling, nothing more.

Giovanni wheeled the gurney containing the corpse of Travis Nash into the examination and autopsy room and shut the freezer door.

A white sheet covered the corpse and he slid it aside, revealing the naked, clay-like body of the man he'd killed twelve hours ago by what had appeared to everyone to be a heart attack. No autopsy had been ordered.

Giovanni realized that if he were going to stick literally to the plot, he would have needed to find a way to have Travis's wife dig up his body and slice off his head with a knife, but burial practices had changed quite a bit since the fourteenth century, and, considering Travis's cremation was scheduled for the following morning, taking his body from the morgue was as close to disinterment as possible.

Since his death earlier in the day, Travis Nash's blood would have pooled in his body cavity, so there wouldn't be much of a mess, just a little seepage.

He unzipped his duffel bag, took out the crosscut saw that he'd used on Brigitte and the governor, placed the blade against the cold, bloated neck of Mr. Nash, and set to work.

Giovanni remembered the night his grandmother died.

He could still see her standing in the kitchen, bent over the sink, her frail fingers scrubbing the dishes, scrubbing, scrubbing, scrubbing, and her soft, papery voice asking him to please put the glasses in the cupboard next to the plates and if he enjoyed the summer with her and was he ready to go back to his father next Tuesday, and then reminding him not to forget his copy of *The Canterbury Tales* that he'd been reading all summer because she'd seen it on the porch earlier in the day.

She was wearing a white apron with a picture of a faded bouquet of lilies embroidered on the front, and there were yellow stains of chicken broth beside the flowers from the times she'd wiped her fingers across the apron while she was cooking.

Yes, he remembered it all: the quiet Kansas breeze blowing through the open window above the sink, the sound of crickets chirping in the dewy shadows outside, the smell of his grandmother's old-lady perfume mixing with the lemon-scented dishwashing liquid, and the fading smell of the chicken dumpling soup that she'd made from scratch for him because it was his favorite.

Yes, and he remembered the knife resting patiently on the counter beside her.

And his grandmother's voice again, "Please make sure those glasses are dry before you put them away, dear. You know how they'll just pick up germs if they're still wet."

"And did his grandmother yell at the boy? Verbally abuse him?"

"Not to my knowledge, Your Honor."

"What about his home life with his father? Was he neglected in any way?"

"He appears to have had a normal, stable upbringing, Your Honor.

His mother died while giving birth, but there is no sign of physical or mental abuse whatsoever from his other family members."

The knife handle looked so shiny and smooth and inviting.

He remembered that. And he remembered wrapping his fingers around it and picking it up and feeling its steady, balanced weight.

He rotated it so that the kitchen light could slant and dance along the blade, where it glistened, glistened, glistened, and then lingered for a moment before sliding off the edge and disappearing into the air around him.

The knife felt right at home in his hand.

Yes, he remembered.

And then his grandmother turned and saw him holding it, and she wiped her hands on her apron and asked what he was doing and would he please put down the knife because knives are dangerous and not to be handled carelessly and he should know that, a boy his age.

And he remembered how glad he was that she'd turned around because he hadn't really wanted to push the knife into her back and this way he could watch her face when it happened.

"Your Honor, the boy is too young to understand his actions. There's no precedent for a child under fourteen years of age being convicted of first-degree murder. He's a deeply troubled young man who needs psychological help. He should be offered counseling, not incarceration."

Everything was clear.

When his grandmother saw that he wasn't going to put down the knife, she took a hesitant step backward, pressing herself against the sink. She was still holding the dishrag, and soapy water was dripping from it and forming a small uneven puddle at her feet on the checkered linoleum floor.

He remembered that, even after all these years.

Giovanni finished with Travis's neck and set the blond, curly haired head in a plastic bag, then wrapped it carefully in a large white linen sheet and placed it in the duffel bag.

It took him only a moment to wash up and then change into the doctor's scrubs he'd brought with him. He stuffed the custodian's clothes into the duffel, covered the body again, and rolled it into the freezer.

Kelsey would be arriving in less than ten minutes.

Good.

He went to the sink to rinse off the saw and prepare the needle.

For some reason, as Giovanni stepped toward his grandmother, the crickets stopped chirping. Maybe they knew. Maybe somehow they could tell what was about to happen.

His grandmother's eyes grew large, and then she dropped the dishrag and tried to push him away, but he was strong for his age, stronger than she was, and she didn't slow him down. Not at all.

Giovanni had cut steak; he knew that cutting meat wasn't easy, and that his grandmother's body would have meat on it, that everyone's does, so he expected that it would be difficult to push the knife into her belly, expected that there would be more resistance, but it was much easier than he thought it would be. Quite easy, as a matter of fact. And pulling it out was even easier than pushing it in because it was slick and shiny with blood and other juices that he didn't recognize.

She didn't scream or cry out, just coughed slightly. A moist cough, and she trembled a little, and then leaned more of her weight against the counter beside the sink, and then sank to the floor.

Giovanni bent over her, and every time he pushed the knife in, it became easier and easier, especially after she stopped quivering so much. And it was quieter then too, after she stopped making those awkward sounds in the back of her throat.

———————————■———————————

Giovanni heard a knock at the morgue's door, and then, wearing the somber, empathetic expression of a concerned doctor, he opened it and found Kelsey Nash in the hallway.

He told her how sorry he was for her loss and apologized for having to call her in so late like this, but then explained that he needed to ask her a few questions about her husband, now, tonight, before the cremation, because it might help clear up some questions that had come up concerning the circumstances of her husband's death.

Kelsey wiped away a stray tear but didn't enter the morgue.

He added that the police feared that Travis might have possibly been murdered, and that once again he was terribly sorry about the whole ordeal, but that this would only take a minute and then no one would be bothering her again.

And at last she stepped hesitantly into the room.

———————————■———————————

As Giovanni returned the knife to the counter he heard the crickets slowly resume their chirping. And he liked that. Liked that the world outside was still normal, that, really, nothing much had changed.

Except for his grandmother, who lay motionless in a widening pool of warm blood that was beginning to find the grooves in the linoleum and make straight, bright lines on the kitchen floor as it spread away from her.

That was something he liked to think about. The red lines traveling away from her like the streaks of sunlight he would make when he drew a sun in the corner of his papers at school.

He watched the blood slide through the grooves in the shiny floor, watched the sunlight escape from the body of his grandmother.

"Giovanni, did your father ever touch you?"

"Touch me?"

"Yes. In a bad place. In a place where your swimming suit covers? On your buttocks or—"

"Is that a bad place?"

"No, no. It's just—maybe a coach or someone? Did Coach Simons ever touch you there? Or your grandmother?"

"In the bad place?"

"Where your suit covers."

"No. Uh-uh. No one. Just good places. Just nice hugs. Nothing in the bad place."

Giovanni motioned toward the freezer. "His body is right over here, ma'am."

Kelsey looked so fragile and shattered by her husband's recent death. She took one step, paused.

"I know how difficult this must be for you." He put a compassionate hand on her shoulder so that she wouldn't be afraid. "I promise you, I'll make this as painless as possible."

And with his left hand, he slid the hypodermic needle from his pocket.

He leaned over so he could look into his grandmother's eyes. They seemed so odd, staring up at the kitchen light without blinking, and they were so round and glossy that they looked like oversized marbles that might roll out of her head at any moment.

"What was it like, Grandma?" His voice sounded large and strong and manly in the empty kitchen. He liked the grown-up sound of his voice, and he repeated the question, even though he knew she wasn't going to answer him. Not anymore.

He watched those glassy eyes for a while, wondering if maybe they would blink, because, even though he was only eleven, he'd heard that sometimes things like that happen. Really, they do. Sometimes people move after they're dead. Reflexes.

But no. Not his grandmother. Even though he waited until the blood stopped spreading and began to grow dark and angry-looking, even then, his grandmother didn't blink.

He placed a finger lightly against the drying blood and found that it had turned sticky and thick and did not feel at all like the warm, soft rays of sunlight that had been landing on his face all summer.

It smelled coppery and warm.

And he liked how it felt on his skin.

Giovanni lowered Kelsey gently to the floor.

The muscle relaxant made her limp but left her conscious, and he could see her eyes moving, telling him that she was aware of what was going on. Her lips whispered silent syllables. Words that never formed.

He wheeled her husband's corpse out of the freezer, removed the sheet that covered it.

"Officially, you're supposed to die of grief," he said. She lay motionless, except for her eyes, her lips, and her chest: her eyes, alert and tracking him, her lips, quivering slightly, her chest rising and falling, rising and falling with each breath. He wondered what it would be like to be conscious but unable to move, able only to anticipate what was about to happen. He wondered if she would be able to cry anymore. He wasn't sure.

Tenderly, he slid one hand under her back and the other beneath her legs so that he could lift her without hurting her.

"I tried to think of a better way to do this, but I couldn't come up with one." He set her on the gurney beside the headless corpse. "I guess you could call this the next best thing."

Since she was unable to offer any resistance, she was pliable, and it was easy for him to position her on her side and drape one of her arms across her husband's bare chest.

He tilted her face toward the place where Travis's head would have been. Her left cheek lay in the pool of congealed blood that had oozed from the damp stump.

"You've kept yourself in very good shape, so that should help. Not as much body fat to insulate you. You'll be with Travis soon."

Despite her paralysis, she was able to make a soft gasping sound that might have been a weak attempt to call for help.

The sounds reminded Giovanni of the ones his grandmother had made so many years ago. That day in the kitchen.

After finishing the dishes, he'd called the police and asked them to come because his grandmother wasn't moving, and he'd told them that he thought he might have killed her with the knife and that there was lots of blood on the floor, all spreading away from her.

And as he waited for them, he carefully dried the glasses and put them away just like his grandmother had asked him to do before he pushed the knife into her stomach and she drifted, twitching to the floor.

"He poses no immediate threat to himself or to anyone else, Your Honor. We recommend that the boy receive counseling and be monitored until his eighteenth birthday, and if he appears to be mentally stable, that he be released under his own recognizance. That's all, Your Honor."

"Any closing comments from the prosecution?"

"We maintain that the boy is extremely disturbed and agree that he be institutionalized and receive the necessary psychiatric care, but this state has a mandatory life sentence for first-degree murder. We request that upon his release from psychiatric care, he serve the remainder of the sentence in prison for this egregious crime."

"All right. We will take a brief recess, and I will announce my decision when we resume at one o'clock. Court is now in recess."

Over the next few years Giovanni's lawyers and the judges and all the doctors and counselors told him again and again that he really didn't understand what he was doing that day in his grandmother's kitchen. And after a while he almost started to believe them.

But in truth, deep down, he knew they were wrong. He did understand.

Yes, he did.

He had killed his grandmother because he wanted to see what it would be like to watch someone die. To see if it would matter to him, if it would make him feel sad or not.

And it had not.

As Giovanni took the sheet that had been covering Travis's corpse and spread it over Kelsey, tucking it up to her neck, he thought fondly of that summer he'd spent in Kansas when he was eleven. The sunlight and the crickets and the memories. The books that he'd read. The stories he'd learned.

He rolled the gurney into the freezer and paused to brush a stray lock of hair away from Kelsey's face.

For a moment, he listened to the moist sounds coming from her throat, sounds that reminded him of his grandmother, then he left the freezer and latched the door shut behind him.

After changing back into the custodian's uniform and placing the doctor's scrubs in the duffel bag Giovanni drove home, carefully avoiding all traffic light cameras.

Tomorrow was going to be a busy day.

18

I did not have pleasant dreams.

I saw myself in the slaughterhouse again, tracking Basque. The stiff, rigid smell of blood in the air. The distant drip of a leaking pipe echoing through the darkness.

Meat hooks hung beside me. Swaying, clanking, even though there was no breeze.

In the dream, I stabbed at the black air with my flashlight, and as I did, a woman emerged. She took one step and then paused and gazed at me with cold, lifeless eyes. I recognized her as Basque's last victim, Sylvia Padilla. Her torso was ripped open like it had been when I found her. Her face doubly pale, drained of blood by death and washed of color by the flashlight's beam.

"Why didn't you save me, Patrick?" She only mouthed the words, but in the dream I heard them as if she spoke them aloud.

Cold lips.

Whispering.

"Why, Patrick?"

And then, footsteps behind me. I whipped around, and my light shone on the faces of more walking dead, all approaching me.

"Why, Patrick?"

Crowding around me, reaching for me.

"Why?"

I pushed them aside, felt my hands smear against their warm, moist wounds, began to run through the dark, my light swinging wildly, shadows splintering, then re-forming, then splintering around me again.

And then I was sprinting through a field and through time and I was in the tunnel of the gold mine again and I was leaning over Heather's body and she opened her eyes and then grinned a dead smile and held the terrible heart out to me.

Her lips, cold lips.

"For you."

But then it wasn't Heather's face anymore, but Lien-hua's, and she was offering me the heart. "Here is my heart, Patrick. For you."

The heart reeked of death.

"No," I yelled in my dream.

I stumbled backward.

She stood up, joined the corpses.

"No!"

And they all called to me, their words beating like a dark heartbeat over and over in my head. "Why, Patrick? Why?"

And then I awoke to a pale shroud of sunlight soaking through the curtains of my room.

I tried to relax, to let the dream fade away, but it refused to let go of me. I looked at the clock, and even though it was just after five, I didn't want to go back to sleep and chance tipping into the dream again, so I climbed out of bed.

The images kept playing like a movie in my head. I slipped into some workout clothes and my rock-climbing shoes and went to the bouldering cave I'd built in our garage—a mini climbing gym with holds bolted to the walls and across the ceiling.

Since Tessa was sleeping over at her friend Dora Bender's house, I didn't have to worry about waking her, so I pulled out my twenty-year-old boombox, popped in some U2, turned it up loud enough to help me forget the dream, moved my car to the driveway, and laid some bouldering mats across the concrete so I wouldn't hurt myself any more than necessary when I fell.

After traversing the walls for ten minutes to warm up, I began to cross the ceiling, hanging upside down, fingers gripping the climbing holds, toes wedged into small cracks or against the holds I'd passed.

Across the ceiling and back.

Arms pumped. Abs screaming. My side throbbed from meeting the axe handle yesterday, but it wasn't as sore as I thought it'd be, so I guessed that no ribs were broken. However, it still ached, especially each time I lost my grip and fell from the ceiling onto my back.

The bouldering pads helped a little, but I could definitely feel the impact.

I worked the routes for forty-five minutes, but as much as I cranked on the moves, I couldn't clear my head. So finally, I gave up and went back upstairs to get ready to meet Cheyenne.

Some people think that an investigator will be immediately reassigned to a different case if a killer mentions his name while corresponding with the authorities or does something to threaten him or his family.

And while the scenario might make for a good plot for a crime novel or cop buddy movie, it's not the way things work in real life. Once you start on a case, especially a high-profile case with a serial killer, you stay on it, regardless of how many threatening phone calls, photographs, or recorded messages the killer might send you.

It has to be this way, otherwise as soon as an investigator started closing in, a killer could simply leave a threatening message or make a taunting phone call and—*voila!*—the one person who has the best chance of catching him would be reassigned. That's just not the way it is.

It'd be too easy for the bad guys.

However, it is true that if they mention your name, it gets personal.

It'd been personal with Taylor and with Basque, and now I felt the same itch, the same intimate anger with this new killer who'd left the recorded message for me in Heather Fain's mouth.

As I stepped out of the shower, changed clothes, and grabbed some breakfast, the message kept replaying in my head, making the case more and more personal each time it repeated.

"I'll see you in Chicago, Agent Bowers."

Maybe coffee would help. Give me a caffeine buzz. Help me think in a new direction.

I decided on Honduran estate-grown French Roast. After all, if Detective Warren was going to shuttle me around for the morning, the least I could do was offer her sixteen ounces of some world-class coffee. I ground enough for thirty-two ounces, brewed the coffee to perfection, filled two travel mugs—adding a little cream and honey to mine—and had just finished downing a bowl of oatmeal when she arrived at the curb.

Toting my computer bag and hugging the two travel mugs against my chest, I maneuvered out the door. I'd never ridden with her before, and now I saw that she drove a scrappy 2002 Saturn sedan. Maroon. Scratched up, mud-splattered. Homey.

Even though it was still early, the sky was already stark and blue, with just a single streak of cirrus clouds layered high in the west. A light, cool breeze wandered through the neighborhood, but other than that, the day had a still, solid feel to it.

Cheyenne rolled down her window. "Good morning, Pat."

"Morning." I set the cups on the roof and patted her car. "I have to say I figured you for a pickup truck kind of girl."

"I'm hard to pigeonhole. Just throw your bag anywhere in the back."

I opened the door and realized that following her instructions wouldn't be as easy as it sounded. The seats and floors were piled with papers, the skeletal remains of at least four trips to KFC, three crumpled shooting range targets, a pair of rusted jumper cables, a mountain bike wheel, a very old pair of men's cowboy boots that I thought it best not to ask about, and a helicopter flight manual. I motioned toward it. "I didn't know you flew."

"Not quite done with my lessons. Just have to pass my solo."

In order to make room for my computer bag I slid the targets aside. They contained some of the tightest center-mass groupings I'd ever seen, so as I positioned my computer bag on the seat I asked her, "How often do you shoot?"

"Mondays and Tuesdays. I try not to miss a week."

After closing the door, I grabbed the travel mugs from the roof and joined her in the front seat. "Looks like you try not to miss the bull's-eye either."

"Part of growing up on a ranch. You need to be able to pick off coyotes from a full gallop."

"Don't tell my stepdaughter about that. She doesn't believe in hunting: 'Nothing with a face should ever be murdered.'" I offered her one of the travel mugs. "Coffee?"

"Naw. I don't touch the stuff."

"Ah, but this is good coffee."

"That's an oxymoron," she said.

OK, now that was just uncalled for. "And here I thought you were a woman of discriminating taste."

She gave me a furtive glance. "I am. When it comes to some things."

OK. This woman was not subtle.

Before I could give her any sort of witty reply, she slid a manila folder across the dashboard toward me. "Some reading material for the drive."

"Thanks."

As I picked it up I noticed a St. Francis of Assisi pendant hanging from her rearview mirror. I would never have pegged her for the religious type.

She really was hard to pigeonhole.

Cheyenne wove through traffic, hopped onto I-70. "By the way," she said, "Heather Fain was poisoned. Same poison that Ahmed Mohammed Shokr died of on Wednesday."

Ahmed was one of the victims in the double homicide on Wednesday. His girlfriend, Tatum Maroukas, had been stabbed with a sword.

There are only four ways to poison someone—inhalation, ingestion, injection, and absorption—so I asked Cheyenne, "Do we know how it was administered?"

"Injected. Potassium chloride."

"So," I mumbled, "they found an overage of intravascular potassium without potassium in the vitreous humor." It was more of an observation than a question.

She looked at me quizzically. "How did you know?"

"It's a big clue that points to potassium chloride. But also, an obvious one. The killer must have known we'd find it."

"You think? I wouldn't suspect many killers would know something like that."

"This guy would. He wants us on his tail."

"How do you know he didn't just make a mistake?"

"Like you said in the mine the other day: it's about leaving a message. He's not trying to cover his tracks, he's purposely choosing to leave them."

She took her time before replying. "One more thing. It was only one woman at the Cherry Creek Reservoir."

"At least that's one bit of good news."

Cheyenne was silent for a moment and seemed to be deep in thought, then she said softly, "A ten-year-old girl found the body parts before the killer phoned in the location."

I felt my throat tighten. And deep inside of me, in the place that matters most, I vowed to get this guy.

I opened the folder and began to scrutinize the files.

19

Tessa would have slept in for at least another two hours if Dora's stupid alarm hadn't gone off.

When Dora just rolled over and ignored it, Tessa turned it off herself, then flopped back onto the trundle bed and stared at Dora's desk. Her computer. The wall.

Dora's breathing became steady again.

Over the past few months her friend hadn't been getting nearly enough rest.

So Tessa let her sleep. She needed it.

Last winter, Dora's parents had gone on a double date with one of her dad's friends, Lieutenant Mason, and his wife. The girl who was babysitting the Masons' baby texted Dora to find out when everyone was supposed to get back and Dora had replied to the text message. While they were texting back and forth the babysitter left the baby alone in the tub. And the little girl had slipped under the water.

Thinking about it still brought Tessa chills.

Only a few people knew that it was Dora who'd been texting Melissa, and as far as Tessa knew, she was the only person Dora had talked to about it. "If I hadn't been texting her," she'd told Tessa one time, "Melissa would have been paying attention to the baby."

"That's stupid," Tessa had said. "It's not your fault." But it hadn't helped. Nothing she'd said had done any good, so finally she just didn't bring it up anymore.

For a while Tessa lay watching the screen saver on Dora's computer scroll through pictures of her family. Tessa had never had two parents around, except, sort of, if you counted the couple of months before her mom died when Patrick was with them.

And all that made it hard to look at the pictures of Dora with her two happy parents.

Tessa picked up her cell, opened the photo suite, tapped to the cover flow view, and flipped through pics of her mom, hoping it might make her feel better, but it did just the opposite. Eventually, she put the phone down, rolled over, stared at the wall, and waited for her friend to wake up.

Cheyenne was quiet as we drove toward Sebastian Taylor's house, and I appreciated the silence because it gave me a chance to review the case files in depth.

The candles surrounding Heather's body were Chantels, a brand carried by nearly all candle and department stores; so trying to track down the purchaser was probably a dead end.

In addition, the recording device could have been purchased at any electronics store, so—just like the candles, almost impossible to track. No prints on the candles or the device.

The forensics team had been able to determine that the candles had been burning for nearly two hours.

The time gap between when the candles were lit and the anonymous tip was phoned in would have given the killer enough time to drive almost anywhere in the Denver metroplex.

The anonymous tip on Friday, the one reporting the location of Sebastian Taylor and Brigitte Marcello's bodies, had been placed while I was in the courthouse.

Emergency Medical Services hadn't been able to track the locations from which either of the calls were made.

The case files included transcripts of both anonymous 911 calls, and in both cases, the caller had said something that caught my attention: "Dusk is coming. Day four ends on Wednesday."

The repeated phrases conclusively linked the double homicides on Thursday and Friday, and also sparked my curiosity.

Dusk is coming . . .

Day four ends on Wednesday . . .

Dusk . . . *A metaphor for death? A deadline?*

Day four . . . *Days of the month? The length of the crime spree? Days of creation, maybe? What did the Bible say God created on day four? Maybe something to do with that?*

I didn't know. Something to look into.

As I mulled things over, I paged to the information about the murders at Sebastian Taylor's house.

He owned a high-end security system with five video surveillance cameras, three of which had been disabled. The other two only showed brief glimpses of a medium-built man in a ski mask.

And the killer had made it personal once again: he'd left a note for me on the workbench in Sebastian Taylor's garage: "Shade won't be bothering you anymore, Agent Bowers." So the killer knew that Taylor called himself Shade, and he knew that Taylor had been sending me messages.

But how? None of that's been released to the public. And how did he find Taylor?

I flipped the page.

After murdering them, the killer had transported Brigitte's body parts to the lake but left Sebastian Taylor's body in the garage. And, although on a personal level the scenario disturbed me deeply, on a professional level it intrigued me.

Typically, killers only transport body parts to dispose of them or take them home as souvenirs. So why leave one body at the house and transport the other across town and then leave it at a public beach?

I considered this: based on the two messages he'd left for me, the murderer knew who I was, knew I'd be at the crime scene Thursday afternoon, and knew I would be testifying in Chicago. So it was likely he also knew about my work.

If that were the case, he was either very stupid—leaving me so many locations, the combination of which would help me track him down. Or he was very smart—perhaps choosing the abandoned mine and the public beach for no other reason than to misdirect the investigation.

And since he'd been able to locate Sebastian Taylor, something no other law enforcement agency in the country had been able to do, I did not think this killer was stupid.

No, not at all.

As Cheyenne wound the car higher into the mountains toward Taylor's house, I finished my coffee and realized that if she were to decide to try hers later, it wouldn't be fresh anymore and consequently she wouldn't enjoy it and might never fall in love with the world's perfect beverage. So, as a favor to her, I drank hers too.

"We should be there in about ten minutes," she said.

I turned to the list of possible suspects.

Tessa heard Dora stirring on the bed but waited to see if she was ready to get up.

Her friend's real name was actually Pandora, but she didn't like being constantly reminded of the story about the girl opening the box and unleashing all of the evil in the world—not exactly the coolest legacy to have. So pretty much everyone just called her Dora.

She had cinnamon hair, shy, brown-black eyes, and a sort of normal, easily forgettable face. The two girls had totally connected the first time they met, even though they had, like, nothing in common.

Oh: except that since Dora's dad was the medical examiner, both of their dads dealt with dead bodies all the time.

So at least there was that.

Finally Dora leaned over the edge of the bed. "Tessa, you awake?"

"Uh-huh."

"Sleep OK?"

"Yeah. You?"

A pause and then, "I kept waking up thinking about ... you know."

"Yeah." Tessa tried to think of something that would get Dora's mind off the baby's death. "Hey, I heard about this cool new Syrup Dive video. We should check it out."

Dora looked at her quizzically. "I thought you hated Syrup Dive? You told me their music was pangelo . . ."

"Panglossian." Tessa shrugged. "Well, maybe I changed my mind. C'mon, I hear the video's sweet."

And so, even though Tessa really *did* think Syrup Dive's music was naively optimistic—she went to Dora's computer and mouse-clicked to YouTube.

Added advantage: you don't have to keep seeing pics of Dora's smiling parents pop up.

"Panglossian." Dora swung her feet to the floor. "That Greek?"

"Latin. I never studied Greek. Just Latin. And a little French."

Dora joined her beside the computer. "Is there anything you don't know?"

"I can't figure out why I don't laugh when I tickle myself."

She found the video.

"And," her friend said, "my story, Pandora's Box. You don't know that. I still can't believe you never actually read it. Considering how much you read."

Tessa had never been all that into Greek myths. "I think I know it pretty well: Pandora was curious. She opened the box and out came all the pain and pestilence and disease of the world."

"Yeah, but that's not all." Dora yawned. "It has a surprise ending."

"I'll check it out this week. I promise."

And then she pressed "play."

━━━━━━━━━━━━━━■━━━━━━━━━━━━

I had just finished Cheyenne's coffee and was about two-thirds of the way through the case files when she broke the silence. "We're here."

Looking up from the papers I saw that we were turning onto the long, sloping gravel driveway that led to Sebastian Taylor's house.

20

Taylor had chosen to live on a dead-end road, which seemed tragically ironic to me, considering the circumstances.

Rustic, yet sophisticated, the amber and tan house wasn't pretentious enough to attract undue attention but still spoke of wealth and affluence just as I'm sure Taylor wanted it to.

In addition to Brigitte Marcello's car, which still sat in the driveway, two cruisers and two civilian cars, including Kurt's, were parked outside the house.

After taking a moment to show our IDs to the half-asleep officer standing guard, Cheyenne and I stepped into Sebastian Taylor's living room.

Lush carpet. Leather furniture. Civil War paraphernalia. Nouveau paintings that must have cost a fortune. I noted that the walls contained no pictures of either of Taylor's ex-wives or any of his four children, and none of this surprised me. A well-stocked liquor cabinet sat near the door to the dining room.

One of the officers from the crime scene unit was dusting for prints in the dining room, and I figured the other CSU members were probably in the garage, where the murders occurred. When I'm working a case I typically carry a pair of latex gloves in the back pocket of my jeans, but there were already extras waiting for us on the coffee table, so Cheyenne and I snapped them on. "Let's start upstairs," she said.

I nodded and we ascended.

Halfway up the steps she cleared her throat slightly. "You've been awfully quiet since we left your house, Pat. What's going on in that mind of yours?"

I took a second to collect my thoughts, then said, "In fifteen years as an investigator I've never come across a double homicide in which the killer dismembered two victims, then transported one of them to a secondary scene where it would be easily located and identified within hours."

"True," she said thoughtfully. "Typically, he would have left them both or taken them both."

We reached the landing. "Exactly."

The upstairs of Taylor's house was small. Just a master bedroom with an attached bathroom, a spare bedroom that he'd left completely empty, a common bathroom, and a landing which he'd turned into a computer workspace. Both the hallway and the bedrooms were decorated with earth tones that were carefully coordinated to match the carpeting.

She led the way to the master bedroom. "What do you think the killer was trying to tell us by transporting only one body?"

"I don't know what he was trying to tell us," I said. "But considering the facts so far, he has managed to tell me one thing."

"What's that?"

The master bedroom's carpet was freshly vacuumed, probably by the CSU searching for trace evidence. The room looked pristine, nothing out of place.

"That he's unique in the way he thinks." I knelt and scanned beneath the bed. Found nothing. Stood and glanced at her.

"In other words," she said. "Hard to pigeonhole."

"Seems to be going around."

"Makes me think of something I once read: it is essential for an investigator to understand his opponent's intellect, training, and aptitude and then respond accordingly."

I paused. "My article last month."

"Yes. It was one of your better ones this year." Her eyes became careful planets orbiting the room in precise symmetry. Occasionally, she would move her lips slightly but then furrow her eyes and shake her head slightly as if she were having a quiet discourse with herself. "I didn't agree with all your conclusions, but I did agree with the section about not expecting a person of inferior or superior intellect to act in conventional ways."

We entered the bathroom.

"Well, that's the one part I can't take credit for." Shaving cream and a razor lay on the counter. A laundry bin sat in the corner. I lifted the washcloth that was lying on top and gently held it against my cheek. Still slightly damp. "It's not a direct quote, but the concept comes from C. Auguste Dupin's approach in 'The Purloined Letter.' I credited him in the endnotes."

"I know," she said. "I read them."

Now this was my kind of woman.

I knew from the case files that the crime scene unit had found strands of Taylor's hair in the shower drain. I saw nothing else of note in the shower area.

"But," she said, "I was surprised you'd cite a fictional story."

"Well, my daughter—that is, stepdaughter—she's a big fan of Poe. She convinced me to read three of his detective stories. Not bad, actually."

"I'll have to check them out."

We took our time exploring the upstairs rooms, then headed to the first floor where we found Lieutenant Kurt Mason sending one of the members of his crime scene unit to examine Brigitte's car.

As he left, Cheyenne approached Taylor's liquor cabinet and pointed to a half-empty wine bottle. "Brunello di Montalcino, 1997. Nice. This man knew his wine." She gestured toward the array of bottles. "But, there's an awful lot of pretty potent stuff there. You think he had a drinking problem?"

Kurt shook his head. "Someone with a drinking problem doesn't leave half-empty bottles sitting around, or keep a shelf full of booze out in the open. He hides the bottles in the cupboard, under the bed, in the closet." Whether or not Kurt realized it, his voice was becoming softer with each word. He knelt and peered through a bottle of vodka. "No. Taylor didn't have a problem. He had a hobby."

Cheyenne and I exchanged glances. I was pretty sure Kurt didn't drink, but I knew that his wife Cheryl had picked up the habit after their baby daughter's death last winter. And, despite all the times I'd visited their home since he invited me to join the task force last January, I'd never seen any half-empty bottles lying around.

Time to change the subject.

"Prints and DNA," I said. "Anything yet?"

Kurt stood, shook his head. "Not a thing."

I looked in the kitchen trash can: a granola cereal box, a few crumpled napkins, orange peels. Closed the lid. "Listen, I've been thinking we should take a closer look at the victimology."

Cheyenne spoke, mirroring my thoughts. "The more you know about the victims' lifestyle, history, and habits, the more you'll know about the killer."

"Yes." She'd obviously read one of my articles from last year too. Impressive. "How is he choosing them? Where did his life intersect with theirs? Let's go deeper. Not just the typical things like acquaintances, place of employment, home address, club memberships. I want to know what route our victims took to work, where they rented their videos, where they bought their gas."

I realized I was giving orders and caught myself. "I'm sorry. I mean, that's the approach I think we should take."

"We'll get Robinson and Kipler on it," Kurt said. He didn't seem bothered by my tone.

"I need to talk to Kipler anyway," Cheyenne interjected. "I'll give them a call." She pulled out her cell and stepped into the dining room.

When she was gone Kurt glanced at the door at the far end of the kitchen. "Have you seen the garage?"

"Not yet."

"C'mon. It's time you had a look."

21

Taylor's garage was a brightly lit sanctum for his freshly waxed Lexus SUV, which sat perfectly centered between the walls. A workbench skirted the west side. The room appeared spotless except for the wide, angular swathe of blood where the killer had done his work.

Most of the evidence had already been removed from the garage and taken to the lab, including the ropes that had bound Taylor, the gag, and his corpse itself; but the manila envelope with the killer's handwritten message to me was still lying on the workbench: "Shade won't be bothering you anymore, Agent Bowers."

I slid the photos out of the envelope and found that they were snapshots of Tessa leaving her high school. Taylor had included a note that read, "She would be such an easy target. You should keep a better eye on her.—Shade."

My fingers tensed, and as I set down the photos I realized that, despite how much I value human life, I was glad Sebastian Taylor was dead.

According to the case files, the tire impressions that had been found two weeks ago beside one of the mailboxes Shade had used matched the tread patterns on Taylor's SUV. I asked Kurt, "Both of Taylor's guns are at the lab?"

"Yes."

"And neither had been discharged? Neither was loaded?"

"That's right."

The door to the house opened, and Cheyenne joined us again.

"I think our guy emptied the guns while Taylor showered," I said. "It was all one elaborate, twisted game."

Cheyenne looked a little confused. "Talk me through that."

"Taylor was well-trained. He never would have carried a gun without a chambered cartridge, and he would have almost certainly gotten a shot off at the intruder if either of his guns were loaded. I'm thinking the killer must have gotten into Taylor's house, found the guns, and emptied them prior to the time Taylor entered the garage. The perfect time to empty the guns would have been while Taylor showered."

One of the CSU members stopped dusting for prints on the doorknob and stepped our way. Brown hair. Early thirties. Inquisitive face. I recognized him as one of the men who'd been waiting outside the mine when we investigated Heather's body on Thursday. We hadn't met yet, so I guessed he was new to the unit. I extended my hand. "Special Agent Bowers."

"Reggie Greer."

We shook hands, then I knelt beside the driver's door and he squatted beside me. "See the blood here, under the car? Taylor must have approached the vehicle and was opening the door when the killer, who was hidden beneath the car, struck."

I gestured with my hand, imitating the slicing motion of the killer's blade. "One, two. First the right leg. See the cast-off splatter over there?" Kurt and Cheyenne nodded. Reggie scrutinized the bloodstains.

With my finger, I traced the outline of the blood spatter. "Taylor was already on his way to the ground when the killer sliced his left Achilles tendon. You can see how the blood spatter from the right leg begins perpendicular to the vehicle and ends parallel to it, so Taylor twisted counterclockwise on his way to the ground. Probably landed on his back. I can't be certain about that, though. Bloodstain analysis isn't my specialty."

I stood and looked around.

Reggie was staring at me. "Blood spatter's not your specialty?"

"That's right." I was studying the sight lines out the window to Brigitte's car. If the lights had been off inside the garage, her headlights would have partially illuminated the room.

Reggie must have been listening in on my conversation with Kurt a few moments earlier, because he said, "But if the killer snuck into the house and unloaded the guns, why didn't he just kill Taylor while he was defenseless in the shower? Why wait?"

"Maybe this wasn't just about killing him. I don't think he wanted it to be over quickly: trap him in the garage, disable him, but leave him the guns to make him think he'd be able to get away. Like a cat toying with a mouse."

"Death isn't enough," Cheyenne said softly. "He wants to see them squirm first."

I heard a cell ring, and both Kurt and I reached for our pockets. When I pulled out my phone, I noticed I'd forgotten to turn it on for the day. Kurt tapped at his screen. "I gotta take this."

He stepped away. I turned on my cell, and Reggie resumed dusting for prints on the doorknob. Cheyenne stood beside me quietly for a moment, then said, "Did you get to the evidence list page in the case files?"

I put my phone away. "No."

She pointed to a receipt on the far end of the workbench. "It's for Chinese takeout. CSU found three empty cartons of food."

"You're kidding me." I checked the time on the receipt. The cashier had rung it up at 8:18 p.m.

"No. Brigitte picked up the food on the way here, but none of it was in her stomach." Then she added grimly, no doubt referring to Brigitte's dismemberment, "We didn't need an autopsy to figure that one out."

But Taylor had showered, changed, and was about to get into his car when he was attacked . . . He wasn't expecting takeout, he was expecting to leave . . .

We could check the incoming calls and text messages on Brigitte's phone, but for now it looked to me like the killer had somehow contacted her and convinced her to bring over the food.

And the food cartons had been empty when CSU found them.

Which meant that he ate the Chinese food while he killed and dismembered those two people.

This guy was the real deal. As cold and disturbing as they get.

"Has Dr. Bender completed the autopsy on Taylor yet?" I asked Cheyenne.

She shook her head. "I don't know."

I speed-dialed his number, and when Eric picked up I apologized for calling him so early, then asked how the sleepover had gone. "Good," he said. "The girls are in Dora's room right now on the computer."

It surprised me that Tessa was already awake, but I stuck to the case. "Eric, when is Sebastian Taylor's autopsy scheduled?"

"I'm leaving for the hospital in about half an hour." Then he added soberly, "It's been a busy week. I've barely been able to keep up. I plan to get started about ten."

I'm not a fan of watching autopsies. I looked at my watch: 9:09.

It struck me that in less than forty-eight hours I would be back on the stand in Chicago. I decided not to think about that. "Is it all right if I swing by and have a look at the body before you get started?"

"Sure. I'll have Lance Rietlin meet you. He's my resident this year. He'll get you whatever you need. Something specific you're looking for?"

"I have a few questions about the wounds, the way he was attacked. I'll see you there."

"OK. See you soon."

Pocketing the phone, I turned to Cheyenne. "We can let CSU finish up here. If we leave now, I think we'll have just enough time to inspect the corpse before Dr. Bender gets started."

She pulled out her keys. "Let me take one more look around. I'll meet you at the car."

22

Tessa and Dora had taken some time away from the videos to shower, dress, and eat a breakfast of cold pizza before returning to the computer to check their Facebook pages.

After ten minutes, Dora slapped the desk.

"I just remembered this other video I wanted to show you." Every one of her words sounded slightly squished because of the strawberry bubble gum she'd popped into her mouth a few minutes earlier. "Have you seen the ones of those kids doing the Rubik's Cube blindfolded?"

"Uh-uh." Tessa had heard about the Rubik's Cube videos and knew they'd been around for a while but hadn't really been that interested in them. But now it sounded like it might make Dora happy, might keep her from thinking about the reason she hadn't been able to sleep so well, so she acted like she was into the idea. "Sure, yeah, let's check 'em out."

"It's pretty insane." Dora was tapping at the keyboard. "You ever try to figure one out?"

"Nope."

"Seriously?"

"Yeah, why?"

Dora shrugged. "I don't know. It's just, you're so into puzzles and stuff." She scrolled to a frozen video image of a Chinese girl about their age holding a Rubik's Cube. "Here's the best one. She does it in less than a minute."

She pressed "play," and Tessa watched as the girl in the video studied the mixed-up cube, waited while someone else blindfolded her, and then twisted the sides until, only fifty-seven seconds later, the entire cube was solved. Then she set it down, removed the blindfold, and smiled.

"Amazing, huh?" Dora pulled her own Rubik's Cube off her bookshelf and handed it to Tessa. All the sides were mixed up. "At first I thought maybe she memorized the moves, but I don't know, she must have twisted it like forty or fifty times."

"Let's watch it again."

They did.

"Seventy-two," Tessa said.

"Seventy-two what?"

"She twisted it seventy-two times."

Reaching across the keyboard, Tessa slid the cursor to the "play" icon and tapped the mouse button. Dora took the opportunity to look in the mirror and pick at her hair.

When the video was done, Tessa began to study the cube Dora had handed her.

"It's wild, huh?" Dora said. "I can't do it. There are like a billion different combinations."

Tessa considered that . . . six sides . . . nine squares on each side . . . "Probably more than that," she mumbled.

"So, see?" Dora said. "That's what makes it so amazing that those kids can solve it blindfolded."

"I think I can do it."

"Do what? Solve it?"

"Yeah," Tessa said. She was already practicing twisting the sides, getting a feel for the way the cube worked, the way one turn would affect the color combinations on the other sides.

"Well, yeah, if you practice for like—"

Dora's dad called to her from the other room, and she tapped a finger against the air. "Hold that thought."

While her friend slipped away, Tessa examined the cube. There were at least three ways to go about solving it. First, cheat. Look up the solution online. Maybe watch an instructional video.

Not exactly her thing.

Second, work the cube until you instinctively knew the patterns, sort of like typing or learning a musical instrument. But that would take days, weeks. Maybe longer.

No, to solve it quickly, you'd need a different approach.

So, math. By assigning a different number to each of the fifty-four squares, solving the cube became nothing more than a slightly—OK, a little more than *slightly*—complex three-dimensional algebraic equation. And since the middle pieces didn't move, and each of the other squares was fixed in relationship to the neighboring square on the adjacent side of the cube, the number of turns needed to solve it shrank exponentially.

She figured that, however mixed up the sides were, the cube could always be solved in fewer than forty turns.

Probably less than thirty.

The girl in the video hadn't been efficient enough in her solution.

Dora returned and plopped beside Tessa on the bed. "My dad is so totally lost this week without my mom around."

"Where is she again?"

"Some real estate convention thing in Seattle. Comes back on Wednesday. Anyway, he has to go to the hospital to do an autopsy and he needs me to run some errands. So I'll have to drop you off at your house by ten."

That gave them half an hour.

"No prob." Tessa mentally assigned numbers to each of the fifty-four tiles on the cube. "I'm ready."

"If you say so." Dora held out her hand. "Let me mix it up."

"It's already mixed up."

"I'll mix it up *more*."

Tessa managed not to roll her eyes. "Whatever." She gave Dora the cube.

Dora turned her back, and Tessa could hear the sides clicking, turning.

In truth, mixing up the cube would be just like shuffling a deck of cards in which three times through was no different than twenty times—the degree of randomness introduced into the order of the cards was statistically identical; you could twist and mix it for five minutes, five hours, or five days and it wouldn't really alter the number of turns required to solve it.

After about thirty seconds or so, Dora turned and handed Tessa the cube.

She studied it. Rotated it 360 degrees. Memorized the color combinations.

"Time me." Then she closed her eyes.

"You can't be serious."

Tessa opened her eyes. "What?"

"With your eyes closed?"

"The Chinese girl did."

"She probably practiced forever."

"Maybe she didn't practice at all. Who knows? I can do it."

"No way."

"OK, how about we put a latte on the line. If I can solve it, you buy me one on the way home."

Dora shrugged. Chomped her gum. "OK. And vice versa. Do I need to get you a blindfold or can I trust you?"

Tessa closed her eyes again. "You can trust me."

"All right, girl." Then a pause. Tessa assumed that Dora was checking her watch. "Ready . . . set . . . go."

She took a moment to mentally review the relationship of the fifty-four numbers.

"I started the time," Dora said.

"Shh." Tessa began turning the sides of the cube, reorienting the numbers in her head with each turn, visualizing them twist and flip around each other as if the cube were transparent and all the squares had the numbers stenciled on them. Calculating, recalculating their position, their movement, their patterns. It wasn't as difficult as she'd thought it'd be.

"That's thirty seconds."

"Quiet."

In her mind's eye, she saw the sides forming, the red side complete, the white side missing only one side piece. She paused. Thought. Twisted.

There. Two sides.

Close.

She worked at the cube methodically. Systematically.

"Fifty seconds."

"Dora, shh!"

Turn, turn.

Turn.

Yes. All the numbers aligned.

There. She punched the cube onto the bed and opened her eyes. "Time."

"A minute four seconds," Dora said. They were both staring at the cube, which was at least as mixed up as before. "Wow." Dora used a friendly kind of sarcasm. "Impressive. I think I'll get a grande."

"Dang," Tessa muttered. "That should have worked."

"Here." Dora stuck the cube into the satchel that Tessa used as a purse. "Take it. It's yours."

"No, that's crazy."

"Seriously. That thing is just way too hard for me." She waited for Tessa to take it. "Go on. It's cool."

Finally, Tessa accepted it. "Sweet. Thanks."

"Oh!" Dora said. "You are *not* gonna believe this. We're getting a dog!"

Dora was the queen of randomness.

"A dog?" Tessa didn't even try to hide her disdain.

"Yeah. Dad says he thinks it'll help. Things have been hard, you know, ever since—"

"Yeah, I get it."

"I know it seems kind of weird to get a dog when—"

"No-no-no-no." Tessa squeezed all the no's together into one word. She knew that coping with grief and guilt wasn't easy, even if something wasn't your fault. Lately she'd turned to journaling and writing poetry to sort through her feelings, but right after her mom died, she'd been into cutting, self-inflicting on her arm, to deal with the pain and loneliness. Getting a pet was a lot better way to cope than that.

"You don't have to explain. But it's just, a dog? C'mon, get a cat instead."

Dora looked somewhat deflated. "What's wrong with a dog? Dogs are man's best friend."

"Well, I have a policy: whenever my best friend starts sniffing my butt and eating his own vomit, it's time to find a new best friend."

"Oh," Dora said. "Wow. Thanks for that image."

"No prob."

"Maybe we oughtta get a cat."

"Good choice."

And then Dora launched into an explanation of how her cousin had gotten a cat when she was visiting her last summer in Orlando and how she'd introduced her to this really hot guy who worked at Disney World—and then Dora sighed and started talking about how much she'd miss Tessa while she was in DC this summer and how she was hoping to get a job at Elitch Gardens after they were done with finals, which she was *totally* not ready for . . .

But Tessa's attention had drifted back to Dora's screen saver.

She carefully averted her eyes and pretended to listen to her friend.

I was outside Taylor's house waiting for Cheyenne when Kurt approached me. He didn't look happy. "That call I got a few minutes ago," he said. "It was the captain. There's something I need to tell you."

By Kurt's tone of voice I was pretty sure the captain hadn't invited us to join him for a beer after work. "What is it?"

"You know how he's not exactly dialed into your techniques . . ."

Here we go. "Yes?"

"Well, last night he talked with your supervisor at the Bureau—Assistant Director Wellington."

Great.

Ever since I'd testified in an internal affairs review a few years ago that had temporarily set back her career plans, Margaret Wellington had been gunning for me with both barrels. I braced myself for bad news.

"She told Captain Terrell that with Basque's trial and the shooting yesterday, she's afraid you might be distracted, not at the top of your game."

I could feel my temperature rising. "The top of my game."

"Her words, not mine. She's sending someone else to work the case with us. Captain Terrell already signed off on it. He's a big fan of those profiling TV shows, so he—"

"She's sending a profiler?" If Margaret was sending Lien-hua, things were going to get very awkward very fast.

"Yeah."

"Did he say who? Was it Special Agent Jiang? Lien-hua Jiang?"

"No. Some guy named Vanderveld. Didn't mention a first name."

Oh, that was even worse. "Jake Vanderveld."

"So you know him."

"Oh yeah. We're acquainted."

Kurt stared at me for a moment, no doubt trying to decipher what lay beneath my words. "Anything I should know?"

Margaret knew how I felt about Jake. That's probably why she'd assigned him to the case.

"Have you noticed how I'm not exactly the biggest fan of profilers?"

"I may have picked up on that."

"Well, he's the reason why." I saw Cheyenne climbing into the driver's seat. "I'll run it down for you later. When does he get here?"

"He's supposed to fly in sometime around noon. I guess he'll probably want to be briefed this afternoon at HQ. I'll let you know when I find out more."

Cheyenne rolled down the window and slipped her key into the ignition. "What's up?" she called.

"I'll tell you on the way." I opened the car door. "Let's go visit the morgue."

23

Amy Lynn Greer sighed.

Her husband Reggie was working a crime scene, so she was the one who'd had to drop their three-year-old son off at day care half an hour ago, even though she had two articles that were both due to her editor by noon.

She would have loved to be covering the murders that Reggie was investigating, rather than writing her column on local politics or the follow-up piece on the amount of drug use in children of professional baseball players who use steroids, but her boss refused to assign her any articles that related to Reggie's cases.

When Reggie had first gotten the job, she'd thought that in her line of work, being married to one of Denver's crime scene unit forensics specialists might have its advantages, but Reggie was under the scrutinizing eye of Lieutenant Kurt Mason, who'd informed him when he got the job that if he *ever* released *any* details about *any* investigation to his wife, he would be without a job and in court facing criminal charges before her story ever ran. Period. She'd met Lieutenant Mason and could tell he was a man of his word.

She took a small break from outlining the steroids story, checked her email, and found five rejection letters, one from each of the literary agents she'd sent her book proposal to.

Five in one day.

That actually might beat her old record.

A knock at the door interrupted her thoughts.

"Yes?"

The door opened, and a vaguely familiar female voice said, "I've got something for you."

Amy Lynn glanced over and saw one of the secretaries, a sandy-haired, thick-wristed woman she could never remember the name of, standing in the doorway, holding an oversized ceramic flowerpot filled with a shiny-leafed plant sprouting a cluster of half-inch-long, purplish-white flowers. The pot was so large she needed to use both hands.

"What's that?"

"Flowers." The woman explained as if Amy Lynn couldn't tell. Her voice was strained with the effort of holding the oversized pot. "Can I set 'em down?"

"Sure." Amy Lynn slid some papers out of the way. She tried to remember the woman's name but couldn't. She thought it was maybe Britt or Brenda or Brett or something preppy and girlish like that.

The secretary eased the pot onto her desk. "So, what's the special occasion?"

Amy Lynn gazed at the flowers.

"There is no special occasion."

Flowers?

Who would send you flowers? Reggie would never do that.

Small clusters of stamen stuck out of the center of each of the feathery-white flowers. The leaves overlapped and grew in layers, each set of two leaves at a perpendicular angle to the ones beside them. The strong minty scent was somewhat familiar, but also unfamiliar at the same time.

She knew how to identify a few kinds of flowers, but mostly just the ones everyone knew—lilies and daisies and roses. She didn't have a clue what kind of flowers these were.

But she was more curious about who might have sent them than what kind they were. "Was there a note?"

The secretary with the all-too-forgettable name fished out a small envelope from where it had fallen behind some leaves.

The envelope was eggshell white and had only four words handwritten on the front: "To Amy Lynn Greer."

She immediately realized that it wasn't her husband's handwriting and that if he'd sent her the flowers he wouldn't have included her last name.

But if not Reggie, who? She had a few sources who were male, and a few friends who were a little more than friends—but none of them would have been brash enough to send her flowers. At least she didn't think so.

The secretary lurked. "I didn't open it." She pointed to the envelope.

"Thank you . . . um, wait, I'm sorry. What's your name again?"

The woman looked hurt by the question. "Brett Neilson. I've been working here for—"

"Thank you, Brett, yes. I'm sorry. I'm not so good with names."

"It's OK," Brett said, but she didn't leave, just stared longingly at the flowers. "My husband never sends me flowers."

Amy Lynn didn't know what to say to that. Finally, she just mumbled, "Well, men. You know." It sounded pathetic when she said it, but it somehow seemed to satisfy Brett Neilson, who gave her a parting half-smile and backed out of the room, pulling the door closed behind her.

After Brett was gone, Amy Lynn studied the flowers again. They had a formal, functional quality about them rather than a flirty, romantic one. And that scent. Was it a spice?

And who sent them?

She had no idea.

The note.

Ripping open the envelope, she found a small slip of card stock paper with a short, cryptic, handwritten message:

> Must needs we tell of others' tears?
> Please, Mrs. Greer, have a heart.
> —John

John?

John who?

She didn't recognize the handwriting.

Amy Lynn considered all the Johns she knew and almost immediately eliminated all of them from her list of people who might possibly send her flowers, especially ones with an enigmatic note like this.

Maybe a reference to a story she'd done? Something about grief? Tragedy? Someone's death?

Amy Lynn turned to her computer and felt excitement stir inside of her for the first time that morning.

Figuring out who sent the flowers was much more interesting than analyzing local politics or writing about the families of drug-abusing baseball players. Her editor would just have to wait.

She shoved her other notes aside, tapped at her keyboard, and began to search through the articles she'd written, looking for references to anyone named John.

24

Cheyenne and I arrived at Baptist Memorial Hospital, one of the oldest and most respected hospitals in the state of Colorado, at 9:46 a.m.

The hospital administration had been renovating the eastern wing for the last six months, and I could see that they still had a long way to go. Local press coverage had emphasized how "patient care had not been compromised in the least" during the current renovations, but over the years I've seen how much spin finds its way into press releases, so I hadn't been completely convinced by the hospital administrator's carefully worded PR statements.

I was stepping out of the car when my cell rang.

"What did we do before cell phones?" Cheyenne said good-naturedly.

"Got into fewer car accidents." I looked at the caller ID picture on the screen.

Lien-hua Jiang.

OK, this was inconvenient. Cheyenne glanced at me. "Excuse me for a minute," I said.

"Sure." She started across the parking lot, and I waited until she was out of earshot.

"Hey," I said to Lien-hua.

"Hello, Pat. How are you?"

"Good. Things are good, pretty good." A stiff and meaningless response. I began to follow Cheyenne but made sure I stayed far enough back so she wouldn't hear my conversation. "How are you?"

"I'm OK. Thanks for asking."

"Well, that's good."

"Yeah." A pause that spoke volumes. "Pat, you know why I'm calling, I think."

Wow. Well, she's not wasting any time, is she?

"I'm thinking maybe I can guess." The words had a bite to them, and I knew it, but I let them stand.

"Please, it's hard enough doing this over the phone. You don't have to make it worse."

"I'm not trying to—" I really did not want to be doing this. Not here, not now. Twenty meters in front of me Cheyenne was entering the hospital. "Look, can we talk about this later, maybe later today?"

"I'm going on assignment to Boston and I don't want to have this hanging over my head. It's nothing against you, Pat. You know that." I could hear pain in her voice but no condemnation. She still cared about me, wasn't blaming me. And that just made this harder.

"It's just . . ." she said. "Things haven't been . . . It's not working."

For more than a month now things had been deteriorating, and we'd both been dancing around the issue, avoiding saying what we both knew we needed to. "Really, Lien-hua, this isn't a good—"

"It's over, Pat."

I felt a sting, a deep sense of finality and regret. "No, we'll talk about it later. Maybe when I get to DC later this week we can—"

"No. Please. It would be too hard for me." Her voice wasn't harsh, but it was firm.

A long pause followed her words. I had no idea what to say.

I tried to formulate the right words, but they escaped me, "So then . . ."

"Yes."

I arrived at the hospital's automatic sliding doors, and they whisked open. I was barely aware of myself stepping inside.

On a better day, either Lien-hua or I might have found something helpful or healing to say before we ended the call, but on this day, neither of us did. A few thick moments of silence fell between us until at last she said good-bye and I said good-bye, and then the conversation was over. Long before I was ready for it to be.

The sliding doors closed behind me, and I stood staring blankly at the phone until I felt Cheyenne's presence beside me.

"Everything all right?"

"Yes," I lied.

I slipped the phone into my pocket, and it felt unusually awkward and uncomfortable. I pulled it out and jammed it back in, harder.

She looked at me with understanding and concern. "No, it's not."

"I'm all right," I said, but I didn't look her in the eye. "Let's go."

———————————————■———————————————

A few minutes later we were being escorted down the hall by Lance Rietlin, a fidgety man in his late twenties who spent the walk telling Cheyenne how much he appreciated being able to work under someone as experienced and respected as Dr. Bender, but I wasn't really listening. Instead, I was trying to convince myself that Lien-hua and I could still be friends, that we would be able to put aside the deep feelings we'd had for each other and move back to the way things were before we started going out—because that's what you tell yourself at times like this.

You tell yourself those things, you hide inside naivety, because the truth is too painful to admit.

And the truth was: from now on it would be difficult to work with Lien-hua; I would be jealous of the attention she gave to other men and I would always wonder if we—I—could have done more to salvage our relationship.

Lance led us down a set of stairs and into the hospital's lower level past a series of custodial supply closets and the physical therapy room. "They're doing some kind of maintenance on the elevators," he explained as we passed the "out of order" signs taped across the doors. "They're supposed to have 'em up and running in an hour or so. But I wouldn't hold my breath."

As my thoughts wandered back to Lien-hua, I realized that getting things out in the open was somewhat of a relief—even though going our separate ways was something I'd never wanted.

We arrived at the morgue and Lance unlocked the door. "Pretty full in there this week. Dr. Bender and I have been . . . Well."

He didn't need to say more.

"Have at it." He swung the door open. The overly sharp smell of hospital disinfectants filled the air. "Eric should be by in about ten minutes."

I noticed Cheyenne glance at her watch.

"I'll be upstairs," Lance said. "Unless you want me to stay?"

"No," I replied. "We'll be fine."

He gave me a small nod. "If you need anything, just call the admitting department. They'll page me." He told me the number, I thanked him, and after he'd stepped away Cheyenne and I entered the sterile white chamber where death is dissected and studied.

The room looked like most of the morgues I've visited over the past fifteen years: stainless steel counters, bright fluorescent lights, microscopes, scales, sanitary disposal units, trays of instruments. An empty gurney.

And, of course, the vibrating electric Stryker saws for cutting through skulls without destroying the tender brain matter inside, Hagedorn needles for sewing up body cavities, skull chisels, bone saws, rib cutters.

Tools of the trade.

The gurneys that bore the dead would be in the freezer.

As I crossed the room, I thought about how we design morgues to be as impersonal and institutional as possible. Despite how messy and nauseating dead bodies are, the place where we probe them is sparkling and clean and carefully sanitized to cover up the smell of decay.

Maybe it's our way of dealing with death, of helping us forget the laughter and tears and smiles of the people we're dissecting.

Maybe that's a good thing—being able to forget.

We reached the freezer, and I stared at the door for a moment.

"OK," I said softly. "Let's have a look at the governor."

25

I unlatched the door to the morgue's freezer. Swung it open.

A swirl of cold air nudged out and encircled me. I could see five gurneys inside.

Dead lips whispering to me, *"Why? Why didn't you do something? Why didn't you come sooner?"*

On each gurney, a cadaver. I recognized the faces of three of them as the victims from earlier this week. Strangely, none of the bodies were covered, and two of the corpses were headless—two, not one. Not just Sebastian Taylor's.

What's going—?

And then as I took my first step into the freezer, I saw her. A woman, seated against the far wall, with the missing sheets from the bodies draped across her shoulders and arms. Her eyes were open.

I rushed toward her, Cheyenne beside me.

As I bent over the woman and felt for a pulse, I realized I'd seen her before at one of the coffeehouses I visit regularly. I didn't know her name, just her face, but somehow, recognizing her made things all the more urgent. Her skin was cold to the touch. Her lips, bluish, cyanotic, but she was still breathing. I found a faint heartbeat. "She's alive," I said to Cheyenne.

"Thank God. Let's get her out of here."

"Ma'am," I said. "We're going to help you." She moved her lips but made no sound. I noticed that she wasn't shivering, which meant she was in the advanced stages of hypothermia.

Cheyenne reached for one of her armpits to lift her.

"Careful." From my rock climbing trips I knew that moving people with severe hypothermia can jar them, cause them to go into shock or cardiac arrhythmia, but I didn't want to say that within earshot of the woman. "I'll get her."

As gently as I could, I lifted the woman. She had a slight frame, but still I felt a twitch of pain in my side where Grant had driven the axe handle into my ribs the day before.

I carried her to the empty gurney in the exam room, and Cheyenne ran ahead of me, pressed the intercom button, and called for a doctor to report to the morgue, stat!

I eased the woman onto the gurney. "We're going to get you warmed up."

As long as she remains conscious, she should be all right.

"It's going to be OK," Cheyenne said, but she must have realized how serious the woman's condition was because she whispered, only for my ears, "I'm not sure we can wait for a doctor."

"She'll be all right."

But as I was evaluating whether or not we should wait for a doctor or go looking for one, I saw the woman's eyes roll back. Cheyenne slapped her cheek firmly to keep her awake. "Stay with me," she said. "Stay with me!" But the woman's breathing was becoming choppier. Cheyenne called, "Pat—"

"I know."

The woman shuddered. Cheyenne slapped her cheek again, but this time she didn't respond.

I grabbed the end of the gurney to push it into the hall. "We have to warm her. Now."

26

As I passed through the door I remembered that the elevator on this level was out of service.

No!

In the wilderness you'd remove someone's clothes and lay beside her to share your body heat, but I figured we could do better than that here at the hospital.

I glanced down the hallway, reviewing the rooms we'd passed on the way to the morgue.

"The PT room," I mumbled and began to wheel the woman down the hallway as fast as I could.

"What is it?" Cheyenne caught up with me.

"Physical therapy, we passed it on the way here. They'll have a whirlpool."

Cheyenne hurried ahead of me and held open the door. I eased the gurney inside. "We're going to help you," I told the woman. "It's all right."

Gently, I took her in my arms.

He locked her in the morgue.

The killer tried to freeze her to death.

The sadistic, merciless nature of his crimes stunned me, nauseated me.

No one else was present, but I saw Cheyenne motion toward me from the far side of the room. "The whirlpool's over here."

The pool had been built into the floor, and as I descended the steps and entered the warm water, I saw Cheyenne reach for the control panel. "Leave the jets off," I said. "It might be too much of a shock to her system."

"Right."

Supporting her weight, I carefully lowered the woman into the water, but she began to shake, weak quivers running through her body. I lifted her a little, then lowered her again, more slowly, while Cheyenne spoke to her, comforting her, reassuring her from beside the pool.

A few moments later the woman coughed and blinked her eyes rapidly. The color was returning to her face.

"He . . ." She was speaking softly, but at least she was speaking. "He left me in . . ."

"I know," I said. "Who was it? Who did this to you?" She shook her head. She didn't know. "What's your name?"

She gasped. Took a breath. "Kelsey."

"We're going to get you warmed up, Kelsey. You'll be OK."

She gave a small nod.

Moments passed. Curls of warm steam rose from the water and meandered around us.

Kelsey's breathing began to grow more normal, more steady. Then I heard running in the hall.

"It's the doctor," I called to Cheyenne, but she was already heading for the door. A moment later a man in doctor's scrubs, a nurse, and Lance Rietlin came hurrying into the room. "Over here!" I yelled as I lifted Kelsey from the water and carefully stepped out of the whirlpool.

"Let's get her on the gurney," Lance said, then helped me lay her down. He touched her hand lightly. "What's your name?"

"Her name's Kelsey," Cheyenne said, then brushed some wet hair out of Kelsey's eyes.

"We need to get you out of these clothes," the nurse said to Kelsey. "Is that all right?"

Kelsey nodded, and Cheyenne and the nurse removed her wet clothes while Lance retrieved some towels and blankets from the linen closet. Then he handed them to the nurse, who quickly and thoroughly dried her off and laid the blankets over her.

The doctor, a balding man in his fifties with a look of permanent worry etched on his face, checked Kelsey's eyes with a penlight. "Whose idea was it to warm her in the pool?"

"Mine," I said. "There was no other way to heat her up. No doctors here, no elevators. She was going into shock. We needed to do something."

"We came down the elevators," he said. It sounded like an accusation.

"They were out of service when I brought them down here," Lance explained.

After a moment of reflection, the doctor seemed to accept that. "All right. Well, let's get her out of here." Then Cheyenne told me she'd reconnect with me in a few minutes, there was a rush and swirl of bodies, she left with the medical crew and I was alone in the room.

I grabbed a towel and wiped it across my face and arms. Right now Kelsey had plenty of people helping her, so I decided to return to the morgue and have a look around, especially now that it was a crime scene for attempted murder.

I threw the towel on the pile. Turned toward the hall.

A man stood in the doorway. "Hey, Pat. Good to see you."

The profiler, Special Agent Jake Vanderveld, had arrived.

27

"Hello, Jake," I said.

He stepped into the room. Four years younger than I am. Handsome. Smart. On his way up. Jake had tousled blond hair, intensely blue eyes, and he wore his neatly trimmed mustache like a badge. Even a decade after graduating with his master's degree in abnormal psychology, he still had the honed physique of the Division I swimmer that he'd been at Cornell.

"So, Assistant Director Wellington tells me you can use a little help on this case." He was staring at my dripping clothes. "I'm glad I was available." He was smirking.

"I thought you weren't arriving until this afternoon?"

"Shifted my schedule around. I figured you'd be glad to have an extra set of eyes on this thing. So that woman they were taking down the hall, what happened?"

As I summarized, I noticed that in the haste to get Kelsey to a room, her clothes had been left on the floor. Jake watched me pick them up, and the gears seemed to be turning in his head. "You took her into the whirlpool?"

"Yes."

"I wish I could have been here to help."

Immediately, I sensed that his words could be taken two ways: either as an expression of genuine concern or as a lame and completely inappropriate joke. His tone of voice made me think it was the latter of the two, but before I could respond to him, my phone rang. I was amazed the water hadn't shorted it out.

Tessa's face came up on my caller ID and I told Jake to hang on a second, then answered the cell. "I'm in the middle of something, Tessa. This isn't the best time to talk."

"Um, Agent Jiang called, like, half an hour ago. She left a message on my cell. Said she'd tried you first."

She must have called before you turned on your cell.

"She must really be trying to get a hold of you," Tessa went on. "You're supposed to give her a shout."

It'd been bad enough talking to Lien-hua with Cheyenne nearby; I definitely did not want to do it in front of Jake Vanderveld. I laid the phone against my chest to muffle the sound. "Hey, could you give me a couple minutes? Call dispatch, get a CSU team over here to process the morgue."

A small grin from him. "I'll see you soon, Pat."

"All right, Jake."

Then he left and I told Tessa, "I talked with Agent Jiang about twenty minutes ago."

"And?"

"And what?"

"Is it official?"

This girl was more observant than most of the agents I work with.

"It's been that evident, huh?"

"That would be a yes."

"Well, I guess, you could say that, yes; it's official. Listen, about lunch—"

"Your decision or hers?"

"Not so much a decision as a mutual acknowledgment." I headed for the hall. "I have to take care of a few things, maybe I can call you later."

"I'm sorry, Patrick." It sounded like she really meant it. "Breaking up sucks."

"I'm a big boy, Raven. I can handle it."

"Doesn't matter how big you are." She paused. I heard her take a sip of something. "It still sucks."

Here I was, getting relationship counseling from a teenage girl. I wasn't sure what to say. "Well, thanks."

Since my clothes were soaked, after I'd had a chance to have a look around the morgue, I would need to get changed, and that meant swinging home. "Are we still on for lunch?"

"Yeah. I was thinking that new vegan place—Fruition. You know all those signs, 'Come to Fruition,' 'Have you tasted Fruition?'"

How exciting. Bean curd, spinach, and chickpeas.

"Are you still at Pandora's house?"

"She dropped me off at home."

"OK." I was almost to the morgue. "I can probably be there in about half an hour. You can pack until I arrive."

"Well, actually, though, I'm pretty busy."

"Oh, really? On a Saturday morning? What are you doing?"

"Dora gave me this Rubik's Cube that I'm trying to figure out. And, oh yeah, I'm finishing up this iced triple grande three pump dolce breve with whip, pumpkin pie spice latte before you get here." She rattled off the name of her drink in one breath.

I stopped walking and stared blankly at the wall. "You're kidding me. Please tell me you're kidding me."

"It's Dora's favorite. I decided to try one. It's good. Should I save some for you?"

This was very troubling. "Admit it. You bought that just to annoy me."

I heard her take a sip. "If I did, you deserve it. You're a coffee snob."

"Not snob, connoisseur—wait a minute. Pumpkin pie spice is seasonal. They only serve that in the fall."

"They had some in the back."

"Oh, please tell me you didn't."

"I did."

"You're drinking mass-produced, factory-packaged coffee that was roasted and ground more than six months ago?"

143

I heard her sip again, a big hearty slurp. "Ahh. Yummy. Maybe I'll go buy you one."

"I'll see you in half an hour for lunch. Get packing. And put that thing down before someone arrests me for child abuse."

One more noisy sip. "See you."

I arrived at the morgue and found Dr. Eric Bender inside, rolling the as-of-yet unidentified headless corpse out of the freezer.

After a quick greeting, I filled him in about the woman we'd just rescued. He listened intently, occasionally shaking his head, and when I was done he said, "You mentioned that her name is Kelsey?"

"Yes."

"Then this was her husband." Eric gestured toward the corpse in front of us. "Travis Nash. He was brought in yesterday morning, myocardial infarction. There was no autopsy ordered, everything pointed to natural causes." He pulled out a file folder and showed me a picture of Travis before he'd been beheaded.

"We need to find out what this man really died of," I said. "But this exam room is now a crime scene—attempted murder. You'll need to either move him or wait for CSU to get in here."

Eric didn't look happy with that, but he didn't argue with me. "OK," he said.

"Can I have a look at Taylor?"

Eric nodded and I followed him into the freezer.

28

I stared at Taylor's headless, mutilated corpse. The case files mentioned that he'd been tortured, but I hadn't realized how extensive the injuries had been until now.

Eric must have noticed me observing the wounds. "This man did not die quickly," he said.

I was mentally reconstructing the way Sebastian Taylor had been attacked, when Eric pointed to the bone protruding from the corpse's right forearm. "Look here. His ulna is fractured, but there were no contusions near the site of the break. His wrist was also fractured."

"What does that mean?"

"I can't tell for certain from a cursory external observation, but most likely the killer used his bare hands." He pointed to the break in the forearm. "Based on the angle and severity of that open spiral fracture, the attacker would need to be unusually strong and has probably studied—"

"Martial arts, close quarters combat, or some type of hand to hand."

"Yes."

The killer found Taylor . . . disabled his surveillance cameras . . . possibly has skills in self-defense . . .

Military intelligence training?

Law enforcement experience?

"OK. Keep me up to speed."

He nodded. "I will."

I found Cheyenne standing beside the doorway to room 228, texting someone. She looked up as I approached. "Kelsey's doing a lot better."

"That's great."

"They have her on a warm saline IV to raise her core body temp." She finished sending her text and slid her phone into her pocket. "An officer's on his way over here to guard the room in case the killer finds out she survived and tries to return to finish what he started."

"Good. Did Kelsey give you a description of her assailant?"

"She wouldn't talk about it. When I asked her, she just closed her eyes and shook her head."

Sometimes victims take weeks before developing enough emotional distance to talk about life-threatening events, so, after an experience as traumatic as getting locked in a morgue, Kelsey's reaction didn't surprise me. But it wasn't going to make our job any easier.

"We'll follow up," Cheyenne said. "If she's willing to talk, I'll call for a sketch artist to come in. Oh, and Agent Vanderveld stopped by."

"Great."

"He seems like a man who is very sure of himself."

"That's one way to put it." I didn't really want to talk about Jake. "Hey, let's have an officer review the hospital's video surveillance cameras to find out when Kelsey arrived. Maybe there's some footage of her attacker entering or leaving the hospital."

"I'll get someone on it."

I quickly briefed Cheyenne on Kelsey's husband. She nodded solemnly, then glanced at her watch. "I can't even imagine what she's going through. I'm going to stay here for a little while. Whether or not she decides to talk, she needs someone with her right now."

"One more thing," I said. "I need to get home and change. Can I borrow your car?"

"Anytime."

I gave her Kelsey's wet clothes, she handed me the keys, and I was on my way.

———■———

Since receiving the flowers nearly an hour ago, Amy Lynn Greer had been searching through every article she'd written in the last year, looking for connections to stories about people named John, Jonathan, or Johnson, and had found a few possibilities, but nothing that looked relevant.

After she'd eliminated the articles that she'd personally worked on, she'd expanded her search to include articles by other journalists.

Still nothing solid.

The phrase about telling of others' tears made her vaguely uneasy, and as an investigative journalist, she didn't like mysteries that she couldn't solve.

A thought that had been nagging her was starting to become more and more intrusive.

Maybe it wasn't just a coincidence that she mysteriously received the flowers while her husband and the rest of the crime scene unit were investigating one of the most gruesome crime sprees in Denver's history.

She decided to give herself one more hour to see if she could uncover anything about the phrase "Must needs we tell of others' tears?" and then, even though she wasn't supposed to, she would call her husband to find out if this might be related to any of the cases he was working on.

All right, then. One more hour.

29

After talking with Patrick on the phone and torturing him about
the pumpkin pie spice latte, Tessa had spent some time lounging
in her room, listening to music and working on the Rubik's Cube,
but she couldn't solve it. Even with her eyes open.

And that really annoyed her.

She had her iPod docked to her stereo, and when the playlist came
to Vigilantes of Love's *Audible Sigh* CD, she cranked the music to
help her concentrate. A little retro, kind of an R.E.M college rock
feel, not quite as edgy as most of the bands she was into, but sweet
lyrics. Bill Mallonee was a genius with words.

When "Black Cloud O'er Me" came on, she couldn't help but
think of her conversation with Patrick. He'd really been into Lien-
hua, and even though he was acting like it wasn't a huge deal, he
must have been hurting pretty badly after breaking up with her.
Talk about a black cloud.

Tessa had started getting used to the idea of the two of them
being together but had noticed their relationship disintegrating for
the last couple of weeks, and it was probably better that they called
it quits now, before either of them ended up getting hurt worse.
She'd seen lots of kids at school drag things out way too long and
then break up. It wasn't pretty.

A carnage of hearts.

Sounded like something Bill Mallonee would write.

So, do what Pat asked. Pack. Cheer him up.

Obviously, since they were only going to be out East for three months, they weren't taking everything, but most of the stuff in their bedrooms needed to go. They'd been clearing out his closet the other night. Maybe she could just finish that before he got home.

Going into his room had always felt a little weird to her, like some kind of invasion of his personal space, but the longer they lived together, the more OK it seemed to her. Part of being in a family. One of the good parts.

She stepped inside. Glanced around.

Rumpled bedsheets on his bed. A half-read copy of Pascal's *Pensées* on the end table beside it, rock-climbing gear thrown on the floor under the window. Ansel Adams prints of Half Dome and El Capitan, two of the places he'd climbed, hung on the wall.

Two photos sat on his dresser. One of the family: Mom, Patrick, and her on the Staten Island Ferry—her mother bald from chemo. The other picture was of him in the Appalachian Mountains when he was a wilderness guide in college. He had a ponytail in the picture, and she'd gotten a ton of mileage out of that.

Scattered around the room were five heavy-duty cardboard moving boxes.

She popped open the one next to the closet and found it half full of dog-eared criminology textbooks and back issues of the *Journal of Environmental Psychology* and the *Journal of Forensic Sciences*, and a clutter of office supplies just thrown on top—pens, scissors, paper clips, pencil holders, USB cords, rubber bands—a pair of dress shoes, and some crumpled-up dress shirts. How he could be so meticulous in his FBI life and such a slob in his single-guy-at-home life had always been a mystery to her.

There was still room in the box, though, and she knew they didn't have a ton of extra moving boxes around so she opened the closet and saw that, apart from a couple pairs of running shoes, and an old backpack, the floor was empty.

But there was a shelf near the ceiling and some camping stuff sticking over the edge.

She dragged a folding chair to the closet, stepped up, and yanked down a first aid kit and daypack.

Only after she'd pulled down the sleeping bag did she see the shoe box shoved against the wall. Between her and the box lay an ocean of thick dust—which was way, way disgusting since the human body sheds over two million dead skin cells every hour and nearly 65 percent of dust found in homes is from human skin.

Ew.

Gingerly, she managed to retrieve the box without touching the layer of human remains. Then she stepped off the chair, closed her eyes, and blew the dead skin off the box.

Eyes open again, she realized it was an old Keds shoe box, which was a little weird since Patrick never had kids and the box wasn't big enough to hold his shoes.

There was stuff in it, but by the weight she could tell it wasn't a pair of shoes. She took one of Patrick's shirts from his dresser and wiped off the box.

And noticed her name written in black magic marker on the end.

But it wasn't Patrick's handwriting, it was her mother's.

30

Tessa sat on the bed, the shoe box on her lap.

Popped it open.

And found a small stack of postcards, two ticket stubs from a Twins game, three genuine arrowheads, a couple dozen letters stuffed back into their opened envelopes, a bunch of photos, a brochure from the Circus World Museum in Baraboo, Wisconsin, a few pictures that Tessa had drawn when she was a kid with big lopsided hearts and crayoned words that read, "I love you Mommy!!"

And turtle drawings.

Eight turtle pictures.

She'd always liked to draw turtles when she was a kid, probably because they were easy—just make a big circle, then add four feet and a smaller circle on top for the head. Bam. A turtle. When she was a kid, they'd seemed like masterpieces.

But now she could see how dorky they were.

Still, when she was a little girl, her mom had always found room for them on the fridge. Always.

And when Tessa saw the turtle pictures, she knew what kind of collection this was—the one special collection everyone has of the stuff no one else would ever understand. Stupid little things that wouldn't even bring you a dime at a garage sale, but that you'd go back into a burning building to save.

Tessa had a box like this too, under her bed.

But as she flipped through her mother's memory box, which she named it on the spot, her heart seemed to snag on something inside of her chest.

Why didn't Patrick ever give this to you? He knows how much Mom meant to you. Why would he keep this from you?

Maybe he'd forgotten about it, pushed it way back there one day and it just slipped his mind.

But maybe not.

Feeling somewhat betrayed, Tessa filed through the box's contents more carefully, taking the items out one at a time and placing them on the bed.

She found a tangled-up kite string and wondered why her mom had kept it. Then she pulled out a shell that she remembered finding during a trip to Lake Superior when she was ten. As she set the shell on the bed, she noticed what lay on the bottom of her mom's memory box.

Her fingers trembled.

A pregnancy test.

And the little plus sign was still visible, even after seventeen years.

She picked it up.

When your mom first looked at this, you were already growing inside her.

It was an obvious truth, totally obvious, but in that moment, to Tessa, it seemed profound.

She was holding the first proof her mother ever had that she was going to have a child, a daughter that she would name Tessa Bernice Ellis—Tessa, derived from St. Teresa of Avila, a mystic who was one of her favorite writers, and Bernice, the name of her mom's grandmother.

As Tessa stared at the plus sign, she thought of what it would have been like for her mom to look at this—still in college, not married, the guy she'd been seeing a total loser. A man who never became a part of his daughter's life, never even visited her.

Not even once.

Tessa felt the old anger, the old hatred, the old loneliness rising again.

Even when she was a kid, she'd realized that nearly all of her friends had a dad around somewhere. Even in families where their parents were separated or divorced, the dad would show up occasionally—in the summer maybe for a couple weeks, or on Tuesday nights, or for a couple weekends each month. Sure, not always, but unless he was dead, he was usually a part of their life.

So when she was about six or seven, she'd asked her mother if her dad was dead.

At first her mom wouldn't tell her, but Tessa wore her down until finally she'd said, "I don't know, Tess. I haven't seen him since the day I told him I was going to have a baby." Then she'd held Tessa close—she still remembered that—and her mother had added, "But just because your daddy isn't here doesn't mean you aren't loved. I get to love you double, from both of us."

But Tessa had pulled away. "But why did he go away, Mommy? How come he doesn't come back?"

Her mom had hesitated at first, then said, "What matters is that I love you and I'm never going to go away. I promise."

But then her mom did go away, not on purpose, but even when she was dying, she hadn't told Tessa any more about her dad.

Tessa figured that her mom had probably kept the truth about her biological father's identity hidden because she didn't want her to grow up hating him.

Well, if that was the plan, it hadn't worked.

Enough with that.

She put the pregnancy test down and looked into the shoe box again, and found a neatly folded-up magazine ad for some kind of real estate company. It'd been ripped out of whatever magazine it was from and half of it was missing, but the part that was there had a picture of a blonde-haired girl, maybe four or five years old, trying on what were probably supposed to be her mom's high heel shoes and necklace. Part of the text of the ad was gone, but the words "homes are not just" were still there. That was it, "homes are not just" . . . something.

But what caught Tessa's attention wasn't so much the text but the jewelry box that lay on a dresser behind the girl in the photo.

Wait a minute.

She looked more carefully at the jewelry box and felt her heart begin to hammer. Then she jumped up and, carrying the picture, hurried to her room.

To her dresser. To her jewelry box.

Yes, yes.

It was nearly identical to the one in the picture. Her mom had given it to her when she was a girl, somewhere around the age of the girl in the magazine ad.

Is that you? Is it possible? Is that you in the picture?

No, the hair was different, the girl didn't really look like her at all, and there was no little mole on the side of the girl's neck like the one on hers.

Then why? Why would she give this to you? It can't just be a coincidence.

She returned to Patrick's room and scanned the remaining contents of the shoe box looking for an answer; didn't find one.

However, she did find one final thing that made her inordinately curious: a key attached to a key ring with a plastic tag with the number "18" written on one side and the words "For Tess" on the other.

In her whole life she'd only let one person call her Tess: her mom.

The key was too small to fit in a normal lock, and even though it was about the same size as the one to her jewelry box, it wasn't the right shape.

She tried it just to make sure, but no, it didn't fit.

Then she heard the front door swing open.

Patrick had arrived to pick her up for lunch.

31

As soon as Tessa heard the door open, she realized she needed more time to read the letters in the box and she didn't really want Patrick to know that she'd found them, so she jammed everything back inside, except for the key, which she put in her pocket, and quickly snuck the box to her room, then hid it under her bed next to her own memory box.

"Tessa, are you ready to go?" he called.

"I'll be right there!" she shouted through her bedroom door. "Gimme one minute."

So, ask him about it, or not?

She thought about the picture of the little girl, the items in the box, all the enveloped letters that she still hadn't read.

He kept this from you. He should have given it to you.

But maybe he just forgot?

Either way she needed to know the truth.

But he's having a hard day, remember? The breakup? A carnage of hearts? Don't accuse him of keeping it from you. It wouldn't be right.

So then, ask him about it, but be tactful.

Yeah, that shouldn't be a problem.

———————————————■———————————————

When I stepped into the house I heard Tessa yell from her room that she'd be ready in a minute—which probably meant I had at least ten—and that was good because it gave me a chance to get dried off and change clothes.

Partly I wished I were back at the morgue, looking for evidence, but my job wasn't to process individual crime scenes but rather to help focus the direction of the investigation.

And that was proving harder than I imagined.

In my bedroom, I noticed that one of the packing boxes was open but nothing more had been packed, which irritated me a little since Tessa'd had all morning and she knew we were leaving for DC on Wednesday.

Deal with that later.

I changed clothes, and as I was putting on my SIG's holster I thought of Grant Sikora and the gun he'd aimed at my head less than twenty-four hours ago. He'd somehow loaded it before it was brought into the courtroom . . .

Or found someone to load it for him.

I speed-dialed Ralph.

"What's up?" he said.

"Are you still in Chicago?"

"Yeah. Helping the field office here deal with the shooting, get some tighter security measures in place for next week . . ." His voice seemed muffled, his words jumbled. It sounded like he had something in his mouth.

"What's that sound? You're not eating more of those yogurt raisins, are you?"

A moment of silence. The faint sound of swallowing.

"Nope."

"Listen, Ralph, about the shooting; that's one of the reasons I called. You're thinking the evidence room, right?"

"Yeah," he said. "The gun was in a sealed evidence bag when it was brought into the courtroom. All someone would have needed to do was get in the evidence room, load the gun, and then wait for it to be brought into the courtroom. After all, why would anyone check to see if a gun that's stored in a sealed evidence bag from a case thirteen years ago was loaded?"

"Exactly. Have a talk with Officer Fohay. He was working the security checkpoint at the courthouse yesterday."

"You got something on him?"

"No. But he had strong views about Basque's guilt, and he mentioned that he works in the evidence room. He would have had access to the gun. If there's any kind of personal connection between Sikora and him—"

"Gotcha. Anything else?"

"I'm concerned about Calvin."

"What? Werjonic?"

"Yes."

I took a few minutes to summarize the previous night's conversation with Calvin. When I was done, Ralph asked what I wanted him to do.

"His office is there in Chicago. I'm wondering if you can keep an eye on him. I'm worried that he might make a move on Basque over the weekend."

"A move? You're kidding me."

"No. I'm not."

A pause. "Basque is secure. After that attempt on his life, they're not letting anyone near him."

"Remember who I'm talking about here. Calvin is one of the smartest criminal scientists to ever live. If he wants to get in there—"

"Yeah, all right," he muttered. "I'll make sure he doesn't pay Mr. Basque a visit. Don't worry."

"Thanks." We ended the call, and when I emerged from the bedroom I found Tessa waiting for me in the hallway.

"Ready?" I said.

"Yeah," she replied. "Let's go to Fruition."

32

Tessa took a seat beside Patrick in a booth at the back of the restaurant.

She'd ordered a California alfalfa salad and Patrick had gotten a falafel burger, probably because it reminded him of meat more than anything else on the menu.

She ate her salad for a few minutes while he smothered his falafel patty with ketchup. In between bites he told her he'd managed to arrive in time to save a woman's life earlier in the morning.

"Are you serious? What happened? Wait. Let me guess; you can't tell me."

"No, not all the details. But I can tell you it felt good to get there in time for once. It felt . . . right."

She watched him eat for a few minutes, and she realized she was proud of him, of what he did for a living, that he made a difference.

"Well, that's cool," she said. It was a little lame, but it looked like he could tell she meant it. Finally, when the time felt right, she asked him about the box. "Hey, um, while I was packing, I was wondering if there's, like, any of my mom's stuff still around?" She downed some of her root beer. "You know, that you haven't already given to me?"

Patrick was eating his falafel burger way too fast to really enjoy it. "Nope."

"You sure?"

He swallowed, wiped a napkin across his chin. "Pretty sure."

"Huh, well, that's weird then, 'cause I found the shoe box."

"The shoe box?"

"Yeah."

"What shoe box?"

"The one with my mom's stuff in it, and I want to know why you never gave it to me."

———————————■———————————

I stopped eating.

"Well?" she said.

"I forgot I even had that."

"How could you forget? It's her special stuff!" The whole atmosphere of the meal had shifted almost instantaneously, and I needed a few seconds to regain my footing.

I tried to explain that when we moved to Denver I'd just stuck the box in the closet and piled some camping equipment in front of it; tried to help her understand that it had been a hard time for me and I hadn't thought any more about it, but she didn't seem to buy it.

When I'd finished, she held up a key. "I found this too. What does it open?"

I couldn't be certain, but I was pretty sure I knew which key that was.

I went for my Coke and used the time it took me to drink it to stall and collect my thoughts.

"Well?" Tessa demanded. "I'm waiting."

You don't have to tell her about it. You could say it was lost or damaged or destroyed. You don't have to let her read it.

I set down my drink. "I'm not positive, but I think that's probably the key to your mom's diary." Rather than elaborate, I waited for her to respond. I finished my falafel burger. It tasted like toasted sand. Even the ketchup didn't help.

"Her diary?"

I nodded. "She gave it to me before she died, but she told me—"

"Mom kept a diary?"

"Yes, before I met her. I think when she was in college. And she said I wasn't supposed to give it to you until—"

159

"Well, where is it? I want to read it."

"Tessa, stop cutting me off. Your mom told me not to give it to you until you turned eighteen."

A short, awkward silence. "Why?"

"I don't know. The point is, if I gave it to you now I'd be breaking the promise that I—"

My ringing cell phone interrupted me mid-sentence. I looked at the screen. Kurt. "Just a second," I told her.

She set the key in front of her and drummed her fingers on the table while I answered my cell. "What's up?"

"We might have something. Someone sent flowers to a reporter at the *Denver News*. He left a note: 'Must needs we tell of others' tears?'"

I was missing something here. "And?"

"The reporter's husband is one of the CSU techs—Reggie Greer. You met him this morning."

I rubbed my forehead. "His wife is a reporter?"

"Don't worry. He knows not to share anything about his cases with her. But here's the thing, she called him wondering if he sent the flowers. She emailed him a photo of the flowers and the note, and he realized right away that the handwriting matched the handwriting on the note the killer left for you in Taylor's garage."

Now he had my attention. "Go on."

"Reggie is still finishing up at Taylor's house. Two officers are giving Cheyenne a lift from the hospital, so she's on her way to the newspaper office right now. Can you get over there? I don't want anyone else touching those flowers until we've had a chance to look at them. Something came up with Cheryl, I'm at home right now, but I'll get downtown as soon as I can."

The *Denver News* building was less than two miles away.

"I'll be there in five minutes."

"All right. The reporter's name is Amy Lynn Greer."

We ended the call, and before I could say a word to Tessa, she blurted, "You have to give me the diary."

"Don't push things right now, Tessa. And don't demand things from me." I stood to go.

"I'm old enough to read it. I'll be eighteen this fall."

"We can talk about the diary later. I need some time to think about this. Your mother was very insistent—"

"Does it tell who my dad is?"

The question took me off guard.

"I never read the diary. I wanted to respect your mother's wishes—"

"Does it tell who my dad is?" Her voice had turned into something solid and cold.

"Tessa, do not interrupt me." I understood that she was upset, but I wasn't in the mood to be cut off every time I started a sentence. "I promised her I'd wait until you were eighteen, and right now you're not giving me any reason to break that promise."

She opened her mouth as if she were going to respond but must have thought better of it because she closed it again without making a sound. The look of anger she gave me was mixed with something more profound—a deep sense of sadness or disappointment—and I felt bad she was hurting.

"We'll talk about this later. Right now, I need to go." I was still standing beside the table; she hadn't moved. "Come on."

Finally, she stood. "Is it a case? Are you taking me along to a crime scene?"

"It's just something I need to look into. Maybe you can call Dora, have her pick you up when we get there."

———————————————■———————————————

All during the drive to the *Denver News* building, Tessa stared out the window, but she wasn't really watching anything. Mostly she was just thinking.

Her mom kept a diary.

A diary.

And she wanted you to have it, but not until you're eighteen.

But why not?

And why was Patrick making such a big deal about it? It wasn't fair to make her wait, especially now that she knew about it. What would it hurt to read it a few months early?

She glanced at her watch.

Dora had agreed to pick her up at one o'clock—still twenty minutes away.

If Dora took her back home, they could maybe look for the diary, but that would mean unpacking everything—and besides, Patrick might have it in his office at the federal building just to make sure she wouldn't have accidentally found it.

That's what she would have done if she had a teenager in the house.

You need to read the stuff in the memory box before you go worrying about the diary—

"Tessa."

"Huh?" They'd arrived at the newspaper building, but she'd been so distracted thinking about her mom and the diary and the memory box that she hadn't even noticed.

"I'll call you on your cell when I'm done." His voice was tense, and he was obviously in a hurry, all of which added to Tessa's curiosity about why they'd left the restaurant so abruptly and rushed over here.

"OK."

He slid a "Federal Car. Official Business" sign onto the dash and then jumped out and jogged up the sidewalk.

She wasn't stupid. She knew he was on a task force with the cops and she'd seen the news about the string of murders over the last couple days. It didn't take a rocket scientist to figure out what case he was working on.

She looked at her watch. Dora wouldn't be arriving for fifteen minutes.

Hmm.

That might be just enough time.

33

I crossed the lobby of the *Denver News*, flipping open my ID as I passed the curly-permed woman doing her nails behind the reception desk near the elevators.

"Amy Lynn Greer's office," I said. "Which floor?"

"Fourth." She slid a clipboard and a visitor's keycard across the counter to me. "You're s'pposed to sign in."

I scribbled my name across the pad, swiped the pass off the counter, and headed for the elevator.

A few moments later, Cheyenne met me beside the elevator bank on the fourth floor. "Good to see you," she said.

"You too." She led me down the hallway past a shrine of journalism plaques and awards that the newspaper had apparently won. "Any updates on Kelsey's condition?" I asked.

"She's recovering. Her body temp was up seven degrees when I left. Almost back to normal. I think she'll make it. She's not talking, though. Still too traumatized. But I asked her if the man who attacked her was Asian, African-American, Caucasian—she stopped me there and nodded. So at least we have that much."

"Do we know why she went to the morgue last night?"

"No, but hospital surveillance cameras show her arriving at 8:19 p.m.; nothing on the guy who attacked her, though. He managed to avoid getting caught on tape."

I considered the implications.

We passed the employee break room and Cheyenne said, "I forgot to mention: Agent Vanderveld's on his way over here. Should be here in fifteen minutes or so."

"Wonderful."

Then, in her endearingly blunt way, she asked, "What's the deal with you two, anyway?"

I was about to blow off her question when I realized I would have to explain things eventually and I might as well just get it over with. "Six years ago I was geoprofiling a case in Albuquerque. Teenage boys were disappearing—three bodies found, three other boys missing."

"I think I might remember hearing about that. They were being abducted from their homes after school?"

"Yes. While their parents were still at work. The sheriff's department was, well, let's just say, less than enthusiastic about my techniques."

"Imagine that."

"I know."

The hallway opened into a large work space, and Cheyenne guided me through a maze of cubicles. Since it was Saturday, I didn't expect the room to be too full, so I was surprised to see nearly two dozen staff members typing, surfing the Internet, and jabbering into their cell phones.

"Anyway, the Bureau decided to send in a behavioral profiler and chose Jake; decided to reassign me to a series of shootings in New York City."

"Pulled you off the case?"

"Yes."

"And so what happened? Vanderveld screwed things up?"

"After two days on-site he became convinced that we should be looking for a twenty-four- to twenty-seven-year-old male Caucasian, single, never married, homosexual who had a history of working with kids and could easily gain their trust. A high school teacher, maybe a coach, someone like that."

"Lemme guess." She stopped walking for a moment. "Wild goose chase."

"Over the next three weeks, two more boys disappeared before an eyewitness saw a thirteen-year-old boy get into a car with the forty-eight-year-old, divorced, Hispanic city commissioner."

"So the only other thing Vanderveld had right in his profile was the killer's gender and sexual preference?"

"Yes."

"Which was self-evident considering the victim selection."

"That's right."

We started walking again.

"The city commissioner lived near the center of the hot zone. If the police would have listened to me, those two boys might still be alive."

I tried holding back the anger that I still carried with me. "But then, here's the kicker: Vanderveld holds a press conference and explains how quickly the case was wrapped up after he arrived. He milked the media attention as long as he could. He didn't even give credit to local law enforcement. He loves the spotlight, and when he's in it, he won't step out."

"But that's not all, is it?"

"No."

"What else?"

"Let's just say I don't trust him and leave it at that."

Just past the watercooler we came to a line of offices along the east wall. Two of the doors were open, and I could see that each office had a window view of the city. I assumed these were the executive offices, or at least the suites for the top-tier journalists.

"Thanks for the heads-up," Cheyenne said, then she knocked on a door that had a small metallic sign: Benjamin Rhodes, Assistant Vice President, Editorial.

"Come in," a man called.

Two people were waiting for us inside the office. The man, whom I assumed was Rhodes, appeared to be in his late thirties. Shaved head. Slightly graying goatee. Black turtleneck, blue jeans, black shoes.

I held out my hand. "Special Agent Bowers. I'm with the FBI.

We're working closely with the Denver Police Department on this case."

"Benjamin Rhodes." We shook hands, then he gestured toward the woman, who did not look happy to see me. "And this is Amy Lynn Greer. One of our top investigative reporters."

Late twenties, sleep-deprived, pretty. She had kinkily curled brown hair and wore a hemp necklace, blue blouse, stylish shoes. I recognized her face from the picture that ran next to a weekly political column that I now realized was hers.

"It's a pleasure to meet you, Mrs. Greer," I said. "I met your husband this morning."

"Amy Lynn will do." Her manner was curt. "I saw your photo come through the wire. Something about a shooting in Chicago yesterday?"

"Yes. It was tragic." Not something I wanted to be reminded of. My eyes tipped past her to the desk. "Are those the flowers?"

Amy Lynn and Benjamin nodded.

Cheyenne stood quietly beside us. I assumed she'd been through introductions and had already taken some time to inspect the flowers.

The plants had narrow towers of purplish-white flowers and thick leaves. I leaned close and smelled a strong minty odor mixed with an underlying scent of the potting soil's earthy decay. "Do we know what kind of flowers these are?"

Benjamin exchanged glances with Amy Lynn. "We're not sure. We were going to call some people in, see if anyone on the floor was a gardener, but when Amy Lynn told Reggie about the note—"

"He asked me to keep it quiet," she said.

"Good," I said.

Earlier that day, on the way to Taylor's house, Cheyenne had mentioned that both Heather Fain and Ahmed Mohammed Shokr had died of potassium chloride poisoning. I didn't know what kind of flowers these were, or what they might be covered with, but I didn't want to take any chances. "Have either of you two touched the plants?"

"I did, a little," Amy Lynn replied. "Why?"

I didn't want to scare her. "Probably should wash your hands."

She looked at me nervously, then stepped out of the room, and I asked Benjamin, "How many people have handled the pot?"

"Well." He looked a little nervous as well. "Amy Lynn, of course. Brett, one of our secretaries. The flower delivery guy who dropped it off. I'm the one who carried it in here."

"Cheyenne," I said. "Can you take Mr. Rhodes and talk with Brett, see if she can give us a description of the man who delivered the flowers? Find out if he said or did anything unusual."

She flipped out her notebook and nodded toward the door. "Mr. Rhodes?"

"Of course."

"And hands," I said, "have everyone wash their—"

"Got it," Cheyenne said.

They stepped into the hallway, I snapped on the pair of latex gloves I carry with me and carefully investigated the petals, then studied the stems to see if there was anything noteworthy about the flowers themselves. Finding nothing, I prodded softly at the dirt, looking for a black recording device like the one I'd found in Heather Fain's mouth.

Nothing.

I heard Amy Lynn return.

"Where's the note?" I asked.

She pointed to the corner of the desk. "Right there. It's signed John."

Picking it up, I read the inscription, then flipped it over and studied the card stock paper it was written on. The paper didn't seem to have any distinctive or unique markings. It would be hard to trace.

"I Googled the phrase," Amy Lynn said. "'Must needs we tell of others' tears?' I didn't find anything."

"All right." I set down the note. "Any friends named John? Any Johns in stories you're currently working on?"

"I looked into that too." She sounded impatient. "The only one I could come up with is John Beyer, the pitcher for the Rockies. I'm doing a piece on steroid use, but I can't imagine how that might be related to the flowers."

It sounded like a long shot to me, but we could send an officer to speak with him.

Carefully, I lifted the pot to investigate the bottom; found nothing unusual. Then I felt around the lip of the pot. I was circling the circumference with my finger when I heard the door swing open behind me. I assumed it was Cheyenne and Benjamin returning.

I caught myself verbalizing my thoughts, "Who are you, John? Why send these flowers?"

And someone said, "That's basil."

But it wasn't Cheyenne's or Benjamin's voice.

It was Tessa's.

I turned. "What are you doing up here?"

Her eyes were riveted on the flowers. "They were trying to tow the car."

"What! Really? No, they weren't."

"OK, you got me, they weren't—but you said 'John'? Just a second ago?" She entered the office.

"You shouldn't be up here." I set down the pot. "You need to go back downstairs."

"You say it's basil?" Amy Lynn asked.

I stepped around the desk toward Tessa. She was staring at me, her eyes growing wide. "Seriously, you said John, right—'Who are you, John?'"

"Yes."

"Excuse me," Amy Lynn said. "But you are . . . ?"

"This is my stepdaughter, Tessa," I said. Since this piece of evidence was apparently connected with the killings, I wanted to get Tessa out of here as quickly as I could. "Come on," I told her. "We're leaving."

"It's a pot of basil and the note's from John . . ." Tessa said softly. The blood had drained from her face.

I looked at her quizzically. "Do you know something about this?"

"I need to go."

"What is it?" I asked.

"It's a pot of basil," she repeated, backing toward the door.

"A pot of basil," I said. "Yes. OK. So what?"

She began to shake her head slowly. "You don't understand. I gotta go. I'm gonna be sick."

Cheyenne and Benjamin appeared behind her, but she pushed past them and ran toward the newsroom.

"Was that Tessa?" Cheyenne asked.

"Yes." I was on my way to the door.

"Is she OK?"

"I'm not sure." I stepped past her. "I'll be right back. Don't let anyone else in this room."

34

I caught up with Tessa at the elevators. She was pushing the "down" button over and over, her hand was shaking. "No," she mumbled. "No, it's not. It can't be."

"Tessa, do you know who sent those flowers?"

She shook her head. "Uh-uh."

"Then what's wrong?"

"Keats."

I noticed a trash can beside her. I tugged off the exam gloves I was still wearing and stuffed them inside it. "Keats?"

The doors opened and she hurried into the elevator. I joined her.

She punched "Level 1" four times and started muttering, "Yeah . . . I think Keats, or maybe Alexander."

"Tessa—"

"But it doesn't matter." The doors closed and she stared at them, anxious, terrified. "It's the same either way."

Her intense reaction was really starting to worry me. "Calm down for a minute and just tell me what you're thinking."

She was tapping her right thumb and forefinger together rapidly. "You don't think it's . . . but then why would someone . . . ?"

I gently put my hands on her shoulders, and when I did, she looked up into my eyes. "Please," I said. "Tell me what's going on."

Finally, she drew in a deep but shaky breath and said, "There was an artist, right? John White Alexander. In like, I don't know, 1896 or 1897 he painted a picture, it's this famous picture called

170

'Isabella and the Pot of Basil.' John White Alexander, see? So that's why John might refer to him."

"OK, so—"

"But he based the painting on this poem by Keats, John Keats. So either way, it's John. You know Keats, the poet?"

"Yes."

"The poem is about this woman. Her lover is killed and . . ."

I thought of Kelsey, her husband, all that had happened in the last two days.

"She digs him up and . . ."

The morgue.

The bodies.

Oh.

I felt a chill. Suddenly, I understood what Tessa was saying, realized why she'd reacted so strongly. "That's enough. I can look it up—"

"The woman, she . . ." We arrived at the ground floor, and the elevator dinged.

"I understand. You don't have to say anything else."

But Tessa wasn't listening to me. She was staring into space. "They take it away from her. The pot, and then—"

"It's OK. Shh . . ."

The elevator doors opened, but Tessa didn't step off, she looked at me instead and bit her bottom lip. "Don't tell me, OK? When you look. Don't tell me. I don't want to know if I'm right."

"OK. I promise."

Tessa nodded and looked past me. "Dora's here."

I knew that Tessa was terribly upset and I wanted to be there for her, but I also needed to get back upstairs, especially if she was right about the pot. "Do you want me to come home with you?"

"No. I'm OK."

We met Pandora Bender in the lobby near the front door, and she assured me she would stay with Tessa. "She'll be all right with me, Mr. Bowers. Don't worry."

"Thank you, Dora," I said, then turned to Tessa. "You're sure you don't need me?"

She nodded. "Yeah. I'm fine."

I touched her arm softly. "Call me, all right? You say the word, I'll come home."

"I know." Dora stepped toward the door, and Tessa mouthed to me, "Don't tell me."

"I won't."

They stepped outside, and I watched them through the darkened windows until they disappeared around the corner of the building. Then I returned to the fourth floor.

To look inside the pot.

35

Only Cheyenne and Amy Lynn were in the office when I arrived. Cheyenne explained that Rhodes had gone to meet with two of the board members, and I wasn't sure if I was glad to hear that or not. I suspected they were discussing how to handle the release of information concerning the flowers, but I didn't have time to deal with any of that right now.

Just one glance at the flowerpot told me it was the right size. I knew we needed to get it to the lab, but first I wanted to find out if Tessa's guess was right, and sometimes I'm just not as patient as I should be. "Amy Lynn, can you give us a few minutes?"

She hesitated.

"Please go and wash your hands thoroughly."

"But I already did."

"Trust me." I didn't have another pair of gloves, but with the back of my hand, I pushed the pot into the center of Rhodes's desk past his MacBook and its aquarium screen saver. "This plant may have substances on it that you would not want to accidentally ingest."

After one last disgruntled look, she left and Cheyenne said, "What's going on? Is Tessa all right?"

I carefully pressed the flowers to the side and observed that the dirt around the base of the plant was loose. "Can you lock the door?"

"Pat, what's—"

"Please."

I pulled out my TSAVO-Wraith and flicked out the blade. "She's

OK, Tessa is," I said. "Thanks for asking." I slid the knife's tip gently into the dirt.

Cheyenne locked the door and then returned to my side. "What are you doing?"

I pushed aside a small triangle of moist soil. Based on the size of the pot I didn't think I would need to dig too deeply. "There's a painting."

I brushed some more dirt away. Slid the blade of the knife about five centimeters into the soil. "And a poem by Keats . . . but the point is . . ."

As I pressed down, I felt the tip of the blade press against something that was not soil.

". . . there was a woman who disinters . . ."

Folding up the knife, I slipped it into my pocket and then used my fingers to gently nudge the dirt away.

". . . the body of her lover."

Beneath my finger I felt something soft and cool and fleshy.

Cheyenne was staring at the place in the pot where I'd been digging. "Pat, you're not saying . . ."

I pushed more dirt aside, and the scent of basil was no longer the most overpowering odor in the room.

Just enough of the pot's contents were visible.

Tessa had been right.

"Oh . . ." Cheyenne's voice trailed off.

"Yes," I said. "It's Travis Nash."

36

43 minutes later

The pot and soil lay on the far end of the steel examination table.

Travis Nash's head lay in front of us.

After delivering the pot to headquarters, Cheyenne had swung me home so I could pick up my car and check on Tessa, but she and Dora hadn't arrived yet. So, we'd returned to police headquarters in our respective cars, parked in HQ's underground parking garage, and then hurried to join the team in the lab.

Now, two forensics specialists were studying the head, carefully using toothbrushes to clear dots of soil from the open, staring eyes.

Jake was speaking quietly with a third lab worker in the corner of the room. The door opened, and Kurt entered.

"Reggie here yet?" he asked.

I shook my head. "No."

"Did CSU find anything at the morgue?" Cheyenne asked.

Kurt strode toward us. He stared grimly at the examination table. "He used the sink, we know that. Didn't leave any prints on the door handles and managed to get into and out of the building without showing up on any of the hospital's security cameras. I assigned an officer to compare the suspect list with the roster of hospital employees to see if it gives us any leads."

"Good," I replied, although I wasn't sure the suspect list was going to be much help.

As investigations like this progress and people call in with tips, names are added to the list of potential suspects generated by the

175

evidentiary aspects of each crime scene. The list usually grows exponentially with time. When I'd read the case files on the drive to Taylor's earlier in the day, there were already 180 names on the list. I've worked cases with tens, even hundreds of thousands of names on the list, and I had a feeling the number of suspects for this case was going to grow quite a bit before it began to shrink. Sometimes the lists are beneficial, but many times the killer's name never even appears, or if it does, it's often buried so deeply in the stack that it gets overlooked.

Reggie arrived, and Kurt began to have words with him on the far side of the room.

As I watched the forensic technicians work, I began to feel useless standing around here, and anxious to move forward on this case—and now at least there were some specific leads to research.

That message: Must needs we tell of others' tears?

The pot of basil.

The Keats and Alexander connection.

I heard the exchange between Kurt and Reggie growing louder, but I was only able to catch bits and fragments of their conversation. Something about Reggie's wife, Amy Lynn.

Then Reggie raised his voice. "I know, but I can stay with her."

"That's not enough." Kurt's tone was sinewy and strong. "We're going to do whatever we need to do to protect her."

"I'm aware of that. But Amy Lynn—"

Before he could finish, Kurt led him into the hall to continue their conversation out of earshot. Obviously, the two of them were not in agreement on how to best protect Reggie's wife now that the killer had sent her the basil, marking her as a potential victim.

We needed to move on this case before the killer had a chance to make that happen.

"All right," I said to Jake and Cheyenne. "It's time for me to go."

"And do what?" Jake asked.

"I think we should start with the Keats poem and the paintings of John Alexander. The victims so far have been posed, their murders so unusual that I'm wondering if maybe the killer is reenacting other violent poems or portraying other paintings."

"Hmm," Jake said. "To create some kind of gallery of portraits of the dead."

"Maybe."

Cheyenne looked around the room. "Well, for the moment there's nothing more for us to do here. We can use the conference room on the sixth floor. The computers up there are actually less than a decade old."

"I'll come too," Jake said. "Give me a few minutes, though." He was staring at the head. "Then I'll be right up."

Cheyenne and I left and found Kurt just outside the door, alone. Reggie was already halfway down the hall. I watched him for a moment and let my gaze become a question for Kurt.

"He wants to let Amy Lynn keep working," he said. "We've assigned an officer to her, but I think we should move her into protective custody. The note, the pot—they connect her to the case. I don't like it." He paused. "I want her safe."

"You need to ask Amy Lynn," Cheyenne said. "Not her husband. It's not your call or Reggie's. It's hers."

She was right, of course, but from my brief meeting with Amy Lynn I didn't get the sense that she was the cautious type. I couldn't see her choosing protective custody.

Kurt let out a thin sigh. "Point taken."

Cheyenne told Kurt where we were going, and he said he'd join us as soon as he'd spoken with Amy Lynn.

Then, as we left, I glanced back into the forensics lab and saw Jake Vanderveld leaning over, staring intently into Travis Nash's lifeless eyes. It looked like he was whispering to himself.

But maybe he was whispering to the ears of the dead.

And I couldn't help but wonder what he might possibly be saying.

Amy Lynn Greer didn't like the fact that no one would tell her why the police and FBI were in such a hurry to remove the flowers after the teenage girl told them it was a pot of basil, or why they'd stationed an officer right outside her door, and she let Benjamin Rhodes know it.

"You can't get involved with this," he said. "Not with your husband's position."

"I'm already involved. The flowers were sent to me." Rhodes looked like he was about to respond, but before he could, she added, "Look, I spent all morning following up on this. I know more about it than anyone else. And you're telling me being knowledgeable disqualifies me from writing about it? What kind of—"

"Amy Lynn, settle down. Let's just see what the police find out first." Rhodes rounded his desk and stood beside the window, hands folded behind his back. "The executive board feels that if we move on this too fast there might be legal ramifications. They want us to sit on it until we have something a little more solid."

"But don't you see?" she said. "That's all the more reason to investigate it now, so we can be prepared to run a story when the time comes."

If the pot of basil was related to the week's previous murders, she could already envision this story shaping up as a true crime book. This was her chance for a big story, a breakout story, and she wasn't about to let it slip through her fingers just because the board wanted to play it safe.

"No," Rhodes said. "I'm sorry."

Amy Lynn was about to let him know what she thought about him and the executive board but held her tongue and simply said, "All right."

"Finish the steroids piece, get your weekly column on my desk. I'll give you till four this afternoon—then we'll see."

"Yes. All right. Thanks." She left his office, brushed past the police officer waiting for her in the hallway and headed for her desk.

No, she wasn't going to spend the rest of her day writing about a baseball player.

She was going to find John.

37

We split up the research.

Cheyenne took the Alexander paintings, I scoured the Internet for Keats poems that might bear some semblance to the murders, and Jake looked for other literary references to pots of basil or to the message about telling of others' tears.

Even though Cheyenne had suggested we use the sixth floor conference room because of the computers, it didn't take me long to realize that they were dinosaurs compared to the laptops the Bureau provided. I switched to my computer, and five minutes later, I noticed Jake had done the same.

Each of us sat in a separate corner of the room and disappeared into our research, and as if by a unanimous, unspoken agreement, we worked quietly for nearly twenty-five minutes typing and surfing and scribbling notes before Jake broke the silence. "Well, let's see what we have."

I looked up and saw him gaze from me to Cheyenne.

"Sure, I'll go first," Cheyenne offered, but she sounded frustrated. "I looked all over Alexander's online portfolio and, apart from two pictures that vaguely resemble the view of the mountains near the mine where we found Heather's body, I'm not seeing any paintings that have a connection to the other murders. Nothing solid at all."

I tilted my laptop's screen so I could read it more easily. "Well, I don't have much either. Just one thing, though. A section of the poem by Keats."

And then I read aloud,

O Melancholy, turn thine eyes away!
  O Music, Music, breathe despondingly!
O Echo, Echo, on some other day,
  From Isles Lethean, sigh to us—O sigh!
Spirits of grief, sing not your "Well-a-way!"
  For Isabel, sweet Isabel, will die;
Will die a death too lone and incomplete,
Now they have ta'en away her Basil sweet.

I summarized, "The theme of despair runs through almost every line: melancholy, despondence, spirits of grief, the lack of singing, and then a lonely death—just like the killer wanted Kelsey to experience in the morgue."

"But she's safe now," Jake said.

I thought for a moment. "I don't see this killer giving up that easily." I turned to Cheyenne. "There's an officer with her now, at the hospital?"

"Yes."

"Let's keep him assigned to her until we catch this guy."

"All right." She wrote something on her notepad. "I'll talk with Kurt."

"One more thing. Keats mentions 'Isles Lethean.' I looked it up: the river Lethe was one of the rivers in Hades. If you drank from it, you would forget your life on earth. You would forget everything."

"Isles Lethean." Jake gazed at the wall thoughtfully. "Maybe the UNSUB is perpetrating these crimes to forget something from his past, to cross the river, so to speak."

Great. UNSUB: Unknown Subject of an investigation. It may very well be the stupidest acronym ever created in FBI history. And that's saying something.

Jake, of course, loved the term.

He went on, "Maybe he's trying to find freedom from his own despondence, his own grief."

There was no way to either prove or disprove his hypothesis, and either way it offered us no specific investigative strategies. After all, who hasn't dealt with grief? Who doesn't want to forget painful memories? Most of the Denver metroplex's 2.8 million people would probably fit that profile.

Still, I let his words pass without comment. "I only managed to get through about thirty of Keats's poems, but I didn't find anything helpful in the ones I read." Then, though I didn't want to, I admitted the inevitable, "It's possible we're on the wrong track entirely, here."

Jake glanced at his computer screen. "I'm not so sure." He motioned to the wide screen television monitor mounted on the conference room wall. "Is there a way we can . . . ?"

Cheyenne deciphered his question and stood. "I'll get it." She powered on the wall-mounted monitor and then fished a USB cord out of a drawer on a nearby console.

Jake took a moment to connect his computer to the USB port on the table, and just as the image from his laptop appeared on the screen, Kurt eased into the room and took a seat.

"Amy Lynn wanted to be in protective custody," he said, then looked at me. "A couple of your boys at the field office moved her to a safe house. And Reggie is not happy."

"So she's safe," Cheyenne said. "That's good. One less thing to worry about."

Something didn't seem quite right, but I couldn't put my finger on it. Jake opened a website, and it appeared on the wall monitor.

"One more thing," Kurt added. "The victimology info you wanted, Pat. Everything we have so far has been uploaded to the online case file archives."

"Good." I filled him in on what Cheyenne, Jake, and I had been discussing and then motioned for Jake to resume.

"Here's what I have." Jake pointed the cursor to the middle of the webpage. "Nothing on the phrase about tears, but I did find something more about the pot of basil. Keats's poem was actually based on a story from the fourteenth century about a woman named

Isabel who digs up her lover's body, severs the head, and puts it into a pot, then plants basil over it." Jake paused, then added, "The story appears in a book that was condemned by the church. It's called *The Decameron*."

I leaned forward.

"A condemned book?" Cheyenne said.

"Yeah. It's by an Italian author named Giovanni Boccaccio." He scrolled down the article. "And by the way, Giovanni is the Italian form of—"

"John," I said.

"Yes."

"Unbelievable," Kurt muttered.

John Alexander.

John Keats.

John Boccaccio.

All three of these men had told the story of a disinterred head in a pot of basil: the first through a painting, the second through poetry, the third through prose.

And now here in Denver, we had a killer who called himself John and had reenacted the story in a fourth way: real life.

By signing the note "John" and sending the pot of basil to a reporter, the killer must have known we would eventually make the connection to either Keats, Alexander, or Boccaccio. I wasn't sure if I should be impressed by this thoroughness, or insulted by it.

All one elaborate, twisted game.

Jake went on, "Apparently, *The Decameron* became a source of literary material for other authors, including . . ." He looked at his notes. "Faulkner, Tennyson, Longfellow, Shakespeare, Chaucer, and of course, Keats—just to name a few. In fact, a quarter of the stories in Chaucer's *Canterbury Tales* as well as its literary structure are based on stories from *The Decameron*."

I could hardly believe it. "Chaucer, Longfellow, Shakespeare, they all based stories on Boccaccio's book? I've never heard of him before."

Jake shook his head. "Neither had I."

"Wait," Cheyenne said, somewhat impatiently. "You said the book was condemned by the church?"

Jake scrolled down the webpage. "In 1370 a monk named Pietro Petroni wrote to Boccaccio warning him that he would be eternally damned unless he renounced the book. Boccaccio later revised the book, but he never recanted. Soon after that, the pope, let's see . . ."

He slid the cursor across the screen until he found his place. "Yeah, Pope Paul IV officially condemned the book, and it was banned from being distributed and read. But that only seemed to make it more popular."

"No surprise there," Kurt said. "The best way to sell a book is to get someone to ban it."

"It's still on the Index Librorum Prohibitorum to this day," Jake concluded.

"The Index of Forbidden Books," Cheyenne said softly. She caught me looking at her questioningly. "Catholic school."

"All right," I said to Jake. "Then it must contain something heretical, or maybe satanic. What did the website say about the book's content?"

He glanced at the notes he'd scribbled on a legal pad beside his keyboard. "The book is about ten people—seven women and three men who are trying to escape the Black Death in the 1300s. In the story, the Plague had infected Florence, and the ten travelers were trying to get to the hills of Fiesole where they could be safe."

I was amazed at how much he'd been able to uncover in only twenty-five minutes.

After a quick breath, he went on. "During the ten-day trip they agree that every day they'll each tell one story. And that's where the title *Decameron* comes from: two Greek words, *deka* and *haemeron*, which mean 'ten' and 'days,' respectively."

Ten travelers. Ten stories. Ten days.

Ten candles surrounding Heather Fain's body.

My heartbeat quickened.

Cheyenne tapped the table impatiently. "Jake, get back to Pat's question for a minute. If the church condemned the book, what kind of stories did these people tell?"

By her tone, I sensed that investigating a book condemned by the church she'd grown up in was bothering her more than just a little.

"Well, one of these indices lists . . ." Jake glanced at his computer, and I saw a new webpage appear on the wall monitor. "Yes. Here. It looks like the stories are pretty much about everyday topics: relationships, politics, religion, corruption, grief, and love . . ."

"So, daily life," Kurt said.

"Pretty much."

I still didn't understand why the church would have condemned the book, but for now at least, the church's specific reasons for banning it didn't matter as much as the connection it might have to the case.

"We need to find out as much as we can about the stories in *The Decameron*," I said.

Jake shook his head. "These stories aren't short, and there are a hundred of them. It'll take us, I don't know, at least a couple days to wade through all—"

"No," I said. "Remember the anonymous tips about the bodies: 'Day Four ends on Wednesday.' We can skip the rest of the days for now and just focus on the stories told on the fourth day. And we need to hurry. Dusk is coming."

38

The four of us downloaded the text to *The Decameron* from the Internet, then Jake offered to investigate the first three stories that were told on the fourth day, Cheyenne took stories four through six, Kurt, seven and eight, and I agreed to study the last two.

Kurt suggested we reconvene in an hour, at 3:30. I figured that the Denver Public Library, which was only a couple of blocks away, would likely have commentaries that might include additional details and background on the stories we were studying, so as the four of us dispersed to do our research, I grabbed my laptop and hit the sidewalk.

Ever since Tessa and Dora had arrived at the house, they'd been lounging on Tessa's bed, going through the items in her mom's memory box, and Tessa had been telling her friend stories about the objects she remembered.

The girls were about to start reading the letters when Dora announced that she'd missed lunch and was *starving* and had to eat something or she was probably going to keel over and die.

Whatever.

But Tessa realized she was pretty hungry too.

So, to the kitchen.

Dora opened the fridge, grabbed a Sprite for herself and a root beer for Tessa. "So he won't even let you see the diary?"

"Not yet, no." Tessa dumped some tortilla chips into a giant bowl. Set it on the counter next to a smaller bowl of salsa. "I need to find a way to convince him to give it to me."

Dora closed the fridge. "How are you gonna do that?"

Tessa shrugged and picked up the bowl of tortilla chips to head back to the bedroom. "I don't know." Then she noticed that the bowl was almost as big as the pot of basil had been.

A shiver.

She set it back down.

OK. Think about something else.

She went for two cereal bowls instead, transferred the chips into them, and then stuck the big bowl back in the cupboard. She hadn't told Dora about the flowerpot and what was probably— almost certainly—inside it. She didn't even want to think about that. "C'mon," she said. "Let's go read those letters."

They grabbed their snacks and returned to the bedroom. But Tessa noticed she wasn't nearly as hungry as she'd been a few minutes earlier.

I found the collections of Boccaccio's writings in the 853s on the third floor of the Denver Public Library, sandwiched between the other volumes of Italian prose.

Of the sixteen books about Boccaccio or *The Decameron*, twelve were translations, two were comparative literature studies of Boccaccio's writings and Chaucer's, and two focused on Boccaccio's other works.

None of the library's five commentaries about *The Decameron* were on the shelf.

I checked the computerized card catalog and found that all five were checked out, but when I asked the library's director which patron had them, she told me she couldn't release that information.

"Yes, you can." I showed her my FBI badge. "And I'll need a list of everyone who's checked them out over the last twelve months."

She shook her head.

"This is a federal investigation."

"And this is a public library." The woman folded her arms. She had a haircut only a librarian could love. "There are laws to protect people's right to privacy, you know."

Technically, she was correct, but the right to privacy isn't a constitutional right, just an imputed right, and can therefore be overridden for things such as terrorist attacks, national security, or imminent threat. "People's lives are in danger," I told her.

"So are people's rights," she replied stiffly. "Come back with a warrant and we'll be glad to help you."

My jaw tightened. Over the years I've requested more than my share of search warrants and I knew we didn't have enough information yet to get one for the library records. Besides, it would take an hour just to fill out the paperwork.

Forget it. You can always follow up on that later. Just get to the stories.

I went back to the 853s and chose the translation with the most footnotes—John Payne's 1947 translation from Italian into English, rather than the 1942 translation we'd downloaded off the Internet.

Then, I began to read the ninth and tenth stories of the condemned book that had, by all appearances, inspired a man to kill at least seven people so far this week.

Giovanni sat at his desk and thought about the next six hours, thought about the man he was going to abduct and the rather unsettling way he was going to die in story number six: the tale of the greyhound and the convent and the silk sheet that would be covered with soft, graceful rose petals the color of bloody sunlight.

And so.

Giovanni had the straight razor and hypodermic needles with him.

He checked the time: 2:53 p.m.

Thomas Bennett would get off work in less than two hours. And he would be dead in less than twelve.

———————————■———————————

It was perfect.

When the authorities had offered Amy Lynn Greer the chance to be sequestered in a safe house for the rest of the day away from the prying eyes of Benjamin Rhodes, it was an offer too good to pass up.

She had her son along, sure, but that wasn't such a big deal. The safe house was stocked with plenty of children's videos and toys.

And she had her computer with her.

That was all she needed.

Earlier in Rhodes's office, the girl whom Agent Bowers had identified as his stepdaughter had become upset when she connected the pot of basil with the name John, and right after that the authorities had hustled the pot away, so Amy Lynn had spent the last hour researching connections between the name "John" and the spice "basil" while her son played with Legos and watched TV in the adjoining room.

And when she found a poem by Keats about a head that was hidden in a pot of basil, she decided it had to be related to the fact that Governor Taylor had been beheaded on Thursday night.

She could hardly believe how big this story was. Even though Sebastian Taylor's death was receiving nonstop media coverage, as far as she could tell, no one else had made the connection to the pot of basil.

The pot had been sent to her.

The killer had contacted her.

Had chosen her.

She could write the story no one else could ever write.

But she needed just a little more information to do it.

One news commentator had mentioned that there had been two anonymous phone calls reporting the location of the bodies.

189

Amy Lynn knew that sometimes audio files of 911 calls get posted online, so she took a few minutes to search for them but came up empty. Which meant, if she were going to find out what those tapes said, she would need to call her source at the police department.

Not her husband. No. She couldn't use him. The man she was thinking of worked in the EMS dispatch office.

It was a friendship she'd never taken the time to mention to her husband. It wasn't anything serious, they'd shared drinks a few times, met for coffee, nothing compromising, but it had paid off for her in three previous stories.

With office buzz in the EMS department, who knows what he might have heard.

She closed the door to the safe house's bedroom to make sure the federal agent watching TV with her son in the living room wouldn't overhear her conversation. Then she pulled out a notepad and called her contact's cell number.

He answered after one ring. "Ari."

"Ari. It's Amy Lynn."

A slight pause. "Amy Lynn."

Dr. Bryant, her journalism professor, had taught her to always start by relating as a person, before ever relating as a reporter. "Otherwise your source might think you're more interested in the story than in him," he'd told the class, then he'd paused and grinned. She still remembered that. "Of course, you are more interested in the story, but knowing how to get the information you want without letting people realize you're using them is the difference between good journalists and great ones."

"You doing OK, Ari?" she asked warmly. Considering his timorous personality, she'd always found it ironic that in Hebrew his name meant "Lion."

"I'm good." He paused. "How are you and Jayson?"

She noted that he hadn't asked about her husband, just her son, but she decided not to remind him that she was a married woman.

"Just turned three. He's talking now. He's a real mama's boy. Yeah, we're good."

"That's great."

"Yeah."

"So, how do you do it? Working, mothering, everything?" It was a subtle compliment bordering on flirtation, and she noticed.

"Lots of day care." *Get to the case. Ask him about the tips.* "Hey, I heard about these calls the last couple days. The homicides. That someone tipped off the police."

Silence.

"Off the record, I was wondering—"

"Amy Lynn, I'm not supposed to—"

"I know, I know. But I won't use your name. I'll just say, 'an anonymous source,' just like we did last time."

"Yeah, but last time they almost found out." He'd lowered his voice. "I could lose my job. They're really worried about leaks with this one, he's been killing two people every day—" He cut himself short.

"Two people a day?" She jotted the words "Mounting Death Toll Shocks City" on her notepad. "So they think he'll kill again before tomorrow?" She spoke without thinking, slipping into reporter mode.

"I didn't say that." Slightly defensive. Not good.

"Of course not. No, you didn't say anything."

"Maybe I should go."

Quick.

"You're right, Ari. Really, look, I'm sorry. I shouldn't have called. The last thing I'd ever want to do is get you in trouble."

Wait. Wait.

"Don't worry about the story. Really. I can . . . It's not that big of a deal."

Wait.

More, a little more.

"It's really good to say hi, though. Good to hear your voice. I should probably go."

Wait.

"Good-bye, Ari—"

"Hang on."

Oh yes.

"One thing." He spoke even softer than before. "But I didn't tell you, though. You have to promise."

This was good. Very good. "No, of course not. You didn't say a word."

"I didn't take either of the tips the guy called in, but I heard people talking."

She waited, pen poised on her notebook.

"He said dusk was coming, that Day Four would be over soon, that he wouldn't stop until he was done with the story. I don't know what it means. No one does. That's it. But don't print it, OK? Just say something like 'the police are investigating the calls.'"

"I promise, I won't print it." It was a promise she wasn't sure she could keep, but it was the right thing to say at the moment. "I wouldn't want to do anything to hurt our friendship. You know that."

"Yeah, thanks . . . um. Hey, I've been wanting to give you a call. It's been awhile since . . . Maybe we could meet for dinner?"

"Yeah, yeah. That'd be great." She needed to end this. She glanced at the closed door to the room she was in. "Wait, here comes my editor. I need to go. OK? I'll call you."

"OK—"

She hurriedly said good-bye, ended the call, and looked down at her notes: dusk . . . day four . . . he's telling a story . . . two victims each day.

Maybe the note John left in the pot of basil has something to do with the story the killer is telling.

Slowly she wrote out the words to the note, thinking carefully about each one: "Must needs we tell of others' tears? Please, Mrs. Greer, have a heart.—"

Wait.

She'd missed a word before. A crucial word—we.

"We tell of others' tears."

Her heartbeat quickened.

Maybe John was in the media as well.

He's one of us.

She pulled up the *Denver News'* staff roster on her computer and began to search for anyone who might have recently written a story about dusk, or the fourth day of something, or someone who'd been off duty at the times of the murders.

She would start there. Then move on to other media outlets until she found the man who'd sent her the flowers.

I was deeply troubled by the two stories I read in *The Decameron*.

If our killer really was reenacting the stories told on day four, when he came to the ninth tale he would commit one of the most shocking crimes I'd ever heard of.

The tenth tale was less gruesome, but it left the door open for even more crimes.

My time was slipping away.

I checked out the copy of the 1947 translation of *The Decameron* and hurried back to police headquarters.

Even though I was anxious to share what I'd uncovered about story number nine, I knew that in order to understand the broader context of *The Decameron* connection, we needed to start with the first story told on day four.

That was Jake's story and he was already waiting in the conference room when I stepped inside.

Kurt and Cheyenne arrived less than a minute later, and the meeting began.

39

Kurt got things under way. "This guy has been escalating, and we have a lot to cover. Let's be thorough, but let's be concise." He nodded to Jake. "Talk to us."

Jake glanced at his notes. "In the introduction to the first story, the storyteller Fiammetta says 'needs must we tell of others' tears,' in reference to the goal they have of telling tragic stories on this day. John simply inverted the first two words to make it into a question directed at Amy Lynn."

"Since the words weren't in order, an online search engine wouldn't have found the phrase," Cheyenne said. "Clever."

If there'd been any doubt at all, that reference locked in the connection between the killings and *The Decameron*.

I caught myself tapping my finger against the table. Stopped.

Jake went on, "This first story is about a father who has some men strangle his daughter's lover. He sends her the dead man's heart in a golden bowl, she pours poison over it, drinks it, and dies."

"And I'll bet she's found holding his heart against her own," I said.

Jake didn't have to glance at his notes. "Yes."

I had a horrifying thought, but one I couldn't shake: *John made Heather drink a bowl of poison that contained her boyfriend's heart.*

"Wait," Cheyenne said. "The anonymous caller said that Day Four would end on Wednesday—that's ten days after Heather and

194

Chris disappeared. And there are ten stories told about others' tears. So that means—"

"He's reenacting all ten stories," Kurt said.

Stillness climbed through the room.

"Well," Jake said at last. "I'm not sure how he'll reenact the second story: it's about a priest who pretends to be the angel Gabriel in order to have sex with a woman who's beautiful but not all that bright."

"What happens to the priest?" Kurt asked.

"He's caught, humiliated, sent to prison."

"He's not killed?" I said.

Jake shook his head. "But he is left for a while in the forest, chained to a tree with a mask fastened over his face so he couldn't call for help."

"The woman?" asked Cheyenne.

"She survives too."

Kurt stared thoughtfully at the wall for a moment and then said, "I don't know of any priests from the area who've been caught recently in sex scandals, but I'll check with Lieutenant Kaison in Sex Crimes, and I'll give Missing Persons a call." He scribbled some notes on his pad.

"All right," Jake continued. "Third story: this one reads like a medieval soap opera. It covers a three-way love triangle gone bad. Really convoluted. In the end, though, one man is poisoned and a woman is killed with a sword."

"So that must be Ahmed Mohammed Shokr's poisoning and the stabbing death of Tatum Maroukas on Wednesday," Cheyenne said.

"Those are my three stories," Jake concluded.

Cheyenne's turn. She stood.

"The fourth story obviously relates to Sebastian Taylor and Brigitte Marcello: a woman is dismembered before her lover's eyes, then dropped into the sea, or in this case, Cherry Creek Reservoir. In the end, her lover gets beheaded."

"So," Jake said reflectively, "the UNSUB dumps bodies where they can be found quickly, calls in tips, leaves notes." He paused, looked around the room. "He's a storyteller. He wants an audience; needs to tell *someone* of others' tears."

"That fits," Cheyenne said. "Story five is about the pot of basil."

Something didn't click. The timing of the crimes was off. "Hang on," I said. "Heather and Chris disappeared on Monday, but they were found on Thursday. If the killer is reenacting the crimes in order, they should have been found first . . . Wait . . ."

"What is it?" Jake asked.

"Remember the temperature in the mine? Forensics measured it at 42 degrees Fahrenheit when they tested the candles. The cooler temperature preserved the body and the heart."

"So they might have been killed on Monday," Cheyenne said.

"Yes. For now, let's call the killer John. If he really is retelling the stories in order and if the priest isn't supposed to die in the second story—"

"He might still be alive." Kurt finished my thought.

"Right."

I felt a small thrill.

Kurt stood. "I'll put this into play right now; see if we have anything unusual—anything at all—involving priests this week." He left the room.

"Hang on, Pat." It was Jake. "The first anonymous tip came in on Thursday; if John killed Heather and Chris on Monday, why wait three days before calling our attention to the crime?"

"Who knows," I said. "Maybe he waited to give himself a head start. Let's not worry about reading his mind, let's just focus on catching him. The first crime occurred on Monday; today is Saturday. That means he's going to be reenacting story number six today."

Jake and I shifted our attention back to Cheyenne.

She began to circle the table. "That one's about a man named

Gabriotto who dies of what Boccaccio calls a 'pus-filled abscess' bursting near his heart. But remember, this was in the 1300s, so I'm guessing maybe a heart attack; it's hard to know what Boccaccio might have been referring to."

"A heart attack?" I shook my head. "Not good."

"Why's that?" she asked.

"Given the number of heart attack victims in the Denver metroplex, it'll be almost impossible to track. It's too vague."

I thought for a moment. "This killer, he's into spectacle, right? What did you say, Jake?—that he's a storyteller, that he wants an audience?"

He nodded.

"Then he'd do something more dramatic than just let a man die of a heart attack. Cheyenne, is there anything else in the story he might use? Anything more unusual? More shocking?"

She'd stopped walking and now I noticed her face turning pale. "Before the man dies, he has a dream that a black greyhound attacks him and eats out his heart while it's still beating in his chest."

40

A chill.

All three of us were quiet.

For a moment we let the impact of her words settle in, and finally, I asked Cheyenne, "What about the man's lover?"

She consulted her notes. "She survives. After laying his body on a silk sheet covered with rose petals, she joins a convent. So, I'm not sure that helps us as much. The greyhound connection, though, I think that's solid."

I nodded. "So do I. Before we go any further, we need to get some officers on this—greyhound owners, vets, kennels, tracks. Let's see if anyone's missing a dog, or if there have been any recent dog attacks. If we're right, John is going to commit this crime today . . ." Then I paused. I didn't want to add the next four words, but I felt like I needed to. "Maybe he already has."

"All right," Cheyenne said. "I'll talk with Kurt and Captain Terrell." She headed for the door.

I offered to join her, but she called over her shoulder, "I'll be right back. Give me five minutes."

After Cheyenne left the room, Jake headed for the snack machines at the end of the hall. I took a moment to jot down the names of the victims and the story details from the crimes we knew about so far, then I tugged out my phone, checked my voicemails, found none, but then remembered I'd promised to call Calvin today.

I tried his number.

No answer. I left a message for him to return my call.

The facts of the case kept tumbling through my mind: the dismemberments, the poisonings, the beheadings, the progression of stories one through five, the pot of basil. The timing and progression—

I still hadn't spoken with Tessa since she'd left with Dora. I speed-dialed her.

"Yeah?" she said.

"It's me. How are—"

"So, was it in there?"

"What do you mean?"

"The pot. Was it in the pot?"

"You said you didn't want me to tell you."

"I know, but I'm just wondering, like, was it or—wait. Don't tell me, OK?"

"OK," I said.

"But it was there, though, right? The head?"

"We're not talking about that."

"Yeah, no, I know. But—"

"Tessa, enough. Is Dora still there?"

"We're reading through my mom's shoe box stuff. It's pretty cool." A pause, and then, "It'd be better if I had the diary."

"We'll discuss that later. How long is Dora staying?"

"She's gotta leave in an hour or so, but I think we're gonna hang out later tonight, I guess. Grab supper. See a movie, something like that."

"Well, if I don't see you this afternoon, have fun. And I want you back by midnight."

Another pause. "Yeah."

"OK, talk to you soon."

"So are you gonna give me the diary?"

"Not if you keep asking me about it."

"That's not even fair. How am I supposed to make my case if I can't ever talk about it?"

"Good-bye, Raven."

Silence.

"I said, 'good-bye,'" I repeated.

No answer. I waited, and finally I realized she'd hung up.

Great.

I was pocketing my cell when Kurt appeared at the door.

41

His face was drawn tight and traced with a weary sadness. "You OK?" I asked.

He nodded and told me that he was fine, and that he had officers following up on all the leads, but I could tell there was something else weighing on his mind.

"It's not just the case, is it?" I said.

After an awkward pause he said, "It's Cheryl . . . but it's gonna work out. Things are just, you know, a little tense right now."

Watching his marriage disintegrate had been one of the most painful things for me over the last five months. "Maybe you should take a little time off, work things through," I said.

He shook off the suggestion. "It'll be all right."

"If there's anything I can do—" But then Cheyenne and Jake stepped into the room, and I thought it best not to elaborate any further.

"Thanks," Kurt said. "I appreciate it."

As everyone took their seats, I said, "Before we go on, let's take a minute to look at what we have so far. Summarize the progression of the crimes."

I borrowed Jake's computer, which was still hooked up to the wall monitor, and typed,

Victims:
    Monday—Heather Fain and Chris Arlington (found on Thursday)
    Tuesday—Unknown. A priest? Still alive?
    Wednesday—Tatum Maroukas and Ahmed Mohammed Shokr

Thursday—Sebastian Taylor and Brigitte Marcello
Friday— Kelsey Nash (survived) and Travis Nash
Saturday—?

We all stared at the list.

"It's a little overwhelming when you lay it all out like that," Cheyenne said, mirroring my thoughts.

No one said anything, and I sensed a focused urgency descend on the room.

After taking a few minutes to review the means of death outlined in each of Boccaccio's stories so far, our eyes fell on Kurt. "Well," he said, "let me give you the nutshell version: in story seven, two lovers die from rubbing poison—from poisonous toads—against their gums, and in the eighth story two ex-lovers die of grief. The man dies when he realizes the woman he loves is happily married to someone else; the woman, when she attends his funeral."

He added a few more details but kept his synopsis brief.

Then it was my turn.

"The ninth tale reminded me of a gothic horror story." I decided to just be blunt. "When Sir Guillaume de Roussillon's wife sleeps with another man, he kills him, cuts out the man's heart, and then gives it to the cook to prepare for dinner."

"Please tell me they don't actually eat it," Cheyenne said softly.

I pulled out the copy of *The Decameron* I'd gotten from the library. "It might be best if I just read this section of the story."

The lady, who was nowise squeamish, tasted thereof and finding it good, ate it all; which when the knight saw, he said to her, "Wife, how deem you of this dish?"

"In good sooth, my lord," answered she, "it liketh me, exceedingly."

Whereupon, "So God be mine aid," quoth Roussillon; "I do indeed believe it you, nor do I marvel if that please you, dead, which, alive, pleased you more than aught else."

A deep silence.

"I'm not surprised this pleases you dead," Jake said, "which pleased you more than anything else, alive. That's cold. That's just brutal. How does the story end?"

"The woman kills herself by jumping out a window."

"Love and tears," Jake mumbled. "Fits to a tee."

"What are you thinking?" Kurt asked.

"It's John's obsession," Jake said, extemporaneously profiling the killer. "All of these stories are about the tragic consequences of love; all cruel, fatal tales of love and loss. That's what the phrase refers to: must needs we tell of others' tears? Through his crimes, John is reenacting the lovers' tears."

No one said anything. Whether it was true or not, it made sense.

Kurt looked at me. "What about the last story?"

"This might be the only one that's not filled with tears," I said. "In fact, when I was reading it, I was thinking that Boccaccio might have added it just to lighten the mood and maybe transition into the next day's tales. In any case, no one dies in the last story; however, a man is drugged and sealed in a large crate."

"Buried alive?" Cheyenne asked.

"No, but the way it's written, you start to think that's what will happen. But in the end, there's no tragedy."

"Just lessons," Jake mused. "About love and death."

"That's right." As I agreed with him, I wondered whether our killer would be content with that ending. I doubted it. "This gives us plenty of specifics to move on," I said. "The greyhounds, the poisonous toads, the priest."

Things were popping.

So many crimes. So many puzzle pieces.

"Kurt," I said, "let's get a warrant to look over the library's records and see who's been checking out Boccaccio's books. Also, let's identify which colleges offer courses on Boccaccio or this *Decameron* book. Start with DU and CU, and move out from there. Our guy might have studied all this on his own, but we can at least compare class rosters with the suspect list."

"We'll go countrywide if we need to," he said.

"And we still need to find out who owns the mine where we found Heather's body. It might give us a lead to finding John."

"Jameson's on it," he said with a head shake. "But there are hundreds of abandoned mines up there, and most of Clear Creek County's records still aren't computerized. It's a mess. He's up in Idaho Springs now, going through the county's plat books one at a time."

We were quiet.

"Jameson knows what he's doing," he added. "If there's anything there, he'll find it."

Jake rapped the table decisively with his knuckle and stood. "I'll work on the UNSUB's psychological profile."

Cheyenne rose also. "All the stories so far have to do with married couples or love affairs, and the victims have all been couples. Here's what I'm thinking: our guy is choosing the victims somehow, but there's no obvious connection between each of the different couples, right?"

"Not that we know of so far," I said.

"And Jake, what did you say? Fatal tales of love and loss?"

"That's right."

"Well, who deals the most with a couple's love and loss? Knows about their loneliness, their grief, their love interests and affairs?"

"Yes, good," I said. "A therapist. Or a marriage counselor."

"Exactly," she said. "A counselor's client list would be confidential; in some cases even family members and spouses wouldn't know the person was seeing him, and it would make it very difficult for us to link the victims."

It seemed like a good angle to me. "Check it out. It might be too obvious of a connection for this guy, but maybe he's not as smart as I think he is." I gathered my things.

"What about you?" Jake asked.

"The geoprofile." I headed for the hallway. "I'm going to figure out where John lives."

———————————■———————————

22 minutes later
4:41 p.m.

Giovanni stared at the dark, tinted windows of Thomas Bennett's gray '09 Infiniti FX50 parked on the second level of the 18th Street parking garage. Because of the tinting, he couldn't see into the car's interior—either the front or the backseats.

Perfect.

This way he wouldn't have to wait underneath the vehicle, he could wait inside it.

Even with the Infiniti's advanced security system, it took Giovanni less than thirty seconds to pick the lock.

And less than three minutes to disable the vehicle's GPS tracking and satellite mapping capabilities.

He situated himself in the backseat, closed the door, and then took a moment to tilt the rearview mirror so that he'd be able to see Bennett's face when he climbed into the car.

He laid the two needles he would be using on the seat beside him.

It was a short walk from the Wells Fargo building where Thomas Bennett worked to the parking garage, so Giovanni didn't think he would have to wait long at all for Mr. Bennett to arrive.

42

I was sitting at my desk in my office on the eighteenth floor of the Byron G. Rogers Federal Building, working on the geoprofile.

And getting more and more frustrated.

Kurt's team had done a good job of compiling victimology information: the victims' street addresses, places of employment and recreation, as well as known abduction sites, and the location where each of the bodies had been found. They'd also analyzed credit card usage and, based on the frequency of the victims' purchases, identified the locations of the gas stations, grocery stores, night clubs, and pharmacies the people preferred to patronize.

Still, the first time I ran the data through my FALCON, the Federal Aerospace Locator and Covert Operation Network, the results were inconclusive. As advanced as FALCON's algorithms and geospatial mapping programs were, I was only able to narrow down the hot zone to about 22 percent of Denver County. Not exactly pinpoint accuracy.

I was evaluating the possible ways that Denver's array of one-way roads might be skewing the killer's perception of the distances between the crime sites when my cell rang. I glanced at the caller ID as I answered.

Assistant Director Margaret Wellington.

Great.

I picked up.

"Margaret, I don't have a lot of time right now—"

"It's a sign of respect to address someone by her title."

My fingers tightened around the phone. "I'm a little busy right now, Assistant Executive Director Margaret Wellington." I could picture her sitting behind her desk at FBI headquarters: power suit, thin lips, piercing eyes, mousy hair.

"I'm expecting a full report summarizing yesterday's shooting at the courthouse to be on my desk by eight o'clock Monday morning."

"That seems reasonable. Now—"

"I'll also be ordering a full investigation of the incident."

A waste of time. The Chicago Police Department already had statements from dozens of eyewitnesses. The only investigation that needed to be done was on how Sikora, or his accomplice, had managed to load the gun before it was delivered to the courtroom.

"Thanks for letting me know."

"Has Jake arrived yet?" she asked curtly.

"Jake arrived this morning." How to put this. "And he's already been an invaluable asset to the investigation." I realized that the words valuable and invaluable are synonyms, just like flammable and inflammable, but it felt better to describe Jake's contributions as invaluable.

She paused, no doubt trying to read any subtext of my words. "Do not patronize me, Dr. Bowers. I can make your life miserable."

Who am I to argue with that?

"Margaret, I have to go."

"I'm looking forward to you teaching at the Academy this summer." Derision underscored each of her words. "Just think, we'll be able to see each other every day for three months."

"I can hardly imagine what that'll be like."

Before she could reply I ended the call and put Margaret and her infatuation with paperwork out of my mind.

I decided to switch strategies on the geoprofile. Maybe if I couldn't find John's home base, I could at least narrow down the routes he took to locate and then transport his victims.

To do that, I reorganized the data and began to study the most likely locations where the victims' travel patterns might have intersected with the killer's.

And the minutes ticked by.

Thomas Bennett stepped out of the elevator, and Giovanni lowered himself into the thick shadows of the Infiniti's backseat to make certain he wouldn't be seen.

He pulled on his ski mask, unfolded the straight razor, and heard the car beep as Bennett remotely unlocked the doors.

The man climbed into the driver's seat.

Closed the door.

Slowly, Giovanni sat up and stared at Thomas's face in the rearview mirror. He was a narrow-jawed man with nervous eyes, and he was so busy fumbling with his keys that he still hadn't noticed that there was a person watching him in the mirror. Giovanni waited. He wanted Thomas to see that he was not alone in the car.

Finally, as Thomas slid the key into the ignition, his eyes instinctively found the rearview mirror. "What the—"

But before he could finish his sentence, Giovanni had already reached around the headrest and pressed the straight razor's blade against the front of Bennett's neck. "Hello, Thomas."

The man's lips began to quiver. "Who—"

"This blade really is sharp, so I'm going to have to ask you to sit still and not fidget. If you move too much, it'll get messy. Trust me. If you understand, nod slowly."

Giovanni eased the blade slightly away from Thomas's neck while the man nodded stiffly.

"All right. I'm going to give you a little something to help you relax."

His eyes were large with fear. "You can have my wallet, I—"

"I'm not interested in your money." Giovanni held the razor

blade firmly against Bennett's neck again to encourage him to remain stationary. "Now, please, just sit still for a moment."

Then, watching him carefully in the mirror and holding the blade steady, Giovanni picked up the first needle with his free hand, placed its tip against the left side of Thomas Bennett's neck—

"No," Bennett begged. "Please."

"Shh."

Depressed the plunger.

And a few seconds later, after Thomas was unconscious, Giovanni climbed out, shifted him to the backseat, and unbuttoned the man's shirt to reveal his chest.

Then he carefully gave him the second injection, rebuttoned the shirt, slid behind the steering wheel, and left for the ranch.

43

Ever since my conversation with Margaret nearly forty-five minutes ago, I'd been doing what I used to think I did best.

I wasn't so sure anymore.

No matter how I reworked the geoprofile, I wasn't coming up with anything solid, and I was running out of ideas.

Though I hated to admit it, I was starting to believe that John might have skewed the results by randomly selecting his victims and crime scene locations.

I rubbed my eyes.

I pushed back from my desk and stood. Stretched my back.

My eighteenth-story office window stared down at the city of Denver, and I leaned my hand against the glass and let my eyes wander through the maze of mirrored high-rise hotels and banks that make up Denver's downtown.

John lived down there somewhere.

Or maybe he didn't. Maybe he was peripatetic, just traveling through.

The muscles in my arm, my shoulder, my neck stiffened in frustration and anger.

You have to find him, Pat. You have to bring him in.

I caught sight of the original Denver courthouse just across the street from my office. It had been built in 1910 as a premier example of turn-of-the-century architecture and as a testament to justice in the West. Even though it was only four stories tall, it was imposing, monumental, and took up an entire city block.

From my window I could read the frieze inscribed in tall letters, spanning the building just below the roof—*Nulli Negabimus, Nulli Differemus, Jutitiam.*

Tessa had studied Latin in middle school, so a few months ago I'd brought her downtown to give her a chance to show off her foreign language expertise. As we'd passed the building I'd looked up and said, "Hey. Isn't that Latin?"

But she'd already noticed the words and was working on the translation. "Yeah, but it's kind of hard to translate." She sounded frustrated, and I was glad it was at least a little bit of a challenge to her. "I guess maybe it'd be 'To no one we will deny, to no one we will defer justice.' But *differemus* could be translated 'discriminate.' So, pretty much it's saying they won't deny justice to anyone or discriminate against them." And then she mumbled, "Yeah. Maybe if you're rich."

Her comment seemed to come out of nowhere, and I had the sense that I should disagree with her about it, but realized that she was at least partly right. So, instead of commenting, I led her around the building to the southwest side to show her the second Latin inscription, but before I could, she pointed angrily at the building. "Can you even believe that?"

She wasn't pointing at the Latin phrase.

"What?" I asked.

"There."

She pressed a light finger against my jaw and turned my head toward the marble lettering above an ornate stone doorway near the corner of the building. The sign had two words: Judges Entrance.

"It's been up there for like a hundred years," she said.

"So? It's where the judges go in."

"You're kidding me? It doesn't bother you?"

"Why should it?"

"It's missing an apostrophe."

OK.

As I was trying to figure out how to respond to that, she scanned the phrase I'd led her to this side of the building to see: "OK. So that one's from Cicero. It's a lot more common. We learned it in Latin class. It means, 'The law does unfairness to no one, injustice to no one.'"

Injustice to no one.

So now, as I leaned my hand against the glass and thought of that day with Tessa, Calvin's words from last night echoed in my mind: *"Our justice system is concerned more with prosecutions and acquittals than it is with either truth or justice. You know it's true. It's just that we're reticent to admit it."*

Tessa might not have agreed with the first inscription, but I was starting to doubt the truth of the second.

Because sometimes the law is unfair.

Sometimes justice isn't carried out.

As I was considering that, I heard a knock at my office door.

I turned. "Come."

But the door was already flying open.

Cheyenne burst into the room and slapped a manila folder onto my desk. "We know who owns the mine."

44

"His name is Thomas Bennett," she said. "He lives here in Denver; works as a weekend auditor at the Wells Fargo bank. He left work about forty-five minutes ago. Either his cell is off or he's not answering. It might be nothing, but we can't get a GPS lock on his car either. His wife said he never turns off his phone and he should have been home by now."

I positioned myself in front of my keyboard. "Do you have his home address?"

"Sure."

"Let's plug it in here, see if he lives in the hot zone. "

She gave me the address and while I updated the geoprofile, she told me she hadn't come up with anything on the therapist or marriage counselor angle. "What about you?" She studied the screen. "Anything?"

"Not so much."

Using a different color for each victim's travel routes, I overlaid the data onto a three-dimensional map of the Denver metroplex. The result looked like a plate of multicolored spaghetti.

She pulled up a chair beside me, perhaps closer than she needed to, but I didn't say anything. "So tell me," she said. "What am I looking at?"

I remembered that she was familiar with some of my research, but I also knew that geospatial investigation wasn't her specialty, so I pointed to the tangle of overlapping colors and said, "I'm trying to find John's home base, so I input Denver's most traveled roads based on the typical daily vehicle congestion at the times of the crimes, then I compared that with the victim's typical travel patterns—but so far, even with Bennett's address it doesn't look like the data is complete enough to give us what we need."

"OK." She drummed her fingers on the desk. "Let's think this through. Location and timing, right?"

"Yes."

"We know when the anonymous tips were called in."

"That's right. And in most of the crimes so far, we know the times and locations of the abductions or murders. I've already input those."

She stood. Paced to my bookcase. "And because of the videos from the entrance to the hospital, we know when Kelsey Nash arrived at the morgue . . ."

"We know when Brigitte Marcello bought the Chinese food she took to Taylor's."

"And," she added, "we know that John flew to Chicago sometime after dumping Brigitte Marcello's body, and that when he returned to Denver he drove from the airport to the morgue."

I was about to say something, then paused. "What?"

"Well, I mean, not for certain, but at least it's probable. Based on the audio message in the mine, we can assume that John traveled to Chicago after disposing of Brigitte Marcello's body."

"I don't like to assume."

"But you *are* assuming—you're working from the premise that John *didn't* fly to Chicago. Doesn't it make sense to run your data at least once, assuming that he did?"

I stared at her for a moment.

It struck me that even though she wasn't in the Bureau and we'd only worked half a dozen cases together over the last year, it was beginning to feel like she was my partner. And I liked how it felt.

"You might have a point," I said.

"It pains you to have to say that, doesn't it?"

"You have no idea."

Thoughts of the cases I'd worked with Lien-hua tried to climb into my mind, but I slid them aside and pulled up the FAA's archives of arrival and departure schedules for the last three days to figure out which airport John might have used.

The ranch lay on the southern edge of Clear Creek County, fifty minutes from Denver and three thousand feet higher in the Rockies than the Mile-High City.

The property contained a few rolling fields dotted with pines and was hemmed in by thick spruce forests and steep rocky cliffs. National forest land bordered the ranch on three sides.

Elwin Daniels had owned the land until three weeks ago when he bequeathed it by default to the man who was watching the blood spurt from his neck.

Red sunlight streaking the air.

And since the property lay at the end of a remote, unmarked dirt road and the good people of Clear Creek County tended to keep to themselves, Giovanni hadn't had any trouble with neighbors stopping by to chat with the reclusive rancher he'd killed.

He turned onto Piney Oaks Road.

Less than five miles to the ranch.

It only took a few minutes to analyze the flight schedules from Denver International Airport and Colorado Springs Airport. While I did, Cheyenne pulled out an oversized map of Denver County and unfolded it on the other end of my desk.

By comparing arrival and departure schedules with the time of Friday's anonymous tip about the location of Sebastian Taylor's body, I realized that John would have needed to fly out of DIA instead of Colorado Springs.

To cover all my bases, I ran the names from the suspect list against the passenger manifests and, considering how careful John had been so far, I wasn't surprised when I didn't find any matches.

Based on the current theories of distance decay, I reorganized the data and calculated the most likely travel routes from Bearcroft Mine to Taylor's house, from Cherry Creek Reservoir to the airport, and from the airport to Baptist Memorial Hospital at the times of day John would have been traveling.

Hit "enter."

The hot zone shifted west of the city.

I felt the familiar thrill of being in the middle of a case as things heat up. "Do you have the list of greyhound owners?"

"Let me check with Kreger; he was heading that up."

She tapped at her phone while I pulled up the satellite imagery of the Denver metroplex. A moment later I heard her identify herself to someone on the other end of the line.

"Ask about the greyhounds," I said. "If anyone from Clear Creek County recently purchased one."

She relayed the question, nodded to me as she listened to the answer, then tipped the phone away from her mouth and told me, "A man named Elwin Daniels. Ten days ago. MasterCard purchase. He lives on a ranch in the southern part of the county."

The location lay less than two miles from the revised hot zone.

I typed in his name. Pulled up his address. Zoomed in using FALCON.

It'd been three minutes since the last satellite pass, but we had footage of a car halfway up the winding dirt road to the ranch. The Infiniti had tinted windows, so it was impossible to see the driver's face. I focused on the rear bumper to try to read the plate number.

Cheyenne spoke into the phone, then said to me, "According to Elwin's DMV records, he's seventy-two years old. So, probably not our killer."

You need to get to that ranch, Pat.

"Cheyenne." I froze the picture. Magnified the image. "Get us a helicopter."

Sharpened the resolution.

Yes.

Got it.

I grabbed the car's license plate, enlarged it, then tapped at my keyboard and ran the numbers.

Beside me, Cheyenne was requesting a chopper. Dispatch must have suggested Cody Howard, the department's chief helicopter pilot, but she told them rather brusquely, "We've been through this before: I don't fly with Cody. Get us Colonel Freeman." Her sharp tone surprised me, but then the name of the man who owned the vehicle flashed on my screen and I stopped worrying about why Cheyenne preferred to fly with the colonel.

The Infiniti belonged to Thomas Bennett.

The owner of Bearcroft Mine.

I sent my chair toppling backward as I stood. "Let's go."

As I sprinted for the hall I yanked out my cell and called dispatch to get some cars and an ambulance to Elwin Daniels's house.

45

Colonel Cliff Freeman fired up the helicopter as Cheyenne and I slipped on our headphones and headset mics so we could communicate en route.

As we took off, I used my cell to pull the DMV photos for Thomas Bennett and Elwin Daniels so that we could visually identify the two men if either of them were at the ranch.

By the time I looked up, we were already soaring over the foothills toward the Rockies.

Giovanni dragged Thomas Bennett's unconscious body into the barn and laid him on the hay-strewn ground.

He took a moment to close and latch the twelve-foot-tall sliding doors so that they could only be opened from the inside. The only other way into the barn was through the tack room.

With the doors shut, the barn was lit only by the sparse lightbulbs dangling from the beams high overhead and the four tiny windows on the east side.

The familiar odor of dried manure and dusty hay surrounded him, but now it was mixed with the stench of the stale urine on the floor of the greyhound's cage.

The cage hung in the middle of the barn, about twenty-five feet away, suspended three feet above the ground by four chains cinched around the beams high overhead.

Giovanni had named the sleek, jet-black greyhound Nadine, after his grandmother whom he'd pushed the knife into when he was eleven. And now that he hadn't fed the dog in four days, he knew she'd be motivated to eat whatever type of meat he offered her.

Even if it were still moving.

A wheelchair sat beside the cage, but the floor of the barn was too rutted and had too many loose boards to wheel Thomas around, so Giovanni picked up the man's legs and pulled him across the hay.

As he passed the horse stalls, the Appaloosa and the black mare—the only two horses currently in the barn—watched him from behind their gates. The Appaloosa neighed and stomped at the hay as he passed, but he ignored her.

He arrived at Nadine's custom-designed cage: four feet wide, eight feet long, and just tall enough for her to stand. Because of its weight, it barely swayed as she paced impatiently back and forth.

He hoisted Bennett into the wheelchair.

From inside her cage, Nadine let out a burst of vicious barks that betrayed the fact that she'd grown up domesticated.

She stopped and locked her eyes on Giovanni. Snarled.

He'd expected her to be in a nasty mood, but the low feral sound coming from her throat surprised him. The amphetamines he'd injected into her throughout the week must have been making her even more aggressive than he'd anticipated. "Easy, girl," he said. "Supper's on the way."

Bennett's limp body slumped in the wheelchair, and Giovanni took a moment to prop him upright.

Then he retrieved a roll of duct tape from a shelf near the tack room and returned to the wheelchair to begin the preparations.

———————————————■———————————————

I spent the flight reviewing what I knew about the case, trying to discern whether Thomas Bennett was more likely the victim or the killer, but I didn't have enough data to confirm or disprove either possibility.

We made it to the ranch in less than nine minutes.

"There!" Cheyenne pointed to the gray Infiniti FX50 parked

beside the barn. A field stretched between the house and the barn, but had so many scattered pine trees and so much uneven terrain that I couldn't see any good landing spots.

I asked Cliff, "What do you think?"

He shook his head. "Closest I can get is that field to the southeast." He pointed to a meadow that lay about six or seven hundred meters from the ranch house.

I wasn't sure how fast Cheyenne could run, but she sure appeared fit. And although I hadn't been jogging much since last winter when I'd been shot in the leg, I'd recovered pretty well and I figured I could make it to the ranch in less than three minutes.

"Up for a run?" I asked her.

A gleam in her eye. "Only if it's a race."

I liked this woman. Liked her a lot. I patted Cliff's shoulder. "Take us down."

He nodded and aimed the helicopter toward an opening in the trees.

46

Giovanni finished duct taping Thomas's left wrist to the wheelchair. Tugged the tape tight. Ripped it off. Set down the roll.

There. Both wrists and both ankles were secure. Thomas wouldn't be leaving that chair.

The spaces between the bars of Nadine's cage were only wide enough for her muzzle, but that didn't stop her from viciously attacking the air less than two feet from Giovanni's arm as he stood nearby.

He felt a spray of her hot saliva on his forearm.

"Almost time," he said, being careful not to get too close to her. "You've been more than patient. Just a few more minutes."

Confident that Thomas couldn't wriggle free, he walked past the cage to retrieve the duffel bag and the bucket of rose petals from the shelves near the maze of round hay bales on the barn's west side.

He carried the duffel bag and the roses back to the wheelchair, set them down, and glanced at Nadine.

The top of the cage could be unlatched and had an opening through which Giovanni had lowered the tranquilized dog a week and a half ago. The cage's only other door lay on the end a few feet from Thomas Bennett's unconscious body. When unlatched, this second opening wasn't large enough for the dog's body, but it was large enough for her head.

That was the feeding door.

Greyhounds are smart, so it hadn't taken Giovanni long to condition Nadine to eat whatever he placed in front of the feeding door.

He unzipped his duffel bag and pulled out a silk sheet, then smoothed it across the ground.

He would be needing that for the body.

Cheyenne beat me to the ranch house, but not by much.

The barn lay a hundred meters past the house on the other side of the field.

We drew our weapons. "You take the house." I tried to hide how out of breath I was. "I'll get the barn."

A quick nod and then she was on her way to the porch.

I rolled under a length of barbed wire fence and ran toward the barn.

Giovanni dipped his hand into the bucket, caressed the rose petals. Smooth. Velvety.

Fragrant.

He cupped a handful and tossed them onto the silk sheet, and they fell in gentle curling patterns that made him think of great, crimson snowflakes. Red on white. Petals the color of blood landing on a silken field of snow.

Jacked on adrenaline, I arrived at the barn built of wooden boards, baked dry in the Colorado sun.

Assess the situation.

Assess and respond.

I checked the Infiniti.

Empty.

Then turned to the barn.

The best way to get killed is to rush into a situation like Rambo. I've known too many agents and police officers who've died in the line of duty because they reacted instead of anticipated.

Be careful. Be smart.

I ran around the southeast corner and tried to picture what lay inside. I'd grown up on a farm in Wisconsin, so I knew barns, and this one probably had a tack room, the seed room, horse stalls, hay bales, dead farm equipment. This barn was nearly twenty-five meters long and twenty wide—larger than I'd thought at first.

Looking for a way in, I circled around the south side, saw that the four-meter high metal sliding doors were closed off. Tried sliding them open.

Locked.

Inside the barn a dog was barking. Wild. Ferocious. I'm not an expert on dogs, so I didn't know what a greyhound sounded like, but this one sounded more like an attack dog than a racer.

No sign of anyone outside the barn.

The dog growled, then barked again.

As I ran around the corner, I noticed a standard-sized door at the far end of the barn. Probably to the seed room or the tack room. Or maybe an office. Or hay storage area. Whatever it led to, I was going in.

The dog's agitated barking told me it wasn't alone in the barn.

I sprinted toward the door.

47

Giovanni was still scattering rose petals when he heard Thomas Bennett stir.

He pulled his ski mask from his pocket. Put it on.

"Where am . . ." Bennett's voice was garbled. He was still waking up. "What's going on?"

"I was hoping you might sleep through this, Thomas." Giovanni was lying but tried to sound as convincing as possible. He emptied his hand of petals and then faced his captive. "It'll be a bit more distressing for you this way, I'm afraid."

The door was locked.

I peered around the corner of the barn and saw no other doors, just a line of small windows.

Back to the door then. I could shoot out the lock, but if the killer was in the barn with Thomas, the sound of the shot would alert the killer and put Bennett in more imminent danger.

Of course, he might have heard the helicopter.

But with all the barking, he might not have.

At least for the moment I decided not to announce my presence. Instead, I yanked out my keys, flipped open my lock pick set, and slipped a pick blade into the keyhole.

Thomas was still disoriented. Giovanni saw him look vaguely in his direction, but a moment later when Nadine growled and sprang toward the bars, the meaty slap of impact seemed to jar him awake.

He stared at the dog, then jerked his head down and gazed at the wheelchair, the bindings. Tried to wrestle free.

Failed.

Tried again, but he was secure.

His eyes widened with confusion and fear. "What are you doing? Where am I?"

Giovanni set the bucket of rose petals on the ground. "How did I do there a moment ago? When I said I hadn't expected you to be awake? Did I have you convinced? It's important for me to know; I've really been working on my acting."

"What?" A tremor in his voice.

"The truth is, I was waiting for you to wake up."

Thomas let his gaze travel around the barn and then land on the dog. "What's going on? Who are you?"

"My name is Giovanni and I murder people, and you're about to become my next victim."

Thomas became frantic. Struggled uselessly to get free. "Let me out of here!"

Giovanni walked to the wheelchair and disengaged the wheel locks.

His captive tried desperately to pull his arms and legs free, but the duct tape snugged tighter the more he strained against it.

He positioned the wheelchair so that the man's knees were under the cage and his chest was less than a foot from the feeding door's opening.

Nadine seemed pleased.

"No," Thomas cried again. "Please stop. Please."

"On Thursday night I gave a man who was about to die the option of wearing a gag," Giovanni said. "I'd like to extend the same courtesy to you, although I should probably tell you that I'm not expecting your situation to last as long as his did, so it might not even be worth the trouble."

Nadine shoved her muzzle through the bars and snapped. Growled.

"Why are you doing this?" Thomas's voice was becoming shrill, girlish.

"I did bring one along however," Giovanni said, ignoring Thomas's question, "just in case, and I'll be glad to accommodate you, if you like."

"What do you want?" Thomas's voice had fallen from a shriek to a whispered plea. "Please, don't do this. You don't have to do this. What do you want? Money? I can get you money. A million. I swear."

Giovanni took that as a no regarding the gag. So, two for two. Maybe his victims weren't taking him seriously enough. Next time he would make sure he'd been unequivocally clear about their situation. He set the wheel locks so that the chair wouldn't roll back from the cage once things got started.

Then he stepped back. "Now, in Pamfilo's story, after your death your wife is supposed to join a convent and live a godly and abstinent life, but in today's culture that seems unlikely. I decided instead that I would just help her along with the abstinence part. The surgery is relatively simple. I'll be visiting Marianne as soon as we're done here. I promise not to make her suffer long. That should be of some comfort to you."

"No, please—"

He placed one hand gently on Bennett's shoulder. "I want you to look carefully at that dog. It's very important to me that you visualize what's about to happen." Then he unbuttoned Thomas's shirt to reveal his bare chest.

To make it easier for Nadine to get to her meal.

———————————■———————————

The lock gave me more trouble than I thought it would, and when I heard yelling from inside the barn, I was getting ready to shoot it out after all—

Click.

Finally.

Gun ready, I pressed the door open, swept the room.

The clean, musky scent of leather.

Saddles, halters, bridles hanging on the walls. Two grooming kits on the floor with fly spray, liniment, and brushes.

The tack room.

Nothing.

No one.

A door on the far wall.

I ran toward it, eased it open, and stepped into the dusty, muted light of the barn.

A network of shadows skirted along the wall. Just to my right, a thick wooden ladder led to the hayloft that darkened this corner of the barn even more. I was still out of sight. Good.

My heart raced.

I edged around the corner of an empty horse stall and scanned the barn.

To the left, rows of hay bales and two horse stalls. Rusted farm equipment. A tractor. A few gasoline cans. To the right, four more horse stalls. Tarps. Boards. Rolls of twine. Several buckets, two containing water, one sweet feed, the fourth empty. A few bridles hanging from hooks on the wall nearby.

A typical barn.

Except for the hanging cage.

And the dog.

There were two men beside the cage. One in a wheelchair, the other with his back to me.

John.

Six foot, maybe six-one. Medium build. Jeans. Black sweatshirt. Black ski mask.

Not much to go on, it could be almost anyone.

I could see the side of the victim's face and I recognized him from his DMV photo as Thomas Bennett. I couldn't see the suspect's hands. I had to assume he was armed.

If I shouted for the killer to step aside, he might kill the man. I needed to move on him, but I needed to play this right.

Nadine snarled, a green fire in her eyes.

"Well, then," Giovanni said, reaching for the feeding door's latch. "Let's get started."

When I heard the words I knew I couldn't wait.

I stepped out of the shadows. "Stop!" I aimed my gun at the suspect's center mass. "Hands to your side and step away from the cage."

Giovanni froze. He recognized that voice.

Bowers.

Impressive.

Impeccable timing.

The suspect didn't move. His back was still toward me.

I edged closer. "Hands to the side and turn around. Do it now or I will shoot. Hands out, now!"

He didn't move.

"He's gonna kill me!" Thomas Bennett hollered.

"Show me your hands!" Then I heard a metallic snap, the suspect lifted his arms, and that's when Thomas Bennett began to scream.

48

The next two seconds were a blur.

The suspect dove toward the jumbled network of hay bales, and I saw the dog thrust its head through a small door in the cage, lunging toward Thomas Bennett's chest.

No!

I eyed down my SIG at the dog.

Giovanni was rolling beneath the gate of an empty horse stall when he heard the shot.

Before I could pull the trigger, a gunshot ricocheted through the barn and the dog slammed against the side of the cage, dark blood spouting from a gaping wound in the back of its head. One of the small windows at the far side of the barn was shattered.

Cheyenne.

She'd fired through the glass, threaded the bullet between the bars of the cage, and hit the dog in the eye in mid-attack at fifteen meters.

Brilliant shot.

Admire her later.

I ran to Bennett but kept my gun trained on the hay bales. "Are you hurt?" He was staring blankly at the dead dog. "Mr. Bennett, are you OK?"

At last he nodded. Swallowed. Nodded again.

We were too exposed. No time to untie him.

No time.

I tried to push the chair to safety, but the wheels were locked. *Quick. Quick.*

With one eye on the hay bales, I unsnapped the locks and yanked the wheelchair across the barn floor, bouncing it over the boards and into an empty horse stall in a shadowed corner of the barn. If the suspect were armed, the gate to the stall would offer at least a little protection.

Cheyenne was outside. She could cover the door in case John tried to escape.

Unless there's another way out.

"I'll be right back," I told Bennett.

"Don't leave me."

"I'll be back."

"Untie me!"

I started for the hay bales as Cheyenne threw open the tack room door.

"He's behind the bales," I shouted to her, and she slid into position to cover the east side of the bales. Bennett kept yelling for help, but for the time being I ignored him. I had to find John.

"Step out now!" I yelled.

I saw shuffling movement somewhere in the darkness, but I had no visual on the suspect. "Hands in the air!" I signaled to Cheyenne that I was heading in, and she ducked behind the tractor to cover me.

———————————■———————————

Giovanni lay still and silent beside the gasoline cans and looked down the barrel of his Wilson Combat Elite Professional .45 ACP at Detective Warren's back.

He had a clear shot at her. Yes. He could shoot her right now and then take out Bowers as he rushed to help her, but he didn't want to do that. Not after all the planning, all the preparations.

Giovanni considered his options.

He doubted the FBI or DPD could offer him any better adversaries than these two.

Well, one way to find out just how good they were.

---■---

The sound of a gunshot sent me pivoting backward behind a horse stall.

I looked at Bennett and saw that he was still struggling to get free.

"You OK?"

"He's shooting at me!" He sounded unhurt.

Cheyenne still sat crouched behind the tractor. I called to her, "Cheyenne, are you—"

"I'm fine."

Then I saw that the bullet had shattered a bucket near the cage and sent rose petals spewing across a silk sheet laying on the hay.

"Drop your weapon!" I yelled.

End this now.

I nodded toward Cheyenne, and she leveled her gun. I rounded the corner of the stall and entered the maze of hay bales.

Nothing.

Heart beating.

Around another bale.

No one.

Where is he?

I edged around the second row of bales near the wall of the barn.

Still nothing. Still quiet.

Maybe there's another way out.

Then, the scent of gasoline.

And then a line of flames, leaping, springing to life from the dry hay near the Appaloosa's stall. The fire raced across the floor to one of the barn's support beams. In the tangled light I saw a figure bolt toward the tack room out of Cheyenne's line of fire.

I aimed. "Stop, FBI!"

Identify the subject. Confirm that it's—

This man wore a gray polo shirt, not a black sweatshirt.

No shot! No shot!

"There's two of them!" I yelled to Cheyenne. I ran forward.

He slipped through the tack room door. A moment later I arrived and grabbed the handle.

Locked.

I shot out the lock, then threw my shoulder against the door, but it wouldn't move. I slammed into it again, but it held fast. He must have propped something against the other side or bolted it shut.

The fire was spreading quickly around me, devouring the hay in great gulps, snaking around the perimeter of the barn.

Smoke billowed toward the ceiling.

A shift in priorities.

Get Thomas and Cheyenne out of the barn. Now.

49

I holstered my weapon and ran toward Bennett as Cheyenne wrestled with the metal sliding doors at the far end of the barn. "Will it flare up if I open the door?" she yelled.

I wasn't sure. The rush of oxygen might cause the barn to fill with flames, but we didn't have any other options. "It'll be fine. Open it!"

Beside one of the stalls I noticed the black sweatshirt.

He changed shirts so you wouldn't shoot him!

Man, this guy was smart. Really smart.

Either that, or there are two men . . .

"Help!" Thomas yelled. I made it to him and grabbed the wheelchair's handles but quickly realized that the fire was spreading too fast to roll him all the way across the barn. I needed to cut him loose. I flicked out the blade of my Wraith and slit the tape binding his right arm.

Cheyenne opened the sliding door.

The barn didn't explode into flames—thankfully, yes, thankfully—"Get out!" I yelled to her, but she ran toward the stalls to free the horses.

I cut Thomas's left wrist free. Bent to cut his legs loose.

Smoke began pooling at the ceiling. The two horses circled in their stalls, snorting, stomping. Tossing their heads.

"Hurry!" Bennett yelled at me.

How is this fire spreading so fast?

As I cut the tape from his left leg, I took a quick glance around the barn. Almost immediately, I could see that the hay and the boards hadn't been strewn randomly across the floor, but were laid in careful, crisscrossed rows. All designed to block the exit with flames.

John was ready for us. He was prepared.

I cut the tape from Bennett's other leg. Put the knife away. "Can you stand?"

"I don't know." He tried but collapsed backward. He shook his head. "Drugged me. Knocked me out."

A quick survey of the barn.

It was bad.

The fire already barred the exit and was moving steadily toward us, sealing us into the corner of the barn that lay farthest from the sliding doors. I couldn't carry Thomas through the field of flames. We'd never make it.

Cheyenne unlatched one of the horses' gates. A black horse reared back, then took off at a dead run, jumping over the two-foot-high ridge of fire now encircling the barn's perimeter, and disappeared out the door.

Cheyenne reached for the Appaloosa's gate, and I had an idea.

"Wait!" I yelled.

I hoisted Bennett over my shoulder and snatched a bridle from a hook on the wall.

Even if I couldn't get Bennett out, Cheyenne could.

50

She must have read my mind because she grabbed the horse's halter to steady her.

"Take Thomas!" I yelled.

"What about you?"

"Don't worry about me." I lowered Thomas to his feet and wrapped an arm around him to support him.

The horse tensed and whinnied, but Cheyenne worked at soothing her, calming her down. Then she shouted to me. "I won't leave you!"

Two of the walls were completely consumed. I grabbed Cheyenne's arm. "You have to go."

"Get me out of here!" Thomas hollered.

I handed Cheyenne the bridle, but she tossed it aside, grabbed a handful of mane, and swung onto the horse's back. "I'll come back for you," she said.

"I'll look forward to it."

With a surge of adrenaline and Cheyenne's help, I hoisted Thomas onto the horse, where he wrapped his unsteady arms around her waist and then slumped forward. I hoped he'd be clear-headed enough to stay on the horse.

The fire climbed the wall to my left, toward the hayloft.

I scanned the barn but couldn't see any way for me to get out. I knew the horse could gallop through the burning hay, but I'd be lucky to make it as far as the cage.

I reached for the latch and studied the chains holding up the cage.

The opening from the sliding doors is nearly three meters high
. . .

The horse stamped and circled. "Open the gate!" Cheyenne yelled.

You can't make the shot, Pat. Not from here.

No, but Cheyenne can.

I pointed to the length of chain attached to the corner of the cage closest to me. "Shoot the base of the chain!"

"What?"

"The chain. The closest one. Shoot it at the base!" Holding on wouldn't be easy, but it'd be a lot easier than crawling upside down across the ceiling of my garage.

She gave me a puzzled look, then I pointed to the fire snaking up the wall toward the hayloft, and at last it registered. She drew her gun. "Open the latch!"

"But—"

"Do it!"

I threw open the gate, but instead of taking aim she kicked the horse into a flat-out gallop.

No!

Now I'll never get—

As the Appaloosa raced through the blaze, Cheyenne swung her gun to the right and fired four shots at the chain as they passed the cage.

A clang.

The cage's corner dropped to the ground, and the chain nearest me swung free.

This woman could shoot a gun.

The chain would be too hot to touch and probably too short to reach the ladder's base, so I grabbed one of the horse blankets and dashed toward the cage.

51

I reached the cage and whipped the end of the horse blanket around the chain. Cinched it tight and ran back to the hayloft pulling the chain with me.

Holding the blanket, I climbed the ladder. The flames that were snaking up the wall raced me to the hayloft.

I scrambled onto the landing and stood. Stared across the barn.

I had a straight shot from the loft to the sliding doors, and the opening was high enough, but I'd need to avoid hitting the other chains and keep my feet above the flames raging across the floor.

But I could do it.

Maybe.

Flames began to finger their way over the edge of the hayloft and lick at the hay around my feet.

You need to go. Now.

I moved the blanket up the chain. Squeezed it.

Took a deep breath.

And jumped.

52

I swung through the barn.

Gauged my timing. Waited.

Flung my body toward the opening.

And let go.

I landed hard on my left side just beyond the edge of the flames, and rolled out the door, through the dirt, rolled, rolled away from the blaze until at last, I pushed myself to my feet and scrambled into the field.

The heat chased me, but with every stride it grew less fierce, less intense.

A quick breath.

Another.

Out of the corner of my eye I saw the barn erupt into a ball of flame that mushroomed into the deep blue Colorado sky. A gust of heat swooped over me, and I had to cover my face with my arm and turn my back to the fire.

When I looked up I saw Cheyenne about five meters away, hurrying toward me, leading the Appaloosa. She'd managed to get Thomas off the horse, and he was leaning against a fence post nearby. "Pat!" she called. "Are you OK?"

"I'm all right." Looking toward the barn, I saw that the gray Infiniti was gone. "You?"

She nodded and let go of the halter. The horse left and joined its partner, who was already more interested in nibbling grass than watching the burning barn. Although they each had some singed hair, thankfully neither animal looked seriously injured.

Police sirens wailed through the neighboring canyons.

If John was in the Infiniti, we might be able to catch him leaving the property.

I pulled out my cell but discovered it was cracked and dead. I must have smashed it when I landed and rolled away from the fire. Cheyenne noticed and handed me hers.

"Thanks." I tapped in Kurt's number and stepped away from Bennett so I could talk in private.

Kurt answered before I could say a word. "Cheyenne, we're on our way."

"It's Pat," I explained. "Cheyenne's here with me. Listen, we're looking for a male Caucasian, medium build, dressed in blue jeans and a gray shirt." I gave him the plate numbers for the Infiniti.

"Gotcha. I'll pass it on."

Then, a thought. "Wait. He changed clothes once. He might have changed again. And it's possible there are two men."

"OK."

I oriented myself to the steep, thickly forested terrain surrounding the ranch and considered the most recent research on the rational choice patterns of fleeing suspects. "If he's on foot," I told Kurt, "he'll tend to bear right and favor southern slopes. He'll head downhill. If he's still in the car, tell your officers to look for him to take a left on Piney Oaks Road, then two rights. He'll avoid the first on ramp to the highway—"

"Pat," he said. He sounded a little annoyed. "We're on it."

"Have Colonel Freeman circle the area. What about road blocks, other air support?"

"Done."

I looked at the barn. "And send a fire truck. He burned down the barn. No known casualties." But even as I said the words I realized that by the time a fire suppression unit arrived, it'd be too late to do any good. Still, it seemed best to have a fire truck on site just in case. "And have the Arapaho forest station send a firefighter unit in case this fire decides to spread."

"I'll call it in," Kurt said. "See you in a minute." We ended the call, and I handed Cheyenne her phone.

"I was coming back for you," she said softly. She was close enough now for me to see the intense concern on her face. "I thought maybe you . . ."

"He tried to kill me," Thomas called to us.

We went to him, and as I walked, I realized that landing on my side hadn't helped my bruised ribs feel better, but I reassured myself that it hurt a lot less than being burned alive.

Kneeling beside him, I noticed that he'd suffered first- and second-degree burns on the right side of his face, neck, and arm, but he didn't appear to have any third-degree burns or life-threatening injuries. "Are you all right?" I asked.

He nodded stiffly.

"You're safe now. Help will be here soon."

He stared at me somewhat suspiciously. "You a cop?"

"FBI. I'm Special Agent Bowers. Did you get a look at the man who attacked you?"

The swirling lights of squad cars and several ambulances appeared on the potholed road leading to the ranch.

Thomas shook his head. "Wore a mask." His voice was strained. "Was he in there? Is he dead?"

No, the car is gone.

"I'm not sure," I said. "Listen to me, Thomas, was it possible there were two men?"

He thought for a moment, then shook his head. "No. I don't think so." His hand was quivering. He turned to Cheyenne. "My wife. You're sure she's safe?"

"The police are on their way to your house. She'll be fine."

"Don't worry," I said to him. "We'll get the man who did this."

Cheyenne stepped away to signal to the patrol units where we were.

"He was gonna kill me," Thomas muttered. "He drugged me. Knocked me out."

He seemed to be speaking to me from another place. "Thomas, did he say anything about the drugs he used on you? Do you know what they were?"

Thomas shook his head and repeated himself. "He was gonna kill me."

I patted his shoulder. "Don't worry. The paramedics will be here in a minute."

He took a choppy breath and nodded and watched the emergency vehicles rumble toward us.

Cheyenne returned and I motioned toward a nearby pine. "Hey, can we talk for a second?" I assured Thomas we'd be right back and he nodded to me, but his attention was already on the approaching ambulances.

"Was the car gone when you got out here?"

"Yes. But we'll get him, Pat. He couldn't have gotten far."

Sweat and dark soot streaked Cheyenne's face. "You sure you're all right?" I asked her softly.

"I'm fine." She took my wrists in her hands and gently turned them so that my hands were palms up. "Are you?"

Only then did I notice the burns on my forearms—not serious. Mostly first degree. They looked like bad sunburns. "I'll be OK."

She was still holding my wrists. I didn't mind.

"You need to soak," she said. "A good, cool bath. And lots of aloe vera."

"Thanks, Mom."

Finally, she let go, and I felt my hands drop to my sides.

"That was an amazing shot," I said. "The chain. Thanks for that." I wanted to ask her about that shot—something was bothering me about it, but I decided that could wait until things had settled down a little.

She shook her head, obviously frustrated with herself. "It took me four shots." She brushed some scorched, matted hay off my shoulder.

Her voice felt as gentle as her touch, and my troubled relationship with Lien-hua seemed like something that had ended a very long time ago.

Cheyenne let her hand pause on the side of my neck. "I'm glad you made it out of there, Agent Bowers."

"I'm glad you made it out as well." I looked into her eyes and saw the fire from the barn reflecting in them, dancing across them.

"You sent me out first," she whispered. "You were willing to stay behind, to—"

"Shh," I said.

At last she let her hand glide from my neck.

And then we were both quiet for a few moments, but our eyes kept carrying on a conversation of their own.

The first ambulance rolled to a stop beside Thomas. Two EMTs jumped out and hurried to him. On the other side of the field, three men wearing CSU jackets were heading toward the house.

I would've liked to keep standing there staring into the rich depths of Cheyenne's eyes, but I knew I needed to get back to work. "I'm going to take a quick look up there before things get crazy."

"Right," she said, her voice losing its softness, returning to normal. We were working a case again. We were professionals. "John likes snakes," she added, and I remembered that she'd searched the house briefly when we first arrived at the ranch.

"He likes snakes?"

"He has half a dozen aquariums filled with them. And one of the rooms in the house is locked, I didn't get in there. I heard the barking and came to help you at the barn."

"I'll check it out."

"I'll see if I can get a more detailed description of the suspect from Bennett."

"Good," I said.

"All right."

An awkward pause. I found it hard to look away from her. "So, I'll see you in a few minutes," I said.

"OK."

Then, simultaneously I stepped to the right and she stepped to the left so that we were standing face to face again.

"Hmm," she said. "Great minds." She grasped my arms, held me gently in place, and stepped past me to the right.

It wasn't easy redirecting my thoughts onto the case, but I closed my eyes, took a couple breaths, then opened them and started for the house.

Soot and ash roiled through the air all around me.

I thought of the heart laying on Heather's chest . . . the wide streak of blood on the floor of Taylor's garage . . . Kelsey Nash huddled on the floor, left to die in the freezer . . . Thomas Bennett bound to the wheelchair beside the cage . . .

Considering the appalling nature of the crimes John had already committed, I wondered what kind of evidence we might discover inside the ranch house.

53

As I neared the house, I reminded myself that, even though we hadn't caught John yet, we were right on his heels and closing in fast.

Helicopters.

Roadblocks.

The net was tightening.

I'll get you, John, I thought. *You're mine.*

But even as the thought crossed my mind, so did another: *Don't be so sure.*

I glanced again at the smoldering remains of the barn and thought of how John had been ready for us, how he'd set a trap that had almost burned Cheyenne, Thomas, and me alive. I thought of how he'd managed to enter and leave the morgue without appearing on any surveillance cameras . . . of how he'd been able to find Sebastian Taylor, one of the most elusive men ever to land on the FBI's most wanted list . . .

And then, as I considered the recorded message in the mine and the handwritten note he'd left for me in Sebastian Taylor's garage, all of the facts, everything, I had a disturbing thought that I wanted to discount, but that I couldn't shake. *Maybe you're not the one closing in on him, Pat; maybe he's the one closing in on you.*

But then I arrived at the house, and my thoughts were interrupted by the shouts that came from one of the CSU members inside.

An officer standing beside the front door rushed inside, and I ran up the steps behind him, close on his heels.

The first thing that struck me was the heat—mid-eighties, maybe higher. Someone had cranked the thermostat. All the lights were off, and when I flicked the switch by the door, nothing happened. The hallway was nearly black.

Turning on my Maglite, I shouldered past the confused-looking officer now blocking my path.

Two CSU technicians stood at the end of the hall staring into the kitchen. "Easy, Reggie. Easy," one of them said. Then, "Where's Harwood with that shovel?"

"What is it?" I asked.

"Rattlesnake," the man said in a hushed tone, as if saying the word softly would somehow make the snake less dangerous. The grimy kitchen window let only a dim haze of light into the room, and as I eased past him, my flashlight beam found the snake: a healthy-sized Western Diamondback, coiled in the middle of the kitchen, rattling its tail.

Beyond the snake, Reggie Greer stood cornered by the sink.

"Forget the shovel," the guy beside me said. "Just shoot it."

"Not with Reggie behind it," I said. "We miss the snake, the bullet could ricochet and hit him."

"Yeah, let's not shoot it," Reggie said.

"There are better ways." It'd been almost two decades since I'd worked as a wilderness guide and had been trained to deal with venomous snakes, but I figured I could at least remember enough to get the snake safely out of the house.

"Got another one in the bathroom!" someone yelled.

I heard the officers around me edging backward. But one set of footsteps was approaching me. A cautious-looking woman with dark hair appeared beside me. I recognized her. Officer Linda Harwood. She carried a shovel and a spade.

"Let me," I said.

I accepted the spade and ventured into the kitchen as she stepped back with the shovel.

The snake wavered its head toward Reggie, then wound its body into a tight circle.

Rattled.

"It's gonna strike," Linda whispered.

"Shh." I lowered the blade end of the spade in front of the snake's head, and the rattlesnake turned its attention to the spade and tracked its movement. Reggie took a nervous step toward the refrigerator. "Stay still," I said. "They're attracted to movement."

He stood still.

The rattler was now focused on the spade. Slowly, I moved the blade toward its head and then twisted the handle, hooking the snake's neck in the crook of the spade like you might do with a real snake pole or snake stick. I slowly rotated the spade, relying on the rattlesnake's natural inclination to coil and hold on.

Lifted it up.

"Back up," I told the people in the hall. "Let me through."

They seemed agreeable enough.

By the time I'd turned around, the hallway was clear.

Carrying the snake, I exited the house and walked to a nearby fence row. Even though I knew that lots of people don't like snakes and would just as soon kill it, I deal with enough death in my life and I don't believe in killing things that don't deserve to die. So I carefully lowered the rattler to the ground, shook it free from the end of the spade, and stepped back. The snake went for cover beneath a scrub pine, where it coiled again and eyed me.

"Where did you learn to do all that?" one of the police officers asked.

"I watch *Animal Planet*," I said.

"Why didn't you just kill it?" he asked.

"It wasn't that snake's time to die."

"There's a bunch of smashed aquariums in one of the bedrooms," an officer yelled from the front steps of the house. "There's snakes all over in there!"

Then it was clear to me why the suspect had killed the lights and turned up the thermostat: he knew we'd sweep the house and he'd entrusted it to his pets to slow us down. The heat would liven up the snakes.

This guy was something else.

I noticed Kurt striding toward me. "Is everybody out?" he yelled.

I deferred with a glance to Officer Harwood. She took a quick count. "Yes."

"All right, that's it," Kurt yelled. "Nobody goes back in. We'll get Animal Control out here. Let's start by processing the exterior doors and the porch."

As people began to disperse and get to work, I walked to Kurt. "Anything on John?"

He shook his head. "Haven't even found the car yet. We're checking every possible route out of here."

"Listen," I said. "I'm going back in the house. There might be something in there that'll lead us to him."

"No, Pat. We can't have anyone getting bitten. Don't worry, I'll have the CSU work with Animal Control, make sure they don't contaminate the scene."

I could understand that he didn't want to put anyone in harm's way, but my mind was made up. "Kurt, if there's even a chance we can find a clue to his whereabouts, or possible associates, we need to move on it now." I pointed to the rattler I'd removed from the house. "I'm good with snakes. I'll go in by myself. I'll be careful."

He deliberated for a few seconds, and then at last said, "All right. Yeah. Do it."

"Let me use your phone."

He looked at me curiously.

"Video," I said. "Mine's out of commission."

He handed me his cell. "Watch your step."

"I intend to."

And then, armed with the spade and the Maglite, I reentered the snake-infested house.

54

The agitated snakes slid through the shadows around me, the sound of their thin, dry rattles cautioning me to be careful where I stepped.

I heeded the warning.

With the house deserted, the snakes seemed to feel at ease exploring the hallway. As they slithered through my flashlight's beam, the light shimmered off their scales, making their bodies look as if they were glistening and wet rather than dry and rough.

And even though I knew how dangerous the rattlesnakes were, I couldn't help but admire their elegant diamond designs as they moved with beautiful, deadly grace across the carpet. I reminded myself that they didn't want any trouble from me any more than I wanted trouble from them, but that didn't settle my pounding heart.

I walked in a circuit through the kitchen, the living room, the dining room. Earlier, Cheyenne had told me that the ranch's owner, Elwin Daniels, was in his early seventies, and now I saw that the dated furnishings, knickknacks, and pictures on the wall bore that out.

By the time I arrived at the bedroom that had held the aquariums, I'd counted more than a dozen rattlesnakes and twice had to slide snakes out of my way with the spade.

The aquariums lay smashed on the floor. Ten more snakes slithered between the shards of glass or huddled against the wall.

Carefully, I took video of the room, getting the perspective from four different locations.

Next, the bathroom.

On the countertop beside the sink lay a toothbrush, razor, and four tubes of toothpaste. I opened the medicine cabinet and found it empty except for six sterilized hypodermic needles. I took video of everything, then went to the last room, the one at the end of the hall.

The room that was still locked.

I laid the spade against the wall and pulled out my SIG and lock pick set.

It took me only a moment to pick the lock.

I eased the door open. A quick glance around the room told me no one was there. Just a few more rattlers.

But when my eyes found the bed, ice slid down my back.

Resting on a pillow and staring unblinkingly at the east wall lay the severed head of Sebastian Taylor.

Insects had gotten to it and were doing their work.

But I could still identify whose head it had been.

The smell turned my stomach.

I tore my eyes off the head and looked at the wall its face was directed at.

Dozens of newspaper clippings had been tacked up, and the orientation of the head brought to mind the illusion that its eyes were reading the articles.

Killers love to fantasize, to relive their murders either by reading about them, watching news reports, or recording the crimes themselves and then watching the videos, so I wasn't surprised to see the articles—the shock came when I directed my flashlight at them and realized that these were not articles about the crimes John had committed in Colorado.

No.

Every one of the clippings was about the grisly crimes committed by Richard Devin Basque thirteen years ago in the Midwest.

55

I checked beneath the bed, then inside the closet, confirmed that no one was lying in wait inside the room.

Then, avoiding the two rattlesnakes near the bed, I approached the wall with the articles.

I recognized each of the sixteen victims' Associated Press photos.

Their names floated through my head: Sylvia Padilla, Juanita Worthy, Celeste Sikora . . .

"Why, Patrick?"

"Why?"

John had kept clippings from the *Milwaukee Sentinel*, the *Chicago Sun-Times*, the *Wisconsin State Journal*, and even some of Wisconsin's smaller local papers like the *Janesville Gazette*, creating a journalistic memorial of the slayings of Richard Devin Basque.

A shrine.

From the time I'd heard the recorded message in the mine on Thursday evening, it'd seemed evident to me that the killer in Colorado had some kind of connection to Basque's trial in Chicago. I hadn't seen how the two cases might be related before, but I did now.

Richard Devin Basque had a fan.

Finally, I came to fourteen articles that covered my arrest of Basque. In each of them, the reporters had included the AP photograph of me. One of the articles, written by a journalist named Zak Logan who'd hounded me for three weeks for an exclusive, described me as "The brave detective who tracked down and single-handedly apprehended the man suspected to be responsible for the brutal slayings of at least a dozen women."

I remembered him now, and how upset I'd been that he'd written that I'd single-handedly caught Basque, as if the other officers on my team didn't even exist.

And in all of the clippings containing my picture, my face had been circled with a red pen.

So, maybe Basque wasn't the only one who had a fan.

Maybe I did too.

56

Getting the video took me longer than I expected, but at last I stepped out of the house and noticed three of the CSU members gathered around Jake Vanderveld, who stood beside the scrub pine where I'd released the snake. He'd corralled the rattler into the open and was holding the shovel vertically, handle up, blade down.

I started toward him, but before I could stop him, he raised the shovel and brought it down decisively, driving the blade through the snake's neck and into the dirt. The head, along with about eight centimeters of neck, flopped onto the ground near the rattler's body, which twisted and curled in the dirt.

"Hey!" I closed the space between us and snatched the shovel from his hand. "What are you doing?"

The snake's body writhed beside my feet.

"It's a rattlesnake," Jake replied, as if that explained anything. He was watching the head, which was still hissing, fangs bared. "It's dangerous."

Officer Harwood stared at the head. "It's still alive."

"Reptilian reflexes," Vanderveld said. "It can live up to ninety minutes. Careful. That head can still bite. Still release venom."

Maybe Tessa's views on animal rights had worn off on me more than I'd realized because, when I saw that none of the CSU members seemed bothered that Vanderveld had just killed that snake for no reason, it irritated me almost as much as what he'd just done.

"Step away, Jake."

He took one step backward. Stared at me coolly.

Out of the corner of my eye I saw the head of the snake lift on its short stump and bite at the air, and as it did I pictured grabbing Jake and lowering him onto the head. *The ambulance is still here. The EMTs could get the poison out. It wouldn't kill him, just make it too painful to sit for a month or so.*

Bad thoughts.

Bad thoughts.

But kind of entertaining, nonetheless.

Finally, Jake just said, in a hey-old-buddy-what's-the-big-deal voice, "Take it easy, Pat. It's just a snake. Let's not lose focus and forget who the bad guy is."

"I haven't lost focus."

He looked like he might reply but remained silent and finally strode toward the house. The snake's body was still curling and coiling, leaving dark smears on the soil from the end of its severed, bleeding stump. The head, with its unblinking eyes, flicked its tongue out and tasted the air.

I wondered how much snakes can feel pain. The head was obviously still alert. Maybe it was suffering, and if Jake was right about it living for ninety minutes, it might suffer for another hour and a half. I thought of Tessa again and her love for animals, her progressive views about animal rights and the sanctity of all life, what she would say if she knew I'd left the snake here like that . . .

And finally, even though I didn't know if the dead snake was still in pain, I picked up the shovel and brought it down four times, ending all doubt.

■

As I turned away from the snake's remains, I saw Kurt approaching me. "We located the Infiniti on an old mining road about a mile from here. No sign of John." His eyes found the bloody blade of the shovel. "What's going on?"

"Nothing." I tossed the shovel aside. "Any indication of which direction he might have fled?"

"No." Kurt was staring at the snake's flattened remains. We

were both quiet for a few seconds, then he said, "Pat, take a break. We'll find John. We're scouring this whole mountainside. Get out of here. We've got three other choppers up here. Freeman can take you back to Denver. It's been a long enough day already." And then he paused as a knot of tension worked its way through his voice. "For both of us."

I noticed him rubbing his wedding ring stiffly between his fingers. "You doing OK?"

It didn't look like he was going to answer me, but then he said quietly, "Do you know how many marriages survive the death of a child?"

It was one of those questions you don't answer with words. I put my hand on his shoulder, but he shook his head and said, "Forget it." Then he shrugged my hand off and took a moment to bury his emotions. "So, what'd you see in the house?"

"Kurt, we can talk about—"

"The house, Pat." His voice had become edgy and hard, and I knew I needed to back off.

"OK." I took a minute to tell him about Taylor's head and the newspaper articles.

He heard me out and seemed to be more interested in the newspaper clippings than the governor's severed head. "You mentioned you got the feeling John was a fan of Basque?" His voice still held a trace of the pain that'd accompanied his remarks about his marriage.

I nodded.

"But Grant Sikora tried to kill Basque," he said. "So if John was involved in any way with coordinating that, he was trying to get rid of Basque, not honor him as his hero." Kurt shook his head. "I don't think those articles are a tribute to Basque."

"What do you think they are?"

"Maybe a scouting report."

I had to let that settle in.

He circled your picture, Pat. Maybe he's scouting—

"Hey." It was Cheyenne. I hadn't noticed her coming our way. "What do we know?"

"John's still at large," I said.

A hundred meters away I saw that the EMTs had placed Thomas Bennett on a gurney and were wheeling him toward the ambulance.

"How's Bennett?" Kurt asked.

"Looks like he's doing all right," she said. "But he's pretty shaken up. They want to keep him at the hospital overnight for observation. We still don't know what he was drugged with."

"Did he give you anything else on his abductor?" I asked.

She shook her head. "No. He said the guy talked in a low whisper, he didn't think he'd be able to recognize his voice if he heard it again."

Kurt scribbled some reminders on his notepad. "I'll make sure there's an officer waiting at the hospital to guard him when he arrives."

"One more thing," she said. "The killer told Thomas that he was going after his wife, Marianne. I called it in, and dispatch already sent a car to her place, but I'm wondering if we can assign a female undercover officer to the house and put Marianne in protective custody just in case John decides to go after her."

"Hmm . . . a UC might be good," Kurt muttered. "As long as she doesn't turn into bait." He thought for a moment. "Let me make some calls." He held out his hand to me.

"What?"

"My phone."

"Oh yeah." I handed it to him. "There's video of most of the house. Email it to me."

"I will." Then he stepped away from me and Cheyenne but called over his shoulder, "Now, get out of here and get some rest. Both of you look like—" His final word was muffled as he walked away, but I figured I knew what it was.

And then Cheyenne and I were alone.

57

The sun edged over the high mountains that folded back against the sky. The Rockies were stealing minutes from the day.

"He let the snakes loose," I told her. Then I filled her in about Taylor's head and the newspaper clippings in the locked room.

She let it all sink in. "We can't release this information about Taylor's head to the press," she said. "If the media jumps on this, it'll only cause more panic, more roadblocks for this investigation."

I didn't have any arguments with that.

We spent a few minutes reviewing all that had happened during the day, talking through the facts, clues, and connections, but I had the feeling both of us were hoping the conversation would turn in a slightly less work-related direction.

As we spoke, I saw that Cliff had found just enough room to land in the field near the house. I didn't remember hearing him fly in. He stood beside the cockpit, glanced at his watch. I wondered how long he'd been there.

"I'm riding back with Bennett," Cheyenne said. She gestured toward the ambulance still sitting near the barn. "I think he could use someone with him right now. Maybe once he calms down he'll be able to give us something more specific."

"I guess I'll keep Cliff company on the chopper." A slight pause. "Good work today, Cheyenne."

"Thank you." She brushed aside a stray tress of hair that had fallen in front of her eye.

"So," I said.

"So."

Twilight tipped over the mountains. All around us the day was wearing thin. The ambulance began to slowly rumble toward us over the pot-holed road.

"You doing anything else tonight?" she asked.

"I'll probably work a little on recalculating the geoprofile now that we know the killer used this location. Maybe follow your suggestion: take a good, cool bath. Break out the aloe vera. All that."

It seemed like maybe there was more to say, but I didn't know what it might be. "Well, OK," I said. "Good night. I'll see you tomorrow. Thanks again for shooting the chain."

"My pleasure."

I headed for the chopper but had only made it a few steps before she called me back. "Wait."

I turned. "Yes?"

A slight pause, then, "Have dinner with me."

I felt a sweep of both excitement and apprehension. "I'm not sure I can—"

"Oh. You have plans already."

"No, I . . ." Tessa had told me she was hanging out with Dora for supper and a movie tonight so I'd be home alone and would probably just end up throwing in a pizza—not exactly what I imagined Cheyenne meant by the word *plans*, but still—

"Oh, I'm sorry." Cheyenne's voice flattened. "You're seeing someone, I—"

"No, no. It's not that. I'm not seeing anyone, I just—"

"The woman on the phone earlier today?"

Man, she was good. "Lien-hua? No, that's over." The words tasted sour in my mouth.

"So then, you're not seeing anyone." Cheyenne said it decisively, and I wondered if she were trying to convince me that it was true. "And neither am I, and we're both hungry and we're both free for dinner. So, all I'm saying is, eat it with me."

I noticed Reggie Greer walking toward the snake's remains, not far from us. "I don't know, Cheyenne . . ."

"I'm not asking you to marry me, just to eat food in my general vicinity."

The ambulance cruised to a stop ten meters away.

Reggie grabbed the shovel and used it to scoop up the snake's remains. "Agent Bowers," he called. "Thanks for helping me out back there in the kitchen." He tossed the dead snake further into the field, out of sight.

"You're welcome." As I answered Reggie, I was still trying to think of what to say to Cheyenne.

"Well?" she said.

A different tack. I lowered my voice, hoping Reggie wouldn't hear. "Maybe I'm old-fashioned, but I've always thought it was the guy's job to ask the girl out."

And then, before I could say another word, she said, "Well, thank you, Dr. Bowers. I'd be honored to join you for dinner."

"I wasn't exactly—"

"Eight, then?"

"Eight—"

"Perfect. I know a great steak place near Union Station that you can take me to." She put her hand on my arm and gave it a soft squeeze. "This time, you can pick me up." Then she told me her address and left for the ambulance.

I caught Reggie Greer grinning at me. "What?" I said.

"That was smooth."

"What are you talking about?"

"Sorry. I couldn't help but overhear. Getting Detective Warren to ask you out and then switching everything around so she wouldn't feel awkward about taking the first step—nice. Very nice."

"Oh yeah, wow," I mumbled. "Thanks."

"And you're a brave man to go on a date with her."

I wasn't exactly sure how to take that. "It's not a date."

Cheyenne disappeared into the ambulance. I really hoped she wasn't hearing any of this.

"Oh." He winked at me. "I get it." The ambulance doors closed.

I folded my arms. "I'm just eating a meal in her general vicinity."

"Sure. Gotcha."

This was going nowhere. "I'm leaving now. Good-bye."

I headed toward the helicopter as the ambulance pulled away.

And as I thought about the upcoming evening, I remembered how understandably upset Tessa had been about the pot of basil.

I borrowed Cliff's cell, and when Tessa didn't pick up, I left a voicemail telling her to have fun at the movie and that I'd just grab supper later and see her when she got home. I explained that my cell was broken, and left Cheyenne's number and told her to "just call Detective Warren if you need to get in touch with me."

She didn't know that Detective Warren was a woman.

Then Cliff and I climbed aboard the chopper, and a few moments later we were soaring above the darkening mountains, flying east toward Denver, where the moon was already beginning to rise.

———————————◼———————————

Tessa was emotionally fried.

After filing through the memory box all afternoon with Dora and realizing how much of her mom's life she didn't know anything about, she'd decided she needed some time to chill before heading out again for the evening.

So after Dora left to take care of a few things at home, she'd started going at the cube again, and finally managed to solve it once, but she still wasn't even close to doing it with her eyes closed.

She'd been working on it a few minutes ago when the phone started ringing, totally distracting her.

But she'd kept her eyes closed. Tried to concentrate.

Generic ringtone. It kept ringing.

Annoying, annoying, annoying.

Finally it stopped, but by then it was too late. She'd completely lost track of where the colors were. Frustrated, she opened her eyes and went to see if whoever had called had left a message.

And found a voicemail from Patrick.

On the vm he explained that he was twenty-five minutes out and to have a good time at the movie and not to worry about him because he would just eat supper later and that he loved her and to call some detective named Warren if there was a problem.

And when she heard his voice, she remembered their last, less-than-cordial conversation.

OK, so hanging up on him might not have been the best thing to do, especially on a day he was obviously stressed about the trial and the pot of basil—oh, that was just way too disturbing—and breaking up with Agent Jiang. Ending the call like that had probably *not* helped her case for convincing him to give her the diary.

Hmm. So, OK.

He would grab supper later, huh? So that meant he hadn't eaten yet.

And come to think of it, except for the chips and salsa she'd had earlier with Dora, she hadn't eaten either.

And that gave her an idea. Maybe, just maybe, if she stopped acting like a whiny little brat, nagging him to give her the diary, he might change his mind about giving it to her. If she showed him that she really could be mature and responsible . . .

Dinner.

Yes.

There weren't too many things that both she and Patrick liked to eat, but spaghetti with meatless sauce was one of them. Perfect.

But, according to his voicemail, she had less than twenty-five minutes to get it ready.

She called Dora and cancelled for the evening, pulled a bag of spaghetti noodles off the shelf, and filled a pot with water. Then she stuck it on the stove and started to prepare a salad while she waited for the water to boil.

58

I smelled the spaghetti sauce as I stepped through the front door. "Tessa?" I set my computer bag next to the couch.

She appeared in the kitchen doorway holding a ladle dripping with marinara sauce and wearing the barbeque apron Ralph's wife Brineesha had given me on Father's Day last year that read "King of the Coals."

"Welcome home," she said. "Supper's on the table."

"What are you doing?"

"Cooking."

"Cooking?"

"Yeah," she said. "C'mon in."

"You're cooking?"

"Uh-huh. Do you want a glass of wine or something with your meal?"

I joined her in the kitchen and saw that the table was set for two. Our finest plates. One wine glass, one can of root beer. "Tessa, what's going on?"

She blinked. "I made supper."

"You hate cooking."

"I'm branching out." She held up two wine bottles. "Red or white?"

I gazed around the kitchen, tried to take everything in. The salad. The simmering sauce. The bowl of noodles. "I thought you and Dora were going out for supper and then seeing a movie?"

"We cancelled." She waved the ladle toward the stove, sending drops of red sauce splattering across the tiling. "I kept the sauce simmering to keep it warm."

I had no idea what to say.

"This is great and everything, but I have dinner plans already."

"What do you mean?"

"I promised someone I'd meet them for dinner."

"Oh." She lowered the ladle. Set it down. "OK." Slowly, she turned toward the stove and then shut off the burner that was warming the sauce.

"No, listen. I'm impressed, though, that you made dinner. I mean, it looks great, really."

Her back was to me. "No, it's no big deal. Seriously."

Oh boy.

"Hey, look. I'll cancel. It's OK. I'll just call my friend and tell them —"

"Is it a woman?" Tessa still hadn't turned around.

"That doesn't . . . that doesn't matter. All I'm saying is that I told him — her — whoever it was that I'd eat in their general vicinity."

Tessa faced me. "Their general vicinity?"

"Yes."

"You may not have noticed, but you keep switching the case of your personal pronouns from singular to plural, using 'them' and 'their' to refer to individuals. You wouldn't bother doing that if you were eating out with one of the guys, so I'm guessing you're having dinner with a woman." She folded her arms. "I'm right, aren't I?"

"It's a professional acquaintance."

"A female one."

"Well, it's —"

"Is it a date?"

"It's not a date."

"What is it?"

"Dinner."

"A dinner date."

"No."

She cocked her head. "You sure?"

"Yes. I'm positive. It's not a date."

"Good." She pulled off the apron and draped it over the top of one of the chairs beside the table. "Then I can come too."

"Um, maybe it is a date."

"Too late. I'm coming. Just gimme a sec to grab my purse."

She disappeared into the other room.

What just happened here?

"Tessa, I'll cancel!" I called.

"Naw, it's all right. I don't mind eating out," she yelled back. "We can have the spaghetti tomorrow."

"That's not what I'm talking about—"

"So, Detective Warren, huh?" She was shouting to me from behind her bedroom door. "Is she that cute redhead who was at the newspaper office?"

I rubbed my forehead. *This can't be happening.* "I'm serious, I'll just call her and—"

"That's rude. Keep your word. Go on your date."

It's not a date!

OK, so options: (1) cancel eating in the vicinity of Cheyenne; (2) lay down the law with Tessa, tell her you're going out and that she needs to stay here—but that would mean leaving her alone with her thoughts of that pot of basil. Besides we'd argued earlier in the day about the diary, and it might be nice to spend time with her tonight letting her know that I wasn't mad at her.

I headed to my bedroom. "All right, you can come," I said to her door. "We leave in twenty minutes."

"Sweetness."

"I'm going to take a quick shower and get cleaned up—I was almost burned alive this afternoon."

"Cool."

I stopped and stared at the door. "It's cool that I was almost burned alive?"

"That you were *almost* burned alive." The door opened a crack, and her head appeared. "If you had been, it would have totally sucked."

Oh. Well in that case.

She ducked back inside.

I showered, changed clothes, and when I returned to the kitchen I found that Tessa had put the food away. Then we left to pick up Cheyenne.

59

I knocked on the door to Cheyenne's condo.

On the drive over, I'd borrowed Tessa's cell and called Cheyenne to tell her about the slight change of plans, but she hadn't answered. I'd left two voicemails, but she hadn't returned either of them.

She opened the door. "Hey."

I hardly recognized her. She wore a stunning black dress that accentuated all the right parts of her figure in all the right ways. I couldn't remember ever seeing her wear makeup before, but maybe she thought this was a special occasion. She looked gorgeous.

"Wow," I said. "I didn't know cowgirls dressed like that."

"I told you before, I'm hard to pigeonhole. How are those arms of yours?"

"Excuse me?"

"The burns."

"Oh. Yes. Good," I said. "Hey, um, did you get my message?"

"Message?"

"Voicemail. I called you about—well, it doesn't matter. I was just trying to tell you that my plans had changed a little." I stepped aside and gestured toward the car. Tessa rolled down the backseat window and waved two fingers at us. "We have company."

"It's Tessa."

I tried to read her tone of voice, but I couldn't tell what she might have been thinking.

"Listen," I said. "It's kind of a long story. If this isn't going to work, it's OK. We can just postpone—"

"No, no, it's fine." Cheyenne stepped onto the porch and swung the door shut behind her. Started for the car. "Like you told Reggie, it's not a date."

And the night was off to a brilliant start.

———————————————■———————————————

On the way to the restaurant, Tessa just happened to mention that she was a vegetarian and just happened to ask if the place we were eating at would be serving any recently slaughtered calves or other inhumanely treated, brutally murdered animals because if they were, it might—she was sorry—but it might totally make her sick.

"We're letting Detective Warren choose the restaurant," I told Tessa, remembering that Cheyenne had told me she wanted to go to a steak place near Union Station. "So wherever she wants to go, we go. And I don't think vegetarian is on the menu."

60

I parked in front of Sahib's Vegan Cuisine and sighed, but I managed not to say anything as we climbed out of the car.

After we were seated and had given our drink and appetizer orders to the server, Tessa gazed around admiringly. "This place rocks. I've never been here before."

"Best Indian restaurant in Denver," Cheyenne said.

"Thanks for, you know, choosing . . ."

"You're welcome."

Tessa leaned toward Cheyenne. "Patrick's been to India four times."

Cheyenne gave me an approving nod. "Really?"

"Just to do a little teaching and consulting in Mumbai. It wasn't really a big deal—"

"Sure it was," Tessa interrupted. "He helped catch five people who were kidnapping girls and selling them into the sex trade."

Cheyenne looked at me solemnly. "That is something to be proud of." I sensed a depth of emotion in her words I'd never heard her express before. "I mean that."

"Thank you."

Then the drinks and naan arrived and we ordered our food. I don't remember the Indian names for everything, but the names didn't really matter. Everything was pretty much just vegetables and rice. Not steak. Not even close.

After the server left, I spent a few minutes helping Tessa and Cheyenne get to know each other, then Tessa said, "Detective Warren, did you know geographic profiling was first developed in India?"

I stared at my stepdaughter quizzically.

What is she doing?

"No, I didn't," Cheyenne said.

I didn't want to talk business tonight, especially knowing how derisive Tessa could be about my work. "I'm sure Detective Warren isn't interested in the history—"

"Actually, I am. Go on, Tessa."

How did I know she was going to say that.

"Well," Tessa said. "For nearly two thousand years the rural villages of northern India have been plagued by gangs of bandits who sneak into the towns at night and attack, rob, kidnap, and murder people, and then escape under the cover of darkness back to their own villages or to their hideouts in the jungle. Isn't that right, Patrick?"

"Yes. They're called—"

"Dacoits," said Tessa. "So, to solve the crimes—and I'm not exactly sure what year they did this, you'd have to ask Patrick—the Indian authorities finally decided to stop looking for the three things detectives in North America usually base their entire investigations on—motive, means, and opportunity. First of all, the Indians didn't care what motivated the crimes—whether it was anger or greed or tradition, or whatever, because it was probably all of the above. And second, they knew that most people in the region had the ability to attack and rob others, so focusing on the means wouldn't have done any good. And finally, as far as opportunity, well, the crimes were always committed during the new moon when it was darkest, so that didn't tell them a whole lot either."

The food arrived and I was glad, if nothing more than to interrupt Tessa's lecture.

"One thing before we dig in," Cheyenne said. "If we want to be culturally sensitive, we need to eat with our fingers." She demonstrated by swiping her thumb and the first three fingers of her right hand along the edge of her plate, scooping up some rice and vegetables, then lifting the food to her mouth.

I knew all of this from my trips to India, but I'd never taken the time to teach my stepdaughter Indian table etiquette.

"Cool," Tessa said. She began to eat with her fingers. Out of instinct, she used her left hand.

Cheyenne smiled. "But always use your right hand."

A slightly offended look. "What about left-handed people?"

"Well," I said. "Indians use their left hands for other . . . chores." I kept my description purposely vague, hoping Tessa would be able to fill in what I left unsaid.

"Chores?"

Cheyenne leaned forward and said softly, "Most rural villages don't have adequate sewer systems, so the people don't use toilet paper."

Stunning dinner conversation, this was.

"What do they . . . ?"

"Water. They wash."

Tessa stared at her plate. "Well, that's informative." I sensed that she was about to ask a follow-up question, but she held back and instead wiped her fingers on a napkin.

All three of us ate for a few minutes, then Cheyenne swallowed some of her vegetable curry and asked Tessa, who was now eating with her right hand, "So what did they look for?"

"Who?"

"The Indian authorities."

"Oh, right. Sorry." Tessa punctuated by stabbing a finger into the air. "Timing and location."

"Just like Patrick," said Cheyenne admiringly.

"Not exactly—" I began.

"Yes," Tessa said. "Just like Patrick."

What has gotten into her?

"They studied how far a person could travel on foot at night, and then reduced the search area to include only those villages within that radius."

She alternated between taking bites of her dinner and expounding on her answer. "Then they evaluated the most likely travel routes, studied land use patterns, and compared those to the proximity of the crimes and reduced the suspect pool even more. Finally, they considered the culture and traditions of the region."

"Culture and traditions?" Cheyenne asked.

"Yes. They knew that the men in the gangs wouldn't attack members of their own caste, so that eliminated even more suspects. At that point they started to look for physical evidence, eyewitness identification, confessions, etc. . . . . But they started by looking at timing and location."

"Wow, I'm really impressed. Where did you learn all that?"

Tessa pointed her gooey, rice-covered fingers at me. "Patrick's books. They're very engaging and informative. Well-researched too."

OK, this was just ridiculous.

I was about to explain that any investigator could have figured out the same approach by just using logic and rational deduction, but Tessa shoved her chair back from the table. "Well. I think I need to use the little girls' room." She paused, then said, "Um, they do have—"

"Yes," Cheyenne said. "They do here."

"Perf."

Tessa wove between the tables on her way to the restroom, and I just shook my head. "I have no idea what's going on with her tonight. I'm really sorry."

"For what?"

"She's not usually like this. Most of the time she's a lot less . . . um, forthcoming."

"She's proud of you, that's all." Cheyenne took a drink, then set down her lassi. "I like her. She's got spunk."

"Yes," I said. "Spunk."

We ate for a few minutes, then I set down my fork. "Cheyenne, let me ask you something."

"Yes?" She took a small bite of her vegetables.

"Back at the barn when you shot the chain . . ." I took a moment to collect my thoughts so it wouldn't sound like I was questioning her judgment. She chewed her food. Swallowed. Waited for me to go on.

"Why didn't you shoot it when you were beside me? You know, before the horse started running. It seems like that would have been a much easier shot than hitting a three-centimeter-wide chain from a galloping horse."

"You're right. It would have been easier."

"So then, why?"

She took one last bite of her meal, then slid her plate toward the middle of the table and dipped her fingers into the small metal bowl of water that the server had provided for patrons to clean their fingers. "I would have needed a few extra seconds to aim, but the fire was spreading so fast I didn't want to chance it. I wasn't confident the horse would make it if I waited."

That seemed to make sense, but I got the impression there was still something more she wanted to say.

"On the horse it was all instinct," she explained. "That's the way I work best—gut instinct. A person can overthink things, you know." In the amber light of the restaurant she looked more attractive than ever. "You trust your head, Pat, and I admire that. I trust my gut."

The ambient sounds in the restaurant seemed to fade away. "And what's your gut telling you right now?"

A gleam in her eye. "That it's hungry for dessert."

Then she let her gaze drift past my shoulder as Tessa reappeared from behind me and plopped into her chair. "Did you say dessert?"

"That's right. As soon as you two are finished."

While Tessa and I worked at our meals, Cheyenne told her about some of the horses she'd owned over the years, and considering Tessa's love for animals, I could see that Cheyenne was making a new friend.

At last Tessa took one final bite, swished her fingers clean, and looked brightly at me. "I'm hungry for tiramisu. They don't make Indian tiramisu, do they?"

"Not usually," I said.

Cheyenne eased back from the table and stood. "Tiramisu sounds perfect. Let's go."

61

Even though she should have been expecting him, when Reggie showed up at the safe house after working a crime scene "in the mountains," it annoyed Amy Lynn. She'd been hoping he would stay at their home, leave her some space to work. Typical for their marriage—she was always looking for more space, he was always looking for more of "an intimate connection."

"You doing all right?" he asked after the two federal agents stationed in the house had stepped into the other room.

"Yeah, I'm fine."

He picked up Jayson, lifted him playfully above his head. "You sure you want to be here?"

"It's been good."

And it had been. She'd been able to throw something together for her weekly column and fudge her way through the steroids piece in time for her four o'clock deadline. Then she'd spent the rest of the afternoon and evening researching the killer. And even though she hadn't found any leads on John's identity after looking through the entire *Denver News* staff and freelance contributors directory as well as the other local newspaper, TV, and radio station staff listings, she was confident she would, given a little more time.

Jayson giggled as Reggie lifted and lowered him. "Maybe after I put this little rascal to bed we can, you know, spend some time together."

"I'm not a wascal!" Jayson said with a playful smile.

"Mmm, that'd be nice," Amy Lynn said, but her thoughts were somewhere else.

A few minutes later while Reggie was in the bedroom tucking Jayson in, she went online and researched websites of true crime publishers. Ideally, she would have been writing a series of articles for the *Denver News* about the killer, but since Rhodes wouldn't give her permission to work on the story and the execs were trying to play it safe, she decided on a slightly different approach.

There were other ways to scoop a story than just through print media.

In fact, posting it online would give her a bigger audience, more exposure, and she could update the information more quickly. Plus it would help her stay ahead of the other news outlets. Keep her out front.

Of course, she would need to write it anonymously or under a pseudonym, but eventually, when the time was right she would reveal her true name.

She was at her computer when she heard Reggie's footsteps. The article was not something she wanted him to see, so she quickly minimized her Internet browser.

"So," he said. She felt his hands massaging the back of her neck. "When will you be ready for bed?"

The massage felt nice. He had strong hands, and he kneaded her tense muscles deeply. "Why?" she said. "Are you sleepy?" She closed her eyes and enjoyed his touch.

"Not so much." His voice had become a whisper. He kept his hands on her neck, kept massaging.

"I'll be there in a little bit. Just a couple things I'd like to check on first."

Strong hands relieving the tension. "Don't be long," he said.

"I won't." The massage stopped. She opened her eyes slowly and heard the door to the master bedroom close.

Then she resumed her typing, and after a few minutes she'd completely forgotten about her husband waiting for her in the room at the end of the hall.

62

We stopped for dessert at Rachel's Café, one of my favorite indie coffeehouses in downtown Denver.

Built on the first floor of a remodeled warehouse, Rachel's had hundred-year-old wooden plank floors, brick walls, and air ducts and pipes snaking across the ceiling. Copies of the *Denver News* lay strewn on the tables. A coffee roaster sat in the corner near the cramped stage.

Just like most independent coffeehouses, Rachel's Café didn't have color-coordinated, matching furniture and didn't sell "green" plush baby seal toys made by child-laborers in China, overpriced espresso makers, or trademarked mints. Instead, Rachel's simply offered an eclectic bohemian atmosphere and exceptional coffee from around the world. My kind of place.

I would have liked to hang out for a while, but since I didn't know why Tessa had been so aggressively nice all night, I wanted to get her home as quickly as possible before she said something to Cheyenne that I would regret. So, I made sure our dessert stop was brief, then we headed for Cheyenne's condo.

Ten minutes after leaving Rachel's, I parked at the curb, but before I could invite Cheyenne to join me outside so that I could say good night, Tessa spoke up: "Be a gentleman, Patrick. Walk her to the door."

"Tessa—"

"Go on."

"That's enough," I said.

"That sounds nice," Cheyenne said. Then she stepped out of the car and waited for me to join her.

I lowered my voice and said to Tessa, "We're going to talk about this when we get home."

"OK."

I opened my door. "I'll be right back."

"Take your time."

As we headed along the path toward her porch, Cheyenne took my arm and managed to slow our walk to a stroll. "Well, Dr. Bowers," she said. "Thank you for eating food in my general vicinity tonight."

"You're welcome. I've been thinking, I'll probably need to eat sometime in the next week or so. Maybe we can do it again?"

"Hmm," she said. "I'll have to check my busy social calendar."

"That full, huh?"

We arrived at the porch, but instead of stepping into the light as I expected her to, Cheyenne paused on the fringe of the night. "You have no idea how popular I am."

"And yet you chose to spend the evening with my stepdaughter and me."

"Yes, I did."

"I'm honored."

The night settled in, calm and sweet and cool around us. "I had fun," she said. "And I really like Tessa."

"She has a way of growing on you." Then I added, "She means the world to me."

"I can tell." Even though I didn't remember either of us edging closer, the space between us seemed to be shrinking. I gazed at her standing in the faint glow of the porch's twilight.

Cheyenne Warren really was a beautiful woman.

Moments eased by.

The sounds of traffic drifted toward me from far away, from some distant city that had nothing to do with the two of us.

Finally I said, "Maybe I should be going. You know. Take Tessa home." But after I'd said the words, I didn't go anywhere. Neither did Cheyenne. It seemed like neither of us wanted the date-that-was-not-a-date to end.

I had the urge to take her in my arms, to hold her, to kiss her and see where everything might lead, but then I remembered Lien-hua and how things had ended with her. I didn't want to start off on the wrong foot with Cheyenne. Didn't want anything to go wrong.

Take it slow, Pat. She's worth it. Don't do anything stupid.

The sound of a car honking on one of the neighboring streets broke the spell, and I eased back a step. "OK," I said. "I guess — "

Cheyenne let out a soft sigh. "That's twice now."

I hesitated. "Twice?"

"Yes. Once at the barn earlier today, and then, just now."

"What do you mean?"

Her eyes were still filled with their usual confidence and strength but also held a touch of disappointment. "That's twice I thought you were going to kiss me and you decided to back away from me instead."

Oh man.

My heart was racing. I felt like I was in junior high again, fumbling for the right words to say to the girl I'd finally worked up the nerve to talk to. "It isn't that I don't want — "

She squinched her eyes shut and hit herself in the forehead with the heel of her hand. "Oh, I shouldn't have said that. I'm always doing that. I just say what I'm thinking. I don't even — it's a bad habit. I'm sorry."

I wanted to tell her that it wasn't a bad habit, that her blunt honesty was one of the things I liked about her, but just ended up saying, "Never apologize for telling the truth. It suits you." And then, "Good night, Cheyenne."

"Good night," she said, and then I gave her a light, friendly hug, but that was all.

And as I turned and walked back to the car I heard the condo's door swing open and then click softly shut behind me.

63

Back at home, I wanted to get to bed, but Tessa only left me alone long enough for me to get my toothbrush in my mouth before she knocked on my bedroom door, walked in, caught me in mid-brush in the adjoining bath. "Why didn't you kiss her good night?"

I spit out the toothpaste. "That's none of your business."

"She's nice. I like her. I think you should've—"

"All right, that's it." I set down the toothbrush. "What are you trying to do?"

"Just saying you should have kissed her."

"No, I mean all night." I grabbed a cup of water. Rinsed out my mouth. "What's going on?"

"Nothing."

"You made dinner for me. You've been playing matchmaker. You even complimented my book. Something must be seriously—"

"Can't I just be nice once in a while without you getting on my case for it?"

"I'm not getting on your case. I just don't understand."

She slung a hand to her hip. "What? Maybe you'd prefer I cop an attitude instead?"

"Well . . ."

"How about a little obstinacy? Would that be better? Or despondency, maybe? Is that what you'd like?"

"Look, it's just that you haven't seemed like yourself tonight, that's all. Usually, you're more quiet and introverted and sort of just annoyed at life in general, and not so . . ."

"Not so what?"

"Aberrantly cheerful."

"Well, that's easy enough to fix," she said.

"Tessa, please." I tried to think of anything that might have happened earlier in the day to cause all this. "Is it leaving for the summer? Is it something to do with that?"

She was silent.

"The shoe box?"

No reply.

What else?

Oh yes.

"Your mom's diary. Is that it? Is that what this is all about?"

The look of pain that swept over her face came so swiftly and suddenly that the whole mood of the room changed in an instant. "I was just trying to . . ." she began, but didn't finish.

The diary must have been more important to her than I ever would have guessed.

"I loved her, you know? More than anything else in the world." Her voice had become something small and fragile. A little girl's voice.

"Come here."

I took her in my arms, and she leaned against me in a way that made my heart break. And as she did, I thought of Christie, the woman both Tessa and I had loved so much, and of the promise she'd asked me to make regarding the diary.

But now, considering how troubled Tessa had become, I couldn't imagine that Christie would want me to keep it from her for five more months.

"Hey, listen." I backed up and gently held her shoulders. I saw that she hadn't actually started to cry, but she was a girl experienced at hiding her pain. "I'll give it to you, OK? Tomorrow. I'll give you the diary in the morning."

"What?" She looked at me with a mixture of hope and skepticism. "Really? No, you won't."

"Yes. I think your mom would understand. I'm sure she never meant for this to be such a big deal, for it to upset you like this."

Tessa looked past me into my bedroom. "So where is it?"

"It's not here." I let go of her hands. "I'll have to get it tomorrow. It's at my office at the federal building."

"Can't you just—"

"Tomorrow. We'll do it tomorrow."

"You're not just saying this as some kind of manipulative parenting thing to—"

"No. I'll give it to you."

She studied my face for a moment and then said softly, "Thank you, Patrick. I seriously mean it."

"I love you, Raven," I said.

She smiled at me then, a soft, unforced smile. "I love you too."

And for a moment, just a moment, the dead bodies in Colorado and the trial in Illinois faded from my mind, and life seemed in sync with the way things should be. Tessa and I were on the same page, and I felt like I was able to give her a gift, a chance to connect with her mother in a way she'd never been able to before.

But almost immediately, I realized that reading Christie's diary would undoubtedly bring back Tessa's feelings of grief and loss all over again, might open old wounds, possibly make her even lonelier than ever.

I tried not to think of those things, and instead I just told myself that this was the right thing, the loving thing to do.

Then Tessa left for her room, but I noticed that the feeling of peace I'd had only a moment earlier had evaporated even before she stepped out the door.

64

I couldn't sleep.

In addition to my questions about giving Tessa the diary, my thoughts had returned to the ranch where we'd found Thomas Bennett and almost caught the killer.

Almost.

But we hadn't.

I tried to put everything out of my mind, but I couldn't seem to relax, and eventually I gave up and grabbed my laptop, propped some pillows behind my back, and surfed to the online case files.

Read them for twenty minutes.

Didn't get sleepy.

Didn't notice anything new.

I checked my email and found, amid fifty-nine junk mails and four internal FBI memos, three messages that caught my attention — one from Kurt, one from Ralph, and one from United Airlines telling me it was time to check in for my 4:04 p.m. flight to Chicago tomorrow.

Oh yes. The trial.

Another thing to think about.

But not at the moment.

I read Ralph's email first.

> Hey,
>
> Why aren't you answering your cell? I hate typing.
>
> Nothing much here. Officer Fohay's clean, tho. Prints didn't match and he had no prior association with Sikora.

Calvin hasn't left his house all day.
Talk to you tomorrow.
Don't waste my time. Just answer your phone.

—R

So, nothing earth-shattering. It would have made things a lot easier if Fohay had been the one who'd loaded the gun; but things aren't usually that simple.

I replied to Ralph, explaining that my phone was dead and that if he needed to get in touch with me to just use my landline or call Tessa's cell.

It surprised me a little that Calvin hadn't left his house. After all, he didn't believe in retirement, worked weekends, and only took Wednesdays off. He'd told me on Friday that he was going to wait and see what happened next. I wondered if maybe something had.

So I emailed him as well, to see if he could pick me up at the airport tomorrow evening to give me a ride to my hotel.

Then I scrolled to Kurt's message:

Pat,

I've attached the video file of the footage you took inside the house. A couple other things:

We found Elwin Daniels's body in a shallow grave near the house. Preliminary time of death looks like eighteen to twenty-one days ago.

No DNA or prints yet, but animal control verified that one of the aquariums contained toads, not snakes—Colorado River toads. Based on the size of the tank and the amount of droppings it looks like our guy had about ten or twelve of them. Problem is, their skin contains 5-MeO-DMT and bufotenin—psychedelic drugs, but when ingested in concentrated doses . . . you get the idea. Looks like John is getting ready for story number seven.

Nothing yet on any missing priests, but Missing Persons is still looking into it. See you tomorrow. We'll have a briefing at 1:00, sixth floor conference room. Get some rest.

—Kurt

P.S. Reggie told me you had a date with Cheyenne tonight. Don't worry. I won't spread the word.

How thoughtful.

Enough with this. I needed some sleep.

I put my computer away, crawled beneath the covers, and closed my eyes.

65

Sunday did not start out well.

My nightmare of the slaughterhouse and the whispering corpses had returned, and when I eased my eyes open, I saw that the day was going to be bleak.

God had decided to send rain to Denver, and the flat gray sky reminded me more of a November morning in Milwaukee than a Denver day in spring.

I opened the window to check the temperature, and a brush of crisp air with some leftover winter greeted me. The temp had dropped more than twenty degrees from the night before, and by the looks of the clouds and the plummeting temperature, I wondered if we might be in for a late-season snowstorm before the end of the day.

But you won't be here at the end of the day.

Oh yes.

Chicago.

After a quick shower I went online, hoping to switch to a later flight, but there were no openings, which meant I would need to leave for the airport by 2:30, maybe 3:00 at the latest, and that gave me less than nine hours to make some progress on this case before flying to the Midwest.

I was definitely ready for some coffee.

I'd just sent some freshly roasted Peruvian beans through my burr grinder when my unlisted landline rang. Cordless, but an older model. No caller I.D., and since I'd emailed Ralph last night telling him to call my landline if he needed me, I figured it was probably him.

I picked up the receiver. "Pat here."

"Congratulations." The caller spoke in a low whisper, the voice electronically disguised. "On getting to the ranch so quickly."

My thoughts zoomed in, focused to a pinpoint. "John?"

"That'll do."

Play this right, Pat. Play this right.

"I'm glad you called." Knowing how this guy had toyed with Sebastian Taylor and then killed him in his own house, I pulled out my SIG and made sure it was loaded and had a chambered round.

"Yes, well, I thought it was time we spoke."

I hurried to Tessa's room. Eased her door open. Walked to her bed. Yes, she was safe. Sound asleep.

I figured John would be too smart for the "So what's your real name? Where are you calling from? What would you like to talk about?" routine, so I decided on a different approach and said, "We almost had you at the barn."

"Yes. Almost."

"Switching shirts was smart. It might have been the only thing that kept me from shooting you."

"Well, then I'm glad I did it."

Into the living room.

To the window.

I studied the neighborhood. "I saw the newspaper articles in the bedroom."

He said nothing.

No unfamiliar cars. No one sitting in the parked cars on the street.

No movement behind the bushes next door, no fluttering curtains in the neighbors' homes. "Why did you circle my face?" I said.

"I admire you."

Speech is individualized by vowels, pronunciation, and the

suprasegmental phonemes of pitch, stress, and juncture, so as I listened to each of his sentences I tried to catch a sense of John's pauses, inflection, intonation, cadence, but didn't notice anything distinctive.

I ignored his comment about admiring me. "We were able to get Bennett out of the barn in time." As I spoke, I finished checking the house room by room. "Saved Kelsey too. You're getting sloppy, and I'm coming for you."

Rather than argue with me, he said, "I wanted to tell you that I'm veering slightly from the text for this next story."

"Veering?"

As we spoke, I looked in the garage. In the car. Under it.

"Updating," he said. "Boccaccio wasn't as politically correct in his collection of tales as today's audiences would demand. So I'm adapting it to better reflect the diversity of our culture."

I had no idea what that meant, but I would remember it. I would use it.

Then he added, "Have you figured out how I'm choosing the victims yet?"

I suspected he'd call my bluff if I tried one, so I was straight with him. "Not yet." I went to the back door of the house, looked into the yard. Clear. "But I will."

"That would really be the key here, I think. The only way to stop me is to get out ahead of me."

"I can think of a few other ways."

A slight pause. "I would congratulate you on rescuing Kelsey, but let's be honest—that was a fluke. You stumbled onto her by accident."

"You fled south down the cliffs, didn't you? Then probably west along that old mining road skirting the national forest. Did you grow up in the area, John? Is that how you know it so well?"

Another pause, and I had a feeling I'd nailed it.

"Remember," he said, "Kelsey was supposed to die of grief, not hypothermia."

Check on her, Pat. He's going after her.

Yes, I would check on her—both her and Bennett—as soon as I was off the phone.

He continued, "And after what she went through Friday night in the morgue—all that time in the freezer with those cadavers—I think there's a good chance she'll die of grief after all, and the story will play out like it's supposed to."

His words "The story will play out like it's supposed to" troubled me.

Remember, Pat? He was prepared in the barn. He was ready for you.

If I was reading things right, Thomas Bennett was in grave danger. "Why did you wait so long before opening the door to the cage, John?"

"Ah yes. Gabriotto's nightmare."

It was a dream.

It was all a dream.

John went on, "What does he really die of, Patrick?"

No, please.

I grabbed the car keys from the kitchen counter.

"You know, don't you? It isn't the greyhound that kills him."

Get to the hospital. Now.

I flew toward the front door but immediately realized that if John knew my phone number he might know where I lived. I couldn't leave Tessa here alone. I ran back to her room.

"You'll need to be calling the hospital now, I suppose," John said. "To check on Thomas. We'll talk again. I'm moving up the timetable. Dusk arrives tomorrow, just like it did in London."

Then he ended the call.

My heart jackhammered.

As I turned on Tessa's desk lamp, I flipped through my mental catalog of phone numbers. Found Baptist Memorial's. Punched it in.

It rang, no one answered.

I patted Tessa's shoulder firmly enough to wake her up, but she groaned and wrapped a pillow around her head.

The phone continued to ring.

Come on. Pick up.

Since I wasn't on a mobile phone, I couldn't take the receiver with me in the car. I had to wait in the house for them to answer.

Pick up!

Finally, a receptionist answered, "Hello, Baptist—"

"This is Special Agent Patrick Bowers with the FBI. I need you to send a doctor to check on Thomas Bennett—I don't know his room number—"

"Sir, I can't just—"

"And get a doctor to Kelsey Nash in 228. And security to both rooms. Do it!"

A slight hesitancy in the woman's voice, but she agreed. "Yes, sir."

I gave her my federal ID number, then tossed the phone onto Tessa's desk. Shook her again. "Tessa."

She moaned. "Turn off the lights."

"You have to come with me. We have to hurry."

"What are you talking—"

I clutched her arm, and I think I might have scared her because she stopped mumbling, blinked her eyes open, and stared at me. "What's going on?"

"I need to check on someone at the hospital and I can't leave you here."

"Why not?"

Because it might be a trick to get me to leave you alone.

"It's important. You can drive to my parents' house afterward. Now, come on."

She glanced at the bedsheets covering her. "I'm in my pajamas."

"Grab some clothes. Be quick." My tone of voice convinced her, and she crawled out of bed. "Where's your cell?" I asked.

She pointed to the purse on her desk.

I fished out her phone, and while she gathered some clothes I left a voice message for Kurt to get to Bennett's room ASAP.

"Go in the hall," she said. "I gotta change."

"You can change on the way."

"Um, that would be a *no*."

"We're leaving." And before she could argue with me anymore, I hustled her to the car.

And I did not drive the legal speed limit on the way to the hospital, but I had a sinking feeling that no matter how fast I drove, I would arrive too late.

66

The doctors didn't get to Thomas Bennett in time.

The officer who'd been stationed at the door gave me the news as I pushed past him and burst into his hospital room. Denver's chief medical examiner, Dr. Eric Bender, who was also the father of Tessa's friend Dora, stood at the foot of the bed where Thomas Bennett's body lay. I didn't recognize the doctor and nurse who stood beside him.

"Pat, I was just going to call you," Eric said somberly.

I walked to Thomas's bed. His chest was motionless. His face contorted. It looked like he had died in agony. His eyes were closed. His body, still.

So still.

I felt a rising sting of failure, defeat. Somehow John had gotten to him. *How? How!*

"Was it his heart?" I asked.

Eric nodded. "Pericardial effusion with necrotizing fasciitis."

I knew that "pericardial" had to do with the heart, and that an effusion was a release of fluid in the body. I didn't know what necrotizing fasciitis was. "In layman's terms."

"Right. Sorry." He shook his head as if to rebuke himself. "Necrotizing fasciitis is sometimes called 'flesh-eating strep.' It's an infection. Very dangerous. Spreads rapidly. It looks like someone injected the bacteria into the sac that surrounds his heart."

"The pericardium," I said.

"That's right. It's not that difficult of a procedure; you just need a long needle, insert it under the xyphoid notch—"

"Early this morning he complained of chest pains," the other doctor interrupted. "We did an EKG, then an ultrasound, and found fluid and air in the pericardium."

"Necrotizing fasciitis can only be treated by removing the infected tissue," Eric explained. "But since it was his heart . . ." He didn't need to go on.

I thought about Boccaccio's story, Gabriotto's death.

"So basically it was pus, right?" I said. "He died of pus infecting his heart?"

Both doctors and the nurse were quiet for a moment, then Eric said, "That would be an accurate description of what happened."

A pus-filled abscess bursting near his heart. Exactly like Boccaccio's story.

Anger and desperation rolled through me. I looked from Eric to the other doctor. "But they did blood work and a tox screen last night when he got here, right? Why didn't they catch it?"

"The lab is twelve hours backed up," Eric said. "Half of it is still being renovated."

"We were going to finish the tox screen this morning," the doctor added.

I cursed loud enough for the nurse to respond by pressing a gentle finger to her lips, and I realized she was probably concerned not just about my language but about me waking other patients on the floor. I stepped back from the bed. Tried to calm down. Refocus.

Movement beside the door caught my attention. The police officer I'd seen in the hallway had entered the room and now looked at me nervously.

"Who was in here last night?" I said.

"No one, sir. I swear." He pointed to the nurse standing beside me. "Not since she came by two hours ago to check his vitals. And I stayed with her the whole time."

We would interview the hospital staff who'd been treating Thomas Bennett, yes, obviously we would, but I doubted they had anything to do with his death. Somehow John had managed to get to him.

"What about the officer from the earlier shift? The one you relieved?"

He shook his head and pointed again to the nurse, then to the doctor. "He told me they were the only people who'd been in here."

I tried to relax, to regroup by letting my mind replay the last twenty minutes—after getting Tessa to the car I'd phoned my mother and arranged for Tessa to stay with her "while I met with the people I needed to" at Baptist Memorial. Then we'd arrived at the hospital, and Tessa, who'd managed to change clothes in the backseat, left for my parents' house.

I'd made two final calls, one to the Bureau's cybercrime division to see if they could trace the origin of the last call received on my landline, and then, since John had somehow gotten my phone number and I didn't want to take any chances that he would get to my family, I called dispatch to have a car stationed at my mother's place.

And now here I was, in the room beside the body of another man I'd failed to save.

My attempt to calm myself down didn't work. I slammed my hand against the wall, and the four people in the room stared at me quietly.

"I'm all right," I said.

No, you're not.

John's winning.

Eric discreetly nodded for the others to follow him to the hall, but I said, "No. I'm leaving."

Then I headed to room 228 to check on Kelsey Nash.

———————————————■———————————————

I found Kurt standing outside her room, speaking with a police officer.

"She's OK," Kurt announced as I joined them. "The doc is in there now."

I peeked through the doorway.

Kelsey was reclining on the bed, conscious and aware. A slim middle-eastern woman in doctor's scrubs bent over her while a male nurse checked Kelsey's vitals. Kurt motioned for the officer beside us to enter the room, and as the man went inside, he left the door partially open. Kurt stepped back so I could monitor what was happening inside the room while we spoke.

"Bennett died of an infection," I told him.

"I know. I was just up there."

I shook my head. "It looks like John covered his bases—whether he died from a dog bite or the infection in his heart, Bennett's death would still match Boccaccio's story."

The doctor wrote a few notes on her clipboard, then made a call from the room's phone.

"Is Thomas's wife safe?" I asked Kurt.

He nodded. "Protective custody. They're bringing her over to see the body. We have a female undercover officer at her house and a car down the street. If John shows up looking for Marianne, we'll be ready for him. Also, we're looking into any possible connections between the ranch and the mine. Nothing so far."

As he finished speaking, the doctor joined us in the hallway. "Ms. Nash is stable," she said. "The lab just called in, and her blood work came back fine. Physically, she's recovering very well. But mentally, emotionally . . ." She hesitated. "I don't know. She hasn't spoken in almost twenty-four hours. I'm suggesting we put her on suicide watch."

"Do it," I said. "Do whatever it takes to help her. She's our only eyewitness."

The doctor nodded. "All right. I'll have her transferred to psych."

I hated to admit it, but it was true: John had been right about Kelsey too.

She was dying of grief.

After the doctor had left, the officer returned to the hallway, and Kurt gave him specific instructions. "You stay with Ms. Nash every second, even while they're transferring her to the psych ward."

"Yes, sir."

"If anything goes down, anything at all, call me. Got it?"

A nod.

A sad kind of tension crept into the hall, wrapped around us, then Kurt said to me, "I can't just stand around here. Walk with me to my car."

We started for the stairs and I asked him if he'd had any luck with the sketch artist last night.

He shook his head. "I wasn't here. Reggie brought him in, but apparently Kelsey wouldn't meet with him, and Bennett had nothing new for us to go on. Oh yeah, Missing Persons found out half an hour ago that no one has seen Father Hughes, one of the priests from St. Michael's, since Tuesday. Apparently, he sent a text message to some relatives in Baltimore, told them he was coming, but never arrived. I'm letting Missing Persons look into it for now. They're keeping me posted."

"He disappeared on Tuesday?" I said softly.

"Yeah, I know. The timing fits for story number two from *The Decameron*. I tried calling you this morning to tell you, but your line was busy."

All at once I realized that Kurt still didn't know I'd spoken with the killer. "You aren't going to believe this. John called me."

"What!"

"I was so focused on seeing if Kelsey was OK that I—"

"Did you get a recording of it?"

"No. Cybercrime is doing a backtrace on it, but I doubt they'll find anything. I'm betting our guy used a prepaid and tossed it."

"So what did he say?"

"Taunted me. Hinted at Bennett's cause of death. I'll transcribe the conversation. We can circulate it to the team, see if it rings any bells with anyone."

"You can remember it?"

"Yes."

"The whole thing? Word for word?"

"Yes."

A slight pause. "OK." The stairwell was just ahead. "One more thing: the warrant for the library records is still going through, but we did find out that DU offers two courses on Renaissance Humanist literature. Only college in the state that does. Both classes cover *The Decameron*. The instructor is an English prof who also teaches a few classes in the journalism department. No one from the suspect list took his classes, but a number of people from the *Denver News* did: Rhodes, Amy Lynn Greer, at least a dozen others."

"The prof's name isn't John, by any chance?"

We descended the steps.

"No. Adrian, Adrian Bryant. But he doesn't look good for this. He was out of town yesterday, speaking at a conference in Phoenix, so he couldn't have been the guy you chased at the ranch."

Arriving at the first floor, we walked past the nurse's station. "Do we have actual confirmation that he was there, or just anecdotal?" I asked.

"We're working on that." The automatic exit doors slid open in front of us.

We stepped outside.

The day was getting colder. The sky, darker.

Kurt gave his watch a quick glance. "I gotta head home. Cheryl's not too happy about my hours this week."

As sensitively as I could I said, "So how are things? Any better?"

He wasn't quick to answer. "They are what they are." I heard deep remorse in his voice. Then he took a deep breath. "Anyway, I'll call Jake and Cheyenne; fill 'em in. Don't forget, we meet at HQ at one o'clock. I know how much you love briefings, and this one's extra special. Jake's going to run down the psychological profile of the—"

"Please don't say UNSUB."

My comment brought a small but welcome smile. "Killer. So I'll see you there?"

I didn't reply.

"Pat?"

"I'm thinking."

I realized that, given the choice between sitting through a briefing led by Jake Vanderveld and swimming through a pond full of leeches, I'd be looking for my bathing suit. But I didn't mention that. It didn't seem like the polite thing to say.

"OK, I'll see you at one. That should give me enough time. There's something I want to look into."

"What's that?"

"The newspaper articles pinned to the wall at the ranch house all concerned Richard Devin Basque. Since John obviously knows about Basque, I want to find out if Basque knows about John."

"How are you going to do that?"

"I'm going to have a little chat with my old friend."

67

Ten minutes after leaving the hospital, I was in my office in the federal building. I turned on my computer's video chat camera, phoned Ralph, and told him that I needed to do a video conference with Basque. As soon as I'd explained why, he said, "I'll take care of it. I'm about ten minutes from the jail. I'll get things rolling; call you back in twenty."

He called me back in twelve.

"It's good to go," he said. "I didn't mention the subject matter, though. I figured you could bring that up."

"Good. What about Basque's lawyer?"

"He said he doesn't have anything to hide; that he doesn't want her there. He already signed a waiver."

Basque was so addicted to control that I wasn't surprised he didn't want Ms. Eldridge-Gorman sitting next to him, telling him what to say.

"It's a power trip for him," I said to Ralph. "Just knowing that I'm asking for his time probably makes him feel important."

"Is that profiling I'm hearing from you, Pat?"

"That's not profiling. It's called induction."

"Sounds like profiling to me."

"It's not profiling."

"Pat the Profiler. That's gonna be your new nickname. Wait till I send out the memo."

"Could we just focus on the case here?"

Then, through the phone, I heard the sound of a door opening. "Wait," Ralph said. "I gotta go. They're ready."

"I wasn't profiling," I said, but he'd already hung up.

Anticipating that I might want to take notes during my conversation with Basque, I positioned a notepad next to my keyboard, directed the camera on my face, and then clicked "record" so I could keep a digital record of our conversation.

By the time I was done getting ready, I heard my computer beep. A gray jail cell wall appeared on the monitor.

Ralph's head filled the screen. Then the image swung to the left as he centered the computer's camera on an empty chair. He looked into the camera again. "Almost got it, Pat the Profiler."

"Could you tilt your head to the side?" I said. "I'm getting an awful lot of glare on this end."

"Ha. Very funny. Laugh all you want." His face appeared again. He slid his hand across his head. "It drives Brineesha crazy."

"Just buy me some sunglasses."

The image of Ralph's face was grainy, and because of the delay between the audio and video, I guessed they were using someone's older, slower laptop. Then I heard the rattle of leg irons and Ralph said, "Here he comes."

There was a moment of blurry movement as Ralph moved back, then Basque situated himself on the chair and faced the camera.

68

Today, Basque wore an orange prison jumpsuit and not the hand-tailored clothes he'd worn at the trial, and for some reason that brought me a small degree of satisfaction. The door clanged shut as Ralph left.

"Hello, Richard," I said.

"Agent Bowers." Even though he was handcuffed, he looked as confident and at ease as ever. "I'd like to thank you again for saving my life. I wouldn't be here today if you hadn't responded so quickly."

My natural response to a comment like that would have been to say, "You're welcome," but I held back and simply said, "Yes."

"Did they find out how Celeste's father was able to load the gun before it was brought into the courtroom?"

"They're looking into it."

"I'm sure they are." He paused, folded his handcuffed hands on his lap. "Does this chat concern the recent string of murders in Denver that I've been hearing so much about?"

"It does." After the attempt on his life I should have guessed he'd be following the news. "I think you might be able to help us find the killer." I stopped for a moment and evaluated whether or not to say it. Went ahead: "He reminds me of you, Richard."

Basque was silent. Finally he nodded slightly. "So, I'm guessing it isn't motives you're interested in. What are we hoping to find out here today?"

"He knows about you. We found newspaper clippings of your crimes. He collected them."

Basque straightened up. "Clippings?"

"Yes. I'm wondering if he ever contacted you."

Like so many serial killers, Basque had reached celebrity status among a certain aberrant segment of society. From my pretrial briefing with Assistant State's Attorney Vandez, I knew that thousands of people had written to Basque over the past thirteen years. Last I'd heard, nine women had asked him to marry them when he was released.

I figured I'd give Basque one small clue to see if it helped jog his memory. "This killer, he likes Renaissance literature."

I've only met a few people in my life with a memory as sharp as Basque's, and now it looked like he was mentally sorting through all of those thousands of letters he'd received in order to identify the man I was referring to. At last, a look of recognition crossed his face. "Giovanni."

That's Boccaccio's first name, the Italian form of John.

"Tell me what you know," I said.

"Well for starters, I don't know who he is. Giovanni's almost certainly not his real name. I never wrote him back." Basque was as consummate a liar as he was a killer, and even though he sounded like he was telling the truth I wasn't sure whether to believe him or not. He must have noticed my skepticism. "You can confirm it with the warden," he said. "Giovanni wrote to me six times, I never replied."

I would contact the warden as soon as I could, but for now I wanted to find out as many details as possible from Basque himself. "What did he write to you about?"

Basque wet his lips, stared directly into the camera, and said, "You."

69

My heartbeat seemed to stop for a split second, and when it picked up again it was faster than usual. "What did you say?"

"Giovanni wrote to me about an FBI agent he was recruiting to play a crucial part in his story. Someone he was planning to bury alive at the climax. Someone he admired."

I shook my head. "That's not enough. It could be any number of people." I could see the gears turning in his mind. It appeared there was something he wasn't telling me. "What else?"

He tapped a finger slowly against his leg. "I'll help you if you do something for me."

"I'm not here to cut deals."

"Hear me out. It's not a deal like you think. It's a favor."

I was tempted to end the call immediately, but then remembered that nothing I'd done so far had slowed down John—or Giovanni or whatever his name was. He always seemed to be one step ahead, just like Basque had been thirteen years ago in the months leading up to the slaughterhouse. In the months so many women died.

Cold, whispering lips.

Basque's victims.

And now, Giovanni's.

So many innocent people, calling to me from their graves.

Basque stared at me from the cell in Chicago, waiting for my reply.

At last I said, "What's the favor?"

"When you return to the stand tomorrow and Priscilla asks you about what happened in the slaughterhouse . . ." He paused.

I'd been trying not to think about the trial, and I didn't like being reminded that I'd be there in less than twenty-four hours. "Go on."

"Don't tell the truth," Basque said.

His words stunned me. "What?" I stared at the grainy picture on my computer screen and tried to decipher Basque's expression. Couldn't.

"When she asks you whether or not you assaulted me, don't tell the truth."

"I won't lie on the stand."

Why is he asking you to do this?

"You've considered it, haven't you?" Basque said. "I think you have. I'm just asking you to do what you want to do, what your gut tells you to do."

Cheyenne's words about following gut instincts immediately came to mind, especially since Basque's comments struck uncomfortably close to home. "If that's your only condition then this conversation is over—"

"He's coming for you, Patrick." Basque leaned forward and his voice seemed to carry a note of genuine concern. "He's playing with you. Be careful. He's got a twist waiting for you at the end that you'd never expect."

"I'll take my chances. Good-bye, Richard."

"I'll be praying for you. Remember, Exodus 1:15–21. Remember—"

I ended the call. I wasn't in the mood for Basque's games. I wasn't in the mood for any of this.

As I was saving the video and uploading it onto the task force's online case files, I felt a wave of anger.

Then confusion.

Then something else. Something deeper and more primal—a desire for revenge, for a rough and final justice to be meted out against Giovanni and Basque. And against all who would mock the dying or take innocent life.

And with those feelings, I sensed myself slipping, tumbling toward something I did not want to become. I remembered a time a few months ago when Tessa had asked me if I was like them, like the people I hunt, and I'd had to admit to myself that there's only a thin line that separates me from them. A single act. A single choice.

Remember who you are, Pat.

Remember.

I stared at my office wall: my diplomas, my awards.

You're Special Agent Patrick Bowers with the Federal Bureau of Investigation . . . the man who caught Richard Devin Basque . . . criminologist, investigator, author . . .

My mind tried to dictate my resume, but the words in my head were cut off abruptly when my eyes landed on the spine of Christie's diary resting on my bookshelf.

And I remembered the most important part of who I am: *You are Tessa Bernice Ellis's stepfather.*

I crossed the room and gazed at the worn, leather spine of the diary—it wasn't one of those small diaries with pages the size of note cards but was the same size as a hardback novel.

Christie was the one who'd first gotten me interested in mysticism and philosophy, and in the last two years I'd read everything I could get my hands on by Guyon, de Fenelon, Merton, and a dozen others. I'd placed Christie's diary between *The Way of Perfection* by St. Teresa of Avila and *Abandonment to Divine Providence* by Jean-Pierre de Caussade, two of my favorites.

I ran my finger along the spine.

The wedding picture of me and Christie sat on the shelf just below the diary. We'd gotten married at a small chapel in Central Park and then stepped outside to have this picture taken. And now, as I looked at her smiling face, I felt the same strange mixture of thankfulness and loss I always feel when I see her.

Christie had chosen Tessa to be her maid of honor. That's how close they were. That's how much they meant to each other.

I took the diary from the shelf.

And I left to give it to my stepdaughter.

———————————————■———————————————

Unit #14
Safe-Lock Self-Storage
5532 Dayton Street
Denver, Colorado

Giovanni dropped six rats into the aquarium that contained his three remaining Western Diamondback rattlesnakes.

The rats tried to climb the glass.

But the snakes closed in.

Over the next fifteen minutes he let the snakes feed while he extracted the bufotenin from the skin and parotid glands of the ten toads he'd killed, dissected, and pinned out on the board in front of him.

After he'd removed the psychedelic drugs from the toads, he consulted a toxicology textbook to determine how much poison he would need for a lethal dose and found that he had more than enough bufotoxin to kill six people, let alone two.

Reading the description of the symptoms was very informative: hallucinations, vomiting, seizures, paralysis, and then ventricular fibrillation. As one book put it:

> Often the hallucinations involve the sensation of bugs crawling across the victim's skin or out of the bodily orifices. Frequently, those experiencing these symptoms will scratch furiously at their skin or attempt to scrub, slice or burn the bugs away.

So, it looked like the next two victims would die just as dramatically as Simona and Pasquino did in Emilia's story, the seventh tale told on day four.

Given the delivery method he'd chosen, Giovanni couldn't be certain if his victims would fatally poison themselves tonight or in the morning, but he was relatively certain that both of them would be dead before noon tomorrow.

Based on their habits, they would be away from home this afternoon. He could place the poison then. And if they changed their pattern, he would alter his plan. Maybe slip over later tonight while they were asleep. Either way, the story would play out just as it was supposed to.

The tragic squeaking and scratching of the last dying rat caught his attention. He watched it until it stopped quivering, just like he'd watched his grandmother stop twitching so many years before.

Finally, the rat stared wide-eyed and unblinking at the world, just like Grandma Nadine had done.

Just like all the people over the years in the different tales he'd told.

The snake opened its jaws and began to swallow its meal.

Giovanni laid the two syringes full of bufotoxin in a narrow metal case, snapped it shut, and slipped it into his duffel bag.

Then he left the storage facility and, since he had a few arrangements to make before the last four stories began, drove to his place of employment where no one knew, no one had any idea, who he really was.

And where, in the greatest irony of all, he was trusted implicitly with people's lives every day.

70

Tessa was showered, dressed, and sitting at my parents' kitchen table waiting for me when I arrived at their house with the diary.

She was sipping a glass of chilled orange juice and had a half-eaten grapefruit in front of her, and although I expected her to ask me where I'd been or complain that I'd dragged her out of bed and made her change in the car, all she said was, "So, um . . . do you have it?"

I couldn't think of anything touching or profound to say, so I simply handed Christie's diary to her and watched her reaction.

She accepted it quietly, stared at it. Turned it over in her hands.

Christie had used her diary partly as a scrapbook, pasting snippets of letters, notes, and postcards inside, all of which made the book fat and lumpy and left the binding straining at the lock. But it gave the diary character, and by the look on Tessa's face, it seemed to appeal to her inquisitive nature.

After a few moments when she didn't say anything, I asked her, "Where's Martha?"

"At church." Tessa still hadn't looked up from the diary.

"She left you alone?"

"She asked if I wanted her to stay home, but I told her I'd be safe with those two undercover cops in the car across the street watching the house."

"How did you—?"

She rolled her eyes. "*Puh*-lease."

OK, so I would need to have a little talk with those two officers.

"So, you fly out today again?" Tessa was looking at the diary, but speaking to me.

"I need to leave for the airport at about 2:30. I'm hoping to be back tomorrow evening."

"And then we leave for DC pretty much after that." She didn't state it as a question.

It was possible that my testimony in Chicago would affect the timing of our trip to DC, but I decided I could deal with all that later. "We're scheduled to leave on Wednesday. Yes." She didn't reply. I tapped her shoulder gently. "All right, well, fill me in when you're done reading it, OK?"

"I will."

Then, leaving the glass of OJ and the remains of the grapefruit behind, she took the diary upstairs to the bedroom my parents let her use when I'm out of town.

■

Despite her overwhelming curiosity, Tessa stared at the diary for a long time before opening it.

When Patrick had first told her about it, she'd been angry, angry, so angry that he'd kept it from her, but then when he told her that her mom hadn't wanted him to give it to her until her eighteenth birthday, she stopped being angry and became something else.

Curious, yes.

Maybe a little afraid.

But why? What was she afraid of?

She stared at it, ran her fingers across the weathered cover.

She kept this from you. Your mom kept it from you.

She didn't want you to know about it until you were eighteen.

But why not?

Tessa slipped the key into the lock. Her heart began to run like a rabbit through her chest as she turned the key, clicked open the clasp. Flipped to the first entry.

November 2

Dear Diary,
   I'm not really sure why I'm doing this, writing to you, I mean, starting a diary. I guess I'm hoping you'll be a place for me to just be myself, the real me, the person no one ever really seems to notice. I guess it's good to have a place like that. I don't know. It's hard to be honest with people sometimes, maybe I can at least be honest with you.

A place to be real.

Nice.

Based on the date, Tessa realized that her mother had started the journal when she was seventeen—the same age that she was now.

You were conceived two years later.

She was tempted to jump around, skim over the entries, kind of like scrolling through someone's blog to see if you really wanted to read the whole thing or not, but she already knew that she wanted to read every page, and, just like reading any book, you cheat yourself if you skip to the end. You miss all the surprises.

"Hey, Tessa." It was Patrick, calling from the first floor. "I left my laptop at home. I have a few things to check on and then I have a meeting at 1:00. You'll be all right?"

"Uh-huh," she hollered through the door of her room.

"I'll see you this afternoon before I fly out. I've still got your cell, OK?"

"Yeah. Just tell those two cops not to be quite so obtrusive."

A pause. "I will. Call me if you need me."

"OK."

Then Tessa turned to the diary's second entry and began to read.

71

I had a quick and rather blunt word with the two officers who were supposed to be watching my parents' house undercover, and then I drove home to pick up my laptop.

Using Tessa's cell I dialed in to my account and checked my voicemail, but my mailbox was empty. When I checked hers, I found a dozen text messages from her friends at school. I wanted her to be able to access them, so I programmed the phone to automatically forward all her messages to her email account.

Then I called the warden from the Waupun Correctional Institution, the maximum security penitentiary in Wisconsin where Basque had spent most of the thirteen years of his incarceration.

I caught Warden Schuler at home grilling steaks for his family, and he made sure he let me know how happy he was that I was disturbing him on a Sunday morning, but I told him it would only take a minute, and then asked if I could get a look at the letters Basque had received while he was in prison.

"Sure, if we had 'em."

"What do you mean?"

"Basque ripped 'em up and flushed 'em."

"Well, you made copies, right?"

"Privacy rights. We can open the mail, inspect it, but we can't copy anything. ACLU would have a field day with that. Sorry."

"What about outgoing mail?"

"Same deal."

For the second time that day, I cussed.

"My sentiments exactly."

"All right, thanks. Have a good lunch."

"I wish I could be of more help." As Warden Schuler said the words, his voice slipped from the annoyance I'd heard at the beginning of the call into a tense kind of uneasiness. "In sixteen years of doing this, Agent Bowers, he's the worst I've seen. Put him away. At the trial, I mean. Don't let him—"

"I won't," I said and ended the call.

With Basque's letters destroyed, there was no way to verify that John had ever written to him, but still, Basque had known who I was talking about right away when I mentioned Renaissance literature so I figured that somehow, they'd been in touch.

John.

Giovanni.

Since the murders were in Denver, and Kurt had told me that the only college in the region that offered medieval literature courses on *The Decameron* was DU, it seemed probable to me that John— or Giovanni, or whatever his name was—would have taken one of those classes.

When I arrived home I went directly to my desk, tapped the spacebar, and woke up my laptop.

According to our information, Dr. Bryant, the professor who taught the classes on Boccaccio, was in Phoenix yesterday. It's tough living in the twenty-first century without leaving electronic footprints everywhere you go, so I accessed the Federal Digital Database, and surfed to the FAA's flight manifest records. Then I checked the passenger lists from all the airlines that fly into or out of the Denver International Airport and the Colorado Springs Airport for yesterday and today, but I didn't find the name Adrian Bryant on any of them.

I expanded my search to include any arrivals or departures over the last twenty days.

Still nothing.

So unless Professor Bryant drove to Phoenix or flew under an alias, it looked like our local Boccaccio expert never went to his conference.

Interesting.

It took me less than three minutes to do an online search and find out that Dr. Bryant wasn't married, lived alone, and didn't own a landline, so it was a good thing for me the National Security Agency keeps searchable records of all the cell numbers and subscriber names from the mobile phone companies operating in North America.

The Bureau's cybercrime division works closely with NSA, so I called them, and a few moments later, I had Bryant's cell number and verification that the GPS location for both his phone and his 2009 BMW 328i sedan were currently at his home address. I told them to monitor the GPS locations and call me if either moved in the next thirty minutes.

To confirm that Bryant was at home with his cell, I tapped in his number, and after he picked up I asked if he wanted to purchase a free vacation package—

He hung up without even pointing out that I'd offered him a chance to buy something that was free.

So, he was at the house. Good.

Sometimes I wonder how crimes were ever solved before we had computers.

A quick look at the clock—11:14 a.m. I needed to be at police headquarters by 1:00, so considering where Bryant lived in Littleton, it might be cutting it close, but I figured I'd have just enough time to drive over, meet with the professor, and make it back in time for Jake's sure-to-be-scintillating briefing.

I made one final call from behind the wheel of my car, and after Cheyenne answered I invited her to join me, and she agreed—as long as I could swing by and get her. "All right," I said. "This time I'll pick you up." And then, realizing how I'd phrased that, I added, "In my car. For the case. To catch the bad guy."

"Right." I heard a smile in her voice. "I'll see you in a few."

Even though Tessa was a fast reader, she was taking her time working her way through her mother's diary.

In a way, reading the entries felt a little weird, like an invasion of her mom's personal space, sort of like stepping into Patrick's bedroom, but way more private. More intimate.

In addition, her mom never used any last names in the diary. Maybe it was a way of protecting people's privacy. Hard to know, but it added a cryptic touch to every entry, and Tessa liked that.

Most of the early entries dealt with her mom's struggles relating to her parents (whom Tessa had met when she was younger, but who'd died before she was six), her boy problems, and overcoming the loneliness and isolation she often felt as a senior in high school. Even her thoughts of suicide.

Not a whole lot different than you.

Tessa knew that sometimes girls reach a point in their relationships with their mothers where they become almost like sisters. She'd never had the chance to experience that with her mom when she was still alive, but now, reading these entries she found herself feeling close to her in a way she'd never felt before.

And of course, with each entry she came closer and closer to the winter day of her mother's sophomore year in college when she was conceived.

She tried not to think too much about that, and to just take the entries one at a time, but with every page it was getting harder and harder not to wonder when her father's real name might appear.

As Cheyenne and I drove to Professor Bryant's house, we reviewed everything that had gone down during the morning. Kurt had already told her about Bennett's death and John's phone call to me, so I focused instead on summarizing my conversation with Richard Basque.

"It looks like you do have a fan, after all," Cheyenne said. "Maybe two."

"How do you figure?"

"It's very possible Basque wrote Giovanni back—that they're closely acquainted. And that would open up all sorts of interesting possibilities."

I had to think about that.

And I did, all during the drive.

In fact, her words were still cycling through my head when we arrived at Dr. Bryant's subdivision on the outskirts of Littleton.

72

I parked across the street from Bryant's red brick home.

Cybercrime hadn't called me back to tell me his cell's location had moved, and since his BMW was still in his driveway, I figured he was probably still here as well.

Cheyenne rang the doorbell, and a few seconds later a blond man wearing Chaco sport sandals, a gray T-shirt, and Patagonia shorts answered the door.

"Dr. Bryant?" I said.

"Yes?" Caucasian. Mid to late forties. Lean. Athletic. A tanned face, taut and wind-lashed. He looked like he'd spent the last twenty years backpacking and running marathons instead of lecturing at a university.

I showed him my ID. "I'm Special Agent Bowers with the FBI, and this is Detective Warren with the Denver Police Department. We're wondering if we could ask you a few questions."

He let his eyes drift from me to Cheyenne. Then back to me. "What does this concern?"

"An ongoing investigation," Cheyenne said.

"May we come in?" I asked.

He looked like he might object but then said curtly, "Of course."

Once inside, I surveyed his living room. New furniture that looked like it had never been used. No television. A violin and music stand in the corner. The smell of freshly brewed coffee in the kitchen, still percolating. Good coffee, the kind they serve at

312

Rachel's Café. A collection of medieval swords and daggers hung prominently on the wall.

A sword had been used to kill Tatum Maroukas on Wednesday.

"That's an impressive sword collection," I said.

"Thank you."

No, Pat, think about it. John would never have used a sword that could be linked to him. He's too smart for that.

I made note of the swords, tried not to assume too much. We could follow up on that later. I got right to the point. "I understand you teach several courses on the Renaissance humanists."

"I do." He'd crossed the room and now stood protectively in the doorway to the hall, arms folded.

On the other side of the living room, an empty Camelbak hydration pack lay draped over the seat of a mountain bike, a high-end 7 Point Freeride Iron Horse caked with dirt. This was a bike that had seen some miles. He saw me admiring it. "I'm meeting some friends to go mountain biking in fifteen minutes. I really don't have time right now to chat."

"They're calling for snow this afternoon," Cheyenne said.

"I'm an avid mountain biker." His tone was turning more and more caustic, and I didn't like it.

"Dr. Bryant," I said. "I understand you were scheduled to teach at a conference in Phoenix this weekend but didn't make it. May I ask why?"

"I had a personal issue come up. I was here at home the whole time. What exactly is this about?"

"An ongoing investigation," Cheyenne said again, less cordially than before. I could feel tension twisting through the air.

"There's a book," I said, "*The Decameron,* by an Italian author named Boccaccio. You're familiar with it?"

"Yes, of course. I cover it in several of my classes."

"Can you think of any of your students who've shown unusual interest in it?"

"Many of my students enjoy Boccaccio's work."

"Avid interest," Cheyenne specified.

"No one comes to mind." He answered the question too quickly to have given it any serious consideration.

I was beginning to lose my world-famous patience. "Dr. Bryant, we are not—"

"We're not very familiar with the book," Cheyenne said, interrupting me, in what I assumed was an attempt to calm me down and draw him out. I was glad she spoke up. The words I'd been planning to say weren't quite as amenable as hers.

"We're told you're the expert," she went on. "Can you take just a moment to give us a quick rundown?"

Dr. Bryant looked like he was about to object but must have thought better of it, or maybe her subtle compliment appealed to his ego. He let out a thin, aggravated sigh instead. "*The Decameron: Prencipe Galeotto* is about seven women and three men who are fleeing the Black Plague—"

"Wait a minute," I said. "What did you just call it? You said something in Latin after 'decameron.'"

"It was Italian," he said impatiently. "*Prencipe Galeotto*. Boccaccio didn't just name the book *The Decameron*. He also gave the book a secondary name, a subtitle: *Prencipe Galeotto*."

"And what does that mean?"

"Galeotto is another rendering of Prince Galahalt, or Galehaut."

"You mean Galahad?" Cheyenne asked. "The knight?"

"No. Galahalt." He didn't hide his condescension. "But yes, he was also one of the knights of the round table. Not one of the most common characters in Arthurian lore, although he does play a significant role in the story."

"And that is?" I asked.

Dr. Bryant let his gaze climb to the clock on the wall, and he must have decided it would be best to just give us what we wanted and be done with it. He gestured toward the hallway. "Come here. I'll show you."

73

Professor Bryant led us to his study.

On the way past the kitchen I saw the coffee brewing. A full pot.

And it got me thinking.

We arrived at the office, and I saw that most if it was taken up by a large desk piled high with papers, notepads, and textbooks. The walls were lined with bookshelves. An iMac sat on his desk.

Wondering if he might be the one who'd checked out the library's five *Decameron* commentaries, I scanned his bookshelves for spines with an 853 Dewey decimal number but didn't see any.

He approached one of the shelves on the east wall. "The legends vary as to Galeotto's origins, but in nearly all of the stories he's the man credited with setting up Sir Lancelot and Queen Guinevere."

Cheyenne was examining the room as well, taking everything in. "But Guinevere was married to King Arthur at the time, right?"

"Exactly. Galeotto arranged for their licentious meeting and encouraged them to kiss." Dr. Bryant studied the spines of the books on one of the top shelves. Based on the titles on that shelf, it appeared he was looking for a commentary on Dante, rather than a collection of Arthurian legends as I'd suspected.

"However," Dr. Bryant said, "as a result of Guinevere's meeting with Lancelot, she consequently fell in love with him and they had an affair that destroyed the famed harmony of King Arthur's court." He pulled a dusty, leather-bound volume from the middle of a group of other dusty, leather-bound volumes. "Boccaccio took the reference to Galeotto from Dante's *Inferno*, one of the three sections in his *Divine Comedy.*"

The *Inferno.*

Great.

The world's most famous description of hell.

"By the way, a bit of trivia." Dr. Bryant was flipping through the pages of the well-worn copy of Dante's *Divine Comedy* he'd chosen from his bookshelf. "Boccaccio was a big fan of Dante. He's the one who gave this book the title 'Divina.' Dante had just named it 'Commedia.'"

Trivia or not, I made a note of it on my notepad.

He stopped paging through the book. "By the time Dante wrote his masterpiece, Galeotto had come to signify unhappiness or disappointment in love . . ." His voice trailed off as he perused the page, then he nailed the center of it with his finger. "Here: Canto V, lines 137–138." He tilted the book so that we could see the passage.

Cheyenne had been standing across the room from me and now edged closer to get a better look at the page.

"See?" Dr. Bryant said. "Dante wrote, 'Galeotto was the book and he who wrote it. That day no farther did we read therein.'"

"So what does that mean?" I asked. "Galeotto was the book and he who wrote it?"

"Well, there are different interpretations, of course, but I would say that Dante means that Galeotto was both a part of the tale and a shaper of the tale. Some literary critics believe that by giving *The Decameron* the subtitle *Prencipe Galeotto*, Boccaccio was placing himself in the role of Galeotto."

"So you're saying that Boccaccio saw himself as a matchmaker of a love affair?"

"Yes."

I considered the implications. "Between whom?"

"His book and his readers."

"But how does that follow?" Cheyenne said. "Lancelot's love

affair with Guinevere was illicit. There's nothing illicit about reading a book."

"You have to remember," Bryant said, "*The Decameron* was written in the fourteenth century. Boccaccio's stories might not be controversial today, but in those days his book caused quite a stir."

Dr. Bryant was slipping into the familiar role of the professor—being the one with the answers, the one in charge, and that seemed to help him open up. He began to pace, although the cramped room gave him little space to do it. "Reading lurid tales was not considered a valuable use of one's time in the 1300s."

"The soap operas of the middle ages," Cheyenne said.

"Something like that." He gazed from Cheyenne to me. "Although I think it would be more accurate to say that the church of those days regarded *The Decameron* in much the same way as they would regard Internet pornography today. Thus, the reason it was condemned."

His eyes flicked, probably subconsciously, to his computer, and I decided that, taking into account his sword collection, his intimate knowledge of *The Decameron*, and his lack of an alibi for yesterday, it might not be a bad idea to have my friends in the Bureau's cybercrime division do a little checking on the professor's Internet surfing history. We should have enough probable cause to get the request cleared.

But maybe not.

Then a thought.

Maybe I wouldn't have to wait for them.

I wrote a few more notes on my pad, then rolled the pen through my fingers. "All right," I said to Professor Bryant. "You're proposing that, to Boccaccio, the relationship between the reader and the text, between the person and the story, was an illicit affair?"

"Yes."

I surveyed the bookshelves again, laid the notepad and pen on his desk. "And Boccaccio was the one bringing them together, playing the role of the knight, Galeotto." I still hadn't seen any 853 commentaries, but the professor had thousands of books.

"That is correct."

Yesterday, Jake had suggested that all of the killer's stories were about the tragic consequences of love: "Cruel, fatal tales of love and loss."

Is John acting as a matchmaker between lovers and death? Is that his game?

Professor Bryant looked impatiently at Cheyenne and me. "Now, if that's all, I really need to—"

My phone rang. "Excuse me." I stepped into the hallway. Through the door I could hear Cheyenne asking the professor about the specific literary significance of the stories told on day four.

As I answered the phone I walked softly to the kitchen to check on something. "Yes?"

"It's me," Ralph said. "I had an agent watching Calvin. She said he was at home, but he wasn't returning my calls so I swung over to invite him to lunch. He's not there."

"What?" I was silently looking over Dr. Bryant's countertops, then I quickly searched his cabinets.

"Somehow he slipped past us."

"He's nearly eighty years old." Quickly, quietly, I checked the contents of the professor's dishwasher.

"I know. I'm looking into it."

"We need to find—"

"I said I know." He turned his words into hammer blows. "I'm looking into it."

"OK," I said. "Thanks."

He ended the call abruptly. I didn't find what I was looking for in Dr. Bryant's kitchen, and, discouraged on both counts, I returned to the study.

74

As I entered the room, I heard Professor Bryant wrapping up his explanation to Cheyenne: "You see, while the ten pilgrims were trying to escape the Black Plague, death was only one step behind them, but of course it would eventually catch up with them, just as it catches up with us all. So, in all of the stories told on this fourth day of the journey, we find the underlying, unstated theme that love itself is a plague, a sickness, that tracks us down and ends unhappily, that love inevitably leads to misery."

Based on what we knew about the killer and his crimes up until that point, Bryant's analysis seemed right on target.

I caught Cheyenne looking at me. I guessed that she was just checking to see if I had any follow-up questions. I shook my head.

She handed Dr. Bryant her card. "Well, thank you for your time. You've been very helpful. Please call us if you think of any students who've shown particular interest in *The Decameron*."

"I will." But by the look on his face I suspected he'd throw the card away as soon as we were out the door.

"And if we have any more questions," Cheyenne said, "we'll be in touch."

"Yes." He led us to the front door. "All right."

"Oh, wait." I patted my pockets. "I forgot my notepad and pen in your office. I'll be right back."

A few seconds later I was in Professor Bryant's office again, this time, alone. I went around the desk to his keyboard and tapped the spacebar to still the fish swimming across the screen and wake up his iMac.

Sometimes you have to poke around for evidence to find out if there's enough reason to even bother getting a search warrant.

At the end of the hall I heard Cheyenne say, "So, when does the semester finish up?"

The desktop screen appeared. I quickly clicked on the apple on the upper left-hand corner, scrolled to System Preferences—

"Two weeks," Bryant told Cheyenne.

I clicked the "Sharing" icon. Turned on "Remote Login" and "File Sharing."

Dr. Bryant's voice drifted down the hall. "If you would excuse me."

I memorized his IP address so I could remotely log into his computer. Heard footsteps. Grabbed my notepad and pen.

Closed his System Preferences.

Turned.

He was standing in the doorway. "All set?" he asked.

I held up the notepad and pen I'd purposely left on his desk a few minutes earlier. "Mission accomplished."

───────────────■───────────────

After Cheyenne and I were in the car, I promptly started the engine and pulled into the street.

"What are you thinking?" she asked.

"He was lying."

"How do you know?"

"The coffee."

"The coffee?"

"It smelled like Geisha beans from Hacienda la Esmeralda's farms in Panama, one of the world's rarest and most expensive coffees."

"You identified the coffee by its smell?"

"Well, that and the fact that I saw the bag while I was on the phone looking around the kitchen, but that's not the point. The point is: he doesn't own a thermos."

She blinked. "He doesn't own a thermos?"

"Nope. Or a travel mug—or if he does, he's hiding them really well. And he made twelve cups. OK, now this is just my gut reaction, but I doubt that someone who buys one hundred dollar per pound coffee would brew that many cups at once unless he was expecting someone. A coffee connoisseur brews small pots to keep his cups fresh. And it was percolating when I walked in, so I don't think he was about to go mountain biking."

"Did you just say your gut reaction? And here I was, thinking you were the guy who doesn't trust his instincts."

"I don't," I said. "That's why we're circling around the block."

"So he lied about going mountain biking," she said. "Do you think that matters?"

"Everything matters."

Cheyenne cleared her throat, ever so slightly, but I noticed. "You know, this is the seventh case I've worked with you, and you've said that at some point in every one of those investigations."

"Really?"

"Yes."

"Must be a quirk." I parked behind a minivan near the intersecting street closest to Dr. Adrian Bryant's house. "Let's see who he's meeting."

A few moments later, Bryant left the house, looked up and down the street, then slipped into his BMW and backed out of the driveway. He didn't take his mountain bike with him. "Hmm," I said. "A slight change of plans for the professor. No visitors, and I guess the biking trip can wait."

"What do you think?" Cheyenne asked. "Follow him or let him go?"

I looked at my watch: 12:32.

In twenty-eight minutes Jake Vanderveld would begin sharing

his psychological profile of the killer. "Follow him. That way we'll have an excuse for missing Jake's briefing."

She took a moment to evaluate my comment. "You're kidding."

"Yes. Maybe."

"Well, you're the one in the driver's seat this time. You can take me wherever you like."

Man, this woman loved her double entendres.

And I didn't mind them so much either.

Maybe if we were lucky, Bryant would do something illegal so we could arrest him and Cheyenne and I would have a good excuse for missing the briefing.

Bryant entered the tangled web of subdivision streets that surrounded his house, and I followed him, staying far enough back so that he wouldn't see me.

And I memorized the route he took as we drove.

75

Tessa heard Patrick's mother return from church and start setting plates on the table for lunch.

The diary didn't include entries every day, and sometimes Tessa's mom would skip a week or even a month just like most bloggers do. And often, instead of writing, she would paste in a letter or a photograph, but still, Tessa walked with her mother like a friend, like a sister, through her first year of college and into the beginning of the summer that followed.

Her mother had just started writing about a guy named Brad who was one year ahead of her in school when Tessa heard Martha's thin, wispy voice float up the stairs. "What can I make you for lunch, dear?"

"I'm not hungry," she called back.

Tessa liked Martha. Patrick had told her one time that his mother had grown up in Georgia, learning to be a proper Southern lady, so Tessa realized she probably wasn't too thrilled about her stepgranddaughter's eyebrow ring, black fingernail polish, tattoo, and love of death metal, but still, Tessa had never felt judged by her and had always respected her for that. Despite their differences, they got along surprisingly well.

Tessa heard footsteps on the stairs.

Martha wasn't exactly spry, and Tessa didn't like the idea that she was making her come up the stairs just to convince her to eat something, so she left the diary on the bed, walked down the hallway, and plopped on the top stair. "Seriously," she told her. "I'm good."

Martha was halfway up the stairs. "Tessa, dear, you need to eat." Martha was a frail, delicate woman with snow-white hair, yet someone whom Tessa had noticed possessed the kind of strength that's hard to measure.

And even though Tessa really wanted to get back to the diary to find out what happened between her mother and Brad, she didn't want to be rude. "OK, sure, just whatever you're having."

"Meatloaf all right, then?"

Tessa stared at her, expecting her face to give away that she was kidding, but Martha just looked at her innocently. Finally, Tessa said, "In the Bible, weren't Adam and Eve vegetarians? Wasn't that the original plan—that humans wouldn't kill to live? And Daniel the lion-den-guy too? Wasn't he—"

A slight finger in the air. "Point taken." Martha gave her an I'm-proud-of-you look. "So, leafloaf, then?"

"Sure, yeah. Leafloaf," she said. "Thanks." Coming from Patrick, "leafloaf" would have sounded like a lame attempt at humor, but from Martha it just seemed sweet.

Then Martha gave her a light smile and descended the steps again, and Tessa returned to the diary to find out if her mother and Brad ever hooked up.

■

Fifteen minutes after leaving his house, Dr. Bryant pulled into the parking lot of the *Denver News* building.

"So," Cheyenne said. "Bryant is an expert on Boccaccio, he owns a sword collection, was unaccounted for yesterday, the head in the pot of basil was sent to this building, he drives over here as soon as we're done talking to him, and remember? Kurt mentioned that Bryant had Amy Lynn in class."

"Yes," I said. "My interest is definitely sparked."

Clock check—we had twelve minutes before the briefing at HQ, and despite my reluctance to attend, I knew we needed to be there.

"We have to go, but let's get a car over here; have a couple officers keep an eye on the professor."

Cheyenne pulled out her cell, and I aimed the car toward police headquarters.

76

Jake was connecting his computer to the wall monitor when Cheyenne and I arrived at the conference room. In addition to Jake, I saw three of the officers who'd been helping us with the case, two FBI agents, and Reggie Greer. Kurt hadn't arrived yet.

A printed copy of Jake's psychological profile lay on the table in front of each of the twelve chairs. As Cheyenne and I took our seats, Captain Terrell, Kurt's boss and the fan of profiler TV shows, stepped into the room and sat beside Jake. The captain was a severe-looking man with short, choppy hair. A cloud of Old Spice cologne trailed behind him as he passed.

Cheyenne leaned close to me, nodded toward him, and whispered, "They say it takes more muscles to frown than to smile."

I kept my voice low. "You're saying his face likes a good workout?"

She winked. "Good. You're keeping up with me."

"Great minds," I whispered.

Then I overheard Captain Terrell ask Jake if he was ready. Jake nodded. "Good to go."

The captain cleared his throat, and everyone settled into their chairs. "First, I want to thank you all for coming in on a weekend," he said. "As you know, the Denver Police Department is always looking for ways to better serve its constituents, so we're honored and privileged to have two federal agents working closely with us on this case." He gave me and Jake a slightly forced nod.

Then he leaned both of his hands against the table. "So let's cut to the bone—this psycho has got to be stopped. We have at least seven deaths on our hands, and this thing is turning into a freakin' PR nightmare. The DPD is gonna put every available resource we have behind finding this guy."

He picked up one of the photocopies of Jake's profile. Waved it at us. "And Special Agent Vanderveld is the man who's gonna help us do it." Then he gave him the floor. "Jake."

Evidently, Captain Terrell had a shade more confidence in Jake's investigative abilities than I did. I flipped open my copy of the profile, began my obligatory perusal.

Jake stood. "Thank you, Captain." He pointed to the printed profiles. "I won't read what you have in front of you, but I would like to highlight a few points." He tapped a button on his laptop, and an FBI logo appeared on the screen.

"We're dealing with someone who was able to find a man on the FBI's most wanted list, then subdue and kill him even though that man was a trained assassin." He clicked his laptop again, and an image of Sebastian Taylor's face appeared.

I looked around.

No one else seemed to notice that what Jake had just said, although it sounded insightful, was entirely self-evident. Just a restatement of information we already knew.

"The UNSUB is a male Caucasian, thirty to thirty-five years of age. The crime scenes show a mixture of organized and disorganized behavior."

Saying that behavior is a combination of organized and disorganized might be an accurate description, but it's completely useless in zeroing in on a suspect. I could see this was going to be a very long briefing.

"He's not your typical sexually motivated homicidal killer. He is divorced at least once and might have lived with his mother after college."

With every one of Jake's statements I could feel my temperature rise higher. This was precisely what I didn't like about profiling—conjecture based on guesswork rather than facts. Considering solely the evidence that'd been left at the crime scenes so far, how could anyone possibly tell that the offender lived with his mother after college? It was ridiculous.

Jake went on, "I recommend direct confrontation with the suspect during interrogation. Ask him questions such as, 'How many other people have you killed?' 'Where did you stash Chris Arlington's body?' 'Where did you get the idea to reenact the crimes from *The Decameron*?'"

"Excuse me," Cheyenne said.

"Yes?"

"Wouldn't it be more prudent at this point to focus our energies on getting someone into custody than designing an interrogation strategy?"

Oh yes. A woman after my own heart.

Jake smiled, but I could tell it wasn't really a smile. "We need to be prepared for whatever comes our way, Detective. The more we understand this killer, the better our chances of catching him and getting him to confess. My goal is to be as thorough as possible."

By the look on Cheyenne's face I suspected she was about to lay into him, but I intervened. "Jake," I said. "Cheyenne and I just spoke with the professor who teaches about *The Decameron* at DU. He seemed to think Boccaccio sees himself in the role of a knight bringing lovers together with loss, grief, or death. You may cover this in your written profile, but what do you make of the Boccaccio connection?"

"Yes, I do cover it," he said. "In depth. But I'll summarize for you."

Gee, thanks, I thought.

"Thanks," I said.

"The UNSUB's fascination with *The Decameron* reveals that he is smart and well-read. High IQ. He's studied medieval literature. Probably a college graduate, maybe even did some postgrad coursework. Within Boccaccio's stories he finds the inspiration and impetus to let his violent tendencies have free rein in his life."

"So," Cheyenne said thoughtfully. "You're saying the killer is smart and has violent tendencies?"

Her sarcasm seemed to be lost on Jake. "Yes," he said.

Smart and violent.

These insights were remarkable. Maybe I ought to be writing this stuff down.

"He doesn't change his signature," Jake said, "because he can't. He kills because he gets something out of the murder. And that grows from the specific nature of each crime. It's more related to the *why* than the *how*. Methods get refined. Murderers learn from their mistakes. But they don't change the why. It's almost always for power, domination, and control. In this case, the power over fate, over life and death. To catch this guy we need to focus not on *where* the crimes occur but on *why*."

He was staring at me as he said the words, and I could sense that he was picking a fight, but I kept my mouth shut.

"So, here's what we look at: couples. Lovers. Victim selection. Why is he choosing these couples? What do they have in common? Where do their lives intersect with his?"

He'd just told us a few seconds earlier that the *where* didn't matter, and now he was suggesting we focus on where the victims' lives intersected with the killer's, which is what I'd suggested more than twenty-four hours ago.

At least now we were getting somewhere.

"The UNSUB's preoccupation with love and death reveals a great deal of inner pain and turmoil," Jake said. "He experienced profound grief in his formative years. Probably the loss of a caregiver. So, we should be looking for a highly educated man who experienced tragedy or betrayal as a child. He's familiar with this region, probably grew up or studied here; and perhaps has access to confidential case files or restricted areas of the Federal Digital Database that allowed him to track down Taylor's residence through the tire impressions that matched his Lexus."

Hmm ... access to the Federal Digital Database? Maybe even FALCON? Now, there's an interesting thought—

But before I could consider it any further or Jake could expand on his statement, the door to the conference room swung open with a decisive bang.

It was Kurt. "Someone posted an article online about the crimes," he said. "She knows about *The Decameron.* She's calling our guy 'The Day Four Killer.'"

77

"Pull it up," I told Jake, whose computer was still connected to the wall monitor.

He tapped at his keyboard, opened his Internet browser, and typed in the phrase "Day Four Killer."

The article "Medieval Manuscript Inspires Brutal Slayings" popped up. Jake clicked the webpage, and we all read in silence.

Overall, the article was little more than conjecture, hypothesis, and armchair profiling, but it did contain a few details that we hadn't released to the media—some of the wording from the 911 calls, the fact that Chris Arlington's heart had been found in the mine along with Heather's body, and information about the attempt on Kelsey Nash's life. The author also mentioned the pot of basil but incorrectly noted that it contained the head of Sebastian Taylor rather than Travis Nash.

Though it wasn't illegal to write about the crimes, it was illegal to publicly share privileged information about an ongoing investigation, as this author had done. I asked Kurt if he knew anything about the author.

He shook his head. "It was written by someone named Deniece Johnson, but as far as we can tell, that's just a pseudonym."

With the head in the pot of basil reference, the obvious choice for the author was Amy Lynn Greer.

But still, the article's too specific for her to have—

"We have a leak," Captain Terrell said. And this time, I found myself agreeing with the fan of profilers.

For a moment everyone in the room seemed to be studying each other, looking for a guilty gesture, a suspicious action. At last, Jake surprised me and said, "I think we should postpone the briefing and look into this. Maybe we can reconvene later this afternoon."

He looked to Captain Terrell for support.

The captain considered the suggestion, then nodded. "Everyone do your homework. Kurt, you and I will look into this article ourselves, track down the author, find our leak." He checked the time. "We'll meet back here at four." A couple of the people looked at their watches and seemed to be ready to argue with the announcement, but in the end kept their mouths shut.

Four o'clock would be perfect since I'd be boarding my plane to Chicago. "Great," I said. "Jake can finish up then."

Then Captain Terrell dismissed everyone, except for Reggie Greer, whom he asked to join him in the hall, and I guessed that the captain shared my suspicion that Reggie's wife Amy Lynn was the author.

Everyone left the room, but I stayed behind. Something in the article had caught my eye. I opened my laptop and surfed to the webpage.

Reread it.

Yesterday, I'd scanned the transcripts of the 911 calls on the way to Taylor's house, and whoever wrote this article had included the phrase "dusk is coming"—a fact that the author definitely shouldn't have known.

And that was something I could look into right away. It was possible the 911 calls would lead us to the leak.

After grabbing my things, I stepped into the hall and was both surprised and pleased to find Cheyenne waiting for me.

"Hey," she said. "I've been thinking about that article."

"Me too. I was hoping to look into the anonymous calls. I need some more details. I think I'd like to hear the audio for myself."

She looked at me with admiration and a touch of suspicion. "How about that? I was thinking the same thing."

"Good. You're keeping up with me."

"Great minds," she said. Then she started for the elevator bank. "Dispatch is in the basement. We can check it out right now."

78

As we entered the elevator, Cheyenne glanced at me. "By the way, I was impressed by your self-control in there, during Jake's briefing."

"Yeah, well, I'm a tactful, self-controlled kind of guy."

"Huh. That's good to know." She pressed "L" for the lower level, which was actually the floor above the underground parking garage. "Then can I ask you a personal question, Mr. Tact?" She watched the elevator doors close.

"Shoot."

We descended.

"What happened between you and Lien-hua?"

OK, that came out of nowhere.

Even though it was a little awkward to talk about Lien-hua, I took it as a good sign that Cheyenne was asking about her. "I'm not exactly sure," I said. "But honestly, it wasn't the old cliché of work being more important than the relationship. We were careful about that." The elevator stopped. Beeped. "One thing maybe: right before we started seeing each other, she nearly died. Actually, she did die, but I was able to bring her back."

"Wow." The doors opened and we exited.

"Yes, well, I think that in time it strained things between us, made for an awkward dynamic, as if there was some sort of an obligation for her to like me, not simply a choice."

We started down the hall.

"In addition, before she died, for a short time I thought she was involved in a biotech conspiracy. She told me she didn't hold that against me, but I have a feeling it affected things . . . then she was on leave for a while . . ."

"If you don't want to talk about this," Cheyenne said, "it's OK."

"Lien-hua is still in DC." Only after I said the words did I realize how out of place they must have sounded. I didn't even know why I'd said them. Maybe to let Cheyenne know Lien-hua wasn't in the picture anymore.

"DC," Cheyenne replied. "So, the same city where you'll be living this summer?"

"Um. Yes." I didn't want to talk about Lien-hua anymore. We were halfway down the hallway. I ventured a personal question. "So what about you?"

"You mean a guy?"

"Yes."

"Nothing serious, not for a long time. This may surprise you, but I've been told I intimidate men."

"You're kidding. Really?"

"Shocking, I know. Although, I should tell you, I was married once, right out of college. We were together about five years."

"Do you mind if I ask what happened?"

A small pause. "Every affair begins with a smile."

With every moment the conversation was becoming more and more intimate, and my judgment told me to stop asking follow-up questions, but I went ahead anyway. "So, were you smiling or was he?"

I'd probably stepped way over the line, but Cheyenne didn't seem to mind. "For a while we both were," she said. "In the end, I left the guy I was smiling at, and Cody left me." She paused and then added, "Cody Howard was my husband."

"Cody Howard, the DPD's helicopter pilot?"

"One and the same."

I didn't see that one coming.

At least that explained why she wouldn't fly with him.

We arrived at the dispatch office, and as she was about to press the door open, I asked her to wait a second. "Listen, I wanted to say, I'm sorry about last night."

"About what?"

"Sorry about when you said you were thinking I was going to kiss you . . ."

"Yes?"

"And I didn't."

A small pause. She looked amused. "Yes, I do remember that, come to think of it."

"So anyway, I wasn't trying to blow you off. I'm just . . . well, I felt kind of bad about how things ended."

"Pat," she said, straightening my collar. "I don't think they ended."

And as I was searching for a reply, she pushed open the door to the EMS dispatch center and stepped inside.

79

Once inside the dispatch room, Cheyenne went to locate the on-duty supervisor while I waited by the door and gazed around the room, which was lit only by the bluish glow of computer monitors and the few remaining overhead fluorescents that weren't burned out.

A sign on the wall to my right read:

Remember the Three Ws!
Where is the Incident?
Are there *Wounds*?
Are there *Weapons*?
Lives depennd on YOU!!

A misspelled word. Overuse of exclamation points. Unnecessary capitalization. Tessa would have gone ballistic.

Nine dispatchers were on duty in the cluttered cubicles, and most of them had at least two computers, two headset mics, and a floor pedal for transferring and receiving calls. Everyone looked wired and sleep-deprived. The room smelled like old bologna and burned coffee. Eight cubicles sat empty.

With the stress, long hours, low pay, and emotional drain, it's not easy to find people to be EMS dispatchers. I don't know of any major city in the U.S. where the emergency services department isn't short staffed and constantly looking to hire. In fact, one recent Johns Hopkins University study found that being a dispatcher in a major metropolitan area is just as stressful as being an air traffic controller. Maybe that's what accounts for the 60 percent annual turnover rate.

And here's the irony: most high schools have more up-to-date computer systems than EMS services do, and yet, even though dispatchers potentially hold a person's life in their hands with every call, most states don't even require applicants to have a high school degree.

When a call comes in, a dispatcher might hear a gunshot, hear a body fall, listen as the line goes dead, and sixty to seventy seconds later he's on the phone again with someone else. The dispatchers never find out what happened to the previous caller unless they read about it in the paper or maybe catch the story on the evening news.

But none of the dispatchers I know watch the local news or read the paper.

It's just too painful.

Cheyenne returned with a man who identified himself as Lancaster Cowler.

He swaggered toward me like an ex-jock but looked like he hadn't done a push-up in the last twenty years. A roll of stomach fat oozed out of the space between his shirt and his belt like the tip of a giant tongue. "Special Agent Bowers," he said, his voice moist and thick.

I shook his hand. "Mr. Cowler, I don't want to keep you long. I just have a couple questions about the anonymous calls reporting the double homicides on Thursday and Friday."

"Woman who took the calls isn't in today," he said. "Weekends off. You know. To be with her kids."

"Can we see if anyone else has accessed those files?"

"Sure." He leaned his head to the side and called to a man sitting beside a pair of computer screens. "Ari, I need you to pull a couple of audio files for us."

The guy looked like he hadn't slept in a week. "Which ones?" His eyes remained glued to the screen on the left, which contained a panel of dispatch codes and a map of Denver with digital blips representing the current GPS location of the city's emergency vehicles.

Cowler ambled toward the man's desk. "Double homicides."

Ari turned to the screen on his right and quickly scrolled through the database of the week's digitally recorded calls. "Do you know the times?" Even though Ari looked over thirty, his face was covered with acne. The only things on his desk that showed he had a life outside of this room were a Star Trooper action figure, a Semper Fi plaque for ten years of service, and a silver ceramic dragon with outstretched wings.

I watched the call times scroll down the screen. "There." I pointed to an entry from Thursday afternoon. "And there." I identified the second call.

Ari tapped at the keyboard and brought up the first file. Cowler studied the screen. "Nope, reference number doesn't show anyone else accessing the files, except the medical examiner's office. But that's typical for them to do before an autopsy."

"Let's hear the first call," I said.

As Ari played the audio, the automated live-read transcription scrolled across the screen:

EMS: "This is 911. How—"

CALLER: "I have something to tell you. I need you to listen carefully."

EMS: "Sir, can you tell me your name?"

CALLER: "There's a body in Bearcroft Mine, three miles south of Idaho Springs. Take Wheelan to Piney Oaks Road. After 5.3 miles, take the dirt road to the right. It ends at the mine. I want you to send—"

EMS: "Who am I speaking with?"

CALLER: "The Rocky Mountain Violent Crimes Task Force. No one enters the mine before they do, or more people will die. You won't find Chris, so don't waste time looking for him."

EMS: *"Sir, are you there now? Are you in any danger—"*
CALLER: *"Dusk is coming. I won't stop until the story is done. Day Four ends on Wednesday."*
EMS: *"Sir—"*
   CALL TERMINATED BY CALLER.

The second audio was similarly concise but listed Taylor's address and Cherry Creek Reservoir as the location for the bodies.

The caller's voice was electronically disguised, and although I couldn't be certain, it sounded like the pitch, pauses, and cadence of the speech on both tapes matched the speech patterns of the man who'd called me earlier in the day.

However, I heard background noise on both recordings. As I was considering what it might have been, Cowler asked me, "What are you hoping to find, exactly?"

Rather than sound arrogant by listing the phonetic and intonation identifiers, I simply said, "I'm trying to listen for anything distinctive, individualized. Anything that could help us match the caller to a suspect." Then I asked Ari to play them again.

Yes, there was definitely something there, although it was a different sound on each tape. "Do we know what those background noises are?" I asked Cowler.

"Background sounds?"

"It sounds like murmuring on the first tape and something else—I'm not sure what—on the second."

"All right, Ryman," Cowler said. "Let's hear 'em one more time." He handed me and Cheyenne headphones, grabbed a pair for himself, plugged them into the system, and then nodded for Ari Ryman to play the audio again.

After we'd listened to the calls again, we all removed our headphones and Cowler shook his head. "It can get loud in here. It just sounds like background noise from the other dispatchers. It's probably nothing."

If there's one thing I've learned over the years it's this: when someone says "it's probably nothing," you should never believe him.

I knew CSU had studied the tapes, but I needed to have them analyzed a little more carefully. However, before I could request a copy of them, a call came in, and the man with the Star Trooper action figure took a quick gulp from a well-worn mug filled with gray coffee and spoke into one of his two headset microphones. "911. Please state the nature of your emergency."

We stepped away.

Apart from the ambient noise, I didn't notice anything unusual about the audio messages.

"Well," Cheyenne said to me on our way to the door. "What do you think?"

I tried to hide the discouragement in my voice. "The phonemes seem to match the ones used by the man who called me earlier in the day, but with the voice distortion the caller used, I doubt I'd be able to recognize the speaker's natural voice if I heard it. I'm still wondering how the author of the online article found out the wording from the calls."

"So am I."

Cowler led us to the door, and I was about to hand him my card and ask him to email me a copy of the audio files and transcriptions but realized that would just take more time—something we didn't have. So instead I asked him if I could use one of the computers for a minute.

He shrugged. "Sure, we have one set aside for DPD use. Right over here."

He led me to one of the empty work stations at the far end of the room.

80

After I'd taken a seat, Cowler showed me how to pull up the audio files. I clicked past the hyperlinks to the Federal Digital Database's GPS and address locators until I came to the audio archives, then I emailed a copy of both the files and transcriptions, to myself and to Angela Knight at the FBI cybercrime division.

I added a request for Angela to run the audio for the calls through a voice spectrograph. "See if you can isolate that background noise for me," I wrote. "And as usual, I need this ASAP. —Pat."

I thanked Cowler, and as Cheyenne and I entered the hallway, I glanced at my watch and realized I needed to get moving if I were going to have time to grab my luggage from home, say good-bye to Tessa, and then catch my flight.

"I have to go," I told her.

"Wait," she said. "Swing by my car first. It'll only take a minute. There's something I've been wanting to give you."

Amy Lynn was putting another video in for Jayson to watch when a call came through on her BlackBerry. She dug it out. "Yes?"

"They came by." It was Ari. He sounded frantic. "What did you write?"

She turned on the television and set a box of snack crackers on the floor for the boy to eat. "Who came by?" She'd lowered her voice. "What are you talking about?"

"Some detectives. You wrote something about—"

"Just calm down. OK?" She stepped away from the television.

"I just don't want anyone to find out that we talked."

"I know."

"Mommy," Jayson said. "Can I watch—"

"Shh!" she quieted him. "You should know better than to interrupt me when I'm talking on the phone." Then she spoke to Ari again. "I'll do some checking, make sure there's no way to link things to you. I'll call you later."

She ended the call without waiting for his reply.

And she smiled.

So, her article was stirring things up. Good.

Time to start working on the second installment.

81

Three minutes after leaving the dispatch office, I was standing beside Cheyenne's Saturn and she was handing me the St. Francis of Assisi pendant that she'd had hanging from her rearview mirror. "What's this for?" I asked.

"St. Francis is the patron saint of the archdiocese of Denver," she explained. "And last year I found out he's also the patron saint against dying alone. I think that's the worst way to die, so I keep this as a . . . well, it helps me remember why I do what I do. No one should have to die alone."

She paused for a moment and then recited the words I'd read the day before from Keats's poem about the pot of basil: "'For Isabel, sweet Isabel, will die; will die a death too lone and incomplete.' When you read that yesterday, I thought of the pendant, but I kept forgetting to give it to you."

"I can't take this, it's—"

"Please. I thought that if you had this at Basque's trial, it wouldn't hurt. I don't know . . . I just . . . As a reminder. I want you to have it. I can get another one easy enough."

Even though she'd mentioned yesterday that she'd gone to Catholic school, I could see now that she was much more devoted to her faith than I would have guessed. She must have noticed my surprise because she said, "What's wrong?"

"I'm just a little . . . I didn't know you were so religious."

"Hard to pigeonhole, remember?"

"Right." I didn't really believe in relics, praying to saints, or good luck charms, but the gesture meant a lot to me. "Thank you." I slipped the pendant into my pocket.

A moment passed. "Well," she said. "I'm going to swing over to visit Kelsey Nash, see how she's doing; then maybe check in with the officers who are keeping an eye on Bryant."

I realized that my feelings for Cheyenne were growing stronger and more intense by the hour, and I began to wonder how much the stress from the case might be affecting my attraction to her—maybe my heart was reaching out to her because it needed something she seemed to offer—comfort, strength, intimacy. Probably all three.

"I'll have Tessa's cell with me," I said. "Keep me up to speed, OK?"

"I'll call you in the morning."

I gave her the number, and she programmed it into her phone. She looked like she wanted to say more.

I hated to consider the possibility that I was using her as a crutch, but I couldn't shake the feeling that I was.

"I should go," I said hastily.

"Yeah."

Then, before the conversation could slip into anything more personal, I said a hurried good-bye and left for my car.

And I didn't look back because I was afraid she might be watching me, and even though part of me hoped that she was, another part of me had started to wonder if it might be better for both of us if she wasn't.

Tessa reached the entry dated November 15 of her mother's sophomore year at the University of Minnesota—just two months before she was conceived.

And her mom was still seeing Brad.

Tessa didn't know if he was her father, but it was appearing more and more likely that he was, and whenever she read his name she began to feel that old mixture of pain, anger, and heartache that she felt whenever she thought of her absentee dad.

Then she read:

November 29

No, no, no, no, no!
So he tells me today he likes this other girl, that he's just "not into me anymore." Not into me anymore??!! We've been going out for six months! And why did he have to tell me he likes someone else? Why couldn't he have just said it's over? Why did he have to mention her—

The entry ended abruptly, but then her mother spent the next dozen or so entries sorting through her feelings about the breakup, and Tessa discovered that her mom had done pretty much the same things she did when she broke up with a guy—ranted, cried, pretended that she'd never liked him in the first place, and then found another guy a little too quickly and fell for him a little too hard.

And that's what happened to her mother on December 20th.

This guy's name was Paul.

Tessa felt a wisp of fear and anticipation flutter through her, and she just couldn't wait anymore. She had to know. She scanned the pages. Raced through the next few weeks.

Into January—her mother broke up with Paul. But they'd slept together a few times. So, unless there was someone else she hadn't written about—

Then February, March.

Her mom had started getting queasy, sick more and more often. *Yes, it has to be him.*

April.

She'd missed her last couple periods, wasn't ready for exams, just wanted vacation to come and was trying to find a job for the summer—

If there was someone else, if she'd slept with someone else, she would have said so . . .

And then Tessa read the entry her mother had written on May 5th, and the world tipped upside down.

> Dear Diary,
> This morning I found out I'm pregnant. It's Paul's. I don't know what to do. I can't have a baby. I can't! This was the worst day of my life.

And Tessa sat motionless, speechless, staring at the page.

Obviously it would be hard for a teenager to hear that she's going to be a single mom. Obviously. Tessa knew that. But still, the words knifed through her.

"This was the worst day of my life."

Her throat tightened so much that she could barely breathe, and her fingers were shaking as she turned the page.

But the next entry was not written by her mother.

Instead, it was a handwritten letter pasted onto the page.

A letter from Paul.

82

Christie,
  I'm sorry for how things are, for how they've been.
But please, I'm the father. Don't do this. I'll do whatever
you want—pay the medical bills, help raise the baby, find
someone to adopt it, but please don't do this. Whatever
you think of me, I'm a jerk, OK, I'm a loser, but let me do
something right here. Let me help. Let me do one good thing.
Please, keep our baby.
—Paul

Tessa did not breathe for a long time. She let her eyes walk through the words two, three times.

All of her life she had hated her father, had thought that he didn't want anything to do with her. So now, even though the main intent of the letter should have probably struck her the most, her initial reaction was shock that her biological father, her real father, had wanted to be part of her life.

His name is Paul.

Your dad's name is Paul. And he wanted to help raise you.

But then the deeper, more obvious impact of the words settled in.

"*Please don't do this . . .*" he'd written. "*I'm the father.*"

"*I'll do whatever you want—pay the medical bills, help raise the baby, find someone to adopt it, but please don't do this.*"

"No . . ." she whispered. "Oh, please no."

"*Keep our baby.*"

The truth slammed into her.

Harsh and brutal.

Her mother, the person Tessa had loved and trusted more than anyone else on the planet, had wanted to abort her and her father, the man she'd always hated, had begged to save her life.

83

Everything Tessa had believed about her mother and her father, all of it, everything, had been a lie.

A lie.

A lie—

The front door to the house banged open, and she heard Patrick's voice: "Hey, guys. I came to say good-bye."

He knew about this. He had to have known!

She snatched up the diary and, using her finger to mark the place, stormed downstairs and into the living room. Patrick stood beside the door. "So, Raven, how's the—"

"What do you know about this?" She held up the diary.

"What do you mean?"

Martha emerged from the kitchen.

"Tell me. Don't lie to me," Tessa said to him. "Did you read it?"

"I told you before, I didn't read it. What's going on?"

"Did you know about this!" She flipped the diary to Paul's letter. "It's a letter from my dad, my real dad. And he's telling Mom that he doesn't want her to get a . . . a . . ." Her voice broke apart, and she couldn't finish her sentence.

Patrick looked at the page but didn't answer.

"Did you know!"

"Here," he said softly. "Let me see that." He took the diary from her and Martha eased a few quiet steps toward them, and then everything sort of came to a standstill while Patrick read the letter.

After a few moments he slowly closed the diary and handed it back to her. "I'm not sure what to say."

"Huh, imagine that."

"You have to remember how much your mother loved you."

"Oh, wow? Really? I guess that's why she wanted to abort me, then—because she loved me so much."

"Listen, she did love you. You know that. It's not right to—"

"To do what? Judge her? She wrote that the day she found out she was pregnant was the worst day of her life. What is there to judge? She didn't want me!"

"She did want you." Patrick reached for her shoulder, but she pulled back. "She was a loving woman, a caring woman—"

"No."

"But she was human."

"Stop it."

"Just as human as you or me. And she—"

"Stop it! I know what you're trying to do. It's not gonna work."

"Tessa." His voice had become firm, but she could tell he wasn't mad. Not really. "I know you're upset, but just stop and listen for a second. Please. She never regretted having you. She told me that you were the best thing that ever happened to her. She told me that before she died."

"June 3rd, Patrick," she said, and she could feel something deep inside of her cracking. "Paul wrote that letter on June 3rd. You know when my birthday is, right? So, do the math. Mom was twenty weeks along when he wrote this letter. You know what that means."

"Tessa. Please don't do this."

"My heart was beating. My brain was working. I could learn things. I could feel pain. Be calmed by music, experience mood swings." She could hear the hurt filling her voice, but she didn't care, didn't try to hide anything anymore. "I could have been delivered and survived, but—"

"Tessa—"

"You know what they do in a late-term abortion? Maybe a D & E? Maybe she could have done that to 'get it taken care of.' They insert a clamp up through the uterus, grab a part of the body, and they—"

"Shh," Martha said.

"—pull it apart—"

Patrick shook his head. "Tessa—"

"—piece by piece and then they crush the head and suction out the pieces. Or a D & X? Stick a surgical scissors in right here." Tessa pointed at the base of her skull. Her finger was trembling. "It would have been right here on me. Right here! They pry open a hole . . . and insert a . . ."

Martha rested her hand gently on Tessa's shoulder. "Don't think about such—"

"Then after they've suctioned out the brains . . . the skull collapses and they . . . they can finally . . ." She felt dizzy, physically ill, and she couldn't say the words. She just couldn't.

Patrick drew her into his arms, and this time she let him. And then she felt Martha holding her too, her frail arm bent around her shoulder. And she was glad they were there.

But that was all she was glad about.

Tessa leaned her face against her stepfather's chest.

And trembled as she cried.

84

I tried to comfort Tessa but had no idea what to say, so I just hugged her and told her that I loved her and tried to think of something, anything that I could do to help.

Moments passed.

My mother found a box of tissues for Tessa, and after a little while she began to control her breathing again.

Finally, she pulled away from me, wiped a handful of tissues across her face, and said softly, "I wish I never read it. The diary. I wish . . ."

"I'm so sorry, Tessa. If I'd known it would hurt you, I never would have given it to you. You have to believe me."

She took a small breath. "I need to be alone." Then she left for her room, and I thought she might slam the bedroom door, but instead I heard it close gently.

So gently that, in a way, it frightened me.

It wasn't at all clear to me what to do—give her some space, or go to her, see if there was something more I could say.

In the past, Tessa had struggled with cutting as a way to cope, and although she'd mostly moved past it, I was concerned for her and I didn't like the idea of standing here doing nothing.

I walked upstairs. Knocked softly on her door.

"Leave me alone." I could tell that she was crying again.

My mother was climbing the stairs to join me.

"Please, Tessa," I said.

"Just leave me alone. I want to be alone."

I tried the doorknob. Locked. "C'mon. Unlock the door."

"I'm OK. I just wanna be by myself."

As I stood there trying to figure out how to solve things, my mother approached and whispered, "She needs some time, Patrick. Let her be for now. She'll come out when she's ready."

"How do you know?" I kept my voice low enough so that Tessa wouldn't hear. "Maybe I can—"

"Listen to your mother," Tessa called from inside her bedroom.

I blinked.

Martha raised a gentle, knowing eyebrow.

"Did you hear me?" Tessa said.

"Yes."

Knowingly, my mother patted my arm and then turned to leave.

"I guess I'll be downstairs then," I told Tessa through the door. "In the kitchen. I won't leave for the airport until you're ready for me to go, OK?"

No response.

I stood in the hallway for a few more minutes, sorting through everything, then Tessa called through the wall, "Don't lurk," and I finally left to join my mother in the kitchen.

I looked at my watch.

As much as I wanted to stay and work through things with Tessa, I definitely needed to leave in the next twenty minutes if I was going to make my flight.

But that was no longer my priority.

Last night I'd told Cheyenne that Tessa meant the world to me. And now I realized how true that was.

I would stay here if I needed to. Even if I didn't make it to the trial.

Still, I did feel a little guilty and conflicted, because even though I hadn't known about Paul or the letter, one time while we were dating Christie had told me about her decision to abort her child.

85

Christie and I had been going out for about four months when she told me the story.

We were both single and in our midthirties and things were getting serious, so we'd finally decided to get everything on the table, see if there was anything in our respective pasts that would make the other person shy away from something long term.

And we chose to share those secrets on a hike in the Adirondacks on a crisp and cool Sunday afternoon in September.

We'd been hiking for a few hours, slowly revealing more and more intimate details from our lives, when I lost the trail and ended up spending nearly half an hour leading her aimlessly through the underbrush looking for it. Finally, I was so irritated at myself that I kicked a log. "OK. Here's one: sometimes I can get impatient."

"Really?"

"Yes." I shoved a branch out of the way. Hard. It snapped back toward Christie, and thankfully she was far enough behind me so that it didn't smack her in the face. "And moody."

"Huh." I couldn't quite read her tone. "I'll have to keep an eye out for that."

Then I found something that might have been a trail, at least at one time, and it was leading vaguely in the direction we wanted to go, so I decided to give it a shot.

As we walked, I told her about the problems I'd had over the years getting along with my older brother, who owned a bait shop in Wisconsin and spent most of his time muskie fishing when he could have been doing something meaningful with his life.

"Well." She stepped over a fallen tree lying across our path. "At least you're not judgmental."

"One of my few virtues."

Then I admitted to a tendency of getting caught up a little too much in my work. Occasionally.

Once in a while.

And then, though it was a little embarrassing, I talked about dealing with some of the temptations all single guys face.

She listened quietly, asked a few questions, but didn't act as if any of this was a big surprise. And then she told me about how she wasn't really good with money and had built up almost twenty thousand dollars of credit card debt and how she hated housework and sometimes got panic attacks when she was really stressed.

The trail ended.

She'd tried to commit suicide twice in high school; she told me that too. And after a long pause, she added that she wasn't able to have any more children.

Then we were both silent.

I got the impression she wasn't finished sharing, so I waited for her to speak. After walking about a hundred meters she suggested we backtrack and as we turned around she said, "I never told you about when I was pregnant with Tessa. Maybe I should have."

We came to an overlook, but she kept walking.

"I was nineteen when I found out I was expecting. I was scared and single, and I wasn't in love with her father." She paused, then added, "And I was ashamed too. My parents didn't take sex outside of marriage lightly. At the time I didn't understand their point of view. Since then, well . . ."

She didn't need to elaborate; I knew she was a strong believer, a woman unashamed of her faith and her Lord, and from the very beginning of our relationship, she'd wanted us to remain, as she put it, "chaste." I'd respected her convictions, although it hadn't made for an easy couple of months.

"In any case"—she'd stopped hiking now and was looking at

the way the trail curved to the east—"I took a long time to decide. But finally, I made an appointment at the clinic: 10:00 a.m. and I even arrived early."

She was staring past me, toward a horizon that lay hidden and out of sight beyond the trees.

"While I was waiting, I started paging through the magazines that were piled on the table between the chairs and as I flipped through them, I started noticing all these ads for laundry detergent and Kool-Aid and vacations at Disneyland. And every ad seemed to have a child in it: holding up a dirty sock, drinking from a Dixie cup, riding down a water slide, but they didn't seem like advertisements for those things anymore. They seemed like ads for kids."

I listened quietly. Took her hand. She curled her fingers around mine.

"I started thinking about all the things a mom deals with—the diapers and the colic and the sleepless nights, the loneliness and the sacrifices. But then, the other things too: seeing my baby walk for the first time, birthday parties, dropping her off on the first day of school, helping her pick out a prom dress."

"It's OK," I said. "We can talk about this some other time."

A tear formed in her eye, and she smoothed it away. "I couldn't do it, Pat. I couldn't go through with it. I went back to my apartment—I took that magazine with me. And then, since I was due in the fall, I canceled my college enrollment and started working fulltime to earn enough money to have the baby." She paused. "It was always just . . . We never had a lot."

"I know."

Christie had never finished college, never owned a home, always worked two jobs. By her tone of voice I could tell she wasn't complaining, but I could also tell how profoundly her choice to have Tessa had changed the entire course of her life. "You gave up a lot," I said softly.

"That's what I thought too," she said. "Until the first time I held Tessa in my arms."

By the time we found the trail twenty minutes later, I'd decided that I would ask Christie Rose Ellis to marry me as soon as I'd picked out a ring.

As a young woman she'd been scared and alone and desperate but had still found the resolve to give up her dreams and pour them into someone else. And she'd done it for fifteen years, even though it had never been easy. A woman who would do that was a woman I wanted to spend the rest of my life with.

As it turned out, though, we only had a few more months together.

Yet, even when she was dying she never told me the name of Tessa's father. She just told me that he was no longer a part of their lives. "You have to trust me on this, Pat, please. It's best for everyone if he just remains a part of the past."

That was all.

And up until fifteen minutes ago when Tessa showed me Paul's letter, that had been enough.

But now, it no longer seemed like it was.

86

Tessa lay on her bed, curled on her side.

She'd stopped crying for the moment, but the pain inside of her was as sharp and real as ever. She couldn't stop thinking about her mom's decision to abort her and she couldn't stop thinking about what happens in abortions. She wished she could just think about it all in the safe, innocuous terms people use: of "terminating a pregnancy" by "having a procedure" to "remove a fetus." But when you know what happens, what really happens, you can't help but hurt, can't help but *feel*.

Especially when you find out those things were going to happen to you.

For a long, teetering moment she wrestled with the urge to get out a razor blade and slice at the emotions pulsing just beneath her skin, but finally, she pulled out her notebook instead, and as soon as her pen touched the paper, the words spilled out.

> i float in stillness—
> the black before-life life.
> somewhere, a heartbeat comforts me;
> and i sleep
> in the sweet, promising riddle of time.
>
> but silence and sirens
> wrap their arms around me,
> whispers of knives and needles
> seep into my skin;
> and in the end,
>   nothing remains except the echoes,

of a fledgling soul dropping alone
into the belly of the day.

Tessa looked at the words, scratched a few out, tinkered with a
couple of the lines, and it felt good to write. Good to get the harsh
images out of her mind.

But even that didn't make the pain go away.

She set the notebook aside and picked up the diary. Stared at
it.

OK. So her mom had eventually changed her mind and had
her baby. Great. Wonderful. But she hadn't *wanted* to deliver her,
that was the point, and Tessa just couldn't deal with the thought
of reading even one more word about how much her mom hated
the idea of having her in her life.

She targeted the trash can on the other side of the room and
launched the diary into it, where it bounced to the bottom with a
thick, angry thud.

Then she pulled out the razor blade she kept hidden in her purse.
She hadn't self-inflicted in a long time, but it always seemed to
help. At least a little.

She rolled up her sleeve, revealing the row of thin, two-inch-
long scars on her forearm. She placed the blade against her arm,
just below the lowest scar.

Stared at it.

She knew that cutting was just a way of exchanging one pain for
another, of course she knew that, but at least it would get her mind
off the diary, at least it was something she could do.

And so she did.

87

"Patrick," my mother said. "You really need to leave for your flight."

Over the last few minutes as I'd thought about Christie, I'd managed to put the case out of my mind, but when my mother said those words, it all came back: the whispering voices, Basque's trial and all the blood and all the bodies.

"Patrick," she said again.

"I know."

My flight left in less than an hour.

I put a call through to United Airlines but found out that all the flights for the rest of the day were already overbooked. Even with my FBI clearance they weren't able to get me a seat.

My mother watched me hang up the phone. "Tessa needs me here," I said. "I'm not going to leave her."

"I'll take care of her. It might be better, considering . . . I just mean that since I'm a woman, she might feel more comfortable . . ."

"I understand, but—"

"It's OK." It was Tessa's voice, at the bottom of the stairs. "You can go, Patrick. I'm fine."

I looked over and saw her standing with one foot on the bottom step and one on the floor.

"Tessa, are you all right?"

She nodded.

"Giving you the diary. I thought it would help."

"It's not that. It's not you. It's Mom."

Even though I understood where she was coming from, it hurt to hear her say those words. "I'm sorry all this has happened."

"It's not your fault." She toed at the carpet for a moment, then looked at me again. "This killer, this guy on trial, you told me that he did terrible things to people, right? To women?"

I remembered the conversation I'd had with her on Friday morning. "Yes."

"And that he made you question the amount of evil we're capable of doing to each other? And that it frightened you?" I wondered if the graphic descriptions of abortions she'd given me twenty minutes earlier were affecting the emotional intensity I heard in every one of her words.

"Yes."

"Then don't let him hurt any more women," she said. "Don't worry about me. I'll be OK here with Martha and the two cops outside who so cleverly switched cars to disguise themselves."

Great.

"Are you sure? Because—"

"Get going already, before you miss your flight."

She'd convinced me. I kissed her on the forehead and told her that I'd be back as soon as I could, by six tomorrow—unless things didn't go as planned—and that I loved her.

"You too," she said softly.

Then I thanked my mother for letting Tessa stay with her, and she told me of course and not to worry, and then I grabbed my suitcase and computer bag, climbed into my car, and drove through the gray Colorado day to the airport.

Just as the first snowflakes began to fall.

3:48 p.m.

225,341 hits.

That's how many Amy Lynn had gotten since posting the article three hours earlier.

She was almost giddy.

The whole idea of a murderer basing his ten crimes on an ancient book gave her the perfect angle for a series of online articles—and for the true crime book she'd already started outlining. And coming up with the moniker "The Day Four Killer" was nothing short of brilliant.

The cable news networks had picked up on it and the entire Denver metroplex was bracing for what one cable anchorman called "The next troubling saga of unimaginable evil."

And Amy Lynn loved every minute of it.

Ever since Ari called her, she'd been doing what she did best, poking around and digging up facts that she wasn't supposed to find out about.

And if she could just track down a little more background about some of the victims, she could have the second article ready to post by tomorrow morning.

She was online, fact-checking the times of the murders, when her phone vibrated. Reggie.

"Hey, dear," she said, playing the role of the loving wife.

"It was you, wasn't it?" His voice was dark and accusatory. "You posted that article? Tell me the truth."

"What article?"

"The one on the Internet. The one everyone is talking about. About the homicides."

"Of course not, no. Rhodes told me not to write about the killings." And she found that it wasn't difficult to say the words. Eventually, after she found a publisher, she could straighten things out with Reggie. Smooth things over, but for now, she needed some space. "Besides, I've been busy on this baseball piece." She'd turned that in yesterday, but it seemed like a reasonable thing to say.

Silence.

"I swear, Reggie."

Still no reply.

"I wouldn't lie to you. You know that."

Finally, he sighed softly. "OK, you're right. It's just, I don't want you involved with any of this."

"I know."

"You know how much I love you. How much I want to protect you."

Good grief.

"I know."

"It's just, I keep thinking I should be the one to protect you and Jayson, instead of some feds." He didn't bother hiding his contempt for the FBI. And then, he set about once again trying to convince her that she didn't need to stay in protective custody. "I could take a few days off. I can take care of you—"

"I know you can."

"How about this: I'll take off work tomorrow. We'll all go home. We'll spend the day together as a family."

She mulled over his proposal and was surprised to find herself actually considering it.

Yes, she'd enjoyed the privacy of being able to work in solitude at the safe house today, but tomorrow she would probably need to get out, follow some leads, do some interviews . . .

"Reggie, I think it'd be great to be with you, but I don't want us to be bothered with all these cops and agents following us around—"

"I can take care of that."

"Are you sure?"

"Yes. Of course."

"I'll leave as long as it's only you."

"Great, that's great. I get off at six tonight. I can pick you up then."

"No. My car is here, remember? I'll meet you at home."

A slight pause. "Yes. OK. It's going to be better this way. You'll see."

They said good-bye and ended the call.

So, this might be just what she needed.

Even if the feds did send some agents to follow her home, once

Reggie got there he could get rid of them. She'd make sure that he did. And then, tomorrow when it was only Reggie with her, she would find a way to slip away. He and Jayson could have a Daddy Day.

Oh yes. This was going to work out very well.

She ignored Jayson's whining in the other room and began to edit her next article.

88

Tessa's arm hurt.

She hadn't been cutting as much recently, and she'd pressed the blade a little too hard. The blood totally weirded her out, and it seemed like there was more than there should have been, and in the end, she'd had to bandage the cut.

But at least Patrick and Martha didn't know. They would have probably been mad, or worse, disappointed.

And the bummer thing was, it hadn't really helped.

Not really.

Half an hour ago, after Patrick left for the airport, she'd driven to her house with Martha to pick up her schoolbooks and clothes. The undercover cops followed them the whole way, ever so stealthily.

How nice.

From past experience, she knew that when Patrick testified at a trial he was sometimes called back to the stand several days in a row, so she wasn't exactly convinced he was going to make it home by Monday afternoon. She threw a couple extra changes of clothes into an overnight bag just in case. Then she grabbed her jewelry box and the Rubik's Cube.

On the drive back to Martha's, she was glad her step-grandmother didn't give her any trite advice on how to deal with everything, because it wouldn't have helped. Instead, Martha just drove quietly beside her, and it seemed to Tessa that maybe that was exactly what she needed.

But maybe it wasn't, because all the junk was still there inside her.

The twisted, angry feelings weren't going away. Not at all.

By the time they made it to Martha's house, Tessa had realized she definitely needed a way to keep herself from thinking about her arm and her mom and her dad and the pot of basil and everything that had happened in the last couple days.

Writing didn't seem to do it. Cutting hadn't really helped.

She needed something else to think about.

Yesterday, she'd promised Dora that she would read the story of Pandora's Box this week.

That should do it.

She surfed to an online version and pulled it up.

It didn't take her long at all to read four different versions of the story of Prometheus and Pandora, and in the end she found that Dora had been right—the story did have a surprise ending. She'd expected that the last thing out of the box might have been disease or famine or death, but it wasn't.

No, actually it was the opposite—

"Is there anything you need, Tessa?" Martha called up the stairs.

"No, I'm good."

As she slid her laptop aside, she noticed her stack of textbooks staring at her, and she remembered her exams coming up in the morning. Normally, she could pretty much ace her tests without studying, but maybe that was just what she needed to do to get her mind off everything.

So Tessa pulled out her trig book and tried to disappear into the numbers and equations, but her thoughts kept drifting back to Paul, the man who'd written to her mother and begged to be a part of her life. And as she thought of him, she realized that her arm was no longer the part of her that hurt the most.

———————————————■———————————————

5:02 p.m.

It was starting to look like I wouldn't be leaving Denver tonight.

Already our flight had been delayed for nearly an hour because of the late-season snowstorm rolling down the Rockies, and the gate agent kept reassuring us that we would still be taking off, but with the amount of snow falling on the tarmac I had my doubts.

At first as I'd waited, I called to check on Tessa. My mother assured me that she'd spoken with her only a few minutes earlier and that she was fine and reading in her bedroom.

Then, since it looked like I'd be using Tessa's phone at least until tomorrow evening, if not longer, I logged in to my federal account and synched her cell with my address book so I would have access to all of my contacts.

When I hung up, I saw I'd missed a call from Cheyenne, so I gave her a shout, and she informed me that she'd just left Jake's second briefing and that it had been "just as informative and productive as the first."

"Too bad I missed it. Any word on Bryant?"

"Here's the thing: when he left the *Denver News* building, Benjamin Rhodes was with him."

"Rhodes? Amy Lynn's boss?"

"Yes. They stopped for a late lunch at a Mexican place near DU and then went to Bryant's house. I just spoke with one of the officers assigned to watch them. He told me that both men are still there."

Interesting.

Then Cheyenne told me that she would call me as soon as she knew more, and after we ended the call, I decided to follow up on Dr. Bryant. I typed in the IP address I'd gotten from his computer when we were at his house and remotely logged on to his system.

He wasn't online at the moment, but I was able to access his browser's Internet history.

And that's where I found the porn sites.

More than a hundred of them—all hardcore S & M sites that exclusively featured men.

I thought about my conversation with Bryant, the pot of coffee he'd brewed, his dinner meeting with Rhodes, his interest in homosexual porn . . .

So, Rhodes and Bryant . . . ?

All loose threads. Nothing solid. But enough to pique my interest.

I was sorting through the possible implications when the gate agent announced that the flight was now boarding, and that because of the delay, they were expediting the boarding process and welcoming passengers in all seats, all rows, to board.

So we boarded. And I let my thoughts flip through the facts of the case.

And less than twenty minutes later we were in the air and I was on my way back to Basque's trial in Chicago.

———————————◼———————————

Giovanni had placed the poison earlier in the afternoon and then driven to Bearcroft Mine.

Now, he turned on his headlamp and entered the tunnel on the west side of the mountain.

This entrance didn't appear on any of the maps still in circulation. And, while it was possible someone had heard about it, Giovanni believed it was far more likely that, now that Thomas Bennett, the mine's former owner, was dead, he was the only person alive who knew it was there.

It took him nearly half an hour to maneuver through the network of tunnels and arrive at the mine's second-lowest passageway.

He lit a lantern and hung it from a hook on one of the wooden beams buttressing the ceiling.

The tunnel ended just a few feet to his right, and beside him was the six-foot-by-six-foot platform that the miners in the 1800s had used to lower the ore carts into the tunnel thirty feet further down. The platform hung from a rope looped through a double pulley attached to the beam above Giovanni's head. He'd replaced the aging hemp rope with a new static nylon one last month. The pulleys reduced the force needed to raise and lower the platform so that a single person could manage it by himself.

A single miner.

A single murderer.

A single storyteller.

He stepped onto the platform, held one end of the rope, and then released the lever on the beam above him. A crude cam device next to the pulleys pressed against the rope, controlling the rate of the platform's descent.

Slowly, he began to lower himself down the shaft.

The tunnel he was heading toward had never been completed when the mine was abandoned in the early 1900s. It spanned only forty feet, and was less than six feet high, which meant that once Patrick Bowers was sealed inside, he wouldn't be able to stand up for the rest of his life.

As he descended, Giovanni inspected the line of plastic explosives he'd threaded down the walls of the shaft. Even though he had no formal explosive ordnance training, with his professional contacts it hadn't been difficult to acquire the C-4 and learn enough rudimentary skills to rig the shaft to blow. He'd practiced in other abandoned mines over the last few months and had become relatively proficient at sealing shut mine shafts.

When he reached the bottom, he tied off the rope, synched his handheld detonator with the four wireless receivers attached to the C-4, and then looked around.

Months ago when he'd first begun investigating this mine, apart from a few pieces of rusting mining equipment, this tunnel had been completely empty, but now it was stocked with enough food and bottled water to keep one person alive for ten to twelve weeks.

After all, it wouldn't have been nearly as satisfying of a climax if Agent Bowers died too quickly after being buried alive.

If the access shaft had been located in the middle of the tunnel, Giovanni might have been concerned about the entire tunnel collapsing when the shaft blew, but since it was on the end and he'd reinforced the tunnel's ceiling braces, he was confident that the tunnel would withstand the explosion.

One more thing to check.

He pulled out the Matheson Analyzer.

When air moves through space it acts like a fluid, so using the Matheson, he tested the computational fluid dynamics of the oxygen level coming from the air flow of a two-inch wide rift in the wall, taking into account that the access shaft would be sealed. It took the mechanism only a few moments to make the calculations.

Yes, the oxygen would be adequate. Bowers would survive until he either starved to death or eventually went insane.

Early in his planning, Giovanni had decided that it would be more frightening for Bowers to see his tomb for himself, to search the walls, the ceiling, the ground for some possible way out, but to find none. And then, to have his light slowly fade. Slowly die as his small, enclosed world was swallowed in darkness forever. So, when the time came, Giovanni would let his captive have a flashlight.

It would make for a much better ending.

Giovanni clicked off his light and let the thick, living darkness sweep over him. He opened and closed his eyes. No visible difference.

This is what it would be like for Bowers in the end.

He listened to his heartbeat, to the steady, even sound of his breathing.

At last, light back on, he checked his watch.

He still had a forty-five-minute drive to Denver.

Tomorrow, before taking care of Bowers, he would be placing two people in his storage unit, and he needed to make sure all the preparations were in place for their stay. So he took one last look around the tunnel that Bowers would die in at the climax of his tale, then Giovanni left Bearcroft Mine and drove through the softly falling snow to Denver.

89

Although I could think of a thousand things I'd rather have been doing, I spent the flight to Chicago typing up my report about the courthouse incident on Friday for FBI Assistant Executive Director Margaret Wellington, detailing the circumstances involving Grant Sikora's death.

When we arrived at O'Hare, I took a moment to email it to her before leaving the airport.

With my email program open, I noticed there weren't any messages from Calvin. But there was one from Angela Knight, my friend in the FBI's cybercrime division:

> Pat,
>
> About those 911 calls.
> We couldn't backtrace either of them. Nothing on the call to your landline either. Whoever made them knew how to cover his tracks.
> Not much on the voice spectrograph of the 911 tapes either, but I can tell you it was the same person on each call.
> The background noise on the first call is internal feedback from the dispatch office. The sound on the second tape is rain falling on the windshield of a car. And no, I can't tell you the make and year—although I am working on it.
> That's it. More later. Be well.
>
> —AK

So, Cowler had been right about the background sounds on the first tape, and while the rain on the second audio didn't prove that John was in Chicago when the call was made, since a storm had been blowing through the city that morning, it did corroborate the hypothesis that he was.

I checked my voicemail.

Nothing.

Then I grabbed my bags, flagged a cab, and rode to my hotel.

Reggie was several hours late getting home from work, but when he finally arrived, Amy Lynn met him with a kiss, told him how good it was to see him, and then pointed out the window to the pair of agents sitting in a car beside the curb. "Let those guys go. I'll be safe with you. You can protect me."

"All right," Reggie said gallantly, "I'll take care of them."

He stepped outside.

Yes, Amy Lynn would spend the night laughing at Reggie's jokes, responding to his touch, pleasing him, so that tomorrow when she needed some time by herself, he would be more trusting, less wary, and it would be easier for her to slip away.

Dr. Bryant, the journalism professor who'd taught her so much about how to use people to get a big story, would have been proud of her approach.

A few moments later, Reggie returned and smiled. "All taken care of."

She gave him a sly grin. "Now, it's just the two of us."

"And Jayson."

"Right," she clarified. "And Jayson."

"But, we can tuck him in early."

"Perfect."

She took Reggie's hand.

Yes, tonight she would be his. And then tomorrow she would be free.

90

The Hyatt Regency Hotel
Chicago, Illinois
10:10 p.m. Central Time

I took a few minutes to unpack, and then, since my body was still on Denver time and I wasn't ready for bed, I decided to put in a little time on the case. I set my laptop on the desk, and, to make room for my notes, I started clearing off the notepad, hotel directory, and local travel guides when I noticed the Gideon Bible beside the room phone.

I paused.

And I remembered.

At the conclusion of my video chat with Richard Basque earlier in the day, he'd referenced a biblical passage, one that I hadn't yet taken the time to read.

I thought I remembered the reference, but I wanted to confirm that I was right, so I accessed the video file of our conversation and played the final seconds.

"I'll take my chances. Good-bye, Richard," I'd said.

"I'll be praying for you. Remember, Exodus 1:15–21. Remember—"

And that's when I'd hung up.

I paged through the Bible until I came to the first chapter of Exodus.

The story was about Moses's birth, and I recognized it from my childhood days when my mother had taken me to church.

In the story, the Hebrews were living in Egypt where the king of the land, Pharaoh, became concerned about how numerous their population was becoming. Fearing that they might side with his enemies in a war, he ordered the Hebrew midwives to kill all the boys born to the Hebrew women.

Then I came to verses seventeen through twenty:

> But the midwives feared God, and did not as the king of Egypt commanded them, but saved the men children alive.
>
> And the king of Egypt called for the midwives, and said unto them, "Why have ye done this thing, and have saved the men children alive?"
>
> And the midwives said unto Pharaoh, "Because the Hebrew women are not as the Egyptian women; for they are lively, and are delivered ere the midwives come in unto them."
>
> Therefore God dealt well with the midwives: and the people multiplied, and waxed very mighty.

The next verse reiterated that since the midwives had feared God, he blessed them and gave them families of their own.

I gazed at the verses for a few moments, thinking through the story. The message of the section seemed clear to me: the midwives had broken the law and then lied to protect innocent lives, and as a result, God had blessed them.

I had to let that sink in.

I read and reread the verses and then began thumbing through the Bible, remembering other stories, other examples of the same principle that protecting the innocent is more important than telling the truth.

Rahab lied to protect the Hebrew spies and was honored by God for her choice.

Jonathan lied to his father about David's location to save him from being murdered.

Even Jesus's disciples didn't tell the authorities "the truth, the whole truth, and nothing but the truth" about his whereabouts because they knew it would mean his certain death. The only one who told the whole truth about his location was Judas—the world's most infamous betrayer.

In fact, as I flipped through the Bible and reviewed the stories that I was familiar with, I couldn't find a single example of God being displeased with someone who lied to protect innocent life.

I've always believed God values truth. I'd never doubted that.

But it looked like he valued something else even more.

During the interview Basque had asked me to lie about assaulting him, then told me to remember these Bible verses . . .

A thought.

A shocking thought: maybe Basque did turn to the Lord, after all.

I could hardly believe I was even considering the possibility.

But what if it were true? maybe Richard Basque realized that if I confessed to assaulting him, he would quite possibly be set free. And, despite his newfound spiritual convictions, he might be drawn into his old habits, his old hungers. Maybe he knew that for justice to be done, he needed to remain incarcerated—

Stop it, Pat. Too much speculation. Too many ifs and maybes. That's not how you work. Stick to the facts. Stick to what you know.

No, Basque's motives weren't at issue here, my testimony was.

The midwives lied to protect innocent lives.

That's what mattered to them more than anything else.

And that's what mattered most to me too.

All right then.

I knew what I would say when I took the stand in the morning.

91

I was sliding my laptop into its case, getting ready to head to the lobby for breakfast when I heard my room phone ring. I answered, "Hello?"

"Sorry if I woke you, my boy."

"Calvin! Where have you been?" Exasperation as well as anger found their way into my voice. "I've been trying to get in touch with you all weekend."

"Yes, and I am sorry about that. I've been a bit occupied. Buried myself in my work, I'm afraid. But I've uncovered something that might affect your testimony today." He took a breath. "No doubt you made the connection to Boccaccio's *Decameron* previous to the media revelations regarding the case?"

"Yes." I wondered if Calvin had discovered the link even before I did. "But how did you—"

"What are you calling him? Not 'The Day Four Killer,' I hope."

"John."

Calvin was quiet for a moment. "Yes, that is appropriate." Then he added, "Patrick, I believe he's done it before."

I dropped onto the bed. "You have evidence he's committed prior homicides?"

"Yes, by reenacting other stories. Specifically, 'The Man of Law's Tale' in England last May. The story is from Chaucer's *Canterbury Tales*. As you may know, more than 20 percent of the stories in *The Canterbury Tales* are based on—"

"Yes, yes," I said. "I know: *The Decameron.*"

"Precisely. Well, in lines 428–437 of 'The Man of Law's Tale,' several people are stabbed and then hacked to pieces while seated at a table. I believe your man, John, reenacted this crime and killed four people last year on May 17th at a wedding in Canterbury, and I'm certain the city of the crime was not chosen randomly."

"No," I said numbly, trying to let all of this register. "I'm sure it wasn't."

"Later in the story, a man's throat is slit and the bloody knife is left in his lover's bed. And this very crime occurred the next day, May 18th, in Gloucester."

"How did you figure this out?"

"Research," he said simply. "But there are two more. In the next section of the tale, a man is killed for lying, perhaps by God; the context leaves it open for interpretation, and he falls to the ground so forcefully that his eyes pop out of their sockets." Then he added grimly, "After removing Dr. Roland Smith's eyes on May 19th, John let him live. The professor committed suicide a week later. At the time of his death, he was England's leading expert on Geoffrey Chaucer."

I sat in stunned silence. The implications of what Calvin was saying were staggering.

"And last, in lines 687–688, a false knight is slain. And on May 20th, a man named Byron Night was killed in London, Chaucer's hometown. That one was harder to connect, but—"

"The progression of the crime spree and the timing of the murder would have made the crime too much of a coincidence."

"Spot on."

"Unbelievable."

As Calvin spoke about this last murder, I was reminded that yesterday, immediately before ending his phone call to me, John had said that dusk would arrive today, "just like it did in London."

It's him, Pat. He was connecting the dots for you.

Could there have been more crime sprees? More murders that we didn't know about, perhaps based on the other authors who drew material from Boccaccio—Tennyson, Longfellow, Shakespeare, Faulkner . . . Right now, I couldn't afford to think about that. It was too overwhelming.

"So, before now," I said, "no one linked the crimes in England because each was so different."

"Yes. A different modus operandi, signature, cause of death, as well as no evidentiary connection between the victims or similar motives for the crimes."

"Linkage blindness."

"Exactly."

Even though Calvin's information bore relevance to the killings in Colorado, he'd started the conversation by telling me that his research had uncovered something relevant to my testimony. "Calvin, a minute ago you said this had something to do with today's trial. What did you mean by that?"

"I no longer believe Richard Basque is guilty of the crimes for which he is being tried."

I found myself staring at the floor in shock. "What are you talking about?"

"I believe John was responsible for at least four of the murders, possibly more. I can't go into all of my reasons at the moment. Remember the DNA discrepancies that Professor Lebreau's students at Michigan State found which precipitated Mr. Basque's retrial?"

I anticipated what he was about to say. "You're kidding."

"No, I believe it is the DNA of the man you refer to as John."

"Do you have any proof?"

"I'm still in the process of collecting it."

My mind raced forward and backward through the case. Sorting, analyzing. One moment, everything seemed to make sense, the next moment, nothing did.

If John, rather than Basque, had committed the crimes thirteen years ago, it would explain the DNA discrepancies, as well as the newspaper articles at the ranch: John wouldn't have been chronicling Basque's crimes but rather celebrating his own.

It might also explain the attempt on Basque's life—since, if Richard Basque were dead, the case would in all likelihood go away and John would never come under suspicion.

I tried to wrap my thoughts around everything Calvin had just told me. "Where are you?"

"Denver."

I rubbed my head. "What?"

"I think I might know who John is. I'm going to—"

A rush of adrenaline. "Who?"

"First, I must try to prove myself wrong."

"You have to tell me." My voice had become urgent. Intense.

"I'm sorry, Patrick, but I'm afraid I no longer have the confidence in our system of justice that I used to. Quite frankly—"

"No, Calvin, wait. I'll be back later today. Wait for me. You have to—"

"Hopefully, this case will be resolved by then."

"Listen to me—"

He hung up.

Immediately, I punched in the number for cybercrime to have them trace the call, even though I expected that Calvin would be too careful to let us find him.

But they did find him, or at least the location of the phone he'd used.

The call had come from police headquarters in downtown Denver.

92

I speed-dialed Kurt and told him what was going on. "Calvin's there, right now, at HQ. He just called me from one of your phones."

"Hang on. I'll be back in a sec." As I waited, I thought of what Calvin had told me: one of the victims in England had been the country's leading Chaucer expert.

John told you he was updating Boccaccio's story for our culture . . .
An idea.

I snapped my laptop open, cruised to my media files. Then, while Kurt spoke on another line with the officers at the headquarters' front desk, I clicked to the video I'd taken of the interior of Elwin Daniels's ranch house.

A media player appeared on my screen.

On the phone, I heard Kurt assigning officers to each of the building's exits. Finally, he said to me, "What do you want us to do if we find Dr. Werjonic?"

"Hold him for questioning." I was dragging the cursor along the video. I knew what I was looking for; it would be somewhere in the middle of the footage. "I have reason to believe that Calvin has criminal intent."

A moment of hesitation. "You sure about this?"

Even though Calvin hadn't made any specific threats on the phone, I knew what he'd been implying. "I believe a man's life might be in danger."

I came to the footage of the bathroom.

"All right," Kurt said. "I'm trusting you on this one, Pat; but I can't believe you're telling me to hold Dr. Calvin Werjonic."

The medicine cabinet.

The countertop beside the sink.

I pressed "pause." Enlarged the image as much as I could and found what I was looking for—tiny, almost indistinguishable stippled marks on the four tubes of toothpaste. "And Kurt, get some officers to Dr. Adrian Bryant's and Benjamin Rhodes's homes immediately. Go to Bryant's first."

"You think one of them might be the killer?"

"No. I think they might be the next two victims."

"What?" he exclaimed.

"I'll explain later." I felt helpless being in Chicago when all this was going down in Denver. "But if you find the men, get them to the hospital immediately. I think they've been poisoned. John put the bufotoxin in their toothpaste."

"You're not making any sense, Pat."

"Just do it, Kurt. Move." He told me he'd get back to me as soon as he had more, and I reminded him to call me on Tessa's phone. As I ended the call I noticed the time: 7:14 a.m.

If I were going to arrive at the courthouse before the protestors and journalists descended on it, I needed to get going.

I grabbed my things and made sure I had Cheyenne's St. Francis of Assisi pendant in my pocket, then I checked out of the hotel, hailed a taxi, and rode to the courthouse so that I could commit perjury.

93

Reggie had just stepped into the bathroom for his morning shower when Amy Lynn Greer received the text message on her Blackberry. The person who'd sent it claimed to have inside information about the Day Four Killer and included a phone number for her to call.

Which she promptly did.

"I work for the FBI," a man told her in a hasty, whispered voice. "I'd like to discuss an opportunity with you."

"What sort of—"

"I have access to police files. I can help you if you'll help me. Are you interested in discussing this matter?"

Oh yes. This was good.

"Yes, of course."

"I'll email you an address. Come alone. We meet at noon. Don't be late. And don't post any other articles until we've spoken in person."

"Wait, how do I know you're really with the FBI?"

"You'll have to trust me."

Of course she didn't trust him; she didn't trust anyone. But that didn't mean she couldn't use him. "I'll be there."

And then he hung up.

She heard the water in the shower turn on. Reggie wouldn't be out for at least ten minutes.

This was her chance.

Jayson stepped into the room, eating a handful of Cheerios.

"C'mere," she called to her son. "You can play spelling games until Daddy gets out of the shower. Mommy has to take care of a few things."

"Wha' dings, Mommy?"

"I'll just be in the other room," she lied. "Don't worry."

She positioned her son in front of the computer and pulled up one of the preschool spelling games. The boy would be fine playing on the computer until his father was done showering.

After Jayson was sufficiently preoccupied, she shoved her Blackberry and digital voice recorder into her purse, grabbed her car keys, and then slipped out the back door.

◼

Ridgeland High School lay just ahead.

Tessa hated battling rush hour traffic so she'd been thankful earlier in the morning when Martha offered to drop her off at school on her way to bridge club.

Martha still hadn't brought up the diary or the whole deal with Paul's letter the day before. But now as they approached the school, Tessa felt like she should probably say something about it.

"Hey, listen, about what happened yesterday. You know in the living room when I . . ."

"We don't need to talk about all that now."

"OK."

They pulled to a stop in front of the school.

"It'll be all right." Martha patted Tessa's leg.

"Yeah. Thanks." But she didn't get out of the car. "OK, so here's the thing: I know you're probably thinking I shouldn't hold it against my mom, that I should forgive her, or whatever, but I'm not going to. I just can't."

Martha was quiet for a long moment. At last she said, "Then you'll hurt whenever you think of her."

It wasn't what Tessa had thought she would say. "I guess I will."

"That's a rather harsh punishment to sentence yourself to, don't you think? For something you had no control over?"

That wasn't what she'd expected her to say either.

Someone behind them honked, and Tessa finally stepped out of the car.

"Good luck on your exams," Martha said. "And take care of that arm."

"How did you—"

"I found the bandage you threw away last night. It was in your trash can. Right on top of the diary."

"Oh, right—wait, how'd you know it was my arm?"

"I've seen your scars, dear."

Then Martha gave her a smile, and Tessa closed the door and crossed the sidewalk.

After a few steps, she glanced back to see if Martha was still there, but she'd already driven away.

Then the five-minute bell rang and Tessa swung her knapsack over her shoulder and walked up the steps, but her mind wasn't on her upcoming exams; instead she was thinking about the diary and the bloody bandage she'd dropped on top of it.

And the harsh sentence she'd handed to herself.

There are a lot of different kinds of scars.

And she had a feeling Martha had seen more than just the ones on her arm.

94

I knew the media frenzy today would be even more intense than it'd been on Friday, and I really didn't want to face any reporters, so I'd made arrangements for Ralph to meet me at the back door of the courthouse. And now as he opened the door and gestured for me to come in, I saw that his face was swollen. "What happened to you?"

"Turns out I'm allergic to raisins," he grumbled.

"You're almost forty years old. How could you only find that out now?"

"Don't ask me. I guess I never ate quite so many at once before. Now, get in here."

I joined him inside. "Maybe you're allergic to being bald."

"That's not funny."

"It's sort of funny."

"Keep it up, Mr. Profiler, see what happens." I started toward the main lobby, but he directed me down the east hallway. "I convinced 'em to set up a secondary security screening area, so people involved in the trial don't have to walk past the protestors. It's this way."

"Good call."

"There's a lot going on," he said. "I need to fill you in on a few things."

"Do you mean Calvin?"

"Calvin?"

"Yes," I said. "I talked to him this morning. Did you know he's in Denver?"

Ralph stopped walking. "You talked to Calvin?"

"Just before I left the hotel."

"What did he say?"

Ralph seemed curious, but something deeper as well, and as I summarized my conversation with Calvin he listened intently, then began walking again. "He didn't mention anything else? Calvin, I mean?"

"No." We arrived at the security checkpoint. "Why? What's going on?"

After the shooting last week, security was even tighter than it had been on Friday, and most of the people passing through were being patted down. Thankfully, Ralph and I didn't have to deal with that, although we did have to hand over our weapons.

"When I couldn't find him yesterday," Ralph said, "I did some checking. Ran a complete background, the whole nine." Ralph wasn't looking at me, and I got the feeling he was avoiding eye contact on purpose. "Medical records included."

I didn't like the direction this conversation was going. "You found something." He was quiet as we gathered our things from the far side of the X-ray conveyor belt. "What is it?"

Ralph eyed the hallway in both directions, then motioned for me to join him in an out-of-the-way alcove at the end of the hall.

"Tell me, Ralph. What's going on?"

After we were alone, he said, "I think there's a reason Calvin has become so interested in seeing justice carried out promptly."

My thoughts leapt ahead to the most obvious conclusion, one that I didn't want to be true. One that couldn't possibly be true. "You're not saying . . . ?"

Ralph didn't answer. I waited. He looked conflicted. Torn. At last he put a heavy hand on my shoulder. "Yeah. That's what I'm saying."

"No." I shook my head. "It can't be. He would have told me."

"I talked to a couple of his family members. As far as I can tell, he hasn't even told them."

A crushing sadness overwhelmed me. "I need to get back to Denver, Ralph. I need to find him."

"You need to testify first."

"No, Ralph. I have to—"

"You just told me Kurt was looking for him," Ralph said firmly. "He'll find Calvin. You'll see him when you get back tonight, it'll all work out. Right now you need to be here at this trial." He tapped my head. "All of you needs to be here."

He was right, of course, but I needed to take a couple seconds to think things through.

"You all right?"

Grant Sikora's dying request flashed through my mind.

"Promise me you won't let him do it again."

"I promise."

"All right," I told Ralph. "I'm good. Let's go."

95

"So, you know what you're going to say up there?" It was Emilio Vandez, and the beginning of the trial was only minutes away.

I thought of the story about the midwives, about how they'd lied to protect innocent lives and God had honored them for it. And, despite Calvin's misgivings about his guilt, I was still convinced that Basque was responsible for the murders—and that he would kill again if he were set free.

"Yes," I told Emilio. "I think I know what I'm going to say."

"All right." He chugged my shoulder good-naturedly. "Then let's do this thing."

I slipped out Tessa's cell phone and found no messages from Kurt about whether or not they'd found Calvin, or if Adrian Bryant and Benjamin Rhodes were still alive. Then the bailiff rose, I shut off the phone, and the trial began.

The opening trial procedures seemed to take forever, but finally, I swore to tell the truth, the whole truth, and nothing but the truth, and then I took my seat on the witness stand—an act that Tessa had pointed out to me one time was an oxymoronic thing to do—and surveyed the courtroom.

Emilio Vandez looked anxious.

Judge Craddock, annoyed.

The jury, exhausted.

Richard Basque, confident.

And Priscilla Eldridge-Gorman looked pleased to be on center stage once again.

She spent a few minutes reviewing the previous week's proceedings, being careful to avoid drawing too much attention to the attempt on her client's life. I suspected she was concerned that bringing up the attempted murder might cause the jurors to become convinced that Basque really was guilty — after all, why would Grant Sikora have tried to kill him if he were innocent?

But she was taking longer than she needed to, and five minutes after I thought he should have objected, Emilio finally did, saying that if she wasn't going to ask me any questions, why had she called me back to the stand in the first place?

Judge Craddock told Ms. Eldridge-Gorman to get on with it already.

"Of course, Your Honor." She plucked up a file folder.

"Just to remind the jurors, immediately prior to the terrible incident on Friday, I had asked Dr. Bowers if he assaulted my client after arresting him thirteen years ago in the slaughterhouse. I would like to resume my questioning there, but, if it pleases Your Honor, may I request that the court reporter read the transcripts of the final moments of Friday's testimony so that the jury can have an accurate accounting of the line of questioning?"

Judge Craddock nodded toward the court reporter, who took a moment to shuffle through a stack of papers and then read: "Counsel: 'Did you break Richard Basque's jaw with your fist? Did you attack him after he was handcuffed?'" He paused and asked Priscilla, "Is that where you want me to start?"

"Yes. That's fine."

The court reporter went on, "Counsel: 'Dr. Bowers. Are you having trouble remembering that night at the slaughterhouse? I'll ask you one last time. Did you or did you not physically assault Richard Devin Basque after he was in your custody in the slaughterhouse? Judge Craddock, please direct the witness to answer the question.' Judge Craddock: 'Dr. Bowers, I advise you to answer the counselor's question. Will you answer the counselor's question?' Witness: 'No.' Judge Craddock: 'No?'" The court reporter paused. "And then . . ."

"Yes," Priscilla said. "That'll be fine." She gazed at me. "Dr. Bowers, you answered no. Was that in response to my question, or to the honorable Judge Craddock's question?"

I hadn't realized I'd actually said no aloud. "I was responding to Sikora's movement toward the gun," I said, "not to your question or Judge Craddock's."

She might have pounced, arguing that I must have been answering either her or the judge, but she didn't go there. I assumed that once again she was avoiding that line of questioning so she could stay clear of what she'd referred to a few moments ago as "the terrible incident."

Instead, she opened the manila folder.

"I have here the original case files from thirteen years ago in Milwaukee. Just to refresh your memory, Dr. Bowers, here's what you wrote concerning the arrest: 'There was an altercation. Later it was discovered that the suspect's jaw was broken sometime in the midst of his apprehension.' Are those your words?"

"Yes, they are, and—"

"I checked the case files." She cut me off, and though it annoyed me, I decided to let her be the rude one. I would bide my time. "And your description of the events fits the one given by my client during his interrogation—that he broke his jaw when you swung a meat hook at his face. But in preparation for this trial when I asked him about his injury, he told me that he was afraid of you and that's why he didn't tell the truth during his interrogation."

She took a moment to gesture toward Basque.

"My client claims that after you pulled your gun on him and he tried to run, you tackled him, handcuffed him, and then beat him. Of course, he might be lying. He might just be saying that to get set free. You could clarify everything right now, and certainly the jury will believe you, Special Agent Bowers, PhD."

Oh, she was good. She was really good.

The truth, the whole truth, and nothing but the truth.

I waited, but her question didn't come.

And as I waited, I remembered that night in the slaughterhouse, the desperate, terrified look on Sylvia Padilla's face as she died . . .

Cheyenne's pendant pressed against me through my pants pocket, and I recalled her comment that dying alone was the worst way to die.

"So, let me get back to my original question," Priscilla said, "the one that I asked you on Friday."

I remembered my conversation with Calvin about justice. And I remembered the midwives protecting those babies.

"Did you or did you not physically assault Richard Devin Basque . . ."

And arresting Basque.

And the satisfying crunch of my fist against his jaw.

". . . after he was in your custody in the slaughterhouse?"

Truth and justice always wrestle against each other in our courts. Always.

On Friday I'd told Calvin that justice isn't served when truth is censored.

Now, I realized Basque wasn't the only one on trial.

So was I.

So was my past. My conscience.

I opened my mouth to answer Priscilla's question.

And hesitated.

"Once again," Priscilla said petulantly, "we wait for an answer."

I made a decision.

"So here we are—" she began.

"This is what happened." And then I told the court the truth about what happened that night in the slaughterhouse.

96

As I related the facts, all of them, I knew I was signing a death warrant to my credibility, and probably to my career. Even worse, I realized I was creating empathy for Basque among the jurors and that those feelings would most likely influence their verdict.

But unlike the midwives or the people in the other biblical stories, at the moment, I wasn't being asked to hand innocent people over to certain death. I was only being asked to tell the truth. If Basque were set free I would deal with that when the time came.

"I hit the defendant in the jaw," I said. "I hit him twice after he was handcuffed, after he was in custody. It wasn't the meat hook that broke his jaw, it was my fist."

Judge Craddock leaned forward and actually seemed interested in the trial. I thought the jury would be surprised by what I'd said, but most of them just looked disappointed instead.

Priscilla smiled. "That's all I have." And for a moment she reminded me of a snake that had just swallowed a mouse. "No further questions, Your Honor."

"Does the prosecution wish to redirect?" Judge Craddock asked.

"Yes, Your Honor." Emilio stood.

I glanced at the clock on the east wall.

12:04 p.m.

Still plenty of time to get to O'Hare for my 1:59 flight, if Emilio didn't drag things out.

But he did.

He composed himself, and before asking me any questions, took his time distancing my actions in the warehouse from the crimes Basque was accused of. "Agent Bowers's reaction only reflects the deep anger any of us would have felt coming face to face with the scene in the slaughterhouse that day," he told the jury. "The evidence tells the story of Mr. Basque's guilt, and it is *the evidence*, and *the evidence alone* upon which you must base your verdict."

Finally, he asked me a few questions, and I answered them, but in the end I suspected the damage had already been done. Regardless of how guilty Basque was, the fact that I'd assaulted him and then apparently tried to cover it up by not being more forthcoming in my original police report would be enough to discredit my testimony.

And as every defense attorney knows, discrediting even one of the prosecution's witnesses—especially the arresting officer—is enough to raise questions in the minds of the jurors. And since our court system requires a jury to unanimously find a defendant guilty beyond reasonable doubt, a few questions were all you needed for an acquittal.

When Emilio finished, Judge Craddock called for a brief recess for lunch, I stepped from the witness stand, and my duties in Chicago were officially over.

12:28 p.m.

As I collected my things and got ready to leave, Emilio came toward me. "Well," he said. "That was a little rocky, but I think we'll be all right." He was putting his best spin on what had just happened, and I could tell. "And I don't think you need to worry about Basque pressing charges. The statute of limitations in Wisconsin for physical assault have—"

"Run out. I know. That isn't really what concerns me." I noticed that Richard Basque was watching me, shaking his head slowly as if to reprimand me for telling the truth.

And then he called to me, "No one is beyond redemption, Agent Bowers."

The old, familiar anger churned inside of me, searching for an opportunity to get out. I didn't reply, just turned away before I found myself giving in to my urges and attacking him like I'd done the night I arrested him.

He didn't say anything more.

Why did he ask you to lie?

I still had no idea.

Emilio was watching Ms. Eldridge-Gorman, who was chatting amiably with her legal team. "However," he said, "it is true that things have become a bit more complicated."

I thought of the weight I'd been carrying all these years, the subtle power Basque had exerted over me by knowing my secret. Now, there were no secrets. "No," I said to Emilio. "Things were complicated. They just became a lot simpler."

Then he stepped away, and I checked my watch.

12:32 p.m.

My flight left in less than ninety minutes and I still had a forty minute drive to O'Hare. It would be cutting it close.

On the way to the hall I called Kurt, asked him about Calvin, and he told me rather bluntly that he would have let me know if he'd found out anything and that I didn't need to keep bothering him about it. OK?

I wasn't sure how to take his sharp tone, and for a moment neither of us spoke, then I said, "Kurt, what is it? What's up?"

"Yeah, it's the . . ." Kurt was a tough man, but I could hear defeat creeping into his voice. Whatever was bothering him was something big. "It's Cheryl," he said finally.

I felt a rush of concern, and I paused beside the door. "What happened?"

Silence.

"Is she all right?" I said. "Did something happen to—"

"She left me."

The words slammed into me. Left me groping for what to say. "Kurt, I'm so . . . I'm so sorry."

"She went to her sister's place up in Breckenridge." It seemed like there was more he wanted to say, but he left it at that.

I wanted to encourage him, to tell him it would all work out, but I knew how long he and Cheryl had struggled to make things work, and there are no easy fixes when things got to this point. Finally, I asked him if there was anything, anything at all, I could do.

"I need some time," he said. "I'm not trying to bail on you, but I need to go up there, maybe take a couple days, see if I can salvage this thing. I can't just let everything—"

"Go. We'll be fine. We'll get John. And if there's anything you need, call me. OK?"

He told me that he would. "Cell reception up there in the mountains is terrible, but yeah, I'll give you a shout." We ended the call, and I was left wishing there was more I could do, but since I didn't have a direct flight, I wouldn't land in Denver until almost six.

Maybe Cheyenne could check in with Kurt before he left. I decided to call her, but first I needed to get a cab, so as I headed to the security checkpoint to collect my SIG and my knife, I phoned for a cab and arranged for it to meet me two blocks from the courthouse. Then I punched in Cheyenne's number.

"Pat," she answered. "That's weird, I was just picking up the phone to call you."

"Did you hear about Kurt and Cheryl?"

A brief silence. "Yeah," she said. "I hate that this is happening."

"I thought maybe you could stop by, see him before he leaves."

"We just spoke in the hall."

Silence spread between us. It was clear neither of us knew what to say.

At last, Cheyenne took a small breath. "I need to tell you: we found the bodies of Benjamin Rhodes and Adrian Bryant at Bryant's house."

Something heavy and dark sank inside of me. "It was the tooth-paste, wasn't it?"

"Yes. They died after scrubbing toxins against their teeth, just like Simona and Pasquino did in the seventh story. And they didn't just die. You know how 5-MeO-DMT and bufotenin are psyche-delic drugs?"

"Yes." I remembered an excerpt from the research notes in the case files: *"Often characterized by hallucinations of bugs crawling across the subject's body."*

"Based on the smears of blood on the wall"—her voice was strained and somber—"Bryant must have pounded his face against it twenty or thirty times before he died. Rhodes got hold of a knife and . . . well . . ."

She left it at that.

More death. More faces to haunt me. More guilt for what I might have done if only I'd pieced things together faster. "OK, let's—"

"Wait," she said. "How did you know John had targeted them?"

"When he called me yesterday he said dusk would arrive like it did in London. This morning Calvin told me he suspected John killed England's leading Chaucer expert last year in London on May 19th—one year ago, exactly, today."

"What? You're kidding me!"

"No, I'll fill you in later. I'm just saying, that's what made me think of our Boccaccio expert, Professor Bryant. Last night, I logged into his Internet browser, and it was pretty clear what his sexual preference was. I put that together with John's pledge to make Boccaccio's story more politically correct." I arrived at the security checkpoint, picked up my knife and gun, and headed for the back door of the courthouse. "Then, when you told me Rhodes went to Bryant's house last night, I remembered they had the same screen saver."

"The same screen saver?"

"An aquarium—the point is, I don't believe in coincidences."

"And the toothpaste?" she asked.

Our exchanges were quicker now and marked with urgency.

"The hypodermic needles and toothpaste tubes at the ranch. John must have been practicing his delivery method. We never had the toothpaste from Elwin's house checked for bufotoxins, did we?"

"No. I can't think of any reason we would have."

"John was probably counting on that."

"But all those details are a little sketchy, aren't they?" Her tone had turned the question into its own conclusion. "Even with all that, you still needed to rely on your instincts."

I hesitated. "I guess so. A little."

As I waited for her to respond, I thought about Bryant and Rhodes—fatally poisoning themselves simply by brushing their teeth. I would never look at a tube of toothpaste the same way again.

"One more thing," she said. As she spoke I realized that during our conversation, for the first time since I'd met her, Cheyenne Warren sounded rattled. "I wondered if I should wait until you got here but—well, here it is: John left you a note in Bryant's medicine cabinet."

I paused, stared out the window at the razor wire fence encircling the nearby Cook County Jail. "Read it to me."

A short pause, and then, "'Agent Bowers, I think we'll do the last three stories tonight after you're back in Denver. It'll make for a great climax. See you soon.—John.'"

Anger. Rage. Building inside me.

"Any word on Calvin?" My tone had become iron.

"No," she said. "Get back here, Pat. We—"

"I'm on my way."

I was at the back door when Ralph caught up with me.

He didn't look like he was bearing good news, although I wasn't sure how things could get much worse. "Talk with me on the way,"

I said as he jogged toward me. "I need to catch my cab. What's up?"

We stepped outside. "Assistant Director Wellington just called."

"Wow. Word travels fast."

"Yeah, well, she's always had it in for you. And now . . ." He let his voice trail off, but I could fill in the words.

"Let me guess. Internal Affairs wants to speak with me?" We crossed West 26th Street toward South Francisco Avenue, where I'd requested for the cab driver to meet me.

"Well, that and you're released from your current duties in Denver until further notice. And your interim teaching position at Quantico has been put on hold pending a full review."

Even though his words weren't a complete surprise, they struck me deeply. Margaret had told me yesterday that she could make my life miserable, but this time I'd helped her along by telling the truth on the stand.

"And," Ralph added, "she didn't think the report you submitted last night was 'adequate in scope and depth.'"

"Of course she didn't."

We made it to Francisco. A cab pulled up to the curb about twenty meters away, and we headed toward it.

"So here's the thing," he said. "I was gonna tell you the news about the suspension, but unfortunately you'd already left for Chicago when I checked my messages. And since your cell is broken, it took me until ten o'clock tonight before I could reach you at home with the news."

"Thanks, Ralph. I owe you one."

"It's a lot more than that by now."

"Right." The cabbie nodded toward me and I opened the door.

"I'll deal with Margaret and Internal Affairs," Ralph called to me. "Get things straightened out from this end. Just catch that psycho in Denver."

"I intend to."

I climbed into the cab.

So, two things to do: find Calvin and catch John. And I needed to do them both before ten o'clock tonight when I would officially be released from my duties with the FBI.

———————————— ■ ————————————

Denver, Colorado
11:56 a.m. Mountain Time

Amy Lynn Greer parked beside the abandoned warehouse.

The man who'd contacted her earlier in the morning had given her the address, but she didn't see any other cars. Maybe he hadn't arrived yet.

Even though she knew that coming here alone was taking a chance, in truth, she was more excited than frightened. This story was worth taking a few chances.

She stepped out of the car.

Since leaving Reggie and Jayson at the house after breakfast, she'd spent the morning driving to locations related to the murder spree: Cherry Creek Reservoir, police headquarters, the Bennett and Nash residences, and so on. At each location she'd taken photos and notes and dictated observations into her handheld voice recorder so she would be able to accurately describe the scenes in her book.

But through it all, her thoughts had been on this rendezvous.

In his email, her contact had told her about an opening in the southwest corner of the chain link fence that surrounded the warehouse, and an unlocked blue door that led into the shipping area. It took her less than a minute to find the broken section of fence.

She slipped through.

Saw the blue door to the building. Went inside.

Thick, dusty air. High windows letting in layered sheets of dirty light.

"Hello?" Her voice sounded thin and small in the room.

"I liked your article." The words came from a shadowy corner on her left.

She didn't recognize the voice, couldn't see a face. "Thank you."

"The profiling elements of it were strong, showed a lot of insight."

She still couldn't see who was talking to her, and now, for the first time, she began to question her decision to come here alone. "Step out so I can see you."

She was surprised when he did.

A handsome man, slightly older than she was, approached her. He explained that he was a profiler, showed her his FBI credentials, and told her his offer.

As he spoke, she could see how much they had in common and how similar their goals were. They spent a few minutes discussing ways they could mutually benefit by collaborating, and then he explained that even though the police weren't releasing any information to the public until they could contact the family members, the Day Four Killer had struck again that morning. "Two people you know," he said.

"Who?"

"Benjamin Rhodes and Dr. Adrian Bryant."

She felt a mixture of grief and surprise, but it was soon overwhelmed by a flush of excitement as she realized her unbelievably good luck: with her close personal connection with the victims—working for one and being the ex-student of the other—she was the perfect person to write the book; almost certainly the only writer who was both personally and professionally qualified.

It would veritably guarantee a contract.

Maybe the profiler knew that.

Maybe that's why he'd contacted her.

She noticed that he was still waiting for her to respond to the news of the two deaths. "Oh," she said. "That's terrible."

"Yes," he replied simply. "Now listen, you can't mention that you have a source at the FBI until the book comes out."

"Of course not."

"And don't post any more articles until I tell you. The timing has to be just right."

She wasn't too excited about the stipulation, but at last she agreed.

"We both know this is the story of a lifetime," he said.

The story of a lifetime.

Yes, yes, it is.

"I want to see any contracts before you sign them."

She felt a thrill. It was happening. Things were finally coming together for her. "Yes. OK."

Then, they nailed down the details: he would remain anonymous until the book launch, and then he would resign from the FBI and travel with her to promote the book. She liked the idea. He was cute. Who knows, maybe their friendship could blossom into something more mutually satisfying than just a working relationship?

She took a moment to dutifully remind herself that she was "a happily married woman." And instead of fantasizing about the cute profiler, she allowed herself a brief reverie thinking about the money and almost certainly the subsequent movie rights for the book.

The franchise would be worth millions.

Yes, especially if the Day Four Killer were able to finish his crime spree and complete all ten stories—

"I get 55 percent," her contact said. "And my name on the cover."

"No."

"Argue with me and I'll make it 60."

"I'm not going to—"

"All right." He turned to go.

She needed him. Couldn't lose him. "Wait. We'll split it down the middle. Fifty each. Plus cover credit."

He seemed to accept that. "I'll be in touch."

"They're watching me. Someone might find out."

"Leave that to me."

"And we won't be the only ones working on a manuscript.

Promise me you'll pass along any information about subsequent crimes as soon as you have it so I can keep writing and stay ahead of the pack."

"I promise. You'll be the first to know about the next victim."

He stepped into the shadows.

And then he was gone.

She waited for a few minutes until she heard the warehouse's door close, then she pulled her digital voice recorder out of her purse and verified that it had recorded the entire conversation.

She would work with the profiler for now, but if she needed to, she would use the audio tape to keep him on a short leash.

Yes, it was happening. The story of a lifetime.

Things were finally coming together.

She immediately emailed three of the literary agencies she'd been in touch with and told them about the qualifications of her coauthor and about her personal connection with the last two victims.

After the emails went through, she left the warehouse to transcribe her conversation with the FBI profiler onto her laptop.

And she realized how much she liked the feeling of being in control.

A feeling she never intended to give up.

No matter what.

97

Tessa Ellis.

Tessa Ellis.

Tessa Bernice Ellis.

On every exam, she'd had to write her name. Her first and last name. And on this stupid chemistry final, her full name.

Tessa Bernice Ellis.

Her mom had complained that the day she found out she was pregnant was the worst day of her life, and then—surprise, surprise—decided to get an abortion.

So here Tessa was: stuck forever with the last name of the woman who hadn't wanted anything to do with her. Who'd wanted to abort her.

Ellis.

As she thought about her name, it occurred to her that she hadn't mentioned to Pandora that she'd read the story.

Later.

No big deal.

Just focus on this test.

But as she stared at her chem exam, her thoughts felt soggy and thick, and even though, normally, the finals would have been a total breeze, with everything that was on her mind, she just couldn't concentrate. Her eyes wandered to the name at the top of the page.

Tessa Bernice Ellis.

As she scribbled down a few more fumbled answers, she realized that if nothing else, if nothing else at all, she at least needed to find out her real name.

But her mom didn't use last names in the diary. So, how was she supposed to find out Paul's last name?

Duh, Tessa: she stuck postcards in the diary. Postcards have return addresses.

Yes. It was possible—

"Two minutes!" her teacher announced. Tessa still had a quarter of the exam to finish.

She waded through the test questions but was still distracted thinking about the diary. She'd already decided that she couldn't read anything else in that thing, I mean, what if her mom wrote about how much she wished she'd gotten the abortion in the first place?

The hall bell rang. "All right," her teacher called. "Set down your pencils and place your tests on my desk as you walk out."

Tessa joined the crowd of kids heading toward the door, turned in her unfinished exam, and went to find Dora in the hall to see if she could look through the diary after school to find her father's last name.

I figured that the note John had left in Dr. Bryant's house promising to complete the last three crimes tonight justified breaking a few FAA guidelines. So, despite the regulations prohibiting the use of mobile transmitting devices on commercial flights, I spent the trip to Denver reworking the geographic profile using my computer's wireless access to the military's defense satellite network through FALCON.

We still hadn't heard from Father Hughes, the priest who'd disappeared on Tuesday. And even though I couldn't be certain that he'd been abducted, considering the timing and progression of the crime spree, I felt that his disappearance was too much of a coincidence to be unrelated, so I added his home, only two blocks from Rachel's Café, and the location of St. Michael's Church to the geoprofile. Then, I included the home and work addresses from the last two victims: Benjamin Rhodes and Professor Adrian Bryant, and the route Bryant had driven to the *Denver News* building.

Using the updated data, I analyzed the distribution and temporal progression of the crimes and discovered that the travel routes of the victims intersected in four geographic regions—near DU, Cherry Hills Mall, a section of downtown, and the neighborhoods surrounding City Park. FALCON told me there was a 58.4 percent chance he lived or worked in one of those four areas.

It wasn't much, but it was something.

Most crimes occur at the nexus of opportunity and desire—the offender sees the chance to get away with something and acts. But John was different. With him, everything was premeditated. Everything was carefully planned. In fact, I couldn't shake the thought that so far we'd only discovered what he wanted us to discover.

As I considered all of this, the advice I'd gleaned from Poe's fictional detective, C. Auguste Dupin, came to mind: "It is essential for the investigator to understand his opponent's intellect, training, and aptitude and then respond accordingly."

That's what I needed to do. Respond accordingly.

I typed three headings into my document and filled in my notes beneath them.

Physical description
  Male, Caucasian, medium build, approximately six feet tall, athletic.

Training
- Drugged or poisoned at least six people. Knows lethal dosages/how to remove a human heart. Medical training? Medical background?
- Subdued Sebastian Taylor. Possible background in martial arts/self-defense?
- Knew how to distribute the hay and boards to most effectively burn down the barn. Diversionary tactics or explosives/ordnance training? Arsonist?
- Blocked the GPS location for the phones he used to make his calls. Hacker? Military/communications experience?

Intellect/Aptitude
- Broke into Taylor's home and Dr. Bryant's home.
- Picked the lock to the morgue. Skilled in disabling security systems, picking locks, locating video surveillance cameras, breaking and entering.
- Avoided leaving fingerprints or DNA. Forensically aware.
- Knew the location of Baptist Memorial's video cameras. Access to blueprints or hospital security?
- Knew to ask for the Rocky Mountain Violent Crimes Task Force and that I was a member.
- Found out my unlisted phone number.

As I examined the list, I recalled Tessa's comments about the Dacoits: to find them, the Indian authorities evaluated the most likely travel routes, studied land use patterns, and compared those with the proximity of the crimes to reduce the suspect pool.

Yes, reduce my suspect pool.

I still hadn't had a chance to follow up on Jake's surprisingly cogent suggestion that the killer might have access to the Federal Digital Database, so now I logged in and pulled up the access directory for all federal, state, and local government employees in the city.

Denver trails only Washington DC for the highest number of federal employees in a U.S. city, and I ended up with a huge list: 21,042 names.

But the list shrank exponentially with each of the search criteria I added: male, Caucasian, height between 5'10" and 6'2", weight between 175–190 pounds. Then I weighted the search with consideration to military or medical background, previous convictions, forensic and hand-to-hand training, inclusion on the suspect list, or residential or work addresses in one of the four hot zones.

I might have landed on the list myself if I were an inch shorter, but as it was, I ended up with fifty-one names.

Finally, I cross-checked those names against the flight manifests to and from airports in the Chicago vicinity on Thursday and Friday. I came up empty with that, but as I looked over the list again, I

did recognize some of the fifty-one names: two dispatch personnel, six police officers, including Officer Jameson, the man who'd
researched the owner to Bearcroft Mine, and Lance Rietlin, the
young resident from the medical examiner's office who'd led me
and Cheyenne to the morgue.

Lancaster Cowler had mentioned that someone from the ME's
office had accessed the 911 transcriptions. That's where Lance
worked. He was also one of the three people who'd responded
when Cheyenne had intercommed for help in the morgue.

I uploaded the list to the online case files and emailed a copy
of it to Cheyenne, asking her to follow up on all of the names,
specifically on Rietlin.

Then the flight attendant announced that we were beginning
our final descent to the Denver International Airport, and as the
seat belt sign went on, I folded up my computer and got ready to
go to work.

Over the last four hours, Giovanni had taken one man and one
woman to his self-storage unit against their will. However, since
then he'd had to follow up on some work-related business and was
only now able to slip back to check on them.

He found that they were both still secure. Still alive.

Good. He would return later tonight to take care of that.

Before leaving the storage unit, he made sure that his duffel bag
was packed with all the necessary items and checked the temperature
of the warming pad: 84 degrees.

Perfect. He placed the pad on the backseat of his car, laid the
cloth bag containing his three remaining rattlesnakes on top of it,
locked the storage unit, and went to find Amy Lynn.

98

4:40 p.m.

"Well?" Tessa said.

"Just chill," Dora replied, her mouth thick with gum. "I'm looking." Earlier in the day, Martha had removed the diary from Tessa's trash can but had returned it to her when she'd asked for it after school.

Now, as Tessa waited As Patiently As Humanly Possible for Dora to find her dad's last name, she twisted and untwisted the sides of the Rubik's Cube, solving it twice—but it didn't count because she had her eyes open.

After five more minutes of waiting, Tessa asked again, "Anything?"

"I'm going as fast as I can, but it's hard. Your mom didn't use last names."

I already told you that!

"I know," Tessa moaned. "Like I said before, don't look so much at what she wrote. More the other stuff. The letters. The postcards. The things she glued in there."

"I am," Dora snapped, in a tone of voice Tessa had never heard her friend use.

"Sorry."

"Yeah. I know. It's just, I'm doing my best, OK?"

A moment of uncomfortable silence crawled through the room.

Finally, Tessa said, "I read your story last night."

"My story?"

"The one about your name. Pandora's Box. I should have read it before, way earlier, I know. But anyway, you were right. I thought it would end with some kind of plague or infection or something, but it doesn't."

Dora looked up from the diary. "So, you know what the last thing out of the box was?"

"Yes," Tessa said. "It was hope."

Dora started slowly thumbing through the diary again.

"I like how it begs her to let it out, and finally when she does . . ."

But Dora had stopped flipping pages and was staring at the diary.

"What?" Tessa asked.

Her friend was silent.

"What is it?" Tessa dropped the cube and crawled across the bed toward her friend. "What did you find?"

Dora answered by handing the diary to her, and Tessa saw the postcard pasted onto the page:

> Christie,
> Found your address online. I still think of you.
> I hope you're well.
> —Paul

It'd been postmarked just three years earlier and sent to the address in New York City where Tessa and her mom had lived before they ever met Patrick.

And it included a handwritten return address: P. Lansing, 1682 Hennepin Avenue East, Minneapolis, MN 55431.

Suddenly, everything about her dad seemed more real than ever. He was an actual person who lived at an actual address on a specific date.

Your last name should have been Lansing.

Tessa Lansing.

Tessa Lansing.

Tessa Bernice Lansing.

She read the note again. It was too brief to really tell her any-thing—except that Paul Lansing had never really gotten over her mom. Quietly, half to herself, half to her friend, Tessa said, "He doesn't say anything about me."

Dora chewed her gum squishily for a moment, then took it out and stuck it to a piece of crumpled paper in the trash. "Maybe he doesn't know about you."

"What?" Tessa watched Dora shove the trash can away from the bed. "What do you mean? When she was pregnant he wrote to her asking—"

"No, I know all that. I mean, what if he didn't know you were even born?"

"That's not possible."

"Why not?" Dora asked.

"I don't know, it's just—he had to."

A slight pause. "Did your mom ever actually say that *he* was the one who moved away?"

Tessa let the diary slide from her fingers and land on the pillow beside her. "Are you saying my mom did instead?"

Dora shrugged. "Sure, I don't know. Why not?" She was un-wrapping a fresh piece of gum. "I mean, she was scared and didn't want him in her life. Maybe she just packed up and left to start over somewhere else."

It seemed unbelievable.

But also, not so unbelievable.

Paul wanted to help raise you. If he knew you were alive, he would have come to be with you, especially after Mom died.

But as Tessa thought about it, she realized that she couldn't remember her mother ever telling her outright that her dad was the one who'd moved away from them. Maybe she'd just assumed that he—

"So, now what?" Dora was chewing again.

Tessa's racing, quivering heart made it hard to think, hard to consider her options. "I don't know."

Maybe she could just pretend that she hadn't found the memory box or the diary or Paul's letter and his postcard, and just go on with life like none of this had ever happened.

Yeah, right. As if that would work.

On the other hand . . . Tessa stared at the postcard. The address.

She grabbed her school backpack, pulled out her laptop, and flipped it open.

"Wait." Dora scooted closer to her. "You're not thinking—"

"Yeah," Tessa said, "I am."

Martha didn't have wireless, but one of the neighbors did, and Tessa was able to jump onto their network. She clicked to an online white pages site and typed Paul Lansing's name in the search box.

Pressed "enter."

99

As soon as the plane landed, I slid out my cell.

I needed to connect with Cheyenne to follow up on any leads generated by the list of fifty-one names, however, I didn't like the fact that John had left a note for me at the crime scene earlier in the day. So, before heading out to spend the rest of the night tracking him, I wanted to make sure that Tessa and my mother were safe.

Maybe if Cheyenne could meet me at my parents' house I could kill two birds with one stone.

I punched in her number, but the line was busy. So I left a voicemail asking her to meet me, ASAP. Then I told her the address, and before I ended the call, I thanked her for the pendant and assured her that my testimony had gone fine.

Which was true, whether or not justice ended up being carried out.

A few minutes later as we were taxiing to our gate, the phone vibrated and I thought it might be Cheyenne returning my call, but when I answered it, I found myself talking to Dr. Eric Bender.

"Oh," he said, "I must have punched the wrong number. I thought this was Tessa's phone."

"I'm borrowing it for the time being."

"Well, hey, now that I've got you on the line, Pat. The reason I called—I need to do another autopsy tonight—an unrelated case, but Dora isn't answering her cell. The thing is . . . I don't want her home alone. Not with John still at large. I just . . . I'm worried."

I completely understood his concern.

The pilot maneuvered the plane into the gate.

"You know that my wife is out of town for the week. Well, Dora went over to be with Tessa after school; I just wanted to ask if she could stay over there tonight. I don't think I can get out of here until 10:30 or 11:00. I can swing by and pick her up if I get off early—"

"No need. She'll be fine. Tessa's at my mom's; the girls can stay there. Two officers are watching the house." The seat belt light went off. I stood. Collected my things. "In fact, I'm on my way to check on them right now. Just one quick question. Your resident, Lance Rietlin, was he working with you on Saturday afternoon?"

"Yeah. We were at the hospital together until almost six. Why?"

Then he couldn't have been at the ranch. He couldn't be John.
Dead end.

"Just checking up on everyone involved in the case." All the passengers were deplaning. I joined the pack.

"Well," he said. "I'll let you know if my plans for tonight change. And can you have Dora give me a call when you see her?"

"Sure. Talk to you soon."

I hung up, exited the plane, escaped the terminal.

And headed to my car.

As Amy Lynn Greer turned her car onto her street, she couldn't help but smile.

Since meeting with the FBI profiler—and digitally recording their conversation—she'd spent a few hours writing, drove to Evergreen to get a look at Sebastian Taylor's house for herself, and then talked with two literary agents in New York who were both interested in representing her—well, her and her coauthor.

And since she'd been careful to keep her Blackberry turned off for most of the day and had an older model car with no GPS, she'd enjoyed the freedom of being alone and not being followed everywhere by a cop or an FBI agent. Still, she knew Reggie would be incensed that she'd slipped away from him. It was time to get home. Kiss and make up.

But as she approached the house she saw that his car wasn't there.

Hmm.

He might be out looking for her. How sweet.

Well, once she got in the house she could see if he'd left a note for her, and if not, just check her voicemail. She turned on her Blackberry. Punched the garage door opener.

Cruised inside.

And then closed the door.

Tessa hadn't found any Paul Lansings in Minneapolis, Minnesota, so she'd expanded her search and eventually came up with eighty-two of them scattered throughout the country.

She knew that her mom had attended college with her dad, so it was easy to see that in each of the cases, either the length of time the men had spent at their current address or their date of birth or the universities they'd attended precluded them from being her father.

Finally, after the last one didn't pan out, she let out a frustrated sigh.

Dora was tweaking her hair. "Nothing, huh?"

"No."

"So what now?"

Tessa sighed. "I don't know. It doesn't look like he's anywhere online, and it's not like you can just erase your personal history. Once something gets posted on the Internet . . . You know."

Dora shrugged. "Could he have moved out of the country or something?"

"Maybe."

For a moment, Dora found a way to chew her gum silently. "You don't think, maybe, I mean . . . you know."

"What?"

"You know, that he, um . . . well . . . that he died."

That was something Tessa hadn't allowed herself to consider. "I don't know," she said softly. As she thought about that, she noticed that Dora had stopped working on her hair and was just staring blankly into the mirror.

She gave Tessa a smile, but her eyes betrayed her.

"What's wrong?" Tessa asked her.

"I was just thinking about him dying and I thought about . . . well . . . "

"Hannah."

"Yeah."

"Seriously, Dora. You have to stop beating yourself up about all that. You didn't do anything wrong."

Dora was quiet.

"You sent a text message. That's it. That's all you did. It was the other girl, the babysitter. She's the one who left the baby alone . . ." Tessa could see this wasn't helping, and going on describing everything would probably only make things worse. But before she could think of anything better to say, or consider the dark possibility of her father's death anymore, she heard the front door pop open, and Patrick calling, "Tessa? Dora? You girls in here?"

She and Patrick had been through enough hard times together, enough weird stepdaughter/stepfather stuff already. The last thing she needed right now was for him to find out she was looking for her real dad without discussing it with him first.

She closed the webpage and then yelled down the stairs, "We're up here."

Amy Lynn stepped into the kitchen and set her purse on the table.

And saw a black duffel bag on the floor, next to the refrigerator. *What in the—?*

But the footsteps behind her cut her off mid-thought.

"Hello, Amy Lynn." She knew the voice and spun and saw a man in a black ski mask. "Welcome to Day Four."

She gasped, couldn't believe who it was, but before she could say a word, before she could move out of the way, he struck her, hard, in the face, and the world went dark.

———◼———

The door to Tessa's room was half open and she could vaguely overhear Patrick opening and closing doors downstairs. He spoke with Martha for a moment, although it was too mumbly to catch what he was saying. Then he came pounding up the stairs and knocked once as he pressed her door all the way open. "Hey, Tessa. Dora." His eyes scanned the room. He walked over and looked in the closet. "You girls all right?"

OK, so that was a weird question. "Why wouldn't we be?" she said. She folded her laptop shut. Dora tucked her legs under her on the bed. Tapped her finger anxiously against a pillow.

"No reason." Patrick looked like he was trying to figure out what to say next. He crossed the room toward the window. "Your exams go OK?"

Tessa shrugged. "I guess so. But I might not get an A in chemistry. Just so you know."

"Well, that'll be good for you. A little variety." He stared intently at the street.

"Way to steer me toward mediocrity."

"Anything I can do to help. Just a sec." He left the room. The doors on the second floor opened and closed, then he returned and addressed Dora. "Hey, your dad called me. He said he needs to take care of a few things tonight and asked if you could stay here until tomorrow."

"Stay here?"

"Yes. He wanted you to give him a call."

Dora looked a little concerned. She pulled out her cell and elbowed past Patrick, who watched her for just a second and then looked back at Tessa.

"What's going on?" she said.

"It's OK. Everything's OK." She could tell he was trying hard to find the right words before continuing. "Are you feeling better? I mean after yesterday, with the diary and everything?"

"Yeah, of course." This was definitely not the time to get into all that. "How was the trial?"

His eyes found the Rubik's Cube sitting on the bed.

I didn't want to talk about the trial.

I picked up the cube.

None of the sides were completed, so it didn't look like Tessa had made much progress. "These things are pretty tough, huh?"

"I do all right. You didn't answer my question about the trial."

"It went about as well as I expected." I moved the cube through a few turns then handed it to her. "Show me."

She accepted it, flipped it around in her hands, studied it, and then quickly twisted the sides until, only a few seconds later, two of them were solved.

"That's great. Good job."

"It's only two sides. Besides, I was cheating. Are they gonna put him away?"

"I'm not sure," I said. "How?"

"How what?"

"How were you cheating?"

Her expression told me that I'd just asked the stupidest question of the week. "I had my eyes open."

"Oh, OK . . . and?"

"There are these kids on YouTube who can do it blindfolded."

"Wow." I took the cube from her again. Scrutinized it. I could hardly believe anyone could solve it blindfolded, unless he'd memorized the pattern of turns. "So have you ever solved the whole thing?"

"Sure, yeah; it's not that hard, you just have to understand how the pieces move in relationship to each other; so when will they decide? The jury, I mean?"

"Tessa, these things take time—"

Dora appeared beside me. Slipped past me into the room. "He said he's gonna do all he can to swing by and pick me up. I told him it was no big deal." She turned to Tessa. "I can borrow some clothes, right?"

"Yeah, no problem."

The girls are fine, Pat. Get back to the case.

I set the cube on the dresser next to Tessa's jewelry box, which she must have brought from home while I was in Chicago. "I have to go. I'll see you two later tonight. If you need anything, call me."

"By the way," Tessa said, "am I ever gonna get my phone back?"

"As soon as I can get a new one."

Both girls told me good-bye, and I turned to go but stopped mid-stride. "Wait a minute." I spun, leaned into her room. "What did you just say?"

"Um, that I want my phone back."

"No. About the cube. Just a minute ago. You said something about solving the cube."

She looked at me quizzically, almost defensively. "I don't know. Just that you have to understand how the pieces—"

"Move in relationship to each other," I finished her sentence for her.

"Yeah, so what? What's wrong?"

"Yes." Thoughts twisting, rotating, clicking in my mind. "That's it. You're a genius."

"Yeah, right," she grumbled. "Stupid tests are skewed toward—"

"I have to go. I'll call you later." My thoughts were spinning forward as I ran down the stairs.

I could see the pieces of the case—one side of the cube where everything fit together so perfectly: the abandoned mine . . . Cherry Creek Reservoir . . . the travel routes from Denver International

Airport to the morgue . . . Elwin Daniels's credit card purchase of the greyhound—one side solved.

Yes, on Saturday, all the evidence pointed to the ranch—because that's where John wanted it to point.

"Have you figured out how I'm choosing the victims yet?" he had asked me on the phone. *"That would really be the key, here."*

I rushed to the car for my laptop, set it on the kitchen table. Opened it up.

Relationships.

Yes, that was the key.

"What did Giovanni write to you about?" I'd asked Basque.

"You," he'd said.

Yes, yes, yes. The tenth story. Someone gets buried alive.

My mother entered the kitchen and must have seen that I was in the middle of something because she quietly returned to the living room to work on a crossword puzzle.

It is essential for the investigator to understand his opponent's intellect, training, and aptitude and then respond accordingly.

But I hadn't been doing that. I'd been investigating John the same way I do other killers: looking at the clues, the patterns, the timing and location of the crimes he'd committed. But John wasn't like other killers. He was smart, so smart that he'd planned out everything from the beginning.

And that's what was going to help me catch him.

I clicked to the online case files.

To "Victim Files."

Chose "New."

John had always been one step ahead.

Yesterday on the phone, he'd taunted me by saying that the only way to catch him was to move out in front of him—and now I realized that he was right, but he'd made the mistake of letting me know where he was going.

He wrote to Basque about you.

He phoned you.

He chose you.

The secret to catching him wasn't going to be studying the victims he'd killed but the ones he'd *chosen.*

And the one victim I knew about, the one piece of the puzzle I hadn't included in the geoprofile yet, was the final victim in the story.

Me.

100

Giovanni left Amy Lynn's unconscious body, now tightly bound, on the kitchen floor, and carried his duffel bag to the master bedroom.

He didn't want their evening together to be interrupted, so he turned on the police scanner he'd brought with him and dialed it to the dispatch frequency.

Then he pulled ten Chantel candles out of the duffel bag, set them on the dresser.

Laid the knives that he would be needing next to them.

And began to light the candles.

Using FALCON, I brought up a map of Denver and overlaid the crime scene locations and victimology information from all of the other victims so far.

Then, just like I would have done for any other victim, I plugged my personal data into the geoprofile: my home and work addresses, typical travel routes, routine activity patterns, everything. And since I knew the scope of my geographic patterns better than any other victim I'd ever analyzed, I had the most detailed victimology information of my career.

At the trial on Friday, I'd told Richard Basque's lawyer that the more locations, the more accurate the geoprofile can be, and now, by including my data, I hoped I might just have enough information.

You have to understand how the pieces move in relationship to each other.

On the flight, when I'd run the numbers, the computer had identified four hot zones, but now when I pressed enter, only one geographic area came up. According to the software's calculations, there was a 71.3 percent probability that the offender worked in, lived in, or frequented a four-block radius downtown.

That was good enough for me to roll with.

I tapped the mouse, and a 3-D image of Denver's downtown appeared on the screen. Using the cursor like an airplane, I cruised between the buildings. They tilted, pivoted, and slid past me like they would have in a high-end, three-dimensional video game. I studied the orientation of the businesses, apartment buildings, streets.

Nearly all of the victims' travel routes—including mine—intersected on the southeast corner of one of those downtown blocks.

I zoomed in.

Reviewed the routes again.

Everything revolved around that one location.

That's where our lives touch his. That's where he's choosing his victims.

Oh yes.

That was it.

The business on the corner.

The place the cube clicked together.

A coffeehouse.

Rachel's Café.

101

I yanked out Tessa's cell. Ran to the door. Punched in Cheyenne's number.

She answered as the door banged shut behind me. "Hey, I'm on my way, I just—"

"Meet me at Rachel's Café. Remember?" I was sprinting to my car. "Where we went the other night. We need to hurry."

"What's going on?"

"It's all about the pieces—how they move in relationship to each other."

"The pieces? What are you talking about?"

"How long will it take you to get there?"

"I don't know. Fifteen minutes."

"Make it ten."

I jumped into the car, floored the accelerator, and peeled away from the curb.

Tessa heard the front door slam, and a moment later Patrick's car roared into the street. She wondered what was up and headed down the stairs with Dora close behind her. "Does he always act this way?" her friend asked.

"No. Sometimes he can be a little impulsive."

"Oh."

Tessa looked around the kitchen, saw Martha in the doorway to the living room. "He took off?"

"Yes." A motherly sigh. "Typical. Do you girls need anything?"

"No, we're fine," Tessa said.

After a light nod, Martha returned to her crossword puzzle in the living room, and Tessa saw Patrick's computer on the kitchen table. He must have been in such a hurry that he left it.

He never left his computer behind. Ever.

Wait a minute.

Martha had already started on her crossword. Tessa put a finger to her lips to tell Dora to be quiet, then she picked up Patrick's laptop and surreptitiously returned to her room.

Very surreptitiously.

After they were inside and the door was closed, Dora asked, "What are you doing?"

"Maybe *I* can't find my father," she said. "But Special Agent Patrick Bowers can." She opened Patrick's email program, found the email address for the FBI's cybercrime division, and typed in an urgent request for them to locate the current residence of Paul Lansing, former resident of 1682 Hennepin Avenue East, Minneapolis, MN 55431.

She glanced up.

Dora's mouth was ajar, a glob of gum perched on her tongue. "You're not seriously going to—"

Tessa signed the email "Special Agent Patrick Bowers." She didn't know his federal ID number but figured that a message coming from his personal laptop would be verification enough.

Pressed "send."

"OK," Dora said softly. "So, I guess you are."

"Now," Tessa said, "all we have to do is wait. They're good at their job. Patrick calls them all the time. I'll bet within an hour we know where my dad lives."

102

Giovanni had used a gag on Amy Lynn Greer without asking for her permission.

Now, he stared at her, lying so still on the kitchen floor, hands and feet tied securely behind her back. And he thought of his grandmother on another kitchen floor long ago.

With sunlight seeping from her.

He'd seen so much sunlight over the years.

He knelt beside Amy Lynn and slapped her face to wake her. It would leave a bruise, but in a few hours that wouldn't matter.

It didn't do the trick, though, so he hit her again, harder, and this time she woke with a start. Blinked. Widened her eyes.

"Don't worry," he told her. "I'm not going to kill you." As he said the words, a thought, a terrible thought, must have crossed her mind because she shrank back as much as she could. Tried to move away from him. "No, I'm not here for that. I'm not going to touch you."

Rapid breathing. Eyes searching, hoping for a way out.

"But although I'm not going to kill you, I'm afraid you will have to die tonight." She made sounds that might have been her way of trying to cry for help, but because of the gag he couldn't understand her words. "I chose you to play a lead role in story number nine. You know what that means, don't you?"

More muffled sounds. She struggled, but he'd tied her well. A tear squeezed from her left eye.

"Yes, that's right. You've read the story. You do know: tonight you're going to kill yourself after you eat the heart of your dead lover."

She shook her head desperately, frantically.

Giovanni looked at his watch. "I sent him an urgent text message on your behalf a few minutes ago telling him to hurry over, so I think he'll be arriving any minute now."

Then he grabbed her ankles and dragged her toward the bedroom. She twisted and struggled; couldn't pull herself free.

"I won't be able to let you hold your hands over your ears, so you'll probably hear some of the sounds. I'm sorry about that. I apologize in advance."

He situated her on the floor of the closet, closed the door, and then went to the kitchen to preheat the oven.

I burst through the door to Rachel's Café.

Smelled the familiar scent of freshly roasting coffee, saw Janie working behind the counter—a sophomore journalism student. Trendy glasses, retro clothes. Newspaper spread in front of her across the counter just like usual.

A man in his early twenties wearing earbuds sat at a table near the coffee roaster, slowly swaying his head to the beat of his music. A pile of college textbooks in front of him. Apart from the two of them, Rachel's was empty.

Janie must have wondered why I was scanning the room. "You all right, Dr. Bowers?" She knew I was a doctor, knew I worked for the government, but that's all I'd ever told her. "Come in to get some work done?"

To get some work done. Yes.

No!

I realized what I'd done: left my computer at home.

No! How could you be so stupid?

Wait.

Tessa's cell. Yes.

"Dr. Bowers?"

You can access the online case files with the cell phone.

"Janie." I pulled out the phone. "This might sound like a strange request, but I have a few pictures to show you and I need you to tell me if you've seen any of these people in here. If any of them are regulars."

"If they're regulars," she said brightly, "you'd know them."

I shook my head. "I'm only here late in the day. I brew my own coffee in the mornings." I tapped the screen of the cell, brought up the online case files. "Can you look at the pictures for me?"

Confusion ghosting across her face. "Sure."

Quickly, I clicked to the "Known Victims" section of the case files and downloaded the photos for Chris Arlington, Brigitte Marcello, Benjamin Rhodes, and all the others. Then I dragged them into the phone's photo suite so Janie wouldn't see the word *victims*.

"It's really important that you look at these carefully," I said.

The front door opened. Cheyenne. "Pat. Are you all right?"

"Yes. Come here."

Janie's eyes flicked from me to Cheyenne to the cell phone. She no longer looked uneasy but frightened, and I figured it might be best to just tell her what I did for a living. I didn't want the college guy in the corner to hear me if he unplugged his earbuds, so I lowered my voice. "I work for the FBI, Janie. And I think maybe you can help us with a case."

"You work for the FBI?"

"Please. Just look at the pictures." I handed her the cell, showed her how to slide her finger across the screen to scroll through the photographs. She stared at the phone for a moment, then began to view the photos one at a time.

Cheyenne stepped closer to me, piecing things together. "Are you thinking this is where John chooses—"

I nodded. "Yes."

Janie tapped the screen. "This woman. Yeah. I've seen her. And this guy too." She flicked back and forth between the two photos, pointing first at the headshot of Heather Fain and then at the picture of Ahmed Mohammed Shokr, the man who'd been poisoned on Wednesday.

"So, this is it," I breathed. "This is —"

"Who is he, Pat?" Cheyenne asked. "Do you know?"

I shook my head.

Janie tapped the screen again, moving to the next two pictures. "This guy's a priest, I recognize him . . . and sure, Dr. Bryant teaches one of my classes. He comes in here sometimes . . ." She flipped through the remaining pictures. "That's it. That's all the people I recognize."

It was a start, but I needed more. I looked around the café and ran through everything in my mind. The timing. The connections. The locations.

Taking the phone, I surfed to the list of fifty-one names, and began to pore over them, looking for someone I might have run into at Rachel's Café.

From where she lay bound and gagged in the closet, Amy Lynn could hear the noise of pots and pans clanging in the kitchen and the indistinct garble of police dispatch codes being called out through a radio.

She was trying to convince herself that the man who'd hit her and then tied her up was not the Day Four Killer. He was the last person on earth she would have ever suspected.

But it *was* him, there was no denying —

She heard the doorbell ring and she tried to scream, to yell for help, but was barely able to make a sound.

The sound of the dispatch radio stopped.

The doorbell rang again.

Then, heavy footsteps pounded through the house. She strained to get free.

The front door opened. She heard a cry. A short scuffle.

A thud.

And then the voice of her attacker, "Well, this isn't quite what I had in mind, but you'll do."

---■---

I whipped through the fifty-one names, but I didn't remember seeing any of the men at Rachel's and I didn't have enough information to figure out which of them might be John.

Then a thought: John sent the pot of basil and the handwritten note to Amy Lynn. She was the only other person besides myself whom he'd personally contacted.

He chose her, Pat. Just like he chose you.

Janie's newspaper lay on the counter. I flipped to Amy Lynn's political column and pointed at her headshot just beneath the title. "Janie, does this woman ever come in here?"

She nodded. "Sure. I've seen her."

"Did you ever see any guys checking her out? Watching her? Maybe following her?"

She shook her head. "No."

"What about guys meeting her here?" Cheyenne said. "Flirting with her? Coming on to her?"

"Usually, she's with this one blond guy. But he wasn't in any of those pictures you showed me."

"Reggie has brown hair, Pat," Cheyenne said. "It's someone else."

I'd only shown Janie pictures of the known victims, not the fifty-one men.

I suspected that many of the government personnel files would be incomplete and lack a photo, so I copied the names, surfed to the Department of Motor Vehicles records and quickly downloaded the driver's license photos for all of the men. I handed the phone to Janie again. "OK, one more time. The guy she came in with; see if he's one of these men."

"I'm not sure I'm really being very helpful—"

"Please," Cheyenne said. "You're doing great."

Finally, with Cheyenne's encouragement, Janie accepted the cell.

And I closed my eyes and rotated the cube in my mind.

Desperately, desperately, Amy Lynn tried to think of a way to get free. But the only things in the closet were shoes, hangers, dresses, blouses.

Something. There had to be something!

Dim light seeped beneath the door.

She peered around the closet.

No. Nothing.

She twisted. Repositioned herself.

Her leg bumped into one of her dresses and she heard the hanger rattling on the bar above her.

And she realized how she could get away.

A puzzle with so many pieces.

Who could have found Sebastian Taylor? Who could have worked with Grant Sikora to plan Basque's assassination? Who could have known the response times and the fact that I was on the task force? Who had access to my unlisted phone number and to—

I opened my eyes. "That's it."

Cheyenne furrowed her brows. "What's it?"

If I was right, the killer had been right under my nose the whole time. And he had the perfect alibi—but I couldn't be sure yet. There was one more thing I needed to check.

I calculated the time difference between Denver and DC and realized that Angela Knight would still be at her desk at cybercrime.

"Pat, talk to me," Cheyenne said. I could tell she was getting frustrated.

"Let me check with cybercrime first, but I think I might know who John is."

103

I used Cheyenne's phone, dialed Angela's number.

Janie was still scrolling through the fifty-one DMV photos.

Maybe I was wrong. Maybe—

Angela picked up. "Hello. This is Special Agent—"

"Angela. It's Pat."

"Oh, I just sent you the address."

"What address?"

"For Paul Lansing."

I blinked. "Angela, I have no idea what you're talking about."

"Six minutes ago you sent me an email request for a locate on Paul Lansing, formerly of Minneapolis, Minnesota."

A rising uneasiness. "I didn't send you a request."

"It came from your computer."

A request for Paul Lansing? From my computer?

You left your computer at your parents' house, Pat!

Paul . . . from Minneapolis . . .

Tessa must have found an old address for her dad.

A mixture of anger and a strange kind of loneliness shot through me. "Angela, you said you already replied?"

"Yes." Her confusion had shifted to concern. "What's going on?"

This can wait. Find John.

"I'll explain later, just don't send me any more emails until I call you back. For now, pull up those audio files I sent you earlier. I'm wondering about the caller's location."

"I told you before, I wasn't able to get a lock on—"

"I know, I know, but can you isolate the background sound on the first call? Separate the audio tracks from the two sides of the conversation, analyze them individually? Can you do that?"

"Sure." But she sounded a little reluctant. "Just a sec."

———■———

Amy Lynn struggled against the ropes binding her hands behind her back, trying, trying to reach another dress. If she could just get hold of a wire hanger, she could use the hooked end to work at the knots.

But even though she'd managed to pull down five dresses so far, no hangers had dropped to the floor.

She heard her captor dragging a body into the bedroom.

Hurry! You need to hurry!

She leaned as far to the right as she could and grabbed one more dress.

Tugged. Rolled.

It slumped to the floor.

And this time the hanger fell with it, bouncing off her shoulder and landing on the carpet beside her face.

———■———

After only a few seconds, I heard Angela mumble, "That's odd," and when she said those two words I knew what she'd found.

"The ambient noise," I said. "It's from both sides of the conversation, isn't it?"

"Yes. But that would mean that the first anonymous tip—"

"Was placed from inside the dispatch office."

"But that's . . ."

"Yes."

"Here!" Janie tapped the phone. "This is the guy." She turned the phone so Cheyenne and I could see the photo. "I saw him come in with that reporter a bunch of times."

Even before I looked at the picture I already knew who she was pointing at—Ari Ryman, the ex-Marine who'd played the audio tapes for us in the dispatch office.

The Day Four Killer.

104

I handed Cheyenne her phone. "Quick. Call HQ, see if Ari Ryman is there."

A flood of emotions crossed her face as she looked at Ari's photo. "The guy from dispatch? You think he's John?"

"Yes, I do. Please, I'll explain in a minute."

As Cheyenne made the call, I turned to Janie. "You're sure? The reporter, she used to come in with that man?"

"Yeah," she lowered her voice. "I think they might have been having an affair. You work here long enough, you watch people, you can usually tell when two people are . . . you know."

I let my thoughts fly through the facts that had led me to suspect Ari: as an EMS dispatcher he would have had access to my unlisted phone number, known the task force members' names and our response time, and been able to pull up information about the hospital and the morgue; he was an ex-Marine.

He would have learned hand-to-hand combat.

The call came from inside the dispatch office.

And he hung out with Amy Lynn Greer at Rachel's Café, the place where the killer apparently hunted for his victims.

Cheyenne pocketed her cell. "Ari Ryman never came back to work after lunch today."

I looked around Rachel's Café again, trying to figure out where he might be.

He comes in here with Amy Lynn. He sent her the note: "Must needs we tell of others' tears? Please, Mrs. Greer, have a heart. —John."

I spun. Faced Cheyenne. "Is Amy Lynn still at the safe house?"
She shook her head. "I don't know." She tapped at her cell again.

I thanked Janie for her help, pocketed Tessa's phone, and was turning to leave when Cheyenne exclaimed, "Amy Lynn left the safe house last night. The GPS for her Blackberry is at her home address, 7881 East 8th Avenue."

"C'mon." I ran for the door. "She's next. The killer wants her to have a heart."

Yes!

Amy Lynn finally managed to grab the hanger.

Frantically, she twisted the wire tip and went to work at the ropes.

We climbed into the car.

So many thoughts—I was furious at Tessa, determined to catch Ari, dreading what might have happened to Amy Lynn Greer and her husband.

No, Pat. In his note at Bryant's house, the killer said he was going to tell the last three stories tonight, after you returned to Denver. So they might still be alive—

I fired up the engine. "Cheyenne, get some cars to the Greer house—"

"Already on it." She had her phone to her ear.

And I squealed the car into the street.

Giovanni removed the shirt of the unconscious man and placed it beside him on the bed. Then he picked up the scalpel.

The candles flickered beside him.

He could hear Amy Lynn squirming in the closet, and he paused for a moment to listen to her. Carrying the scalpel, he crossed the room, opened the closet door, and found that she'd pulled half a dozen dresses onto the floor. She'd managed to get hold of a hanger and was trying to use the tip of the wire to work her hands free.

"I'm impressed," he said. "Really, I am. That was a good idea. Keep working on that. I'll be back in a few minutes to check on you. Let's see how far you get."

He returned to the bed, positioned the scalpel's blade against the man's bare chest, and was just about to press down when he heard Detective Warren call for dispatch to send two squads to 7881 East 8th Avenue.

Giovanni stopped.

They'd found him. They were coming.

So.

He looked at the man on the bed, then at the blade in his hand.

A change of plans.

He set down the scalpel and went to remove Amy Lynn from the closet.

"Two squads are on their way to her house," Cheyenne said. "Now, fill me in."

In a handful of seconds I summarized the hypotheses that had led me to suspect Ari.

Cheyenne listened. Tracked with me, then shook her head. "But motive? What's his motive?"

"We'll ask him when we find him."

So many sides of the cube to lock into place. It was hard to prioritize. I could think of at least four people we needed to call immediately.

I took us around a corner so fast I almost lost control. "Cheyenne, make some calls for me, OK?"

"Shoot."

"Try to get a hold of Reggie and Amy Lynn. Tell her to report immediately to the FBI field office, not police headquarters. Her life's in grave danger."

I still couldn't believe that Tessa had used my computer to email the FBI's cybercrime division to look for her dad. She should have just asked me for help. Not gone behind my back.

I definitely needed to calm down before talking with her. Sort out what to say.

So I didn't call her, but I did call dispatch. "Tell the officers who are watching the house to go inside, confiscate my computer, and stay with the girls."

A slight hesitancy. "Yes, sir."

I shot through a red light and merged onto I-25.

Amy Lynn lay in the trunk of her own car.

The man had freed her legs, but her hands were still tied behind her back. She was still gagged.

They were backing down the driveway.

She heard the garage door rattle shut, and as the car rolled into the street, in a moment of dark and ironic clarity, she realized that unless she somehow found a way to escape, she was going to end up as nothing more than a chapter in someone else's book.

And it would be the story of a lifetime.

Hers.

The car accelerated.

She didn't care if the gag and the sound of the engine stifled her cries, Amy Lynn kicked against the trunk's latch as hard as she could.

And screamed.

Amy Lynn Greer wasn't answering her cell, but Cheyenne did reach Reggie. They spoke for a few moments, then she filled me in: that morning, after discovering that Amy Lynn had left the house, he'd dropped his son off at day care and gone looking for her.

"He told me that he didn't put out an APB on her because he

wanted to find her himself, to protect her. That he was embarrassed he'd let her out of his sight."

I smacked the steering wheel with my hand. "That's just great."

I accelerated. Slid into the left lane.

"This afternoon he got a GPS lock on her Blackberry. Apparently she placed a call to New York City while she was near Sebastian Taylor's house, so he drove up there to look for her, but she was gone. About twenty minutes ago he received a text message from her that she was at home. He's on his way there, but he's still a good fifteen minutes out."

We called Jake, filled him in; I thought of calling Kurt, but he was still in Breckenridge trying to salvage his marriage, so we gave a shout to his boss, Captain Terrell, instead. Cheyenne told him, "We think it's Ari Ryman," and something caught in my memory.

I began to mumble, "Ari . . . hurry . . . Ari . . . hurry."

A couple seconds later, Cheyenne ended the call to Terrell and stared at me. "Are you all right?"

"He didn't say 'hurry.'"

She shook her head. "Who didn't say hurry?"

"On Friday when Grant Sikora was dying, I told him the paramedics were coming and I asked him who'd gotten him the gun. He answered, 'Hurry . . . You have to get . . . hurry . . .'"

She connected the dots: "You're thinking he said, 'Ari. You have to get Ari.'"

"I can't be certain, but yes. I think he was giving me a name, not asking for help."

"Considering everything we know now, that would make sense," Cheyenne said.

Yes, it would.

In fact, too much sense.

If Grant had said Ari's name, that changed everything.

"Cheyenne, I want to see the work schedules from last week. We're looking for anyone who's had anything to do with this case.

Police officers, detectives, CSU members, also hospital staff and medical examiner's personnel. Call Baptist Memorial and police headquarters; have human resources upload them to the online case files — "

"What are you thinking?"

"I'm thinking I don't want to jump to conclusions. I have a theory. I'm hoping I can prove myself wrong." I flashed past two cars that had to be going at least seventy-five.

We would be at the Greer house in less than four minutes.

On the way to police headquarters, Giovanni radioed dispatch to requisition a task force helicopter and a pilot for Special Agent Bowers.

Almost no one else could have convinced them as quickly and easily as he did to clear the chopper. "Colonel Freeman is on call here at the station," they told him. "He'll be waiting for you on the helipad."

"Thank you."

End call.

Though Giovanni hadn't expected things to play out quite like this, he'd planned for a number of contingencies and he was prepared: he had a police department ID badge with him so that he could enter the staff parking garage underneath headquarters. From there, he would take Amy Lynn up the service elevator to the helipad on the roof.

And fly to the mine.

Tessa knew she was in deep trouble.

A little while ago as she and Dora were waiting for the reply from the cybercrime people, Dora had paged through the rest of the diary, and just about the time she was finishing, the two dopey cops who'd supposedly been protecting the house for the last couple days had come in, taken Patrick's computer from the bedroom, made Dora and her join them downstairs in the living room, and now, they weren't letting either of the girls leave the room or make any calls.

Patrick must have found out about the message she'd sent.

Which meant it was too late to erase it before he saw it.

Which meant she was dead meat.

Especially since she'd read the reply from FBI headquarters just before the cops arrived.

———————◼———————

We were close.

Two minutes, maybe less.

Cheyenne lowered her phone and cursed. "HQ says they'll have the work schedules posted 'within the hour.'"

"Within the hour? We don't have—"

"I know," she said between gritted teeth. "I know."

What else? What else?

The timing of Thomas Bennett's death . . . the flight schedules . . . the time Brigitte Marcello bought the Chinese food . . . the candles in the mine had been burning for two hours . . .

I was deep in thought when the phone rang, jarring me. Kurt's caller ID came up and I answered it, heard static, then my name. "Pat, the —aptain called." His voice cut out. "I —eard what's going on."

"Take a left here," Cheyenne shouted.

I bounced over the curb, then pounded the gas.

"Listen, Kurt." I knew there was spotty reception in Breckenridge, but I hoped he'd be able to catch what I was saying. "The tire impressions we found two weeks ago from Sebastian Taylor's car. Who processed them?"

"What?"

"The tire tracks. Who did you send to investigate them?"

" —eggie."

Reggie Greer.

"There!" Cheyenne called. "Turn right. Four houses down."

No sirens.

No flashing lights.

The patrol cars should be here by now!

Kurt said something I couldn't make out.

"Did the *Denver News* do a story on Hannah's death?" I said. "Did they do an article?"

"Ye—"

"Who interviewed you?"

He lowered his voice. "I'm here wi— Cheryl, I can't . . . I'm —osing you."

"Was it Amy Lynn Greer?"

"—es."

"You and Cheryl are in danger, Kurt—"

"I'll —all you back."

"Kurt!"

Then nothing. I slammed the phone against the dash.

We arrived at the Greer house.

I jumped out of the car, drew my SIG, and ran toward the porch.

105

Brown.

Stucco.

Two story.

Around us, twilight in the city.

Cheyenne flared to the right. "I'll get the back."

No cars in the driveway. The house was dark.

"Watch for snakes," I yelled.

"Got it!"

Onto the porch. I tried the doorknob.

Unlocked.

I pressed open the door, gun in one hand, flashlight in the other. "Reggie? Amy Lynn?"

Silence.

I swept the beam of light across the living room. Scanned for rattlers. Saw none.

Steady, Pat. Steady.

Assess and respond.

Then I heard the squeak of another door and Cheyenne's voice calling for Amy Lynn. A flashlight beam cut through the dining room. I shouted out my location; Cheyenne acknowledged, and I edged into the kitchen.

No one. A few baking pans beside the stove. The oven light was on.

It'd been preset to 450 degrees.

The temperature gauge flipped to 440 as I approached.

Story number nine: he kills the woman's lover, cuts out his heart, and then feeds it to her for dinner.

A deep tremor. Primal dread.

I didn't want to look in the oven, but I knew I had to. I surveyed the room one more time.

Reached for the oven door. Prepared myself.

Opened it.

Empty.

Thank God.

A quick glance at the countertops, the sink. No dirty dishes. No blood. No meat.

It looked like John had turned on the oven but hadn't had a chance to finish his tale.

"He might still be here!" I called to Cheyenne.

I closed the oven. Shut off the heat.

Cheyenne yelled from the end of the hall. "Pat. In here."

She sounded concerned but not in danger, so I took a few seconds to make sure each room was clear as I moved down the hallway to join her.

No people; no snakes.

I found her in the master bedroom where she was on the phone, leaning over the bed, and checking someone's pulse. I couldn't see who it was, only that his shirt had been removed. Then I realized she was talking with 911 and I stepped around her. And saw who was on the bed.

"Calvin!" I rushed to his side.

"He's unconscious," Cheyenne said, "but his pulse is steady." She had the phone to her ear but was talking to me. "They're sending an ambulance."

Why aren't those squads here yet?

Eight Chantel candles flickered on the dresser. Two had winked out.

Gently, I touched Calvin's forehead, and as I did wondered if the killer might have left him alive as some kind of trap, a way of toying with the mouse—of toying with me.

The closet door was slightly ajar.

Cheyenne saw me glancing at it. "I checked inside. It's clear."

I took a look. Six dresses on the carpet. A metal hanger with a straightened hook.

I headed for the hall.

"What is it?" Cheyenne asked.

"I'm going to have one more look around." I spoke softly. "I'll be right back."

And as she monitored Calvin, I left the room to make sure no one was waiting for us anywhere else in the house. Or in the garage.

———————————■———————————

Dora and Tessa were in the living room with the cops. Martha had stepped into the kitchen, and Tessa saw her discreetly pick up the phone.

Tessa was still distracted, thinking of how furious Patrick was going to be when he arrived, and she didn't realize that she was nervously toying with her necklace until she felt Dora's hand on her arm.

"You all right?"

"Yeah."

But she didn't let go of the necklace's black stone.

"I need to tell you something," Dora said. "I was gonna tell you upstairs, but then the cops came in."

"What is it?"

"Your mom tells why at the end of the diary, why she bought you that jewelry box when you were a kid."

Tessa stopped fiddling with the necklace. "Tell me."

"To remind her of the day she changed her mind."

And then Dora told Tessa about the last three entries in her mother's diary.

106

I finished a careful inspection of the house and found no one. Amy Lynn's purse was in the kitchen. I took a quick inventory of its contents and saw that the last text message had been sent to her husband's cell.

I returned to the master bedroom, where I saw that Calvin was still unconscious. Taking slow, shallow breaths.

Cheyenne was laying a blanket across his chest.

I knelt beside the bed. "How is he?"

"He seems stable. His breathing is steady. Paramedics should be here any minute."

"When they get here they need to do blood work right away and a complete tox screen."

"It's all in play," she said. "They're bringing a doctor with them."

I glanced at the candles.

- Based on the negligible amount of wax flow, I could see they hadn't been burning long at all.

The oven had heated up to 440 degrees . . .

I heard a car stop outside the house, then a car door slammed. I unholstered my SIG and called to Cheyenne, "Stay with Calvin."

I hadn't quite made it to the front door when it flew open.

"FBI!" I yelled.

"Don't move!" the man hollered.

I knew that voice.

"Jake, it's me. It's Pat."

Jake Vanderveld stepped into the room, and although I never thought I'd hear myself say it, I added, "It's good to see you."

"You too, Pat. What do we know?"

———————————◼———————————

We were in the bedroom and Cheyenne and I had just finished filling Jake in. "For now," she concluded, "it looks like Calvin is doing OK."

"Do we know if Amy Lynn was even here?" Jake asked.

"Her purse is here, but not her keys. And her car is gone," I said, then pointed toward the closet door. "Drag marks from the bedroom door to the closet, but not away from it. John had her in there, but then he led or carried her away."

"Any idea where?"

I shook my head. "Her car doesn't have GPS, and her Blackberry is still in her purse." Then a thought. "Cheyenne, let's get an APB on her and send some patrol cars to Daniels's ranch, just in case—"

I was interrupted when Jake's phone came to life. He answered it and then stared at me in surprise. "He's standing right here," he said, then he offered me the cell. "For you."

"Who is it?"

"Police headquarters."

I took the phone. "Special Agent Bowers."

"Agent Bowers?" A woman's voice, and she sounded even more surprised than Jake had been. "We've been unable to reach your pilot or your cell number. We thought Agent Vanderveld might be able to—"

"My pilot? What are you talking about?"

A slight pause. "Sir, your helicopter took off three minutes ago without—"

Oh, not good. "I didn't request a helicopter."

"You didn't—"

"Who boarded the chopper?"

Another pause.

"Who!"

"I'm not sure, sir. But we need a flight plan and—"

"Listen to me." I realized I was yelling into the phone, but at that point I didn't care. "The second chopper, is it there?"

"Yes, sir."

"A pilot, is there a pilot available?"

"Sir, I don't understand; you're telling me you're not in the heli—"

"A pilot! Is Cliff there?"

"Colonel Freeman is in the helicopter that you—or that someone . . ." She couldn't seem to collect her thoughts. "Cody Howard's here."

Cody was Cheyenne's ex-husband, the pilot she refused to fly with, but I could deal with that in a minute. "Get him to the helipad and have him fire up the chopper. I'll be there in five minutes. And tell air traffic control at Denver International Airport to get the transponder codes for the chopper that just took off. We need to know where it is. Do it."

The longest pause yet. "Yes, sir." End call.

I tossed the phone to Jake. "John's got a chopper, but he's only a few minutes out. We've got him. Cheyenne, you're with me."

Jake nodded toward Calvin. "I'll stay here with him until the paramedics arrive."

"Good."

"Be careful," Jake said.

That's not exactly my specialty, but I decided not to bring that up. "I will."

Cheyenne and I bolted to the car.

107

Through his headphones, Giovanni heard that Agent Bowers had requested the second chopper. Perfect. Things were going to work out after all.

Five minutes earlier, when Giovanni had appeared on the helipad with the razor blade against Amy Lynn's throat, Cliff Freeman had just stared at him in shock, but he'd finally climbed into the cockpit when Giovanni removed the woman's gag and she pleaded for her life.

Now, they were roaring over the Rockies, just a few minutes from Bearcroft Mine.

Giovanni sat in the backseat beside the woman. Her hands were still bound behind her back.

He snapped the straight razor open and held it close to her face to make sure that he had her undivided attention. "Do you remember at the house when I told you I wasn't going to kill you, that you were going to kill yourself instead?"

She shrank back against the seat.

"Well, that time has come."

"Leave her alone," Cliff yelled from the cockpit, "you son of a—"

Giovanni swiped the blade against the man's right forearm deep enough to make him cry out but not deep enough to disable him. "Please," Giovanni said. "Do not interrupt us again."

Then, he turned to Amy Lynn and began to unbutton the top of her shirt.

◼

Amy Lynn tried to lean away from him, but there wasn't any place to go. "Please, no," she begged.

He unbuttoned the second, then the third buttons. "I told you before, I'm not going to touch you. Now, please, sit still."

"No, don't—" But she was too terrified to finish her sentence. He was picking up the cloth bag he'd brought with him, the one he'd taken briefly to the other helicopter on the helipad before making her get into this one.

The thick, coiled contents of the bag stirred.

"Officially," Giovanni said, "you're supposed to jump from a window, but I don't think we'll attempt that at this point. I can always toss your body out later, so—"

Suddenly, the chopper pitched to the right as Colonel Freeman let go of the control stick. He reached back and tried to wrench the razor from Giovanni's hand, but Giovanni sliced the man's wrist. A deep cut. Blood spurt across the cockpit.

"Get the stick or I'll slit her throat!" He noticed that the colonel had—thankfully—leaned his leg against the control stick to keep the helicopter from crashing.

Freeman shook his head. "No! Put down—"

Giovanni held the blade to Amy Lynn's neck. "Do it or she dies."

He hesitated for a moment, then finally faced forward, blood spurting from his wrist, leveled off the helicopter, cursed, and threatened Giovanni, but Giovanni didn't mind.

"And press your knee against that cut or you'll bleed out."

Giovanni waited until Freeman obeyed, then he untied the string that was cinched around the bag's opening. He would bandage the man's wrist in a minute, but first he needed to take care of Amy Lynn.

He lifted the sack toward the top of her shirt.

"No!" she cried.

"Remember, I'm not going to kill you. In this story you have to kill yourself. Rattlesnakes are attracted to movement. So, if you don't want to die, you'll want to sit very still."

He nudged the fabric of her shirt away from her skin so there'd be enough room, then he tipped the three-foot-long rattlesnake down the front of Amy Lynn's shirt.

———————————————■———————————————

She screamed.

And as she felt the dry, muscular body of the rattlesnake flex against her bare stomach and glide across her abdomen, Amy Lynn Greer did not stay still.

Not at all.

108

Air traffic control told us the location of the other chopper, and when I heard the coordinates in my headphones I told Cody, "I think he's going to Bearcroft Mine. I know where it is. Head toward the southern edge of Clear Creek County."

"Roger that."

He tilted the chopper to the southwest, and we flew into the dying sunlight.

Cheyenne and Cody still hadn't spoken to each other. Even though I had no idea how messy their divorce had been, from the tense silence I got the impression it'd been tough on both of them.

For a moment, I was reminded of my own troubles with Lienhua, but before I could give those much thought, I saw movement on the floor next to the first aid kit—

And I realized what it was.

"Be still!" I yelled.

The rattlesnake glided across Cheyenne's shoe and began to entwine her ankle.

She froze.

I would have grabbed something to attract the snake's attention, but it cocked its head back, and I was afraid it might strike, so I flashed my hand toward its face so it would bite me instead of her. It bared its fangs and rattled, but with my other hand I was able to grab it just below the head before it decided to strike.

The snake's ropey body writhed wildly in my hand, but I held on.

With my free hand, I went for my knife. I didn't really want to kill the snake, but considering the circumstances, I thought even Tessa would forgive me.

There comes a time for all things to die . . .

The rattler hissed and thrashed. Tried to twist its head toward my arm.

And this snake's time had come.

I pulled out the Wraith. Flicked out the blade. And took care of the rattlesnake.

Its body flopped to the floor of the helicopter, I dropped the head beside it and ended its misery with the heel of my shoe.

Cheyenne swallowed. "Thank you."

"Lift your feet. There might be more."

She propped her feet against the seat in front of her. "I saw that," she said. "You were going to let it bite you instead of—"

"Shh. Please. Help me look."

And together we scoured the cabin, hunting for more snakes.

Giovanni left Amy Lynn's body on the helicopter.

He'd warned her to sit still. If she had, the rattler might not have struck the front of her neck, and her throat might not have swollen shut in less than a minute.

Having a hostage would make it easier to lure Agent Bowers into the tunnel, so he decided to let the pilot live for the time being. He made sure he could control the man's bleeding, and then took him into Bearcroft Mine.

I didn't find any more snakes in the cabin and I was about to check the cockpit when I heard Cody cry out in pain.

The helicopter dipped toward the mountains, pitching me forward.

"It bit me!" he cried.

"Get the stick!" I hollered, but he wasn't listening. I scrambled forward and grabbed the control stick but only managed to momentarily stop our descent. "You have to—"

"Cody, get the controls!" Cheyenne cried. She dove toward the cockpit, and I slid to the right as she took the stick, then I scoured the floor for the snake. Saw nothing.

"It got me!" Cody yelled. Thankfully, he'd kept his left hand on the collective pitch lever, but he was holding his right hand against his thigh.

Cheyenne was trying to level us off. Two days ago she'd told me she was taking helicopter flight lessons. I really hoped she knew how to land.

"Where's the snake?" I yelled. Cody just shook his head.

Based on where he was pressing his hand against his leg, I guessed the rattler had struck him on the inside of his thigh near his femoral artery—a terrible location for a bite.

With every beat of his heart, the venom was pumping through his body, destroying more tissue, causing more bleeding, slowing his respiration.

The more his heart races, the quicker he'll lose consciousness.

"Relax, Cody." I was still searching for the snake. "Try to stay calm." He was shaking. I let my eyes tip toward the window for a moment, and I recognized the surrounding mountains. We were close to Bearcroft Mine, less than a mile away.

I scanned the floor again.

And saw the snake weaving beneath the control pedals.

"Everyone be still."

But Cody followed my gaze, and then shrieked and yanked his feet off the pedals. The helicopter pivoted sideways through the air and started to drop.

"No!" Cheyenne hollered.

The world was whipping around, spinning. A blur. I saw the snake slide across the floor toward me.

I grabbed for its neck. Missed. Got the body.

Cheyenne shoved Cody against the door to get her feet to the pedals.

Another rotation, another, and then finally, somehow, Cheyenne pulled us out of the tailspin, but we were less than a hundred meters from the ground and falling fast.

"Level us off!" I yelled.

Still holding the snake I reached for the knife but realized I must have dropped it when I rushed to grab the controls.

I felt the snake's body tense for a strike.

OK. Drastic measures.

Rattlers can strike faster than the human eye, but not faster than a speeding bullet.

109

I drew my SIG.

The chopper was so wobbly and the snake was wavering its head so much that I wasn't sure I could hit it, but I could definitely shoot something else.

Even though the cockpit wasn't pressurized, with the downward force of air from the rotors I figured there'd be enough suction.

I fired at the window to my right.

As the glass exploded outward, the air in the cockpit rushed after it, tugging the snake's body with it.

I let go.

No more snake.

"I'm taking us down!" Cheyenne yelled.

I was cool with that.

A pair of sunglasses and a storm of papers shot out the broken window.

I studied the terrain below us.

The road leading to Bearcroft Mine was just a few hundred meters north of us. A meadow that looked flat enough for Cheyenne to land in lay beside it.

"There!" I pointed.

About half a mile further up the mountain, the other helicopter was already on the ground near the entrance to the mine.

Good enough. I could run from here.

As Cheyenne took us down, I radioed for backup and requested an ambulance for Cody, and then, remembering the mine's deep, narrow shafts and the killer's intention to bury someone—me—

alive, I told them to call in the Arapaho National Forest's high angle rescue team. I sometimes climb with the guys on the team, and if we needed a vertical rescue, they were the ones to do it.

We were twenty meters from the ground.

Cheyenne fought to keep us steady.

Cody was drifting into and out of consciousness.

Ten meters.

I swept my eyes across the floor, looking for more snakes.

All clear.

Five meters.

And then we were settling onto the field. A small jostling, but that was all.

"Beautiful landing," I said. We were alive. We were on the ground. "Perfect."

A breath.

A small moment.

A chance to think.

Both Cheyenne and I were OK, but Cody appeared to be only partially conscious. I tried rousing him. No response. I felt his pulse. Thready. Gauged his breathing, considered the EMS response time. It didn't look good. "Cheyenne, I'm not sure he's going to make it unless we can get him to a hospital." We still had our headphones on; the rotors were still spinning overhead.

She stared at me. "How?"

"Fly him."

She shook her head. "I can't do that."

"I have to go after John. We can't leave Cody alone."

"I know, but I'm not . . . No. I can't do it."

"Yes, you can. You just brought us out of the tailspin and landed with no problem." I saw my knife on the floor. Retrieved it. "Trust your gut—"

"We'll get some paramedics up here."

Arguing about it was getting us nowhere. I carefully sliced Cody's pants leg to take a closer look at the bite.

The area surrounding the wound was already black and distended. We both stared at it.

He was in bad shape, and she could tell. She laid a gentle hand on his knee and closed her eyes, took a long breath, then let it out slowly. "OK." She opened her eyes. "But I'm coming back to help you." A fiery intensity shot through her words.

"I'll look forward to it."

We moved Cody to another seat, then she situated herself in the cockpit.

"You'll do fine!" I yelled. I'd exited the helicopter and was standing just outside her door. I had to shout to be heard over the roar of the motor.

"Find him," she hollered. "Stop him!"

"I will!"

I reached for the door, but before I could close it, she grazed her hand against mine. She said nothing, but communicated everything.

But in that moment I found myself wishing it was Lien-hua with me instead of her. I felt vaguely guilty and squeezed her hand gently, then let go and waved her off. "Go!"

I closed the door and she repositioned her headphones and tapped at the controls in front of her. Then I ran from the churning whirlwind kicked up by the rotors, and after I'd made it about ten meters I turned and watched her lift off into the purple Colorado dusk.

A little shaky, but not bad.

As she flew away, I bolted up the road toward the mine.

Tessa was having a hard time wrapping her mind around everything that Dora was telling her.

Apparently, it wasn't Paul's letter that had changed her mom's mind about the abortion. "You're telling me it was a bunch of magazine ads?" she said. "Like that picture of the girl and the jewelry box?"

Dora nodded. "That's what she wrote in her diary."

The doorbell rang.

The two officers stared at each other for a moment.

Another ring. Martha stood. "I'll get it."

"No," the shorter of the two cops said. "We're on it." Both officers headed to the door.

They unsnapped their holsters.

The taller cop eased the door open, and Tessa saw Dora's dad, Dr. Bender, standing on the front porch. "What's going on in here?" He sounded upset. "Is it true you wouldn't let my daughter call me?"

Tessa glanced up and saw Martha smile at her with a sly, grandmotherly smile, and she remembered seeing her on the phone a few minutes earlier.

Yeah, you go girl.

"Dora," Dr. Bender said. "Go get your things. I'm not leaving here without you."

I arrived at the other helicopter and found a pool of blood on the floor of the cockpit and thin streaks of it splayed across the control panels, the seats.

He cut Cliff. Cut him bad.

No sign of Cliff or the killer, but Amy Lynn's body lay in the backseat.

She wasn't moving, and when I felt for a pulse I realized that her neck was grotesquely swollen. With no pulse, no breathing, and a blocked airway, I couldn't administer CPR. There wasn't anything I could do for her—then a thick ridge gliding beneath her shirt confirmed to me what the killer had done.

I felt my teeth clench.

As a small gesture of respect, I shook the snake out of the bottom of her shirt. Kicked it out of the chopper.

I knew the killer would be ready for me, but Cliff was obviously bleeding profusely, and I wasn't about to wait around for backup to arrive. I grabbed the chopper's first aid kit, removed a roll of athletic tape, and jammed it into my pocket.

A trail of blood led from the helicopter to the mine. I aimed my gun at the entrance. Pulled out my flashlight.

And entered the tunnel.

110

Just inside the entrance.

Cool air.

Silence, except for the faint plink of water dripping somewhere out of sight.

I swept my light around the tunnel. Saw the rough-hewn support beams, the minerals shimmering in the walls, the narrow-gauge tracks at my feet. The place where John had left Heather Fain's body.

For a moment I envisioned her corpse lying there, Chris Arlington's disembodied heart resting on her chest, the ten candles surrounding her. I felt my anger grow into resolve. John's gruesome story had started in this abandoned mine a week ago, and it was going to end here, tonight.

No sign of anyone in the tunnel.

The blood trail ended at my feet. At the far reach of my flashlight's beam, an intersecting tunnel led to the east. I jogged to it, turned off my Maglite, and crouched low. After a breath to steady myself and my gun, I stepped around the corner, flicking on my light again. Its beam sliced through the black air.

No one.

I shut off the flashlight and peered into the darkness—first this tunnel, then the main one, but saw no other lights. Heard nothing.

Which tunnel did they take?

Maglite on once again, I inspected both branches of the mine.

Nothing in the main passageway, but at last, about five meters into the adjoining tunnel, I found more blood.

After only a few paces it disappeared.

The drops of blood were oval, and based on their size, shape, and proximity, I decided the men must have been moving quickly. The trail was still damp but easy to miss on the dark soil.

I took a moment to mark the tunnel so Cheyenne and the high angle rescue team could find it when they arrived, then I sprinted down the passageway toward the next intersection.

Dora zipped her school backpack closed. "So, I guess I'll see you tomorrow?"

"Yeah," Tessa said. "And hey, thanks for all your help today, you know, with the diary."

"No problem. I hope you find your dad."

"Me too."

Dora swung her backpack over her shoulder and as she turned toward the door, it bumped Tessa's jewelry box off the dresser and all her necklaces and earrings spilled across the carpet.

"Oh, I'm so sorry!"

"It's all right." Tessa leaned over to pick them up. "It's no big deal."

"Almost ready?" Dr. Bender called from downstairs.

"I'll be right there!" Dora shouted. She was kneeling beside Tessa, helping her pick up the jewelry. "Seriously, I should have been more careful. Making a mess of things. Pandora, right? Makes sense."

Tessa paused, her hand on the jewelry box. "Wait. What did you say my mom wrote? About this box?"

"She wanted to remember the day she changed her mind."

"Right." Tessa lifted the box, tipped everything out of it and handed it to Dora

"What are you doing?"

"I want you to have it."

Dora's face was full of surprise. "No, your mom gave this to you."

"Remember the story, your story? The last thing out of the box?"

"Dora!" Dr. Bender's voice rolled up the stairs. "Everything all right?"

"I'll be right there!" she yelled.

"This morning Martha told me I shouldn't punish myself for something I had no control over."

"You mean your mom not wanting to have you."

"Right. But you're doing the same thing. That baby's death wasn't your fault. I want you to remember that. Hope. A new start. The last thing out."

Dora finally accepted the box. "Thanks," she said softly. "I get it."

As they were leaving the room, Tessa saw the diary lying on the bed.

She picked it up and headed for the stairs.

———————■———————

Nothing.

I'd been traveling through the tunnel as quickly as I could, but after ten minutes I still hadn't found either Colonel Freeman or the killer.

The trail of blood stopped and started intermittently but always appeared at intersections or at the top of the wooden ladders that led deeper into the mine. John was controlling Cliff's bleeding, using the blood to guide me.

Like a lamb to the slaughter.

I would descend a ladder or series of ladders, come to another tunnel, head in the direction of the blood, then the trail would disappear until I arrived at another intersection or shaft marked with more blood, and then I would descend once again.

All one elaborate game.

But this time he wasn't going to win.

Earlier, when I'd started wondering if Grant Sikora had told me Ari's name and I'd learned that Ari had been seen in public with Amy Lynn, I'd started to doubt that he was John.

The real killer was too meticulous, too careful. Based on all that we knew about him, with his intellect, his aptitude, he never would have told Sikora his real name. Or for that matter, been seen publicly with Amy Lynn.

Even the idea of calling in the tip from the dispatch room was too perfect. Too tidy. It left a giant arrow pointing directly at him.

The circuitous route marked by blood led me deeper and deeper into the more primitive, less maintained sections of the mine. Here, more fissures and cracks ran through the walls. Fewer support beams braced the ceiling, and I could see evidence of more cave-ins.

But if Ari wasn't the killer, who was?

I still didn't know.

I descended three more ladders, all marked faintly with blood, and I was about to start down a fourth when I heard movement below me. I clicked off my light. Listened.

Nothing more.

I stared through the darkness and saw a faint hint of light coming from somewhere in the tunnel where the ladder terminated about fifteen meters below me.

Keeping my light off, I descended as quickly as I could, feeling for the rungs with my feet, my hands.

I'd made it to the tenth rung when I heard a voice, definitely a voice. I froze. Listened.

Yes, it was Cliff, that much I could tell. And though I couldn't make out most of what he was yelling, I did hear the words "rigged" and "blow" before he was abruptly cut off.

I began to descend again, watching carefully for any movement below me.

Thoughts tumbled through my mind.

The evidence room in Chicago . . . the dispatch center in Denver

. . . the location of the hospital's security cameras . . . who could have gained access to them all?

He's forensically aware. He knows poisons and toxins, arson, self-defense, how to mask GPS locations . . .

I reached the tunnel.

Strategically, I was in a terrible position. If John had a gun trained on the end of the ladder, as soon as I climbed down it would all be over.

I needed to find out if there was anyone waiting for me, and it looked like there was just enough light to do it. I wedged my legs against the side of the shaft, clung to a rung with one hand like I did when I climbed across the ceiling of my garage, and held my gun in my other hand. Then, I dipped my head down into the tunnel for a fraction of a second. Saw no one.

Quickly, I repositioned myself, and then, gun ready, dropped to the ground.

Still no one.

Just a thin smear of light easing toward me from around a bend about ten meters away. Flickering. Wavering. Probably from a lantern or a torch.

I thought of the candles surrounding Heather Fain's body.

All ten were burning when we arrived.

All ten.

The wax flow told us they'd been burning for two hours.

And there were candles at Reggie's house too.

The killer sent him a text message to hurry home.

Reggie had tried to keep Amy Lynn out of protective custody . . . He was the one who took the sketch artist to visit Kelsey Nash, and Thomas Bennett . . .

Three of the candles went out while we were investigating Heather's body.

Two were out in the Greers' bedroom.

Reggie was called in to process the mine, the ranch house, Taylor's garage, the tire impressions . . . The pot of basil was sent to his wife . . .

It was all so perfect. So clever.

A lamb being led to the slaughter.

The oven was still preheating.

Yes.

That was it. That was the key.

The cube twisted. The final side clicked into place.

The killer couldn't have been Reggie.

Only one person could have pulled off these crimes.

Slowly, carefully, SIG steady, I moved through the tunnel toward the man who'd proven to be one of the most brilliant criminals I'd ever met.

John.

Giovanni.

The Day Four Killer.

My friend, Lieutenant Kurt Mason.

111

The tunnel's bend and the lambent, flickering light lay just in front of me.

"Kurt," I called. The word echoed eerily through the dusty air. "Let Cliff go. It's time to end this."

"Congratulations, Pat," he replied from somewhere around the bend. "Welcome to the story."

I took a deep breath, leveled my SIG, and stepped around the corner.

Cliff stood ten meters away, a strip of duct tape across his mouth.

Kurt was behind him, a straight razor against his throat. He'd twisted Cliff's arm behind his back to subdue him.

I sighted down the barrel. "Hands to the side."

"You called my name just now. You knew I was the one. How?"

Blood was dripping from Cliff's right arm, forming a dark stain on the ground. Based on the amount of blood he'd already lost, I was surprised he was still conscious. He needed medical care and he needed it fast.

"The oven. It was still preheating when we arrived."

Confusion. "The oven?"

Kurt had carefully positioned himself behind Cliff so that only the edge of his face was visible. I aimed my gun at his eye. "I'm not kidding, Kurt. Put down the blade." But even as I said the words I knew I couldn't make the shot. Cheyenne was the only person

I'd ever met who could have put a bullet into Kurt's eyeball from this distance.

"You're not going to shoot me, Pat. Tell me about the oven."

A quick survey of the tunnel: a lantern hung from a support beam between us. On Kurt's left—a platform that'd probably been used to lower ore carts hung about a meter down in an access shaft. Even from where I stood I could see C-4 explosives wired to the shaft walls. Considering Cliff's words "rigged" and "blow" I had a pretty good idea of what Kurt had in mind. A ceiling beam above the platform held a double pulley and the release mechanism for the rope.

"You should have bought better quality candles," I said.

He didn't reply.

"How long does it take for an oven to preheat to 450 degrees?"

He took a moment to think. "So you knew the killer hadn't been gone long."

"Yes. And two of the candles on the dresser had blown out, even though they'd only recently been lit. So that got me thinking about the mine. How could all ten candles have been burning when we arrived? All ten burning continuously for two hours? Three went out in the short time we were processing the scene."

"Ah," he said. "Very nice."

"You were the first one in the mine, Kurt, you told me so. You didn't light the candles when you left Heather's body, you lit them after you responded to the 911 call, just before the rest of us arrived."

"You really are good, Pat, but that's all circumstantial."

"Maybe I'm learning to trust my gut." I pressed my finger against the trigger. "Now, I'm telling you, put your hands to the side."

"That's not going to happen. Toss me your gun."

"Drop the razor blade, Kurt, or I swear, I will shoot you."

He looked at the blood tipping from Cliff's right hand. "Do you really want to keep stalling? Don't let him die like this, Pat. He has a family. I'll let him live if you work with me here. Now, please, toss your gun to me."

A torrent of anger and desperation.

Think, Pat. Think.

Options: (1) fire, and chance killing Cliff; (2) stall, and watch him die; (3) comply, and buy some time.

Kurt's face was just barely visible. Just barely.

Take the shot, Pat. Take it.

I drew in a small breath.

Aimed.

Aimed.

But I couldn't do it. I just couldn't chance hitting Cliff in the face.

Comply, Pat. Buy some time.

I let go of the SIG's grip, let the gun hang from my trigger finger. Then, slowly, I lifted my hands. "There's no way out of this, Kurt." I couldn't believe this man had been my friend. That I'd ever trusted him. "Backup will be here any minute."

He shook his head. "You were alone when you entered the mine. Cheyenne left in the chopper. We have plenty of time. Now, throw me your gun. Watching someone's throat being slit is very disturbing. Once you see it happen, the image never goes away."

I saw Cliff quiver. Kurt gestured toward the shaft wired with the C-4. "Not something you'd want replaying in your mind for the next three months."

Three months?

I stared at the shaft for a moment and realized what he was saying.

He pressed the straight razor tighter against Cliff's neck, and a thin line of blood appeared.

"OK!" I yelled.

"Next time it's deeper."

"All right. I'm doing it." I bent toward the ground.

"Slowly."

I tossed the SIG halfway between us.

"Don't worry," I said to Cliff. "I'm going to get you out of this."

He gave me a small nod.

"Now, your knife and your phone," Kurt said. "All the way to me this time."

"Let me stop his bleeding, Kurt. Then you can—"

"Throw them to me."

I deliberated for a moment, then tossed my Wraith to him. It landed at his feet and he kicked it to the side, sending it clattering down the shaft. Then I threw him Tessa's phone, which he smashed with his heel.

"My stepdaughter is not going to be happy about that."

"Empty your pockets, Pat. Easy. Don't try anything."

All I had with me were my Mini Maglite, my car keys, and the roll of athletic tape from the chopper's first aid kit. I began holding them up one at a time. "Cheryl's not at her sister's, is she, Kurt?"

"She's with Ari. Back pockets."

"Dead? Are they dead?"

He didn't answer. I pocketed the flashlight, keys, and tape. "Where are they, Kurt? You can at least tell me that."

"Turns out Ari rented a self-storage unit. I'll be visiting the two of them when we're done here. Now, let me see your back pockets."

If he's going to visit them, they're still alive.

I showed him that my back pockets were empty, then faced him again just in time to see him press a needle against Cliff's neck and depress the plunger.

"No!" I sprinted forward.

"Stop!" Kurt wrenched Cliff's head back, blade at his neck.

I froze but watched for a chance to make a move. My gun lay just a few meters in front of me.

Cliff's eyes rolled back, he went limp, and Kurt eased him to the ground.

"What did you give him?" I yelled.

"It's just to knock him out. To give us some time alone. Back away from the gun."

I held my ground.

He pulled a Wilson Combat 1911, aimed it at me. "Step back."

I did.

"Farther."

He waved me back until I was too far away to dive for the SIG, then he folded up his straight razor and slipped it into his pocket. Kept his gun out, kicked mine down the shaft.

"Kelsey was supposed to die in the freezer, wasn't she?" I said. "And she could identify you, so that's why you sent Reggie in with the sketch artist, why you didn't enter her room at the hospital. Are you going back for her? Calvin too? No loose ends?"

He didn't reply, and I took that as a yes.

He pulled out a pair of handcuffs. Threw them to me. They landed at my feet. "Normally, I prefer ropes, but it's too hard for a person to tie himself up." He gestured toward the cuffs. "Put them on."

I didn't move. "Besides London last year, were there other stories? How long have you been doing this?"

He waved his gun at the handcuffs. "Cuff your hands behind your back, Pat. When you get to the bottom I'll leave you the key."

I still didn't move, and he fired the 1911, sending a cloud of dirt exploding at my feet.

"Put on the cuffs or the next bullet goes into your leg."

I believed him. I picked up the cuffs. "I'll find a way out."

"There is no way out. Not after the shaft is blown shut."

"You don't know me. I'll get out."

"I do know you, Pat. Remember? I'm the one who requested that you join the task force. I've been watching you. I know you very well. There's no escape. I made sure. Now, put on—"

"Good."

He narrowed his eyes. "Good?"

"That there's no escape." As I spoke, I surveyed the pulley system, the release lever, the ropes, above the shaft. "Because it might take us awhile to dig you out after I leave you down there, and I wouldn't want you going anywhere." I clicked the cuff around my left wrist.

He watched me carefully, with a bit of caution. "Go on. The other wrist."

I thought of a plan and began to click the other cuff around my right wrist—

"No. Behind your back—hang on. First, throw me your keys. You have a lock pick set on your key ring. I've seen it."

Oh, this was not good. Not at all.

I pulled out my Maglite to get to my keys.

"You can keep the flashlight. I want you to spend a couple days exploring your new home."

I tossed him my keys and slipped the flashlight into my back pocket. "Where's Father Hughes? According to Boccaccio's story, the priest is supposed to survive. Is he still alive?"

"It's hard to say. He's chained to a pole, just like Father Alberto in Pampinea's story. But now that he's been up on Dover's Ridge for a nearly week, and it snowed yesterday, I don't think his chances are very good."

The smoldering anger inside of me flared up. I needed to relax or I'd make a mistake. A fatal one.

"Now, the other cuff."

If I snapped it shut, I'd have no way to escape. It'd all be over. "Will you be the one to find him? The hero?" I put both arms behind my back.

"There are several ways things might play out. That's one of them."

"And Cheryl and Ari?"

"I'm shifting Amy Lynn and Cliff to story eight—"

"You said you were going to let Cliff live."

"I lied to you, Pat. And as far as Ari and Cheryl, I still need to tell story number nine, so it looks like I'll be serving Mr. Ryman's heart to my wife for dinner tonight."

Kurt had planned out every detail, every contingency, and although I could think of a few loose ends, there weren't many, and I had a feeling he'd already taken steps to wrap them up.

Think, Pat. Think!

I had my hands behind my back, but I hadn't snapped the second cuff. "But why, Kurt? Why kill these people?"

Kurt thought for a moment. "It's interesting to watch people die."

He said no more, and his stark, simple answer sent a chill slicing through me.

"But what about Hannah's death?" I said. "You grieved when she died. I watched you."

"I don't grieve. I act." He aimed the gun at my face. "Now, finish with the cuff. I want to hear it snap shut."

I was no longer sure I could get away. "You've been planning this since her death, haven't you? When Amy Lynn interviewed you, that's when you chose her for the story."

I felt the bump of my Mini Maglite in my back pocket.

Yes, that's it.

"Are you Galeotto? From Dante's *Inferno*? Is that it? You see yourself as a knight who brings lovers together with death?"

"Bryant gave you that." Then he started toward me. He must have had enough of my stalling.

I pressed the cuff against my back and clicked it shut.

"Turn around." He stopped walking, kept the gun on me. "Let me see."

I turned. Showed him my wrists, handcuffed together.

"OK," he said, "come here."

Then I faced him, and as I slowly approached him, I fished my flashlight out of my back pocket and began to unscrew the cylinder from the cap that houses the lightbulb.

Respond accordingly.

All right.

I believe I will.

112

I was able to unscrew the cylinder, but that wasn't the part I needed. I slipped the flashlight's casing into my back pocket.

More time. A little more time.

I surveyed the tunnel again. The rock walls and ceiling reminded me of the climbing cave in my garage—how could I use that to my advantage? The lantern? Throw it at him? Find a way to his gun?

Kurt kept his 1911 trained on me but used one finger to tap at a remote detonator that he held in his other hand. I saw the display screen flash thirty seconds, but he didn't start the countdown. He slipped the device into his pocket.

I stopped walking. "So thirteen years ago in the Midwest. Was it you or Basque?"

"It wasn't me. But the crimes drew my interest." He came toward me.

Just a little longer. "You were a fan."

"No. A competitor. For an audience. Like I told you on Saturday, the articles were my scouting report." He grabbed my arm and pulled me toward the platform that hung one meter below us in the shaft that was wired to blow. "Now, it's time for story number ten."

I let him lead me. "And Basque's trial—you loaded the gun?"

"Last month in the evidence room."

When we got to the edge he took out the detonator. "Climb down," he said.

I didn't move. "Before I do I have a small word of advice for you, Kurt."

"What's that?"

"Never leave a handcuffed man who knows how to pick locks alone with the wire spring of his Maglite."

And then, I was on him.

113

A look of shock flashed across his face as I knocked the gun from his hand and punched him in the jaw as hard as I could, just like I'd done with Basque.

And it felt just as good.

Kurt stumbled backward, then straightened up. "All right, let's do this thing." I was about to go for his gun when he flicked out his straight razor. He tapped the detonator's screen, and the countdown began. :29

:28

"Time to end the story, Pat."

He rushed me, sliced at me, but I leapt to the side. I grabbed his forearm, and as he drove the razor blade toward me, I pivoted backward and both of us tumbled onto the platform.

We crashed onto the boards, and he managed to hang on to the straight razor, but the detonator spun from his hand.

I saw the screen.

:23

He swiped the blade at my neck, but I pushed him off me and scrambled to my feet.

I was on the wrong side of the platform, trapped in the corner farthest from the tunnel.

He held the razor against one end of the rope that passed through the cam. Severed it. The platform teetered but held.

It would drop if he cut the other end.

:20

He eased backward toward the ground so he could get off the platform before cutting the rope. "Good-bye, Pat."

"Bye, Kurt."

I leapt and grabbed the wooden beam holding the pulleys, then swung my legs up and kicked him with both feet, hard, in the chest.

:17

He slammed backward onto the platform, and before he could get up, I lifted my feet to the ceiling, just like when I'm rock climbing. I planted one foot against the cam holding the end of the rope and the other against the release lever. Kicked hard. Wedged it all the way open.

And the platform dropped.

:13

"No!" Kurt's scream slit through the air around me.

I kept the countdown going in my head, flung my legs to the side. Landed on the ground beside the shaft.

:10

Heard the solid crunch of impact from the bottom of the shaft. "I'm coming for you!" he hollered. He didn't sound seriously hurt.

I ran to Cliff, dragged him toward the bend.

:06

Around the corner.

:04

The explosion would be deafening. I knelt beside him.

:02

Pressed my knees against his ears —

:01

—squeezed my hands over mine.

Boom.

A thunderous crash, a sweep of sound.

Then, air choking me. Dust. Dirt. Rocks falling around me.

A crack against my head.

And everything went black.

114

53 minutes later

Eyes closed.

Movement beneath me. A thousand buzz saws whirring in my head.

A slight sway, the ground bouncing. Or maybe it wasn't the ground. Maybe it was all a dream, another dream. I groaned and heard a voice, sweet and close, a woman's voice. "Pat."

My head was throbbing, pounding. "Lien-hua," I mumbled.

"It's me. I'm here."

"I knew you'd come." I opened my eyes to a blurry world, and saw her leaning over me. "We can still . . ." I whispered. "We'll try again . . . I need you."

But as I blinked away the dream, Lien-hua's face became vapor, and Cheyenne's appeared in its place. Behind her I saw metal walls. A ceiling. Shelves of first aid supplies. We were inside an ambulance.

"I'm sorry," I said softly. "I thought—"

"Shh." She brushed her hand across my forehead. "It's OK. Are you . . . do you know where you are?"

I nodded slightly. "It was Kurt." My voice sounded raw and dry.

"We know," Cheyenne said. "Cliff woke up before you did. He told us everything." She shook her head in disbelief. "It's unfathomable."

"Yes." Even though I'd had more time than she had to process everything, I was still reeling from the fact that Kurt was the killer.

I tested my limbs. Tried to move. Other than my aching head, I seemed to be all right. A paramedic sat beside Cheyenne.

I gave her a faint smile. "So you found my trail?"

"It would have been hard to miss with those strips of first-aid tape at every intersection."

"And Cliff, he's OK?"

"He will be. Flight for Life took him." She gestured around the vehicle. "You get the meat wagon instead."

"Fair enough." My thoughts were still muddy. "Cody?"

"I actually managed to make it to the Evergreen hospital without crashing. He's doing all right—even thanked me for saving his life, so I guess we're on talking terms again. Small miracles."

The paramedic, a Latino man in his early thirties, laid two fingers against my wrist, checked my pulse. I had no idea how long I'd been out.

I tried to sort through the jumble of memories that were all fighting for my attention: entering the mine . . . following the trail of blood . . . talking with Kurt before the explosion . . .

"Dover's Ridge," I mumbled to Cheyenne, "look for Father Hughes on Dover's Ridge, he's chained to a pole . . . maybe a telephone pole from a power line, I don't know . . . and Cheryl and Ari are in a storage . . . a self-storage . . . check under Ari's name." I could feel myself fading, but I saw Cheyenne pull out her cell. "I don't know which . . . you have to check . . ."

"I will. Relax."

I tried to think, but everything was becoming a blur. Faintly, I saw the paramedic lean over me while Cheyenne tapped at her phone. The fringes of the moment grew fuzzy.

And I sank into sleep again.

Dreams. Voices. Whispers. Promises made and broken.

Then, soft pressure on my right hand and I was opening my eyes again.

Still in the ambulance. Cheyenne beside me, her hand on mine. She was speaking with someone on the phone.

I eased my hand out from under hers and asked the paramedic how long I'd been out.

"Just a few minutes. We found you about an hour ago. Your climbing buddies on the high angle rescue team are good."

I nodded. "What happened to me?" My voice still didn't sound natural.

"A rock fell on your head. Looks like a concussion, other than that—"

"Prop me up."

It took a little convincing, but finally he tilted the head end of the gurney upright. Cheyenne was still on the phone, so I asked to borrow his. Somewhat reluctantly, he handed it to me.

I tapped in cybercrime's number. I was afraid I might go unconscious again, so as soon as Angela picked up I explained that I didn't have much time to talk. "Tell me about Paul Lansing. I think he might be my stepdaughter's biological father."

She didn't answer right away.

"Angela, what is it?"

"Here's what you need to know for now: he lives in the mountains of Wyoming. No driver's license. No bank accounts. He doesn't own a phone or a computer; doesn't use credit cards or pay utility bills."

"He's living off the grid," I mumbled.

The ambulance slowed down.

"His record is squeaky clean," she said.

"Too clean?"

"Maybe."

"Listen, pull together whatever you have on him. I'll call you when I get to my computer. Just wait for my call, OK?"

"All right."

"Keep digging. See what you can find."

"I will."

Through the windows in the back of the ambulance I could see that we'd reached the hospital. Angela's words troubled me. A man doesn't usually disappear into the mountains and drop off the map unless he's running from something.

The paramedic accepted his phone back and Cheyenne finished her call, then asked, "Pat, do you know if Kurt survived the explosion?"

"I think he had enough time to get into the tunnel before the shaft blew. But I'm not sure."

"Are there any other ways out of that passageway?"

"I don't think so. He chose that tunnel for one reason: there was no possible escape." I wondered how long it would take a rescue team to dig him out. Maybe weeks. Maybe they wouldn't even bother. That was a satisfying thought.

Cheyenne considered my words for a moment. "Thomas Bennett and his wife owned the mine. She should know if there are any other passages."

"Good thought," I said.

The ambulance stopped, and the paramedic opened the back doors as Cheyenne phoned headquarters for Marianne Bennett's number.

Two EMTs rushed toward us from the hospital, and with the help of the man who'd been riding with me, they wheeled me out of the ambulance.

"I'll see you inside," I called to Cheyenne, and then the emergency room doors slid open and the three men pushed me into the building.

---

6 minutes later

My nurse set down the blood pressure cuff. "The doctor will be with you in a minute."

"Thank you."

I'd been so groggy in the ambulance that I hadn't thought to ask

Cheyenne how Calvin was doing. So, as soon as the nurse stepped out of the exam room, I stood to go find him.

I felt a little wobbly, but managed to make it two steps before the door opened again.

Cheyenne.

A small smile. "Going somewhere?"

I leaned a hand against the wall. "Just to see how Calvin is doing."

"I was just with him. No change." She looked at me with concern. "You shouldn't be walking around."

"I'm OK."

I took my hand off the wall and showed her I could stand on my own, but she took my arm to support me. "Pat, since Friday you were nearly burned alive, bitten by a rattlesnake, sealed in a mine, blown up, and crushed by a boulder."

"Imagine if it'd been an eventful couple days," I said.

She offered me a half smile.

She'd left the door slightly ajar. Behind her I could see the front doors of the hospital.

"Thanks for getting me out of that mine," I said. She was still holding my arm.

"I told you I'd come back for you."

Her words brought to mind the comments I'd made as I was awakening in the ambulance. I'd been mumbling Lien-hua's name, that I was glad she'd come back. That I needed her.

Gently, I removed Cheyenne hand from my arm. "Cheyenne, when I woke up in the ambulance, I thought that you were someone else."

"Lien-hua."

"Yes."

"It's all right. I know. You were groggy."

I searched for the best way to balance honesty with sensitivity. Obviously, I liked both her and Lien-hua, but I felt like I needed to be straight with her. To tell her everything.

Cheyenne must have sensed that I was struggling with what to say. "Really, Pat. It's all right. I understand. You don't have to explain."

Here's where things got tricky. "Well . . . you see . . . maybe I do."

Silence.

"Oh," she said softly. Her tone mirrored the distance that was already stretching between us. "I see."

"Listen, maybe I just need some time to sort out my feelings."

"Right, sure, that makes sense."

Her voice was breaking, a thin crack ran through every word. *She's as lonely as you are, and you hurt her.*

You hurt her.

I wanted to take her in my arms, to hold her, to tell her I was sorry, but I knew that if I did, it would be a way of making a promise that my heart wasn't ready to keep.

"Cheyenne, this is really—"

"Can you tell me one thing, Pat. Please?"

"Of course."

"Over the last year I've asked you out more than once and the timing was never right—and I understood all that, but . . ." She took a gentle breath. "Is there a chance it ever will be?"

Oh man.

This wasn't how things were supposed to go. "Cheyenne, you're an amazing woman and I . . . I mean, if I wasn't—"

But she cut me off by holding up her hand. "No, that's good. That's enough."

"I'm sorry."

"Please. Don't be. The truth," she said softly, "it suits you."

In the moment that followed, our eyes said good-bye and I felt helpless, trapped by my feelings toward these two women who both seemed, in different ways, to be out of reach: Lien-hua, because of my past. Cheyenne, because of Lien-hua.

Then through the doorway, I saw Tessa and my mother entering the emergency room.

"Maybe we can talk more about this later," I said.

Cheyenne turned to see who I was looking at. "That's OK. I think we've talked about it enough." Her voice carried no animosity, and for some reason that only made me feel worse.

Before I could respond, she stepped away and flagged down Tessa, then she disappeared around the corner and my mother and stepdaughter hurried to meet me in the exam room.

And I realized it was time to talk to Tessa about her father.

115

My head still ached, but other than that I felt passable, so after assuring my mother that I was all right, I asked her to wait in the lobby for a few moments to give me and Tessa a chance to talk.

She didn't look convinced that I was OK. "They told us a boulder fell on your head."

"A small boulder," I said.

She smiled in a careful, concerned way. "All right, but we're not leaving this hospital until a doctor looks you over."

"Deal."

That satisfied her and she left for the lobby as I guided Tessa toward a nurse's station, where we found out that Calvin was in room 131.

"Patrick," Tessa said. "I'm really glad it wasn't a bigger boulder."

"Thank you. That's kind of you to say."

We headed down the hall and I was about to bring up the cybercrime email when she mentioned she'd seen Detective Warren leaving my room. "I recognized that look on her face."

"What look?"

"Please."

I didn't like where this was going. "Tessa, I wanted to talk with you about—"

"So, pretty much: boy meets girl. Boy falls for girl. Boy loses girl. The end."

I held back a small sigh. "Pretty much."

"What kind of a story is that, anyway?"

The story of my life.

"I guess sometimes things don't work out like you hope." It was all I could think to say.

"Is Detective Warren what you were hoping for?"

Definitely time to change the subject. "So you're looking for your father?"

She took a few steps before answering. "My last name should have been Lansing."

"Did you read the email from the cybercrime division?"

"Yes."

"And you want to meet him?"

"Yes, I do."

A terrible whirlwind of emotions blew through me. Even though Tessa wasn't my daughter, it felt like she was, and it stung to hear her words. But even though I had serious reservations about this man, I said, "OK."

"OK?"

"If Paul Lansing is your father, your real father, you have every right to meet him." How to put this. There really was no delicate way. "But . . ."

We passed room 123.

"But?"

"Do you remember how you felt yesterday when you found out your mother struggled with the decision about whether or not to have an—"

"Abortion. Yeah. I remember."

I took a small breath. "Have you thought about the possibility that Mr. Lansing doesn't . . ."

"What? That he doesn't love me? Doesn't want anything to do with me?"

"It's possible," I said.

Room 127. Calvin's room lay just ahead.

She worked her jaw back and forth for a moment, then said, "I just want to know the truth. I mean, he is my father." Then she looked my way. "You understand, right?"

A moment of awkward silence. "Yes. I do."

We arrived at Calvin's room, I pressed open the door and saw him lying on the bed. A doctor I didn't recognize was reading his charts. Jake Vanderveld stood beside the bed.

Calvin wasn't moving, and I feared the worst. "What do we know?"

The doctor looked my direction. "He's stable, but he still hasn't regained consciousness."

Tessa had met Calvin a few times, and I noticed a cloud of worry on her face. "Is he all right?"

"Can you wait with my mother?" I said. "We'll talk more in a minute, OK?"

She was still eyeing Calvin.

"Tessa, go sit with Martha. I'll be there in a little bit."

She finally backed into the hall but then looked at me. "You meant it, though, right? That I could meet my dad? It wasn't just—"

"I meant it. We'll set it up, I promise. Now, please." I gestured toward the waiting room.

After one more lingering glance at Calvin, Tessa left.

And I pulled the doctor aside to tell him that his patient was dying.

116

I explained to the doctor that I didn't know what Calvin's condition was, but that Special Agent Ralph Hawkins did. I gave him Ralph's number and he immediately left the room to make the call.

I went to Calvin's side. My mentor. My friend. He looked so old and frail.

"So it was Kurt?" Jake said.

"Yes," I said simply.

"Amazing. You knew him all this time and yet never suspected a thing."

"It's hard to know people." I felt a knot of tension in my chest. "To really know them. What they're capable of."

"That is true, Pat. That's a good observation."

Jake took a slow breath, then went on. "They found the priest. That man and the woman, too, in the storage unit. They're all OK. Looks like we got to them all in time."

It was nice to hear some good news.

My attention shifted back to Calvin. I had so many questions: How did he know to go to the Greers' house? Why did he call me from police headquarters? What evidence led him to suspect that Richard Basque was innocent?

I'd seen Calvin taking notes at the trial. Maybe his notebook would give me some answers.

His clothes and personal items were in the chair beside the nightstand. I walked to them.

"Her laptop is missing," Jake said abruptly.

"Excuse me?"

I didn't see Calvin's notebook, but I found a slip of paper in his pants pocket.

"Amy Lynn Greer's," Jake said. "It looks like she was the one who posted the article online. But it's hard to tell for sure because her laptop computer is missing."

Calvin had written Dr. Renée Lebreau's name and phone number on the piece of paper—she was the law professor at Michigan State University who'd found the DNA discrepancies that had led to Basque's trial. The sheet also contained a cryptic message: H814b Patricia E.

I had no idea what it meant.

Another mystery.

I memorized the information and returned the paper to its place.

"You ask me," Jake said, "Kurt took it. Destroyed it."

I couldn't understand why we were even having this conversation about the computer. "Well, maybe we'll find something on her digital voice recorder." I didn't find any other answers to my questions in Calvin's things, so I returned to his side.

Jake's demeanor shifted. Cooled. "Her what?"

"I saw a voice recorder in her purse when I was at the house."

Jake seemed to be internally debating something.

"What is it?" I asked.

He checked his watch and stood. "I have to go. Captain Terrell and I have a press conference coming up." He patted my shoulder. "Don't worry, Pat. I'll make sure everyone knows how much you helped us with the case."

The more I spoke with Jake, the more my headache returned. "Please," I said, "don't bother. Just tell them the truth—that we never would have solved it without your profile."

"Thanks, Pat. That means a lot."

"You're welcome."

After Jake left, I sat in silence for a few minutes beside Calvin. Then, I said softly, "We got him. We got Kurt."

In his current state I didn't know if Calvin could hear me, but I added, "And I told the truth today. On the stand. I don't know if it was the best thing to do, but I'm glad I did it. We'll see what happens next."

Calvin lay still. Silent.

A few moments later the doctor returned and told me that he'd just spoken with Calvin's internal medicine doctor in Chicago.

"And?"

"And I'm sorry, but it's the family's wish that his condition remain confidential. You'll have to take it up with them."

Not the news I wanted to hear, but this wasn't the time to argue. I figured I could contact Calvin's family tomorrow. "I have to go," I said, "but I need you to call me if his condition changes. You can do that much. That's not breaking any kind of confidentiality."

The doctor nodded. I gave him my office number, quietly told Calvin that I would see him again soon, and then left the room to regroup with Tessa and my mother.

I checked the time: 10:02 p.m.

So, unless Ralph had been able to pull a few strings with Internal Affairs, I was officially on administrative leave from the FBI.

117

One week later
A dirt road
52 miles west of Riverton, Wyoming
2:51 p.m. Mountain Time

Our flight had landed two hours ago, and while I drove the rental car toward Paul Lansing's remote cabin in the mountains, Tessa sat beside me, her eyes closed, trying to solve the Rubik's Cube that her friend had given her.

All around us, sunlight cascaded across the Wind River Range, but clouds were moving in.

We were less than ten minutes from the cabin.

Over the last week, Angela hadn't found out anything negative about Paul Lansing. No red flags. And in a strange way, that bothered me. I'd promised Tessa that she could meet him and Angela hadn't uncovered anything that gave me a reason to break that promise.

So here we were.

However, there was no way I was going to leave Tessa alone with Lansing. Not for an instant.

I watched the clouds gather in the west, and Tessa, with her eyes still closed, said, "Have you heard any more about Dr. Werjonic? Since this morning?"

She twisted the cube.

Click. Click.

"Still no change," I said.

Calvin's family had chosen to keep his illness confidential, and even though I could have gone through some back channels to find out the details, I'd respected their wishes and let that information remain between them and his doctors. The family was furious enough that Ralph had discovered Calvin's health issues before they had and I didn't want to disturb the waters any more. Calvin was stable, he was being treated, and they were keeping me informed about his condition. That was enough for now.

I'd placed a call in to Professor Renée Lebreau to see what H814b Patricia E. might mean, but hadn't yet heard back from her.

So, nothing on that front either.

"Almost there . . . almost there . . ." Tessa mumbled, twisting the cube's sides in quick succession.

A bit of good news, though: Ralph had managed to expedite the Internal Affairs review and since I hadn't been with the FBI when I physically assaulted Basque, I'd only ended up with an official reprimand. My first students for the summer arrived in two days.

"Got it!" Tessa held up the cube. Opened her eyes.

None of the sides were solved.

She groaned. "Ugh!" She threw the cube over her shoulder and into the backseat. "It's impossible! I'm never gonna get that thing!"

"Don't feel bad," I said. "This morning on our flight while I was watching you work on it, I thought about those people on YouTube who solve it blindfolded. I think there might be a secret to it. It's so obvious that I didn't even consider it at first."

"What secret?"

"Just start with a solved cube, film someone blindfolding you, then mix up the sides, remove the blindfold, and then play the video backward."

A pause. "You're kidding me."

I shrugged. "We can check it out later, but I'll bet we'll be able to tell if we watch the videos closely enough."

She let her hands drop to her lap. "Oh, that so sucks. I spent all week on that stupid thing."

"Well, Raven," I said. "Sometimes the process of solving a problem is more valuable than coming up with a solution."

She stared at me.

I glanced at her. "What?"

"Dr. Phil?"

"What? No. I don't watch Dr. Phil."

"That was so from Dr. Phil."

"No, it wasn't."

"Oprah then."

I looked back at the road. "That's ridiculous."

"You just averted eye contact. Ha, it was Oprah. I knew it."

I drove for a few moments. "I was channel surfing once. I stumbled across it. I only saw a couple minutes."

"Yeah, right." She tried to say the words sarcastically, but I heard a smile underneath them.

"It's still good advice."

"It's not advice. It's an aphorism."

"Right."

We arrived at the intersection of Glory View and Eastern Timber Roads.

To get to Paul Lansing's house we needed to drive half a mile up Glory View, then jump onto an old logging road that terminated at his cabin. I slowed down, maybe more than I needed to, hesitated for a moment, then turned onto Glory View.

Tessa picked up the diary from the floor. Set it on her lap. She fingered it for a moment, then said, "So, ninety minutes. That's all it took for them to decide?"

I was slow in replying. I knew this was going to come up, I just didn't know when. "That's the way it goes sometimes," I said. "Some juries don't need long to deliberate." The news of this morning's verdict had been all over the TV screens at the airport. And since my name and face were part of the Richard Basque saga, I'm sure it hadn't even taken Tessa two seconds to connect the dots.

"So what happens now? He just goes free? Just like that?"

Emilio Vandez had filed for a mistrial, but for now the answer to her question was yes. "That's the way the system works. Mr. Basque was found not guilty."

"But he is guilty, though, right?"

"He was found not guilty," I repeated, although I knew it wasn't the answer she was looking for. "According to the law, he's an innocent man."

A stretch of silence.

"According to the law," she said.

We rumbled up Glory View Road.

I didn't reply.

More clouds gathered overhead.

"He'll go after other women, won't he?"

"No. I won't let him do that. I made a promise that I wouldn't let him hurt anyone else."

She stared at me. "How are you going to do that?"

I thought about it. "I'm not sure."

The space between us seemed to widen, and after a few moments she said, "You knew, didn't you? All this time? That mom was going to abort me?"

For a long time I considered how to answer her, finally opted for the truth. "Yes, I knew. It was a magazine ad. That's what changed her mind."

"Of a little girl. With a jewelry box in the background."

I looked at her curiously.

"The story doesn't end in pain," she said softly, cryptically, then added, "But you never told me because you thought it would hurt me, right?"

This was an incredibly difficult conversation to have. "Tessa, sometimes to protect people you can't be completely open with them . . . It's . . . I guess what I'm trying to say is, it's hard to balance the truth with compassion."

"Thank you."

Her words caught me by surprise. "You're glad I didn't tell you?"

"No," she replied. "But I'm glad *why* you didn't tell me."

We arrived at the entrance to the dirt road that led to Paul Lansing's house, and I let the car idle.

"So," I said. "Do you still want to do this?"

I hoped that she would say no, that sometime during the drive she would have changed her mind and decided that all of this had been a mistake and that things would be better for everyone if we just went back home.

But instead, she nodded and laced her fingers across the top of the diary. "Let's go."

A thousand questions curled around me.

And whether I liked it or not, the answer to the most important one lay just up the road.

As the sun slid behind a cloud and a few lonely raindrops plopped onto the windshield, I pulled around the corner and drove toward Paul Lansing's home.

EPILOGUE

Time collapsed into nothingness.

A week might have passed. Or a month. Or more. There was no way to tell. In a darkness this deep, time meant nothing.

But eventually, Giovanni became aware of motorized sounds high above him in the shaft that he had blown shut.

Someone was digging him out.

And so.

More time slid by, hourglass sand he couldn't measure.

Eventually the sounds became louder, clearer, as more boulders and rubble were removed.

At last, slivers of light began to pierce the shaft, sliding like glowing sabers through the thick, dark air.

Like rays of summer sunlight.

Then muffled voices.

Indistinguishable, but they grew more distinct as the pile of debris was cleared.

Someone called, "Hello? Are you there, sir? Are you all right down there?"

"I'm hurt," Giovanni replied, working on his acting once again. "Please, I need help." He flicked out his straight razor and stepped to the edge of the shadows.

Within minutes, the last three boulders were removed, and two S.W.A.T. members rappelled down the shaft, each man heavily armed and wearing body armor. But that didn't matter to Giovanni, because he could still get to their necks.

As soon as they dropped into view he introduced them to his blade.

Sunlight spilled and sprayed around him.

Wet screams echoed through the tunnel.

And the Knight began to tell a brand-new story to the curious, waiting world.

Look for the next Patrick Bowers thriller, *The Bishop*, in summer 2010.

ACKNOWLEDGMENTS

Special thanks to Sonya Haskins, Pam Johnson, Rhonda Bier, Pamela Harty, Jennifer Leep, Tricia Hafley, Jeff Walker, Geoff and Linda Stunkard, Kristin Kornoelje, Lizbeth Burkhardt, Dave Beeson, Dr. Todd Huhn, Detective Sharon Hahn, Eden Huhn, Liesl Huhn, William Cirignani, Chris Haskins, Pam and Dr. John-Paul Abner, Shawn and Carly for giving me a place to get away to write, Al Mosch and the gang for the tour of Phoenix Mine, Eddie Jones for the greeting card, Amy Lynn for your name, and Randy, Jerry, and Delberta, for your hospitality.

I am indebted to the writings and research of Dr. D. Kim Rossmo and Dr. David Canter for information about geographic profiling and the Dacoits. For anyone interested in geospatial investigation, I highly recommend their books.

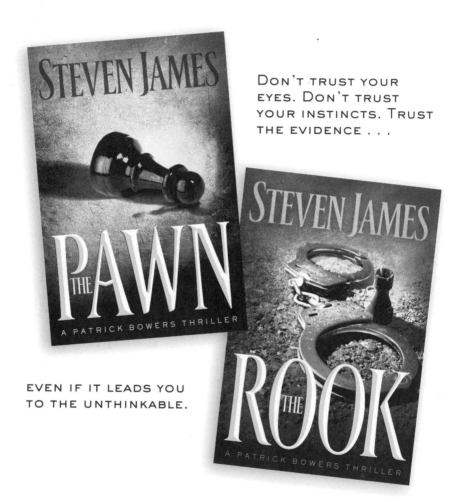